INSTANT *NEW YORK TIMES* BESTSELLER

"It's been ten years since Ian Caldwell cowrote *The Rule of Four*. *The Fifth Gospel* was more than worth the wait. For those who might compare it to *The Da Vinci Code*, don't. This marvelous book stands alone and will become the very high standard for any novel in this genre. Masterfully plotted and extraordinarily researched, and written in a voice that never rings false, *The Fifth Gospel* is that rare story: erudite and a page-turner, literary but compulsively readable. It will change the way you look at organized religion, humanity, and perhaps yourself."
—DAVID BALDACCI

"A novel of betrayals and cover-ups, but mostly of sacrifice, of commitment and of love, with credible characters, twists and turns of plot, and a fascinating theological rationale . . . Although the mystery and the tension mount inexorably throughout the novel, there's none of the cheap end-of-chapter cliffhangers beloved of hack thriller writers. Everything in *The Fifth Gospel* rings true because Ian Caldwell spent ten years researching and writing the novel."
—THE CATHOLIC HERALD

"The second novel from Ian Caldwell, coauthor of the bestselling *The Rule of Four*, kicks off at 90 mph and doesn't slow down. Caldwell's skill as a writer is evident in his ability to weave detailed descriptions of biblical Scripture, Catholic history, and Vatican geography into the story while keeping the action going. . . . He has created memorable characters with complex relationships, deep love, and longstanding hurts. . . . Ultimately, Caldwell's novel is about faith—in God and in family."
—ASSOCIATED PRESS

"You are going to hear a lot about how this book took ten years to write and how it's minutely researched and erudite. Forget all that. This thing reads like a rocket. Jump on and hold tight."
—MARY DORIA RUSSELL, AUTHOR OF *THE SPARROW*

"*The Fifth Gospel* is nothing short of groundbreaking—a literary feast wrapped around an intriguing murder mystery. Caldwell writes with precision and passion as he takes us on an emotional journey deep into the workings of the Vatican and deeper into the hearts and souls of the men and women who have devoted their lives to the Church. *The Fifth Gospel* is a cathedral where skeptics and believers alike may enter and all will leave transformed."
—NELSON DeMILLE

THIS SMART, SUSPENSEFUL THRILLER . . . IS A MUST-READ FOR DAN BROWN FANS." —*PEOPLE*

IAN CALDWELL is also the coauthor of *The Rule of Four*, which spent forty-nine weeks on the *New York Times* bestseller list and has been translated into thirty-five languages. He lives with his wife and children near Washington, D.C.

THE
FIFTH
GOSPEL

ALSO BY IAN CALDWELL

The Rule of Four (with Dustin Thomason)

THE
FIFTH
GOSPEL

a novel

IAN CALDWELL

SIMON & SCHUSTER PAPERBACKS

NEW YORK   LONDON   TORONTO   SYDNEY   NEW DELHI

Simon & Schuster Paperbacks
An Imprint of Simon & Schuster, Inc.
1230 Avenue of the Americas
New York, NY 10020

First Simon & Schuster trade paperback edition August 2016

SIMON & SCHUSTER PAPERBACKS and colophon are registered trademarks of Simon & Schuster, Inc.

For information about special discounts for bulk purchases, please contact Simon & Schuster Paperback Special Sales at 1-866-506-1949 or business@simonandschuster.com.

The Simon & Schuster Speakers Bureau can bring authors to your live event. For more information or to book an event, contact the Simon & Schuster Speakers Bureau at 1-866-248-3049 or visit our website at www.simonspeakers.com.

Interior design by Kyoko Watanabe
Map by Paul J. Pugliese

Manufactured in the United States of America

10 9 8 7 6 5 4 3 2 1

The Library of Congress has cataloged the hardcover edition as follows:

Caldwell, Ian, 1976-
    The fifth gospel : a novel / Ian Caldwell.—First Simon & Schuster hardcover edition.
        pages; cm
    I. Title.
    PS3603.A435F54 2015
    813'.6—dc23
                        2014041909

ISBN 978-1-4516-9414-7
ISBN 978-1-4516-9415-4 (pbk)
ISBN 978-1-4516-9416-1 (ebook)

For Meredith.
At last.

Gardens
1. Mater Ecclesiae priory
2. Casina of Pius IV
   (Pontifical Academy
   of Sciences)

Museums
3. Library
4. Courtyard and
   underground vault
5. Belvedere Courtyard
6. Sistine Chapel

Apostolic Palace
7. Secretariat of State
8. Courtyard of Saint Damasus
9. Palace of Sixtus V

Vatican Village
10. Autopark
11. Belvedere Palace
    (including Pharmacy and
    Health Services)
12. Annona (supermarket)
13. Parish church
14. Saint Anne's Gate
15. Swiss Guard barracks

Saint Peter's Basilica
16. Confession booths
17. High altar
18. Piers containing
    reliquary rooms
19. Saint Peter's Square

20. Former jail
21. Governor's Palace
22. Palace of the Tribunal
23. Casa Santa Marta

Gardens

21

N
W   E
S

Walls

0   400 feet
0   100 meters

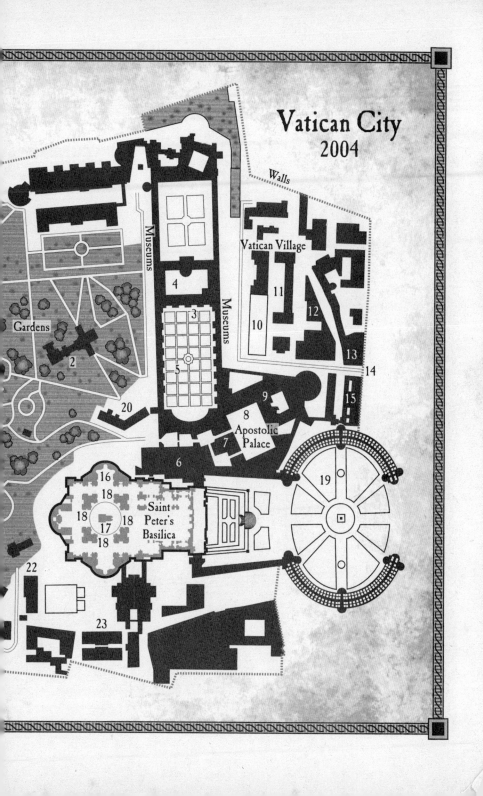

HISTORICAL NOTE

TWO THOUSAND YEARS ago, a pair of brothers set out from the Holy Land to spread the Christian gospel. Saint Peter traveled to Rome, becoming the symbolic founder of Western Christianity. His brother, Saint Andrew, traveled to Greece, becoming a symbolic founder of Eastern Christianity. For centuries, the church they helped create remained a single institution. But one thousand years ago, west and east divided. Western Christians became Catholics, led by the successor of Saint Peter, the pope. Eastern Christians became Orthodox, led by the successors of Saint Andrew and other apostles, known as patriarchs. Today these are the largest Christian denominations on earth. Between them exists a small group known as Eastern Catholics, who confound all distinctions by following Eastern traditions while obeying the pope.

This novel is set in 2004, when the dying wish of Pope John Paul II was to reunite Catholicism and Orthodoxy. It is the story of two brothers, both Catholic priests, one Western and one Eastern.

PROLOGUE

M<small>Y SON IS</small> too young to understand forgiveness. Growing up in Rome has given him the impression that it comes easy: strangers line up at the booths in Saint Peter's, waiting for a turn to confess, and the red lights on top of the confessionals blink on and off, meaning the priests inside have finished with one sinner and are ready for the next. Consciences must not get as dirty as bedrooms or dishes, my son thinks, since they take much less time to clean. So whenever he lets the bath run too long, or leaves toys underfoot, or comes home from school with mud on his pants, Peter asks forgiveness. He offers apologies like a pope offers blessings. My son is two years shy of his own first confession. And for good reason.

No little child can understand sin. Guilt. Absolution. A priest can forgive a stranger so quickly that a boy can't imagine how hard he will find it, someday, to forgive his own enemies. Or his own loved ones. He has no inkling that good men can sometimes find it impossible to forgive themselves. The darkest mistakes can be forgiven, but they can never be undone. I hope my son will always remain a stranger to those sins much more than my brother and I have.

I was born to be a priest. My uncle is a priest; my older brother, Simon, is a priest; and someday I hope Peter will be a priest, too. I can't remember a time when I didn't live inside the Vatican. There has never been a time when Peter didn't.

There are two Vaticans in the eyes of the world. One is the earth's most beautiful place: the temple of art and museum of faith. The other is the sausage factory of Catholicism, a country of old priests who wag the eternal finger. It seems impossible for a boy to have grown up in either of those places. Yet our country has always been full of children. Everyone has them: the pope's gardeners, the pope's workmen, the pope's Swiss Guards. When I was a kid, John Paul believed in a living wage, so he paid a raise for every new mouth a family fed. We played hide-and-seek in his gardens, soccer with his altar boys, pinball upstairs from the sacristy of his basilica. Against our will we went with our mothers to the Vatican supermarket and department store, then with our fathers to the Vatican gas station and bank. Our country was barely bigger than a golf course, but we did everything most children did. Simon and I were happy. Normal. No different from the other Vatican boys in any way but one. *Our* father was a priest.

Father was Greek Catholic rather than Roman Catholic, which meant that he had a long beard and a different cassock, that he celebrated something called Divine Liturgy instead of Mass, and that he had been allowed to marry before being ordained. He liked to say that we Eastern Catholics were God's ambassadors, middlemen who could help reunite Catholics and Orthodox. In reality, being an Eastern Catholic can feel like being a refugee at a border crossing between hostile superpowers. Father tried to hide the burden this put on him. There are a billion Roman Catholics in the world and just a few thousand of our type of Greek, so he was the sole married priest in a country run by celibate men. For thirty years, other Vatican priests looked down their noses at him as he pushed paper back uphill to them. Only at the very end of his career did he get a promotion, and it was the kind that came with wings and a harp.

My mother died not long after that. Cancer, the doctors said. But they didn't understand. My parents had met in the sixties, in that blink of an eye when it seemed anything was possible. They used to dance together in our apartment. Having survived an irreverent time, they still prayed together with feeling. Mother's family was Roman Catholic, and had sent priests up the Vatican ladder for more than a century, so when she married a hairy Greek, they disowned her. After Father died, she told me that it felt strange to have hands anymore, what with no one to hold them. Simon and I buried her in a plot beside my father, behind the Vatican parish church. I remember almost nothing from that time. Only that I skipped school, day after day, to sit in the graveyard with my arms around my knees, crying. Then Simon would be there, somehow, and he would bring me home.

We were only teenagers, so we were left in the care of our uncle, a Vatican cardinal. The best way to describe Uncle Lucio is that he had the heart of a little boy, which he kept in a jar by his dentures. As cardinal president of the Vatican, Lucio had devoted the best years of his life to balancing our national budget and preventing Vatican employees from forming a union. On economic grounds he opposed the idea of rewarding families for having more children, so even if he'd had time to raise his sister's orphaned boys, he probably would've objected on principle. He put up no fight when Simon and I moved back into our parents' apartment and decided to rear ourselves.

I was too young to work, so Simon left college for a year and found a job. Neither of us knew how to cook, or sew, or fix a toilet, so Simon taught himself. He was the one who woke me for school and handed me money for lunch. He kept me in clothes and warm meals. The art of being an altar boy I learned entirely from him. Every Catholic boy, on the worst nights of his life, goes to bed wondering if animals like us are really worth the dirt God shaped us from. But into my life, into my darkness, God sent Simon. We didn't survive childhood together. *He* survived it, and carried me through it on his back. I have never escaped feeling that my debt to him was so great it could never be repaid. It could only be forgiven. Anything I could've done for him, I would've done.

Anything.

CHAPTER 1

"Is uncle simon late?" Peter asks.

Our housekeeper, Sister Helena, must be wondering the same thing as she watches our dinner of hake overcook in the pan. It's ten minutes past when my brother said he would arrive.

"Never mind that," I say. "Just help me set the table."

Peter ignores me. He climbs higher in his chair, standing on his knees, and announces, "Simon and I are going to see a movie, and then I'm going to show him the elephant at the Bioparco, and then he's going to teach me how to do the Marseille turn."

Sister Helena does a little shuffle in front of the frying pan. She thinks the Marseille turn is a kind of dance step. Peter is horrified. Lifting one hand in the air, the posture of a wizard performing a spell, he says, "No! It's a dribbling move! Like *Ronaldo*."

Simon is flying from Turkey to Rome for an art exhibit curated by one of our mutual friends, Ugo Nogara. Opening night, still almost a week off, will be a formal affair to which I wouldn't have a ticket myself except for the work I did with Ugo. But under this roof, we live in a five-year-old's world. Uncle Simon has come home to give soccer lessons.

"There's more to life," Sister Helena says, "than kicking a ball."

She takes it upon herself to be the feminine voice of reason. When Peter was eleven months old, my wife, Mona, left us. Ever since, this wonderful old nun has become my life-support system as a father. She's on loan from Uncle Lucio, who has battalions of them at his disposal, and I have trouble imagining what I would do without her, since I can't pay what even a reasonable teenage girl would expect to earn. Fortunately, Sister Helena wouldn't leave Peter for the world.

My son disappears into his bedroom and returns holding his digital alarm clock. With his mother's gift for directness, he sets it on the table in front of me and points.

"Sweetheart," Helena assures him, "Father Simon's train is probably just running behind."

The train. Not the uncle. Because it would be hard for Peter to understand that Simon sometimes forgets fare money or becomes absorbed in conversations with strangers. Mona wouldn't even agree to name our child after him because she found him unpredictable. And though my brother has the most prestigious job a young priest can hope for—he's a diplomat in the Holy See Secretariat of State, the elite of our Catholic bureaucracy—the truth is that he needs all the grueling work he can get. Like the men on our mother's side of the family, Simon is a Roman Catholic priest, which means he'll never marry or have kids. And unlike other Vatican priests, who were born for the desk and the ample waist, he has a restless soul. God bless Mona, she wanted our son to take after his dependable, unhurried, satisfied father. So she and I made a compromise when we named him: in the gospels, Jesus comes upon a fisherman named Simon, and renames him Peter.

I take out my mobile phone and text Simon—*Are you close?*—while Peter inspects the contents of Sister Helena's pan.

"Hake is fish," he announces, apropos of nothing. He's in a classifying stage. He also hates fish.

"Simon loves this dish," I tell him. "We used to eat it as kids."

Actually, when Simon and I used to eat this dish, it was cod, not hake. But a single priest's salary stretches only so far at the fish market. And as Mona often reminded me when planning meals like these, my brother—who is a head taller than any other priest inside these walls—eats as much as two ordinary men.

Mona is on my mind now, more than usual. My brother's arrival always seems to bring with it the shadow of my wife's departure. They are the magnetic poles of my life; one of them always lurks in the other's shade. Mona and I knew each other as children inside the Vatican walls, and when we met again in Rome, it felt like God's will. But we had a cart-and-horse problem—Eastern priests have to marry before they're ordained, or not marry at all—and in retrospect Mona probably needed more time to prepare herself. The life of a Vatican wife isn't easy. The life of a priest's wife is even harder. Mona kept working full-time until almost the day she gave birth to our blue-eyed baby who ate like a shark and slept even less. Mona nursed him so often that I would find the refrigerator empty from her attempts to replenish herself.

Only later would everything come into focus. The refrigerator was empty because she had stopped going to the grocery store. I hadn't noticed this because she'd also given up eating regular meals. She prayed less. Sang to Peter less. Then, three weeks before our son's first birthday, she disappeared. I discovered a bottle of pills hidden under a mug at the back of a cabinet. A doctor at Vatican Health Services explained that she had been trying to bootstrap herself out of depression. We must not give up hope, he said. So Peter and I waited for Mona to come back. Waited, and waited.

Today, he vows that he remembers her. These memories, though, are really details from photographs he's seen around the apartment. He colors them with knowledge gleaned from television shows and magazine advertisements. He hasn't yet noticed that women at our Greek church don't wear lipstick or perfume. Sadly, his experience of church seems almost Roman Catholic: when he looks at me, what he sees is a lone priest, solitary, celibate. The contradictions of his own identity are still in his future. But he names his mother constantly in his prayers, and people tell me John Paul behaved in a similar way after he lost his mother at a young age. I find comfort in that thought.

At last the phone rings. Sister Helena smiles as I hurry to answer it. "Hello?"

Peter watches anxiously.

I'm expecting the sounds of a metro station or, worse, an airport. But that's not what I hear. The voice on the other end is faint. Far away.

"Sy?" I say. "Is that you?"

He doesn't seem to hear me. The reception is poor. I take this as a sign that he's closer to home than I expected. It's hard to keep a signal on Vatican soil.

"Alex," I hear him say.

"Yes?"

He speaks again, but the line is swimming in static. It occurs to me that he might've made a detour to the Vatican Museums to see Ugo Nogara, who's been struggling with the pressure of finishing his big exhibit. Though I would never say so to Peter, it would be just like my brother to find an extra soul to tend on his way in.

"Sy," I say. "Are you at the museums?"

Down at the dinner table, suspense is killing Peter. "He's with Mister Nogara?" he whispers to Helena.

But on the other end of the line, something changes. There's a burst of hissing I recognize as wind blowing. He's outdoors. And here in Rome, at least, it's storming.

For a moment, the line clears up.

"Alex, I need you to come get me."

His voice sends an uncomfortable tingle up my back.

"What's wrong?" I ask.

"I'm at Castel Gandolfo. In the gardens."

"I don't understand," I tell him. "Why are you there?"

The wind sets in again, and a strange noise slips through the earpiece. It sounds like my brother moaning.

"Please, Alex," he says. "Come now. I'm—I'm near the east gate, below the villa. You need to get here before the police do."

My son is frozen, staring at me. I watch the paper napkin slip off his lap and drift through the air like the pope's white skullcap caught in the wind. Sister Helena, too, is watching.

"Stay right there," I tell Simon. And I turn away, so Peter can't see the look I know is in my eyes. Because the sound in my brother's voice is something I don't remember ever hearing there before. Fear.

CHAPTER 2

I DRIVE TO CASTEL Gandolfo in the teeth of a north-riding storm. The rain is angry, hopping off the cobblestones like fleas. By the time I reach the highway, the windshield is just a drum the sky is beating. On all sides, cars slow up and pull onto shoulders. As the constellation of red lights vanishes, my thoughts turn to my brother.

When he was young, Simon was the boy who would climb a tree in a lightning storm to fetch a stray cat. One night, on the beach in Campania, I watched him swim into a school of glowing jellyfish to bring back a girl who got caught in a riptide. That winter, when he was fifteen and I was eleven, I went to meet him at the sacristy of Saint Peter's, where he was an altar boy. He was supposed to take me for a haircut in town, but on our way out of the basilica, a bird flew through a window in the dome, two hundred feet up, and we heard the thump of it landing on the balcony. Something inside Simon needed to see it, so we ran up those six million stairs, and at the top we reached a fingernail ledge of marble. It looped in a circle over the high altar, with nothing but a guardrail between us and thin air. On the ledge was the dove, flopping in circles, coughing little ink-spots of blood. Simon walked over and picked it up. That was when someone shouted, *Stop! Don't come any closer!*

Across the dome, leaning on the rail, was a man. He was staring at us with red eyes. Suddenly, Simon went running at him.

No, signore! he shouted. *Don't!*

Then the man lifted his leg over the rail.

Signore!

Not even if God had given Simon wings could he have gotten there in time. The man leaned forward and let go. We watched him drop through Saint Peter's like a pin. I heard a tour guide down there saying *bronze stolen from the Pantheon*, and still the man was falling, smaller than an eyelash now. Finally there was a scream, and a little starburst of blood. I sat down. The joints in my legs had buckled. I can't remember moving again until Simon came to pick me up.

All my life, I've never understood why God sent a bird through that window. Maybe it was to teach Simon the feeling of something slipping through his fingers. Our father died the following year, so maybe it was a lesson that couldn't wait. But the last image I have in my memory of that day, before the workmen hustled everyone out of the church, is of Simon on that ledge, arms outstretched, frozen, as if trying to put the bird back into the air. As if it were just a matter of getting a vase back on a shelf.

That afternoon, the priests reconsecrated Saint Peter's, the way they always do when a pilgrim jumps. But no one can reconsecrate a child. Two weeks later, our choirmaster slapped a boy for being out of tune, and Simon jumped out of line and slapped him back. For three days they canceled choir practice while my parents tried to knuckle Simon into an apology. The soul of obedience he had been, all his life. Now he said he would rather quit than apologize. In the blueprint of how we became the men we are, that is where I locate the foundation. Everything I know about my brother rises unwavering from that point.

The decade of Simon's life between the beginning of college and the beginning of his diplomatic training were hard ones in Italy. The bombings and assassinations of our childhood had mostly ended, but there were volcanic protests in Rome against a bankrupt government that was collapsing under its own corruption. During college, Simon marched with the university students. During seminary, he marched in solidarity with the workers. By the time he was invited to enter the diplomatic ranks, I thought those days were behind us. Then, three years ago, in May of 2001, John Paul decided to travel to Greece.

It was the first trip by any pope to our homeland in thirteen centuries, and our countrymen weren't happy to see him. Nearly all Greeks are Orthodox, and John Paul wanted to end the schism between our

Churches. Simon went there to see it happen. But hatreds are something my brother has never understood. From our father he inherited an almost Protestant immunity to the verdict of history. Orthodox blame Catholics for mistreating them in every war from the Crusades to World War Two. They blame Catholics for luring Orthodox away from their ancestral Church for a new hybrid form of Catholicism. The mere existence of Eastern Catholics is a provocation to some Orthodox, yet Simon couldn't fathom why his own brother, a Greek Catholic priest, wouldn't join him in Athens for the trip.

The trouble arrived even before Simon did. When news spread that John Paul was going to touch down on Hellenic soil, Greek Orthodox monasteries rang funeral bells. Hundreds of Orthodox took to the streets in protest, carrying banners that read ARCH-HERETIC and TWO-HORNED MONSTER OF ROME. Newspapers carried stories about holy icons that had begun bleeding. A national day of mourning was declared. Simon, who had made arrangements to sleep in the rectory of my father's old Greek Catholic church, arrived to find that Orthodox reactionaries had vandalized the doors with spray paint. He said the police wouldn't help. My brother had finally found the underdog he was born to defend.

That night, a small group of Orthodox hard-liners broke into the church and disrupted the liturgy. They made the great mistake of stripping the parish priest of his cassock and stomping on the antimension, the sacred cloth that makes a table an altar.

My brother is almost six and a half feet tall. His sense of obligation toward the weak and helpless is intensified by the knowledge that he is larger and stronger than anyone he meets. Simon vaguely remembers pushing an Orthodox man out of the sanctuary in an attempt to save the Greek Catholic priest. The Orthodox man says Simon threw him. Greek police say he broke the man's arm. Simon was arrested. His new employer—the Holy See Secretariat of State—had to negotiate his immediate return to Rome. That was why Simon never saw firsthand how John Paul dealt with the same hostilities, with much better success.

The Greek Orthodox bishops made a point of snubbing John Paul. He didn't complain. They insulted him. He didn't defend himself. They demanded he apologize for Catholic sins from centuries ago. And John Paul, speaking on behalf of one billion living souls and the untold Catholic dead, apologized. The Orthodox were so amazed that they agreed to do something they had refused to do until that moment: to stand beside him in prayer.

I've always hoped that John Paul's performance in Athens was a corrective to Simon's behavior. Another lesson sent down from heaven. Since then, Simon has been a changed man. That is what I tell myself, again and again, as I drive south from Rome into the heart of the storm.

■ ■ ■

IN THE DISTANCE, CASTEL Gandolfo comes into view: a long hilltop breaching over the weird prairie of golf courses and used-car lots that yawn south from the outskirts of Rome. Two thousand years ago, this was the playground of emperors. The popes have been summering here for only a few centuries, but it's enough to qualify the land as an official extension of our country.

As I round the hill, I see a carabinieri squad car at the bottom of the cliff—Italian policemen from the station across the border line, sharing a cigarette while the storm rages. But Italy's laws have no force where I'm going. There's no sign of Vatican police in this slashing rain, and their absence allows the pinch in my chest to begin to loosen.

I park my Fiat where the hillside sinks into Lake Albano, and before stepping out in the rain I dial a number on my phone. On the fifth ring, a gruff voice picks up.

"Pronto."

"Little Guido?" I say.

He snorts. "Who's this?"

"Alex Andreou."

Guido Canali is an old childhood acquaintance, the son of a Vatican turbine mechanic. In a country where the only qualification for most jobs is blood relation to someone else with a job, Guido has been unable to find better work than shoveling manure at the pontifical dairy on this hilltop. He's always looking for a handout. And though it's no accident our paths don't cross anymore, I'm looking for some help of my own.

"It's not Little Guido anymore," he says. "My old man died last year."

"Sorry to hear that."

"That makes one of us. To what do I owe the call?"

"I'm in town and need a favor. Could you open the gate for me?"

From his surprised tone, he has no inkling about Simon. More good news. We negotiate a deal: two tickets to the upcoming exhibit, which Guido knows I can get from Uncle Lucio. Even the proudest sloth in our country wants to see what my friend Ugo has done. When I hang up, I follow the dark trail up the hill to our meeting place, where the wind sharpens to the high hissing sound I heard behind Simon's phone call.

I'm surprised—and at first, relieved—to see no signs of trouble here. Every time I've collected my brother from the police in the past, he's been part of some agitation. But there are no villagers picketing in the square here, no Vatican employees marching for better wages. At the north end of the village, the pope's summer palace looks abandoned. The two domes of the Vatican Observatory rise from its roof like lumps on the head of the cartoon characters Peter watches on television. Nothing is amiss here. Nothing even seems alive.

A private walkway leads from the palace to the papal gardens, and at the garden gate I see a pixie of cigarette light hovering in a black fist.

"Guido?"

"Hell of a time for a visit," the cigarette says, then drops in a puddle to die. "Follow me."

As my eyes adjust, I see that he looks exactly like the late Big Guido: pug-faced, with a broad beetlelike back. Manual labor has made him a man. The Vatican directory is littered with staff Simon and I knew as children, but my brother and I are almost the only priests. Ours is a caste system in which men proudly replace the fathers and grandfathers who shined floors or fixed furniture before them. It can be hard, though, to watch old playmates rise to a higher station, and there's a familiar tone in Guido's voice when he opens the metal lock, points to his truck, and says, "Get in, *Father.*"

The gates here are to keep out the riffraff, and the hedges are to keep out their eyes. An Italian village sits on either side of our land, but you'd never know it. The spine of this hill, half a mile long, is a private wonderland for the pope. His property at Castel Gandolfo is bigger than the entire Vatican, but nobody lives here, only some gardeners and workmen and the old Jesuit astronomer who sleeps during the day. The real inhabitants are potted fruit trees and avenues of stone pines, flower beds measured in acres, and marble statues left behind by pagan emperors, now mounted in the gardens to give John Paul a smile on his summer walks. From up here, the view is from lake to sea. As we drive down the unpaved garden path, there isn't another living thing in sight.

"Where were you looking to go?" Guido says.

"Just drop me in the gardens."

He raises an eyebrow. "In the middle of *this*?"

The storm rages. His interest piqued by the strangeness of my request, Guido turns on the CB radio to see if there is any chatter. Yet it, too, is silent.

"My girl works down there," he says, lifting a finger off the wheel to point. "In the olive groves."

I say nothing. I give tours of this place to new recruits at my old seminary, so in daylight I would know the landscape better. But in the darkness, in this driving rain, all I can make out is the strip of road before the headlights. As we approach the gardens, there are no trucks, no police cars, no gardeners with flashlights sloping through the rain.

"She drives me up a wall," Guido says, shaking his head. "But Alex, the ass on this girl." He whistles.

The deeper we drive into these shadows, the more it blooms in me that something is deeply wrong. Simon must be alone in the rain. For the first time, I consider the possibility that he's hurt. That he's been in some kind of accident. Yet on the phone he mentioned the police, not an ambulance. I replay our conversation in my mind, searching for something I misunderstood.

Guido's truck jackknifes up a road through the gardens and comes to the edge of a clearing.

"Far enough," I say. "I'll get out here."

Guido looks around. "Here?"

I'm already descending.

"Don't forget our deal, Alex," he calls out. "Two tickets to opening night."

But I'm too preoccupied to respond. When Guido is gone, I take out my phone and call Simon. The coverage up here is so spotty that there's no reliable connection. Just for an instant, though, I hear another mobile phone ring.

I move toward the sound, fanning my flashlight into the distance. The hillside has been carved into a vast staircase, three monolithic terraces that descend one after another in the direction of the far-off sea.

Every inch is planted with flowers arranged in circles within octagons within squares, not a petal out of place. The space up here is infinite. It creates a wild anxiety in me.

I'm about to shout Simon's name into the wind, when something comes into view. From up here, on the highest terrace, I make out a fence. The eastern border of the pope's property. Just before the gate, the beam of my flashlight tangles with something dark. A silhouette dressed entirely in black.

The wind snaps at the hem of my cassock as I run toward it. The earth is choppy. Clods of mud are turned up, grass roots sticking out like spider legs.

"Simon!" I call toward him. "Are you okay?"

He doesn't answer. He doesn't even move.

I'm lurching toward him now, trying to keep upright in the slicks of mud. The distance between us shrinks. Yet he doesn't speak.

I arrive in front of him. My brother. I lay hands on him, saying, "Are you okay? Tell me you're okay."

He's soaked and pale. His wet hair is painted to his forehead like a doll's. A black cassock clings to his ropy muscles the way a pelt clings to a racehorse. Cassocks are the old-fashioned robes that all Roman priests once wore, before black pants and black jackets came into style. In this darkness, on my brother's looming figure, it creates an almost ghoulish impression.

"What's wrong?" I say, because he still hasn't answered me.

There's a thin, distant look in his eyes. He's staring at something on the ground.

A long black coat lies in the mud. The overcoat of a Roman priest. A greca, named for its resemblance to a Greek priest's cassock. Underneath it is a hump.

Not in any imagining of this moment have I conceived of something like this. At the end of the hump is a pair of shoes.

"My God," I whisper. "Who is that?"

Simon's voice is so dry that it cracks.

"I could've saved him," he says.

"Sy, I don't understand. Tell me what's going on."

My eyes are drawn to those loafers. There's a hole in one of the soles. A feeling nags at me, like a fingernail scraping against my thoughts.

Stray papers have blown against the high fence that separates the pope's property from the border road. Rain has pasted them to the metal links like papier-mâché.

"He called me," Simon murmurs. "I knew he was in trouble. I came as soon as I could."

"*Who* called you?"

But the meaning of the words slowly registers. Now I know the source of that nagging feeling. The hole in those loafers is familiar.

I step back. My stomach tightens. My hands curl up.

"H-how . . . ?" I stammer.

There are suddenly lights moving down the garden road toward us. Pairs of them, no bigger than BBs. When they come closer, they resolve into police cruisers.

Vatican gendarmes.

I kneel down, hands trembling. On the ground beside the body is an open briefcase. The wind continues to tug at the papers inside it.

The gendarmes begin jogging toward us, barking orders to step away from the body. But I reach over and do what every instinct in my body requires. I need to see.

When I pull back Simon's greca, the dead man's eyes are wide. The mouth is cocked. The tongue is stuffed in its cheek. On my friend's face is a dull grimace. In his temple is a black hole leaking a pink nubbin of flesh.

The clouds are pressing in. Simon's hand is on me, pulling me back. *Step away*, he says.

But I can't take my eyes off it. I see suit pockets turned out. A bare patch of white skin where a wristwatch has been removed.

"Come away, Father," says a gendarme.

Finally I turn. The gendarme has a face like a leather knuckle. From his needlepoint eyes, from his frost of white hair, I recognize him as Inspector Falcone, chief of Vatican police. The man who runs beside John Paul's car.

"Which one of you is Father Andreou?" he says.

Simon steps forward and says, "We both are. I'm the one who called you."

I stare at my brother, trying to make sense of this.

Falcone points to one of his officers. "Go with Special Agent Bracco. Tell him everything you saw."

Simon obeys. He reaches into the pocket of the greca for his wallet and phone and passport but leaves his coat draped over the body. Before following the officer, he says, "This man has no next of kin. I need to make sure he receives a proper funeral."

Falcone squints. It's a queer statement. But coming from a priest, he allows it.

"Father," he says, "you knew this man?"

Simon answers in a faint voice. "He was my friend. His name was Ugolino Nogara."

CHAPTER 3

THE POLICEMAN LEADS Simon out of earshot to answer questions, and I watch the other gendarmes rope up the clearing. One studies the eight-foot fence beside the public road, trying to understand how an outsider penetrated these gardens. Another stares at a security camera mounted overhead. Most gendarmes were city cops in another life. Rome PD. They can see that Ugo's watch has been stolen, that his wallet is gone, that his briefcase is pried open. Yet they keep working over the details as if something doesn't square.

In these hills, people's love for the Holy Father is fierce. Locals tell stories about popes knocking at their doors, making sure every family in town had a chicken in its pot. Old-timers are named in honor of Pope Pius, who shielded their families from harm in wartime. It's not the walls that protect this place, but the villagers. A robbery here seems impossible.

"Weapon!" I hear one of the officers call.

He's standing at the mouth of a tunnel, a giant thoroughfare built for a Roman emperor as a covered path for after-meal walks. Two more gendarmes jog to the opening, guided by a pair of gardeners. There is grunting. Something large topples over. Whatever the police find, though, isn't the gun they were hoping for.

"False alarm," one of them barks.

My chest shudders. I close my eyes. A wave of emotion rolls through me. I've watched men die before. At the hospital where Mona was a nurse, I used to anoint the sick. Say prayers for the dying. And yet I have trouble swallowing back this feeling.

A gendarme comes by, taking pictures of footprints in the mud. There are police everywhere in these gardens now. But my eyes return to Ugo.

What is his special claim on my heart? His exhibit will make him, now posthumously, one of the most talked-about men in Rome, and I'll be able to say I had a hand in that. But what won me over were his battle scars. The eyeglasses he never found time to repair. The holes in his shoes. The awkwardness that evaporated once he began talking about his great project. Even his neurotic, incurable drinking. Nothing on earth mattered to him except his exhibit, and on it he lavished every waking thought. He existed for its future. That, I realize, is the source of my feelings. To this exhibit, Ugo was a father.

Simon returns now, followed by the gendarme who questioned him. My brother's eyes are blank and wet. I wait for him to say something. Instead it's the officer who speaks.

"You may go now," he says. "Fathers."

But the body bag has just arrived. Neither of us moves. Two gendarmes lift Ugo on top of it and stretch the sides around him. The zipper makes a sound like velvet ripping. They begin to carry him off when Simon says, "Stop."

The policemen turn.

Simon lifts a hand in the air and says:

"O Lord, incline Your ear."

Both gendarmes lower the body bag. Everyone within earshot— every cop, every gardener, every man of every caste—reaches up to remove his hat.

"Humbly I ask," Simon says, "that You show mercy on the soul of Your servant Ugolino Nogara, whom You commanded to pass out of this world into the region of peace and light. Let him be partaker with Your saints. Through Christ the Lord, amen."

In my heart, I add those two essential Greek words, the most succinct and powerful of all Christian prayers.

Kyrie, eleison.

Lord, have mercy.

Hats return to heads. The bag rises once more. Wherever it is going, it goes.

There is an aching stillness between my ribs.

Ugo Nogara is gone.

■ ■ ■

WHEN WE REACH THE Fiat, Simon pops open the glove box and feels it out with his fingers. In a faint voice he says, "Where's my pack of cigarettes?"

"I threw it away."

The screen of my mobile phone says Sister Helena has called twice. Peter must be frantic with worry. But there isn't enough service here to get a connection.

Simon scratches his neck needfully.

"We'll get you some when we get back," I tell him. "What happened back there?"

He breathes out the corner of his mouth, a plume of invisible smoke. I notice his right hand squeezing the top of his right thigh.

"Are you hurt?" I ask.

He shakes his head but readjusts himself to make that leg more comfortable. His left hand reaches into the other sleeve of his cassock, dipping into the French cuffs that priests use like pockets. He's looking for cigarettes again.

I turn the key. When the Fiat comes to life, I lean forward and kiss the rosary Mona hung from the rearview mirror long ago. "We'll be home soon," I say. "When you're ready to talk, let me know."

He nods but doesn't speak. Drumming his fingers against his lips, he stares toward the clearing where Ugo lost his life.

WE COULD GET TO Rome faster driving elephants over the Alps. My father's old Fiat is on its last cylinder, down from the original two. There are lawn mowers with more horsepower these days. The dial of the car stereo has rusted in place at 105 FM, Vatican Radio, which is broadcasting the rosary. Simon takes the string of beads off the mirror and begins to finger it. The voice on the radio says: *Pontius Pilate, wishing to satisfy the crowd, had Jesus scourged and handed him over to be crucified.* Those words cue the usual prayers—an Our Father, ten Hail Marys, a Glory Be—and the prayers plunge Simon into faraway contemplation.

"Why would anyone rob him?" I ask, unable to bear the silence.

Ugo had almost nothing worth taking. He wore a cheap wristwatch. Carried a wallet whose contents would barely have covered the train fare back to Rome.

"I don't know," Simon says.

The only time I ever saw Ugo with a wad of cash was after he'd traded money at the airport following a business trip.

"Were you on the same plane home?" I ask.

They've both been working in Turkey.

"No," Simon says distantly. "He got in two nights ago."

"What was he doing here?"

My brother glances at me, as if trying to sift meaning from gibberish.

"Preparing his exhibit," Simon says.

"Why would he have gone walking in the gardens?"

"I don't know."

There are a handful of museums and archaeological sites among these hills, in the Italian territory surrounding the pope's property. Ugo could've been doing research there, or meeting with another curator. But the outdoor sites would've closed when the storm came through, and Ugo would've been forced to find shelter.

"The villa in the gardens," I say. "Maybe that's where he was headed."

Simon nods. The voice on the radio says, *Weaving a crown out of thorns, they placed it on Jesus' head, and a reed in his right hand. And kneeling before him, they mocked him, saying, "Hail, King of the Jews!"* The next round of prayers starts, and Simon follows it, leaving chips of dirt on the beads as they move under his thumb. He's never been a fastidious priest, but he's always been trim and tidy. As the mud dries on his skin, he stares at the spiderwebs of cracks forming in it, and at the flakes of dust stripped off by the rosary.

I remember the two of us sitting just like this, shortly after Peter's birth, on the night I drove Simon to the airport for his first posting overseas. We listened to the radio, watching planes swim into the air overhead, leaving contrails like angels. My brother believed that diplomacy was God's work, that negotiating tables were where religious hatreds went to die. When he accepted a post in lowly Bulgaria, where fewer than one in a hundred people is Catholic, Uncle Lucio wrung his hands and said Simon might as well work for the pork lobby in Israel. But three out of four Bulgarians are Orthodox Christians, and ever since my brother's trip to Athens, it had been his project to promote the reunion of the earth's two biggest Churches. That kind of idealism had always been Simon's besetting sin. Priests in our Secretariat of State are promoted on a timetable—bishop in ten years, archbishop in twenty—which explains why so many of the world's hundred fifty cardinals are Secretariat men. But the ones who fall short tend to be the ones waylaid by good intentions. As Lucio warned him, a maharaja has to choose between leading his people and cleaning up after his elephant. In that metaphor, Mona, Peter, and I were the elephant. Simon needed to extricate himself from us before his sense of obligation slowed him down.

But then Simon posted to Turkey, and God tossed him a new charity case: Ugo Nogara. A lost sheep. A fragile soul struggling with the masterpiece of his career. So I can imagine what my brother must feel at this moment. An agony not entirely different from what I would feel if something had happened to Peter.

"Ugo's in a good place," I remind him.

This is the conviction that helped two boys survive the deaths of their parents. Beyond death is life; beyond suffering, peace. But Simon is still too raw to absorb Ugo's death. Instead of thumbing the rosary, he grips it in his hand.

"What did the gendarme ask you?" I say.

There are wrinkles under his eyes. I can't tell whether he's squinting into the distance or whether a handful of years in the Secretariat has done this to a man only in his early thirties.

"About my phone," he says.

"Why?"

"To see what time Ugo called me."

"What else?"

He stares at the phone in his hand. "Whether I saw anyone else in the gardens."

"Did you?"

He must be swimming in darkness. His only dim answer is, "Nobody."

Loose thoughts tangle in my mind. Castel Gandolfo goes quiet in the fall. The pope leaves his summer residence and returns to the Vatican, so the Swiss Guards and gendarmes no longer keep detachments on the grounds. Tourist spots are deserted by evening because the last daily train to Rome leaves before five, and if the pickpockets here are anything like the ones in Rome, they become more aggressive once the easy prey is gone. For a second I'm haunted by the image of Ugo in the rain, in the empty town square, hunted down by one of them.

"There was a carabinieri station right across the road," I say. "Why didn't Ugo call them?"

"I don't know."

Maybe he *did* call them, but they refused to cross the Vatican border. And if Ugo called our Vatican emergency number, 112, I doubt it would've worked out here.

"What did he say to you on the phone?" I ask.

Simon lifts a hand. "Please, Alex. I need some time."

He retreats into himself, as if his memory of the phone call is especially painful. Simon must've been en route from the airport when it came. Maybe he told his driver to take an immediate detour, but it still wasn't enough.

I remember how he flew home right away when I called him with the news that Mona had left me. He vowed to stay as long as it took for me to feel human again. It took six weeks. Lucio begged him to return to the embassy. Instead, Simon helped me canvass Rome with flyers, helped me phone relatives and friends, helped take care of Peter while I meandered self-indulgently through the city, visiting the places where I had fallen in love with my wife. Later, when he returned to Bulgaria, our mailbox was flooded with envelopes addressed to Peter, each containing photos Simon had shot around the capital: a man losing his toupee in a city breeze; an accordion player with a monkey; a squirrel in a mountain of chestnuts. They became the wallpaper of Peter's room. The ritual of reading the letters became my new beginning with my son. That was how I learned what Lucio had meant. While Simon snapped photos, lesser priests were climbing the ladder. Finally I told him that Peter and I had turned the corner. No more letters. Please.

The city lights have begun to rain color on us. Simon's eyes are moving, sizing up the vista beyond the windshield. It's been more than a month since he saw this skyline, more than a month since he breathed Roman air. Tonight was supposed to be a homecoming.

Quietly I say, "Did you see any of the garden gates left unlocked?"
But he doesn't seem to hear me.

■ ■ ■

THE VATICAN APARTMENT BUILDING where Simon and I grew up,
and where I still live with Peter, is called the Belvedere Palace, because
in Italian you can call anything a palace. Ours is a brick shoebox built a
hundred years ago by the pope because he got tired of seeing housewives
and children in his private stairwells. *Belvedere* means "pretty view," but
we don't have one of those either; just the Vatican supermarket on one
side and the Vatican parking garage on the other. Employee housing, is
what it is.

We live on the top floor, across the hall from the Brothers of Saint
John of God who run the Vatican Pharmacy on the ground floor. From a
few windows we can see the back of John Paul's apartments in the papal
palace—a real palazzo, by anyone's standards. In the small rear lot, a
gendarme is doing what God made Vatican policemen to do: check cars
for parking permits. We are home.

"Do you want me to ask Brother Samuel for a pack you can smoke?"
I ask as we climb the stairs.

Simon's hand is shaking. "No, don't wake him. I've got a stash inside
somewhere."

A second gendarme, passing us on the steps, can't help noticing
Simon's bedraggled appearance. Out of respect, though, he looks away.

I stop.

"Officer," I blurt, wheeling around on the stairs, "what are you doing
here?"

From down the stairwell he looks up. He's a cadet, with the eyes of
a child.

"Fathers . . ." He kneads his service cap. "There was an incident."

Simon frowns. "What do you mean, an incident?"

But I'm already racing up the stairs.

MY APARTMENT DOOR IS open. Three men are huddled in my living
room. In the kitchen, a chair has been thrown on its back. A plate of
food is shattered on the floor.

"Where's Peter?" I shout. "Where's my son?"

The men turn. They are Hospitaller Brothers from next door, still wearing white lab coats over black habits after a day of work at the pharmacy. One of them points down the hall toward the bedrooms. He says nothing.

I feel disoriented. In the hall, a credenza is overturned. The hardwood floor is littered with papers. Staring up at me, innocent and fragile, is my father's icon of the Christ child. Its red clay frame has been smashed by the fall. From behind the bedroom door comes the sound of a woman sobbing.

Sister Helena.

I push open the bedroom door. They're both here, huddled on the bed. Peter sits in Helena's lap, cocooned in her crossed arms. Opposite them, on the bed where Simon slept as a boy, a gendarme is taking notes.

". . . taller, I suppose," she is saying, "but I never got a good look."

The gendarme abruptly looks up at Simon, who has arrived behind me, giant and storm-swept.

"What happened?" I say, rushing forward. "Are you hurt?"

"Babbo!" Peter says, squirming out of her arms to reach me.

His face is pink and puffy. The moment he reaches my embrace, he begins crying again.

"Oh, thank heaven," Sister Helena exclaims, rising from the bed to greet me.

Peter trembles in my arms. I pat him, searching for injuries.

"Unharmed," Helena whispers.

"What's going on?"

She places a hand over her mouth. The pouched skin beneath her eyes weakens. "A man," she says. "Came inside."

"What? When?"

"We were in the kitchen. Having dinner."

"I don't understand. How did he get in?"

"I don't know. We heard him at the door. Then he was inside."

I turn to the gendarme. "You caught him?"

"No. But we're stopping everyone who tries to cross the border."

I press Peter against me. The officer in the parking lot wasn't checking permits, then.

"What did he want?" I ask him.

"We're looking into that," the gendarme says.

"Were other apartments robbed?"

"None that we know of."

I've never heard of a burglary in this building. Petty crime is almost nonexistent in our Vatican village.

Peter nuzzles my neck and whispers, "I had to hide in the closet."

I stroke his back and ask Helena, "Did he look at all familiar?"

The village is small. Sister Helena lives in a convent, but Peter and I know almost everyone who lives inside these walls.

"I never got a look at him, Father," she says. "He was beating on the door so loudly that I lifted Peter out of his chair and carried him in here."

I hesitate. "Beating on the door?"

"And shouting, and shaking the knob. He got inside while I was still carrying Peter. It's a miracle we got to the bedroom in time."

My heart is thudding. I turn to the gendarme. "So this wasn't a burglary?"

"We don't know what it was, Father."

"Did he try to hurt you?" I ask Helena.

"We locked the bedroom door and hid in the closet."

I look down and find my son gazing at the pale, mud-spattered figure of his uncle. Their faces are both deranged with shock.

"Peter," I say, stroking his stiff back, "it's okay. You're safe. Nothing bad is going to happen."

But he and Simon are locked in a frightening stare. Their blue eyes flash at each other. There's an animal quality to my brother's gaze, which Simon is trying but failing to master.

"Sister Helena," I repeat in a whisper, "did he try to hurt either of you?"

"No. He ignored us. We heard him moving around out there."

"What was he doing?"

"It sounded like he went to your room. He was calling your names."

I press Peter against me, shielding his face against my shoulder. "Whose names?"

"Yours and Father Simon's."

My skin crawls. I feel the gendarme staring at me, gauging my reaction.

"Father," he says, "can you shed any light on this?"

"No. Of course not." I turn to Simon. "Can you think of anything?"

My brother's stare is distant. All he says is, "What time did it happen?"

There's an unsettling note in his voice. It suggests something to me that seems irrational at first, but that spreads like ink through my thoughts. I wonder if this attack could be related to what happened to Ugo. If the person who killed Ugo might've come here next.

"It happened only a few minutes after Father Alex left," Helena says.

Castel Gandolfo is twenty miles from here. A forty-five-minute drive. It would've been almost impossible for the same person to have committed both attacks. Nor can I think of a reason. The only thing connecting us to Ugo is the work we did on his exhibit.

Simon gestures at the closet. "How long were you in there?"

"Super long," Peter says appreciatively. At last someone is focused on his suffering.

But Simon's stare drifts toward the window.

"More than five minutes?" I ask, sensing what my brother really wants to know.

"Much more."

The gendarme, then, wasn't being honest with us. From the door of this apartment, the border is only a one-minute jog. No one will be caught at the gates tonight.

The officer folds up his notebook and stands. "There's a car waiting for you downstairs, Sister. You shouldn't walk home in the dark."

"Thank you," Helena says, "but I'll stay the night here. For the little one's sake."

The cop opens the door a mite wider. "Your prioress is expecting you. A driver is waiting in the hall, ready to walk you downstairs."

Sister Helena is a willful old nun, but she won't let Peter see her argue with the police. She gives him a good-night kiss, and as she cups his cheek, her mottled hand trembles.

"I'll call you later," I tell her. "I have some more questions."

She nods but says no more. Peter nestles deeper into my arms as she leaves. His fingers are balled up, clutching the hem of the soccer jersey he wears everywhere. Its red bib is smeared with half-dried tears. As I cradle him, I spot the trunk pushed against the closet door. Sister Helena would've left the closet first, to phone the gendarmes. She would've had

Peter stay behind for his safety. So my son has been hunkering alone in a dark closet.

Feeling him pant on my neck, I realize it's half an hour past his bedtime. I can sense his exhaustion in the sheer weight of his body. "Do you want something to drink?" I whisper.

We make our way out to the kitchen, and he points to the shattered plate on the kitchen tile. "I did that," he says. "On accident."

I raise the overturned chair. Helena must have snatched him right out of his seat, all forty pounds of him. From a shelf I take down the Orange Fanta, a drink reserved for special occasions. It's been Peter's favorite ever since he saw Cardinal Ratzinger drinking it at the Cantina Tirolese in town. As he buries himself in the plastic cup, I stare over his shoulder at the mess in the hall. It extends toward my bedroom. For some reason, it passes over Peter's. This seems to confirm Helena's recollection of events.

"It's storming outside," Peter says, surfacing from the orange lagoon.

I nod absently. Maybe he's thinking about the man out there, the intruder, who hasn't been caught. I watch the gendarme return from a tour of my bedroom. As he passes Peter's door, Simon emerges. The gendarme asks something, but my brother answers, "No. My nephew's been through enough for one night."

"Babbo?" Peter says.

I turn. He's waiting expectantly.

"Yes?"

"I said, did the car break down in the rain?"

It takes me a second to understand. He's wondering why Simon and I were late coming home. Why he and Sister Helena were all by themselves when the man came.

"We . . . had a flat tire."

The Fiat breaks down often. Peter has become an authority on leaking oil and faulty alternators. I worry sometimes that he's becoming an encyclopedia of misfortunes.

"Okay," he says, watching his uncle shut the door after the police.

Now the apartment is ours again. When Simon sits down beside his nephew, his size reassures Peter, who moves to the edge of his chair like a butterfly sunning itself on a branch.

"They'll come back tomorrow," is all Simon offers.

I nod. But what we need to navigate now, we can't discuss in front of Peter.

My brother puts a giant hand on his nephew's hair and musses it. His cassock sheds a dust of dried mud everywhere.

"Did you have to lift the car?" Peter asks.

"What?"

"When you changed the tire," Peter says.

Simon and I exchange a look.

Foggily Simon says, "I just used a . . ." He snaps his fingers in the air.

"Jack?" Peter supplies.

He nods and stands abruptly. "Hey, Peter, I need to get cleaned up, okay?" He glances at me and adds, "Ubi dormiemus?"

Latin. To prevent Peter from understanding. It means "Where will we sleep?"

So he and I agree. It may not be safe to stay here.

"The Swiss barracks?" I suggest. The safest place in our country after John Paul's apartments.

Simon nods and trudges back toward the shower, doing his best to disguise a slight limp.

WHEN HE'S GONE, I tell Peter to collect his favorite pajamas. Then I boot up our computer and wait impatiently for the old CPU to search my e-mail for Ugo's name. My thoughts are uneasy. My ears search the air for sounds outside in the hall.

Two dozen messages surface. All were written this summer. The last, from two weeks ago, is the one. As I reread it, I wonder if my eyes are fooling me. My judgment right now probably isn't sound. But when I hear the familiar thump of water locking in the pipes, I print it and fold the paper into my cassock, then follow Simon into the bedroom Mona and I once shared.

I find him holding his dirty cassock over the laundry bag that our mother once embroidered with the words GENESIS 1:4: GOD SEPARATED LIGHTS FROM DARKS. He looks even more agitated than before. I feel the same way. It's settling over me now that Peter was in danger. That Sister Helena may have saved his life.

"Who would've done this?" I whisper.

Notching one of my drawers out of its track, he searches the hole for his emergency cigarettes. On this very dresser our father kept two ash-trays because one wasn't enough. Until John Paul outlawed it, smoking was the national pastime. But Simon's expression doesn't lighten when he finds what he wants. The drawer won't go back in its slot, so he shakes it and the whole dresser lurches.

"Why would they come for *us*?" I ask.

Flicking off his towel, he steps into his underwear. Now I see why he's been favoring his leg: the skin is purple. Something has been cinched around the muscle.

"Don't say it," he says, seeing that I've noticed.

When Secretariat men enter the world of cocktail receptions and three-fork dinners, they feel they've betrayed the spirit of the priest-hood. So they turn to old solutions. Some whip themselves. Some wear hair-shirts or chains. Some do what Simon has done: tighten a cilice around their thigh. These are quick medicines for the pleasures of em-bassy work. But he should know better. Our father taught us the Greek way: fasting, prayer, sleeping on a cold floor.

"When did you—?" I begin.

"*Don't*," he snaps. "Just let me get dressed."

There's no more line on the reel. We need to get out of here.

Peter appears in the doorway, holding a mountain of dinosaur sleep-wear. "Is this enough?" he says.

Simon quickly steps into the closet.

"Come on, Peter," I say, leading him back toward the kitchen. "Let's wait for Uncle Simon out here."

CHAPTER 4

THE SWISS GUARD barracks is down the street from our apartment. Outsiders are forbidden, but Simon and I spent many nights in these halls after our parents died. The recruits let us join their training runs, share their weight room, crash their fondue parties. My first hangover was born inside these walls. Most of our old friends have flown back to Switzerland for new adventures, but the rest have become officers. When the cadets at the desk call up for orders, we're immediately waved through.

I'm agog at how young the new halberdiers seem. Other than their required stint in the Swiss military back home, they look fresh from high school. Once, these were the men I most admired in our country. Now they're overgrown boys, ten years my junior.

Three long buildings form the barracks, each separated from the next by an alleylike courtyard. New men bunk together in the building that fronts the Rome border. The officers' building, where we're headed, is the innermost one, backing to the papal palace. We take the elevator up and knock at the apartment of my closest friend in the Guard, Leo Keller. His wife, Sofia, answers the door.

"Oh, Alex, how awful," she says. "I can't believe what happened. Come in, come in."

News travels fast in this barracks.

Peter exclaims, "Can I feel the baby?" And before Sofia can answer, he places both hands on her pregnant belly.

I begin to pull him back, but she smiles and places her own hands over his. "Baby has hiccups," she says. "Can you feel them?"

She is a pretty woman, slight in figure like Mona was, similar in posture. Even her hair is reminiscent of my wife's: a shale color that's been brightened by the Roman sun so that it sometimes makes a red halo around her face, like filaments of steel wool about to catch fire. It's been a year since she and Leo were married, but I still find myself staring at her, seeing what's not there. The memories of Mona she brings back, and the appetites a man feels for his wife, make me blush. They also make me aware of a loneliness I've otherwise done well to bury.

"You three, come sit," she says. "I'll get you something to eat." But then she seems to change her mind. "Ah, ah, I see, no." She's staring over my shoulder, at Simon. "I'll stay with Peter here. You Fathers get a drink downstairs."

She has seen something in his eyes.

"Thanks, Sofia," I say. Then I kneel before Peter and add, "I'll be back soon to tuck you in. Best manners, okay?"

"Come on," Simon whispers to me, tugging at my cassock. "Let's go."

THE SWISS GUARD CANTINA is downstairs in the barracks. It's a dim place, dungeonlike, where the permanent haze is punctured by a few grim chandeliers. The walls, decorated with life-size murals showing this five-hundred-year-old army in its ancient heyday, were actually painted during John Paul's lifetime. They're so embarrassingly cartoonish that for an artist to have created them in the shadow of the Sistine Chapel seems to require a belief in the existence of purgatory.

Simon and I drift to an empty table in the corner, looking for something stronger than wine. Because of his size, he must work hard at his drinking to feel any effects. Wine, though, is what they have here, so Simon's first little goblet is already behind him when I say, "Why would someone come looking for us?"

He rubs a thumb against the ridged glass of the thick goblet, armored like a grenade. His voice is full of darkness. "If I find out who did that to Peter . . ."

"You really think this could be related to what happened to Ugo?"

He pulses with emotion. "I don't know."

I take the printed sheet from my pocket and slide it across the table. "Did he ever say anything like this to you?"

It takes him only a few seconds to read. Then he slides it back in my direction, frowning. "No."

"Do you think it could be something?"

He leans back and pours another glass. "Probably not." His giant finger alights on the page, pointing to the date on the message. Two weeks ago.

I read the words a second time.

Dear Ugo,

Sorry to hear about that. From now on, though, I think you should ask someone else for help. I can recommend several other scriptural scholars who would be more than qualified to answer your questions. Let me know if you're interested. Best of luck with the exhibit.

Alex

Below it is Ugo's original message. The one I was replying to. These are the last words he ever wrote to me.

Fr. Alex—Something has come up. Urgent. Tried calling you, but no answer. Please contact me immediately, before word of this gets out. —Ugo

"He never said anything about this to you?" I say.

Simon shakes his head dolefully. "But trust me," he says, "I'll find out what's happening."

In his tone is a touch of Secretariat superiority. Stand by while we save the world.

"Who would've known you were staying at the apartment tonight?" I ask.

"Everyone at the nunciature knew I was flying back for the exhibit." The nunciature: the Holy See embassy. "But," he adds, "I didn't tell them where I was staying."

His tone suggests that this bothers him, too. The Vatican has a small phone book that lists the home and work numbers of most employees, including my own. But it provides no addresses.

"And how," I ask, "could anyone have gotten from Castel Gandolfo to here so fast?"

Simon is a long time answering. He rolls the glass between his palms. Finally he says, "You're probably right. They couldn't have."

And yet he says it without any relief, as if he's just trying to assuage me.

Distant church bells toll ten PM. The change of shifts begins. We watch as guard patrols appear in their night fatigues, returning from duty, making the room repopulate like a tide pool. It becomes clear that this will be no refuge from the shocks of tonight. These men, while on duty, have heard the news trickle in from Castel Gandolfo. Simon and I are celebrities in a way we hadn't anticipated.

The first man to sit down beside us is my old friend Leo. We met the spring of my third year of seminary, at the funeral after the only other murder I can remember on Vatican soil. A Swiss Guard had killed his commanding officer in this barracks before turning the service weapon on himself, and Leo was the first man on the scene that night. Mona and I nursed him through more than a year of recovery, including double dates with women who saw no upside in an underpaid foreigner who was bound by oath not to discuss the memory that haunted him. When Mona left, though, it was Leo who helped Simon tend to *me*. At his wedding to Sofia this spring, I was scheduled to officiate until Cardinal Ratzinger honored them by volunteering. Now, after years of heartache, we will both have sons. I'm gladdened to see his face tonight. Ours is a friendship of survivors.

Simon lifts his glass an inch, acknowledging Leo's arrival. A handful of cadets follows their leader to our banquet table. Soon beer and wine make the rounds. Glasses clink. After hours of compulsory motionlessness, arms and mouths move with gusto. The men here usually speak in German, but they toggle to Italian so we can participate. Not realizing that we're anything more than their leader's friends, they begin asking each other questions that are grotesquely military.

What caliber was the round?

Forehead or temple?

One shot had enough stopping power?

But when Leo explains who the guests are, everything changes.

"You're the one whose apartment got robbed?" one of the men says to me excitedly.

I begin to see how these stories will spread through the Vatican village. My first instinct is that this is dangerous for Simon. Secretariat men must avoid scandal.

"Have the gendarmes caught anyone?" I ask.

There's confusion about which event I am referring to, until Leo says, "Not for either one."

"Did any of my neighbors see anything?"

Leo shakes his head.

Ugo's murder, however, is what captivates these boys.

"I heard they wouldn't let anyone see the body," one cadet says.

Another man adds, "I heard there was something wrong with it. Something about his hands or feet."

They're mistaken. I saw Ugo's body with my own eyes. Yet before I can speak, other men make callous jokes about stigmata. Simon thumps a fist on the table and growls, "Enough!"

The silence is instant. He is the sum of authority in their world—tall, commanding, priestly. At thirty-three years old, I realize, he may also seem old.

"Do they know how someone could've gotten into the gardens?" I ask.

The men twitter like birds on a wire. The consensus: no.

"So nobody saw anything?" I press.

At last it's Leo who speaks up. "*I* saw something."

The table grows hushed.

"Last week," he says, "when I was running third shift at Saint Anne's, a vehicle pulled up to request entry."

Saint Anne's is the gate beside this barracks. Swiss Guards are posted there at all hours to check incoming vehicles from Rome. During third shift, though, the border gates are closed. No one is allowed into our country at night.

"It's oh-three-hundred," Leo continues, "and a cargo truck starts flashing its lights at me. I wave it off, but the driver steps out."

The men grimace. This isn't the protocol. Drivers must lower their windows and display their IDs.

"I approach," Leo goes on, "with Vice Corporal Frei in a supporting position. The driver has an Italian license. Lo and behold, he also has a permission of entry. Guess whose signature is on this permission."

He waits. These men are still young enough to be thrilled by the possibilities.

"It was signed," Leo says, "by Archbishop Nowak."

There are whistles. Antoni Nowak is the highest-ranking priest-secretary in the world. The right-hand man of Pope John Paul.

"I tell Vice Corporal Frei to call upstairs," Leo continues, "to confirm the signature. Meanwhile, I have a look in the truck bed." He leans forward. "And there's a *coffin* back there. With a sheet covering it, and Latin words written on top. Don't ask me what they say. But under the sheet is a big metal casket. And I mean *big*."

All around the table, the halberdiers cross themselves. Every man in this barracks, hearing of a metal casket, shares the same thought. When a pope dies, he's buried in a triple coffin. The first is cypress, the last is oak. But the middle one is made of lead.

John Paul's health has been the subject of urgent concern. He's weak. He's been unable to walk. His face is a mask of pain. The Cardinal Secretary of State, the second-most powerful man in the Holy See, has broken the code of silence by saying retirement is possible, that if the pope's health prevents him from ruling, it's a matter of conscience whether he must step down. Journalists circle like vultures, some of them offering to pay Vatican villagers for any whiff of intelligence. I wonder why Leo is risking a story like this in front of such an unseasoned audience.

But he answers that question by saying: "And who should I find sitting on the bench beside this casket? The name on the ID says: 'Nogara, Ugolino.'" Leo raps the table gently with his knuckles. "A minute later, we get the callback. Archbishop Nowak confirms the permission of entry. My truck pulls away, and that's the last I ever see of the coffin *or* Nogara. Now: someone please tell me what *that* means."

It has the ring of a ghost story. A waking dream that has intruded on dark third-shift hours. These are superstitious men.

Before anyone can respond, Simon stands up. He murmurs something that sounds like *I'm sick*, or possibly *I'm sick of this*. Without apologizing or saying good-bye, he walks out of the cantina.

I get to my feet and follow him, my body feeling clumsy beneath me. Leo's story has added a giant new circumstance to Ugo's death.

These Swiss Guards have missed it, because the days are gone when any Roman Catholic with a few years of school would've known Latin. But my father raised his sons to read both Greek and Latin, so I know the words Leo saw on that coffin drape. They form a prayer:

Tuam Sindonem veneramur, Domine, et Tuam recolimus Passionem.

In the dark, Leo must've been unable to form anything but a vague impression of the box's dimensions, because this coffin was much too big for a pope. I know, because I saw it once with my own eyes.

I know what Ugo was hiding.

CHAPTER 5

SEVEN HUNDRED YEARS ago in a small French village, a Christian relic surfaced for the first time in Western history. No one knows where it came from or how it got there. But slowly, like all relics, it trickled up into better hands. The royal family of that region came to own it. And in time they transferred it to their Alpine capital.

Turin.

The Shroud of Turin purports to be the cloth in which Jesus Christ was buried. On its surface is a mysterious, almost photographic image of a crucified man. For five centuries it has lain in a side chapel of the cathedral in Turin, so carefully cared for and protected that it's displayed to the public only a few times each century. Just twice, in half a millennium, has it been removed from the city: once when the royal family was fleeing Napoleon, and again during World War Two. That second journey brought it to a monastery in the mountains near Naples, where the cloth was protected in secrecy. It was on the way to that monastery that the Shroud, for the only time in history, passed through Rome.

The only time in history, until now.

Most relics are kept in special vessels called reliquaries. Seven years ago, in 1997, a fire in the Turin cathedral nearly destroyed the Shroud while it lay in its silver reliquary. Afterward, a new vessel was designed: an airtight box made of an aeronautic alloy, designed to protect the precious cloth from anything. The new box, not coincidentally, resembles a very large casket.

Over that casket is draped a gold cloth embroidered with the traditional Latin prayer for the Shroud. *Tuam Sindonem veneramur, Domine, et Tuam recolimus Passionem.*

We revere Your Holy Shroud, O Lord, and meditate upon Your Passion.

I am sure, to a moral certainty, that what Leo saw in the bed of that cargo truck was the most famous icon of our religion. The capstone of the historic exhibit that Ugo Nogara created in the Shroud's honor.

■　■　■

I MET UGO NOGARA because I made it my business to try to meet all of Simon's friends. Most priests are good judges of character, but my brother used to invite homeless men over for dinner. He would date girls who stole more silverware than the homeless men. One night, when he was helping nuns operate the Vatican soup kitchen, two drunks got into a fight, and one pulled a knife. Simon stepped in and wrapped his hand around the blade. He refused to let go until the gendarmes came.

The next morning, Mother decided it was time for therapy. The psychiatrist was an old Jesuit with an office that smelled like wet books and clove cigarettes. On his desk was a signed picture of Pius XII, the pope who said Freud was a pervert and Jesuits shouldn't smoke. My mother asked if I should wait outside, but the doctor said it was only an informal evaluation, and if Simon needed treatment, she would have to wait outside as well. So my mother, in tears, took her one chance to ask if there was a medical term for Simon's problem. Because the term in all the magazines was "death wish."

The Jesuit asked Simon some questions, then asked to see where the drumstick of his thumb was sutured back to his palm. Finally he said to my mother, "Signora, are you familiar with a man named Maximilian Kolbe?"

"Is he a specialist?"

"He was a priest at Auschwitz. The Nazis starved him for sixteen days before poisoning him. Kolbe volunteered for this punishment in order to save the life of a perfect stranger who would have been killed instead. Would you say this is the sort of behavior that concerns you?"

"Yes, Father. Exactly. Do you have a name in your profession for men like Kolbe?"

And when the Jesuit nodded, my mother cracked a hopeful smile, because anything with a name might have a cure.

Then the doctor said, "In my profession, signora, we call them martyrs. And in the case of Maximilian Kolbe, we call him the patron saint of this century. A death wish is not the same as a willingness to die. Take heart. Your son is just an unusually good Christian."

One year later, Mother escaped her greatest fear: that she would outlive Simon. And the last thing she said to me before she died, other than *I love you*, was: *Please, Alex, watch over your brother.*

By the time Simon finished seminary, it looked as if he might not need the watching. He was asked to become a Vatican diplomat, an invitation that only ten Catholic priests, out of four hundred thousand in the world, receive each year. It meant studying at the most exclusive Church address outside Vatican walls—the Pontifical Ecclesiastical Academy. Six of the eight popes before John Paul were Vatican diplomats, and four were Academy men; so other than the Sistine Chapel during a conclave, no place on earth is likelier to house a future pope. If Simon remained in diplomatic service, the sky was the limit. All he needed to do was avoid giving away the family silverware.

Still, it seemed a surprising choice for my brother. There are two dozen departments in the Holy See bureaucracy, and if Simon had chosen a job at almost any other, he could've stayed at home. Everyone would've welcomed him at our father's old haunt, the Council for Promoting Christian Unity, or he could've made a statement by joining the Congregation for the Oriental Churches, which defends the rights of Eastern Catholics. Uncle Lucio, like most Vatican cardinals, had been given a few extra appointments outside his bailiwick, so he had suggestions of his own: the Congregation for the Clergy, or the Congregation for the Causes of Saints, where he could help nudge Simon up the ladder. And of all the reasons Simon had for turning down the Secretariat, the biggest was our family's history with its leader, the Vatican's second-in-command, Cardinal Secretary of State Domenico Boia.

Boia came to office just as communism was collapsing in Eastern Europe. The Orthodox Church was reemerging after years of enforced atheism behind the Iron Curtain, and John Paul tried to offer it an olive branch—only to find his new secretary of state standing in the way. Cardinal Boia mistrusted the Orthodox Church, which had split from Catholicism one thousand years ago in part because of disagreements over the pope's power. Orthodox consider the pope to be, like the nine patriarchs who lead their Church, a bishop worthy of special honor—first among equals—but not a superpower, not infallible. This seemed dangerously radical to Boia. So began a silent struggle in which the second-most powerful man at the Vatican tried to save the pope from his own good intentions.

His Eminence began a campaign of diplomatic snubs against the Orthodox that would set back relations by years. One of his most ardent helpers was an American priest named Michael Black, who had once been my father's protégé. In Simon's eyes, no department could have embodied hostility toward our father's ideals more than the Secretariat. Yet instead of refusing the invitation, he seemed to take it as a sign. God wanted him to take up our father's work of trying to reunite the Churches. And the Secretariat was where He wanted it done.

At the Academy, while other men studied Spanish or English or Portuguese, Simon studied the Slavic languages of Orthodoxy. He turned down Washington so that he could go to Sofia, capital of Orthodox Bulgaria. There, he bided his time until something came open in Ankara, the same nunciature where Michael Black was now working.

I knew that Simon had taken up Father's old torch, but what he intended to do with it, I thought even he himself didn't know. Then, a week before I met Ugo for the first time, Uncle Lucio called.

"Alexander, were you aware that your brother has been missing work?"

I was not.

Lucio clicked his tongue. "He was reprimanded for disappearing without cause. And since he won't talk to *me* about it, I'd appreciate it if *you* would find out why."

Simon's excuse was office politics: Michael Black had reported him, out of spite. A week later, though, my brother was unexpectedly in Rome.

"I'm here with a friend," he said.

"What friend?"

"His name's Ugo. We met in Turkey. Come have dinner with us at his place tonight. He'd like to meet you."

———

NEVER IN MY LIFE had I been to an apartment like Ugolino Nogara's. Most families who work for the pope rent Church-owned apartments around Rome. My parents, with Lucio's help, had been lucky to win a flat inside the walls, in the employee ghetto. But here, before my eyes, was how the other half lived. Nogara's apartment was inside the papal palace, right at the corner where the Vatican Museums met the Vatican Library. When Simon answered the door, Peter ran eagerly into his uncle's arms, but my eyes drifted into the vast space behind them. There were no frescoes on the walls, or ceilings worked with gold, but from front to back the apartment ran so far that screens had been put up to divide it into smaller rooms, the way cardinals once did at conclaves. The west wall had a view of the courtyard where scholars from the Vatican Library sipped drinks at a secluded café. To the south, where the crown of trees parted, the rooftops made a path straight to the dome of Saint Peter's.

From deep inside the apartment came a boisterous voice.

"Aha! You must be Father Alex and Peter! Come in, come in!"

A man came loping at us, arms outstretched. At first sight of him, Peter tucked himself into the protective recess of my legs.

Ugolino Nogara had the dimensions of a small bear, with skin so sunburned that it seemed phosphorescent. His eyeglasses were held together with a thick knot of tape. In his hand sloshed a glass of wine, and after he kissed me on each cheek, the first thing he said was, "Let me get you a drink."

Those would be telling words.

Simon tenderly took Peter by the hand and spirited him away, offering him a gift from Turkey. I found myself alone with our host.

"You work at the nunciature with my brother, Doctor Nogara?" I asked while he poured.

"Oh, no," he said with a laugh. He pointed to the building across the courtyard. "I work at the museums. I've just been in Turkey to put the last touches on my exhibit."

"Your exhibit?"

"The one that opens in August."

He winked, as if Simon had surely told me. But in those days, no one knew yet. Rumors hadn't circulated about the black-tie opening night, the reception in the Sistine Chapel.

"So how did you meet?" I asked.

Nogara loosened his tie. "Some Turks discovered a poor fellow in the desert, passed out with heatstroke." He pulled off his eyeglasses to show me the tape. "Facedown."

"They found Ugo's Vatican passport," Simon called out, beginning to drift back, "so they phoned me at the nunciature. I had to drive four hundred miles to find him. He was in a city called Urfa."

Peter, detecting adult conversation, slumped into a corner, staring foggily at the Attila the Hun comic book Simon had brought him from Ankara.

Nogara's face came alive. "Father Alex, imagine it. I was in a Muslim desert, and your brother, God bless him, arrived at my hospital bed in full cassock, with a basket of dinner and a bottle of Barolo!"

I noticed Simon didn't smile. "I didn't realize alcohol was the worst thing for sunstroke. Though someone else *did* know that."

"I could not inform him," Nogara said with a grin, "because after a few glasses of that Barolo, I had passed out."

Humorlessly, my brother rubbed the rim of his glass. A thought began to gnaw at me. An explanation for what I was seeing. Nogara was a curator, which meant he had a special incentive for befriending Simon. His superior was the director of the museums, who answered to Uncle Lucio. Access to Lucio could explain how Nogara had landed an apartment like this.

"So what were you doing out there in the desert," I said, "when you have such a beautiful place here? Peter and I would kill for a flat like this."

The more closely I looked, though, the odder the apartment seemed. The kitchen was nothing but a portable refrigerator, a pair of hot plates, and a jug of bottled water. A clothesline was hung across the room, but I saw no sink or machine to do the wash. It felt improvised, as if he'd just moved in. As if friendship with Simon was paying dividends more quickly than he'd expected.

"I'll tell you a secret," Nogara said. "They gave me the space up here because of my exhibit. And my exhibit is the reason I asked your brother to invite *you* here tonight."

A buzzer sounded, and he turned to check the food cooking on the hot plates. I glanced at Simon, but he avoided my eyes.

"Now," Nogara said, and a sly look crept across his face, "allow me to set the stage." He lifted his wooden spoon like a conductor's baton. "I want you to imagine the most popular museum exhibit in the world. Last year, that exhibit was a Leonardo show in New York. Seven thousand people visited it on an average day. Seven *thousand*—a small town, moving through those galleries every twenty-four hours." Nogara stopped theatrically. "Now, Father, imagine something bigger. Much bigger. Because my exhibit is going to *double* that."

"How?"

"By revealing something about the most famous image in the world. An image so famous that it outdraws Leonardo and Michelangelo combined. An image that outdraws entire *museums*. I'm talking about the image on the Shroud of Turin."

I was glad Peter couldn't see my reaction.

"Now, I know what's going through your mind," Nogara said. "We carbon-tested the Shroud. The tests revealed it to be a fake."

I knew it better than he could possibly imagine.

"Yet even now," Nogara continued, "when we exhibit the Shroud, it attracts millions of pilgrims. At a recent exhibition it drew two million people in eight weeks. Eight *weeks*. All to see a relic that has allegedly been disproved. Put that in perspective: the Shroud draws five times as many visitors as the most popular museum exhibit in the world. So imagine how many will come once I prove that the radiocarbon dating of the Turin Shroud was wrong."

I faltered. "Doctor, you're putting me on."

"Not at all. My exhibit will show that the Shroud is indeed the burial cloth of Jesus Christ."

I turned to Simon, waiting for him to say something. But when he kept silent, I couldn't do the same. The carbon-dating had stunned our Church and crushed my father, who'd pinned his hopes on the scientific authentication of the Shroud as a rallying point between Catholics and Orthodox. Father had spent his career trying to make friends across the aisle, and before the announcement of the radiocarbon verdict, he and his assistant Michael Black had coaxed and urged and pleaded with Orthodox priests from around Italy to join them at the press conference in Turin. Risking the displeasure of their bishop, some of those priests came. It would've been a milestone, if it hadn't been a catastrophe. The radiocarbon tests dated the linen cloth to the Middle Ages.

"Doctor," I said, "people's hearts were broken sixteen years ago. Please don't put them through that all over again."

But he was undaunted. He served us plates of food in silence, then rinsed his hands with bottled water and said, "Please, begin eating. I'll return in a moment. It's important that you see this for yourself."

When he disappeared behind a screen to fetch something, I whispered to Simon, "Is this why you brought me here? To listen to this?"

"Yes."

"Simon, he's a drunk."

My brother nodded. "When he blacked out in the desert, it wasn't from heatstroke."

"Then what am I doing here?"

"He needs your help."

I ran a hand through my beard. "I know a priest in Trastevere who runs a twelve-step program."

But Simon tapped his head. "The problem's up here. Ugo's worried that he won't finish his exhibit in time."

"How can you be helping him with this? You really want to relive what happened to Father back then?"

Every television in our country had been tuned to the news conference when the lab results were announced. That night, the only sound in the Vatican was of children playing in the gardens, because our parents needed time to be alone. The experience wounded my father in a way he would never recover from. Michael Black abandoned him. Phone calls from old friends—from Orthodox friends—dried up. Father's heart attack came two months later.

"Listen to me," I whispered. "This is not your problem."

Simon squinted. "My flight to Ankara leaves in four hours. His flight to Urfa isn't until next week. I need you to keep an eye on him until he leaves."

I waited. There was something more in his eyes.

"Ugo's about to ask you a favor," he said. "If you don't want to do it for him, then I want you to do it for me."

I watched Nogara's shadow approach us down the hallway. It paused there, while his body was still out of sight, and like an actor preparing his entrance onstage, he made the sign of the cross with one hand. In his other hand was something long and thin.

"Have faith," Simon whispered. "When Ugo tells you what he's found, you're going to believe in him, too."

NOGARA REENTERED CARRYING A bolt of fabric. He unspooled it along the clothesline strung across the room, then said, in a reverent tone, "I'm sure this needs no introduction."

I froze. Before me was an image that had lain undisturbed in my memory for years: two silhouettes, the color of rust, joined together at the tops of their heads, one of a man's front, one of his back. On top of the silhouettes were bloodstains: along the head, from a crown of thorns; on the back, from scourging; and under one rib, from a spear in the side.

"A one-to-one reproduction of the Holy Shroud," Nogara said, raising a hand to point, but never allowing his fingers to touch the cloth. "Fourteen feet long, four feet wide."

The image created a strange tension inside me. The ancient tradition of Eastern Christians, both Catholic and Orthodox, is that holy icons are portraits of saints and apostles that have been accurately copied and recopied for centuries. Of all these images, the Holy Shroud is king, the image at the heart of our faith.

It is also our greatest relic. The Bible says that the bones of Elisha raised a dead man to life, and that sick people were healed by touching the garments of Jesus, so to this day every Catholic altar and every Orthodox antimension has a relic inside it. Almost none of these can claim to have touched our Lord, and only one—the Shroud—can claim to be his self-portrait. Never has so important a holy object been shunned.

Yet even after the carbon dating, the Church never transferred the Shroud to a museum, never quietly swept it under the rug. The cardinal of Turin said it was no longer correct to call the Shroud a relic, but he didn't order the cloth removed from the cathedral. It took John Paul a decade after the radiocarbon tests to visit it again. When he came, though, he called the Shroud a gift from God and urged scientists to keep studying it. This had been the Shroud's place in our hearts—in my heart—ever since. We had no answer for the radiocarbon tests. But we believed we hadn't heard the last word, and until that word came, we would not abandon the defenseless. We would not forsake the forsaken man.

My inner turmoil increased when I saw that Peter was paying attention now as well. I'd never spoken to him about the Shroud. The complexity of my feelings about it would've been unfair to heap on a child.

"The first thing you must know," Nogara said, "is how the Shroud covered Jesus' body. It wasn't draped on top of him like a sheet. It was laid *under* him, then back *over* him, in a band. That's why we have a front image and a back image."

He pointed to gourd-shaped holes cut into the cloth. All of them were in a pattern that matched the folds in the linen. "But the marks I want to focus on are these. The burn marks."

"Who burned it?" Peter asked.

"A fire broke out," Ugo said. "In 1532, the Shroud was being kept in a reliquary made of silver. The fire melted part of it. A drop of molten silver landed on the Shroud, burning through every layer of the folded cloth. The damaged linen had to be repaired by Poor Clare nuns. Which brings me to my point."

Nogara plucked a trade journal from a bookshelf and handed it to me. The cover said *Thermochimica Acta*.

"This coming January," he continued, "an American chemist from the national laboratory at Los Alamos will publish an article in that scientific journal. A friend at the Pontifical Academy of Sciences sent me an early copy. See for yourself."

I flipped through the pages. They might as well have been written in Chinese. "Enthalpies of Dilution of Glycine." "Thermal Studies of Polyesters Containing Silicon or Germanium in the Main Chain."

"Skip to the end," Nogara said. "The last article before the index."

And there it was: "Studies on the Radiocarbon Sample from the Shroud of Turin."

It contained pictures of what looked like worms on microscope slides, and charts I couldn't fathom. At the beginning of the text, though, in the abstract, were two sentences whose gist I understood:

Pyrolysis-mass-spectrometry results from the sample area coupled with microscopic and microchemical observations prove that the radiocarbon sample was not part of the original cloth of the Shroud of Turin. The radiocarbon date was thus not valid for determining the true age of the shroud.

"The sample wasn't part of the Shroud?" I said. "How is that possible?"

Nogara sighed. "We didn't realize how much work the Poor Clare nuns had done. We knew they had sewn patches over the holes. We didn't know—because we couldn't see—that they had also woven threads *into* the Shroud to strengthen it. Only under a microscope could they be distinguished. So, inadvertently, we tested a fabric that mixed original linen with repair threads. This American chemist is the first to have discovered the mistake. One of his colleagues has told me that parts of the sample weren't even linen. The nuns made their repairs with cotton."

A cool energy spread through the room. In Nogara's eyes was a controlled giddiness.

"Alli," Simon whispered, "this is it. This is finally it."

I fingered the chemistry journal. "The exhibit," I said, "will be about these scientific tests?"

Ugo allowed himself a smile. "The tests are only the beginning. If the Shroud is really from 33 AD, then what happened to it for the next thousand years? I've spent months digging deeper into the Shroud's history, trying to answer the biggest mystery of its past: where was it hiding for thirteen centuries before it suddenly appeared in France? And I have some very good news." He hesitated. "If I may interrupt your meal, I'd like you all to come somewhere with me."

From a drawer he collected a thick ring of keys to the column of bolts and chains on the front door. Then he tucked a plastic bag from his refrigerator into his pocket.

"Where?" Peter asked.

Ugo winked. "I think you're going to like it."

■ ■ ■

DARK WAS FALLING AS we followed him through the palace halls to the rear doors of Saint Peter's. The sampietrini, the janitors of the basilica, were starting to nudge tourists out the exits. But they recognized Ugo and left the four of us alone.

No matter how many times I've entered that church, it has always given me a shiver. When I was a child, my father told me that Saint Peter's was so tall, three whales could stand head-to-tail inside it, like a circus act on a unicycle, with enough room left for them to wear the Coliseum as a crown. On the floor, the sizes of other famous churches are measured out and engraved in gold letters, like tombstones of little fish in the belly of the leviathan. It is a place made by human hands, but not to human scale.

Ugo brought us toward the altar beneath Michelangelo's dome and pointed to the four corners around us. In each corner stood a tower of marble.

"Do you know what's inside these piers?" he asked.

I nodded. The piers—each one of them almost as large as the Arc de Triomphe—were mountains of solid concrete and stone, built to support the immense dome. Inside each one was a narrow channel, a man-size wormhole, rising to a hidden room. On special occasions, the canons of Saint Peter's would display the extraordinary contents of those rooms.

Relics.

Five hundred years ago, when the Renaissance popes set out to re-build the greatest church in human history, they put four of Christianity's most hallowed artifacts into the reliquaries of these piers. Then four statues were built, thirty feet high, signaling the relics that lay inside.

"Saint Andrew," Ugo said, pointing to the first. "The brother of Saint Peter. The first-called of the apostles. His skull was put in this pier."

Ugo pivoted. His finger was now pointing to a statue of a woman carrying a giant cross.

"Saint Helena," he said. "The mother of Constantine, the first Christian emperor. She visited Jerusalem and returned with the True Cross. The popes placed wood from that cross in this pier."

The third statue was of a woman rushing forward with her arms outstretched. Between her hands was perhaps the most mystical of the basilica relics.

"Saint Veronica," Ugo said. "The woman who wiped Jesus' face as he carried the cross toward Golgotha. On that cloth, a mysterious image of his face was left behind. In this pier, the popes placed that cloth."

At last he turned to the fourth statue. "Saint Longinus. The soldier who pierced Jesus on the cross, wounding him in the side with his lance. In this pier, the popes placed Longinus' lance."

Nogara turned to face us. "As you may know, only *three* of those relics are still here. In a gesture of goodwill, we gave the skull of Saint

Andrew to the Orthodox Church. But Andrew's head never belonged here anyway. This basilica's relics should tell the most important story in Christianity." A quiver began to form in Nogara's voice. "The True Cross, the veil, and the spear are all relics of our Lord's death. What belongs in the fourth pier is a relic of His Resurrection. John Paul, when he inherited the Shroud, was going to move it here. But the radiocarbon tests created a climate of doubt in which it was impossible to transfer the Shroud from Turin. Now we're finally going to fix that. My exhibit is going to bring the Shroud home."

He lowered his voice so that Simon and I had to lean in to hear.

"I have found ancient texts describing an image of Jesus that was kept in a city called Edessa for centuries before the Shroud appeared in France. That Turkish city is now called Urfa and is where your brother rescued me in the hospital. I've tracked our Turin Shroud to that location no later than the four hundreds AD. Now I want to do more: I want the finale of my exhibit to prove that this so-called Image of Edessa came from Jerusalem in the hands of the disciples themselves. And, Father Alex, that is where my work involves *you*."

Before continuing, he reached into his pocket for the plastic bag he had taken from the apartment. From inside it he produced something odd: a plastic spoon resembling a drumstick. He lowered himself to Peter's level and said, "Peter, I need to speak to your father alone for a moment, so I've brought something for you."

The tip of the spoon was covered with something pale and lumpy.

"What's *that*?" Peter asked.

"Suet. And it has magical powers in this basilica." Ugo led Peter to an open space near the altar. "Hold it out just like this, and pretend you're a statue. Don't move a muscle."

A moment later, a dove descended from the dome. It landed on the suet and began to feed. Peter was so surprised that he nearly dropped the spoon.

Ugo whispered to him, "Now go anywhere you like. Take your new friend for a walk. I've found the birds here are quite tame."

Peter was enchanted. With the dove only inches from his hand, he began to drift through the empty nave, careful as if it were a candle he was holding. All of us fell silent for a moment, watching him.

Then Ugo turned back to me. "As I was saying, I've been hoping to prove that the disciples brought the Shroud from Jerusalem to Edessa. This proof, of course, has been difficult to find. But I believe I'm finally on its trail. You see, Edessa was one of Christianity's early capitals, and in the mid–one hundreds AD a gospel was written there. This gospel came to be called the Diatessaron, which I'm sure you know is Greek for 'made out of four,' because its text was a fusion of the four existing gospels into a single document. Since the Shroud would've been in Edessa at the very moment this gospel was written, I believe its writer may have mentioned the Shroud in his text."

I began to interrupt him, but Ugo held up a hand.

"The challenge of confirming this is, of course, that the Diatessaron is extremely rare. Our only surviving copies are translations into other languages, written centuries later. All original copies were destroyed by the bishops of Edessa themselves when they decided in favor of the four separate gospels. At least, so the story goes. But recently I seem to have discovered otherwise."

I blurted, "You found a manuscript of the Diatessaron? In what language?"

"It's a diglot. Syriac on one side, ancient Greek on the other."

I was agog. "That would be the original text."

The Diatessaron had been written in one of these two languages and then translated into the other so quickly that no one today knew which came first.

"Unfortunately," Ugo continued, "I don't read either tongue well. Father Simon tells me, however, that *you* read one of them fluently. So I wondered if you might be willing to help me—"

"Absolutely. Do you have pictures?"

"Alas, the book is . . . not easily photographed. I discovered it in a place where I wasn't supposed to be looking, so I can't bring the book to you, Father. What I need to do is bring *you* to the *book*."

"I don't understand."

He squirmed. "The only other person I've told about this is Father Simon. If word got out, I would lose my job. Your brother assures me you can keep a secret?"

For just a glance at that book, I would have promised Ugo almost anything. I had spent my life since seminary as a gospel teacher, and the first principle of my profession was that a small handful of ancient manuscripts had given the world its entire text of the gospels. The life of Jesus Christ as most modern Christians know it is a fusion of several texts, all slightly different, all breathtakingly old, stitched into a single version by modern scholars who even now continue to make changes based on new discoveries. The Diatessaron, because it was constructed by that same process of fusing older texts, could reveal the gospels as they existed in the 100s AD, long before the earliest complete manuscripts that had come down to us. It could add new facts to what we knew of Jesus' life and make us question the facts as we thought we knew them.

"I can fly to Turkey as soon as next week," I said. "Sooner if you need me to."

The pulse was becoming thready in my chest. It was June; I didn't have to teach class again until the fall. There was enough money in my savings account for two airplane tickets. Peter and I could stay with Simon.

But Ugo frowned. "I'm afraid you misunderstand," he said. "I'm not asking you to come back to Turkey with me. The book is *here*, Father."

CHAPTER 6

As I FOLLOW Simon out of the canteen and up toward Leo's apartment, my mind contains a single thought: the Shroud is here. The burial cloth of Christ is within these city walls. I wonder if it's already locked in one of the piers of Saint Peter's. Maybe the news will be public soon.

The Shroud's arrival lends Ugo's exhibit new significance. The truck's papers were signed by Archbishop Nowak, which means it was John Paul who ordered the Shroud moved. For sixteen years, since the radio-carbon tests, the Church has made no official pronouncements about the Shroud. Suddenly that seems about to change. My thoughts about Ugo's death, and the intruder at my apartment, begin to tip in new directions. I wonder if this is what Ugo was trying to tell me in his e-mail. That he had succeeded in bringing the Shroud here, only to encounter some kind of problem.

Something has come up. Urgent.

Christian relics can unearth the most subterranean feelings. Last year at Christmas, Peter and I watched TV footage of a huge brawl among priests and monks in Bethlehem over nothing more than which side of the Church of the Nativity they were allowed to sweep. Earlier this year, an armed guard had to be posted inside an international Shroud conference, and the Shroud's priest-caretaker had to flee the conference hall because of violent reaction to a decision to have the surface of the cloth gently cleaned. If word of the Shroud's transfer got out, no doubt most people in Turin would be thrilled to learn of Ugo's plans to authenticate and honor it, but a small fringe might react differently. The only other violent attack I remember at Castel Gandolfo was inspired by strange religious delusions: when I was ten years old, a disturbed man tried to attack John Paul in the gardens, before leading Italian police on a highway chase back to Rome and charging them with an ax. In his pockets were found notes filled with ravings about emulating the gods. I wonder if it's possible the moving of the Shroud triggered something similar. If so, then I thank God Peter and Helena weren't hurt.

I jog to catch up to Simon, wondering what his own thoughts are. But my brother has already disappeared. When I make my way inside, Sofia emerges from the nursery and says, "He went up there."

She points toward the rooftop. The most solitary place in the building.

I begin to follow, but she puts a hand on my arm and whispers, "Peter needs you."

I turn toward the nursery. Inside, I find my son sitting up in his makeshift bed. The light is dimmed and the floor is strewn with books and stuffed animals from the nearby crib. Peter is breathing so hard he looks as if he's been running.

"What's wrong?" I say.

The air around him is wet and warm. He reaches out his arms.

"Nightmare?" I ask.

This is the age when night terrors and sleepwalking begin. Simon fell prey to both. I raise his gangly body into my lap and stroke his head.

"Can we read about Totti again?" he whispers, half-delirious.

Totti. The starting second striker for Roma.

"Of course," I tell him.

He leans forward and paws the dark floor for his book. But he's careful not to exit my lap. I've already left him once.

"It's over, Peter," I promise him, kissing the damp back of his head. "There's nothing to be afraid of. You're safe here."

I stay beside him for a while after he falls asleep again, just to be sure. By the time I slip out, Leo has returned home, and Sofia is heating him a plate of food. In the kitchen I see him rub her belly while leaning across it for a kiss. Before they can invite me to join them around the table, I excuse myself to look for Simon on the rooftop.

■ ■ ■

HIS HAIR IS WINDSWEPT and wild. His face is drawn. He is staring down at the lights of Rome the way I imagine a sailor's widow would stare at the sea.

"You okay?" I ask.

His hand, tapping for cigarettes from his emergency pack, is unsteady.

"I'm not sure what to do," he murmurs, not turning to look at me.

"Me either."

"He's dead."

"I know."

"I called him this afternoon. We talked about his exhibit. He can't be dead."

"I know."

Simon's voice grows thinner. "I sat beside his body, trying to wake him up."

A dull pang forms in my chest.

"Ugo poured himself into this show," my brother continues. "Gave it everything." He lights a cigarette. A look of grinding disgust crosses his face. "Why let him die a week before opening night? Why let him die right on the doorstep?"

"Human hands did this," I say. A reminder of where his anger should be directed.

"And why bring *me* there?" he continues, not listening.

"Stop. None of this was your fault."

He blows a long plume of smoke into the darkness. "It *was* my fault. I should've saved him."

"You're lucky you weren't there. The same thing could've happened to you."

He glares bitterly at the sky, then peers down at the empty spot where we used to play as boys. One of the Guard families would inflate a plastic swimming pool on this terrace. All that remains is a water stain.

I lower my voice. "Do you think this could have to do with the Shroud? Moving it here from Turin?"

Tendrils of smoke creep from his nostrils. I can't tell whether he's considering it.

"No one could've known it was moved here," he says flatly.

"Word could've gotten out. People hear things. The same way we just did from Leo."

It would've taken a team of men to load the new Shroud reliquary onto a truck. Priests to open the chapel. Then more men and more priests to unload it here. If just one of them had mentioned the news to a wife, a friend, a neighbor . . .

"Ugo was on the truck that night," I say. "Anyone else who was involved would've seen him. Maybe that's why they came after him."

"But they didn't see you or me. Why come after us?"

"What do you think happened, then?"

Simon flicks an ash off the tip of his cigarette and watches an ember tumble through the darkness. "Ugo was robbed. I think whatever happened at the apartment had to be different."

Yet there's the slightest wobble in his voice.

My phone rings. I check the screen.

"It's Uncle," I say. "Should I take it?"

He nods.

On the other end of the line, a deep, slow voice says, "Alexander?"

Uncle Lucio always seems discommoded by people who answer their own phones. He can't understand why the rest of us don't have priest-secretaries.

"Yes," I say.

"Where are you right now? Are Simon and Peter safe?"

He must already know about the break-in. "We're fine. Thanks for asking."

"I'm told you were both at Castel Gandolfo earlier tonight."

"Yes."

"You must be very upset. I've had the guest rooms prepared for the three of you to stay here tonight, so tell me where you are and I'll send a car."

I falter. Simon is already shaking his head, whispering, "No. We're not doing that."

"Thank you," I say, "but we're staying with a friend at the Swiss Guard barracks."

There's no answer, just a familiar silence, the courier of my uncle's displeasure. "Then I want you to meet me at the palace tomorrow," he says finally. "First thing. To discuss the situation."

"What time?"

"Eight o'clock. And tell Simon, too. I expect to see him as well."

"We'll be there."

"I'm glad to hear it. Good night, Alexander."

Unceremoniously, the line goes dead.

I turn to Simon. "He wants to meet us at eight."

The news makes no impression.

"So," I say, "maybe we should get some sleep."

But Simon announces, "You go ahead. I'm going to sleep right here."

Here. In the open. Under the pope's window.

"Come on," I say. "Come inside."

But it's hopeless. The refusal to sleep in a bed is a common self-deprivation among priests, and healthier, at least, than cinching a rope around his thigh. Finally I give in and tell him I'll come get him in the morning. He needs to be alone. I'll say a prayer for my brother tonight.

■ ■ ■

LEO AND SOFIA ARE in bed when I return. This is their way of giving me the run of the apartment. I'd hoped to talk to Leo about what he heard at the cantina after we left, but it will have to wait. A set of sheets lies on my old companion, the sleeper sofa, veteran of ancient benders. Its former geography of stains is gone, victim of a woman's touch. From beyond the distant bedroom door I make out faint sounds that can't possibly be lovemaking; my friends are too considerate for that. But like most priests, I'm not one to gamble on human nature.

When I check on Peter in the nursery, he's entwined in his sheets. His Greek cross, which he's found some reason to remove from his neck, is slipping from his hand onto the floor. I scoop it up and place it in our travel bag, then kneel beside the window. There's a Bible here, the Greek one I packed, which he and I use as he learns to decipher words. Placing it between my hands, I try to bury my emotion. To master the fear that lurks in this darkness and the rage that burns when I think of Peter threatened in his own home. Wrath runs deep in a Greek heart. It is the first word of our literature. But what I'm about to do, I've done hundreds of times for Mona.

Lord, as I pray forgiveness of my own sins, so I pray forgiveness of theirs. As I ask You to forgive me, so I forgive them. As they are sinners, so am I. Kyrie, eleison. Kyrie, eleison.

I repeat it twice, wanting it to stick. But my thoughts are a muddle. I know there's a good reason why the Swiss Guards have posted more men outside the barracks. A reason why Lucio is calling us to his apartment. When I told Peter we were safe, I wasn't even being hopeful. I was lying.

As my eyes adjust to the darkness, I look at the animals Sofia has painted on the nursery walls. Dangling from a hook on the door are hangers of baby clothes she's sewn herself. Even more than usual, I feel the ache of Mona's absence. Her family still lives here. A handful of cousins and uncles, most of them plumbers, used to brandish lengths of pipe at boyfriends they disapproved of. If I asked for their protection, they would probably take shifts watching over Peter and me. But I would sooner leave town with Peter than put us in their debt.

In the darkness, I unbutton my cassock and fold it. Lying down beside my son, I try to imagine how to distract him tomorrow. How to erase his memory of tonight. I rub his shoulder in the dark, wondering if he's really asleep, hoping that he could use my reassurance right now. Since Mona left, there has been no diminishment in my number of lonely nights. Only a fading in their sharpness, which has a sadness all its own. I miss my wife.

I wait for sleep. I wait, and wait. But I feel I've been waiting all my life.

The gospels say Jesus prepared his followers for the Second Coming by speaking a parable. He compared himself to a master who leaves his estate in order to attend a marriage feast. We, his servants, don't know when the master will return. So we have to wait by the door for him, with our lamps kept burning. *Blessed are those servants whom the master finds vigilant on his arrival.* I remind myself that if I have to wait a lifetime for my wife to return, it's no longer than any other Christian has waited these past two thousand years.

But the waiting, on nights like this, feels like an ache that rattles from an infinite emptiness. Mona was shy and coy and dark. She echoed some uncertainty within me about who I was and why I needed to exist after my parents already had Simon. I didn't pay her much attention when we were kids because I was two years older than she was. But then, she was also too self-conscious to be noticed much. Growing up a girl inside these walls probably contributed to that. The pictures in her parents' apartment show a cheerful, round-faced child who became more attractive each year. At ten she's nondescript: dark shaggy hair, watery green eyes, thick cheeks. By thirteen that has changed; it's clear that she'll be something someday. By fifteen, just as I'm preparing to leave for college, the metamorphosis is beginning. And she knows it: for the next three years, there are new hairstyles and experiments with makeup. It's as if she's peered over the walls into Rome and has seen what a modern woman looks like. Her parents' photographs are carefully cropped, but Mona herself once pointed out to me the low necklines and high skirts still visible in some of them. She told me about the secret excursions into Rome to buy high heels and jewelry, the excursions during which she discovered that the whistles and catcalls weren't aimed at other women.

I've often wondered whether there was a trauma in her life that she never told me about. There's only one surviving picture of Mona when she was training to be a nurse, and she's very thin, with sunken eyes. She explained to me that the work came as a shock after the ease of high school. I always understood this as a request not to pry. I wasn't the first man she'd slept with, but even so, our marriage night was awkward. I had underestimated the psychological toll of making love to a priest-in-training. Accustomed to the company of other men, I was never ashamed of nakedness, or of walking around our home half-clothed. I thought it would demystify the cassock for Mona to see that I was human underneath it. Yet it was almost a week before we consummated the marriage. I began to fear, after the days of false starts, that our love would be mechanical and cringing.

It was not. Once she had exhausted her own defenses, she became eager. My lips bled from where she'd bitten me. From the way certain neighbors avoided my eyes, I knew they were offended by the sounds they heard from upstairs. We both looked forward to meeting each other again each night. It was, in a life of discipline, an opportunity for freedom and pleasure.

A life of discipline. *That* was what should've worried me. Some of our neighbors had misgivings about a priest with a wife, no matter what we did in bed. Mona felt their disapproval keenly. Every social event introduced more problems. Gatherings of priests are designed so that single, celibate men will be surrounded by other single, celibate men. Priests drink and eat together, play soccer and smoke cigars together, visit museums and tour archaeological sites together. To bring an attractive woman to a priestly gathering is a cruel faux pas. Yet to decline invitations because one has a wife is a sure way to stop receiving them. Mona and I agreed that I must go to a certain number of events, just to stay on the list. I encouraged her to spend these evenings visiting friends in Rome, or with other Vatican housewives. I was aware, though, after a time, that she spent the nights alone.

It's unfair to blame the culture of our country. We could've lived outside the walls, in a Church-owned apartment in Rome. Certainly we had no illusions about what Vatican life entailed. But there was one great difference between us, and I discovered it only after we were married. Namely: that my parents were dead, and that her parents were pretending not to be.

Signor and Signora Falceri lived on the next street over, in an apartment building near the gendarme barracks. They had been supportive of our marriage and made no fuss when Mona left the Roman Catholic church for the Greek Catholic one. But I hadn't known, until the marriage began and the pretenses ended, how miserable Mona's mother was. Mona's father was a Vatican Radio technician who'd made the mistake of marrying a woman he didn't respect. Signora Falceri was a passable cook with a gentle sense of humor whose failings weren't immediately clear to me. Only later did Mona explain that her father came from a large family and wanted many children. Her mother had nearly died in childbirth with Mona, and the doctors had discovered a defect in her womb that made it dangerous for her to bear again. Now, when they came to visit us, they visited separately. Mona didn't cherish seeing her father. But it was visits from her beloved mother that left my wife in ruins.

A Greek doesn't need to be told that tragedy runs in families. I knew Mona harbored a certain fear of becoming her mother. When Peter's first two trimesters went peacefully, we took it as proof that the curse had been lifted. Then, in the final trimester, we almost lost him twice. The doctors reassured us that Peter was far enough along to survive, but it seemed as if Mona's body had begun to reject him. In the end, she was rushed to the delivery ward because the umbilical cord was strangling him. When our son was finally delivered, the obstetrician called him Hercules because he had survived a noose snaked twice around his neck. Mona would later cry that she had tried to kill her son.

In the months that followed, the woman I married disappeared. I have more memories of my mother-in-law nursing Peter with a bottle than I have of Mona nursing Peter with a breast. Signora Falceri kept Mona company while I was at work, and to this day I can't see that woman's face without thinking how she tortured my wife. While Mona sat on the couch, eking out some desperate happiness from the madness in her brain, her mother, as if offering loving advice, would announce that our present struggle was nothing compared to what would come later. That we must not delude ourselves. That sadness was a flower. I have searched whole libraries for the source of that proverb—*sadness is a flower*—and in all the world there is no rabbinic gloss to uncoil it. She meant, I believe, that Mona's new temperament had a dark beauty, which we must come to accept. Also: that it would only grow. I'm sickened to think of how many days I let mother and daughter sit on the couch, watching television, while that miserable woman, seeing her own child slowly dying, poisoned her anyway. Peter doesn't see his grandparents today. He asks why. I lie to him, and think to myself that someday I will explain.

When word spread that Mona had left us, families at our church reached out. They cooked us meals. They organized a babysitting schedule so that I could return to work. Eventually Sister Helena took over many of these duties, but even now, no priest at our church receives more generous Christmas gifts than I do, and it would embarrass the most hardened pirates to see the booty Peter receives on his name day. I've always detected an undercurrent of pity and inevitability in this kindness, as if a Greek boy who married a Roman girl was taking a certain risk, and now my life has become the honorable aftermath. The parishioners don't mean anything by it. All Christians believe the business of human life is to pay down the debt on old sins. These good people helped support me until the day came when I could shoulder my debt myself.

I had a fantasy once, which I thought I would carry with me always. It was the fantasy of my wife's return. I would encourage her to take shifts at the hospital again. I would take care of Peter full-time until she was ready to know him better. Then she would discover that our son is not an omen, not an emblem of her failures. He is precocious, conscientious, and good-hearted. Teachers praise him. He is invited to many birthday parties. He has my nose and Simon's eyes, but he has Mona's thick, dark hair; her round face; her cheerful smile. He will be grateful someday that he looks more like his mother than his father. In my dreams Mona would discover, through him, that she had never completely left. That we could rebuild what we once had, since the foundation we set together continues to rise.

But I've lost that fantasy, as surely as I've sloughed my old skin. To my surprise, I've discovered I can be whole without it. Only one part of it stubbornly remains: I want Peter to understand that his mother's love for him isn't a fiction I've created. I want him to understand that there are sources of himself that lie outside of me. From Mona come his deep intuitions of difficult truths, his fondness for jokes and riddles, his magical love of animals. His mother would fascinate him. I want nothing more than to share them with each other.

Wherever Mona is today, I imagine her full of regret for the life we shared, or else for her decision to end it. It would've broken me to feel regret on that scale, but I never did. Every time I looked back, Peter pointed me forward. I am still midstream in the voyage I began with my wife. Every night I thank God for my son.

CHAPTER 7

Wᴇɴ ɪ ᴡᴀᴋᴇ, the floor beside me is empty. Peter's gone.

Fumbling into the hallway, I find Leo and Sofia looking up from their breakfasts at the kitchen table. Leo points to the balcony, where a tiny body is hunched up like a cricket, bent forward over squatting legs, coloring with a crayon.

"He's making a card for Simon," Leo explains.

I smile. "I'll take him up to the roof."

Sofia whispers, "Father Simon's not there."

The look on Leo's face supplies the rest. They don't know where he's gone.

When I dial my brother's mobile, he picks up on the fourth ring.

"Where are you?" I say.

"At the apartment."

"Are you okay?"

"Couldn't sleep. When I get back, I'll take you and Peter to breakfast."

Leo and Sofia are both watching me. Sofia must've been tending to Peter since he woke up. The poor woman is still wearing her bathrobe.

"No," I tell him. "Don't go anywhere. We'll meet you there."

ɪɴ ᴛʜᴇ ʟɪɢʜᴛ ᴏꜰ day, it seems eerie that the apartment is unchanged. The wreckage hasn't all burned off like the darkness. Peter's hand is clamped to mine as we enter. He steps over toys as if they're poisonous mushrooms. In the kitchen, the broken plate is gone, the spilled food cleaned up. All the windows are open. Simon is sitting alone at the table, pretending that he hasn't been smoking.

Peter dashes away from me to give Simon the handmade card. There are four stick figures holding hands: Mona, me, Peter, and Simon. On closer inspection, however, Mona is wearing a habit. My heart sinks. It's Sister Helena.

Simon lifts Peter onto his lap and squeezes him. After admiring the card, he presses his lips into the thicket of wild hair. "I love you," I hear him whisper. "Babbo and I won't let anything happen to you."

The sink is empty. Dishes washed and cleaned. The sponge looks as if it's been wrung dry with an industrial winch. I'm surprised Simon was able to stop himself from cleaning the whole apartment.

"What time does Sister Helena come with the laundry?" he asks.

I'm too distracted to answer. Now that the mess in the kitchen is gone, what remains is more obvious.

"Earth to Alex," Simon says.

"Peter," I say, "before we get breakfast, could you go wash your hands?"

Nervously he traipses down the hall.

"What's wrong?" Simon asks.

Surely he has noticed it, too. I point to the areas where the damage is concentrated. The credenza by the door; the bookshelves; the side table where the phone is kept.

Simon shrugs.

"He was looking for something," I say. "He opened everything with doors. Except *that*."

Eastern Christians keep a special corner in their homes where icons are arranged around a book of the gospels. In our apartment the icon corner is modest—just a dressed-up curio cabinet where Peter and I pray. But in the attack it wasn't touched.

"He must've known what that was," I say.

Nothing but sacred objects are kept in an icon corner. The intruder knew there was no need to look there for whatever he wanted. Almost no Italian layman would've known so much about our rituals. Last night's ideas about a deranged intruder inspired by religious madness already seem impossible.

Before Peter finishes in the bathroom, I quickly follow in the man's footsteps. Sister Helena heard him calling for Simon from the hall outside Peter's room. The hall leads to the bathroom and, across the way, to my bedroom. The bathroom is untouched; so was Peter's bedroom. I feel an electric tingle down my neck. It looks as if the intruder went straight to the master bedroom.

My bed is undisturbed. If the dresser drawers were rifled, then Simon erased all sign of it when he dressed after showering last night. But when I look more carefully, I see one shelf was touched: the one where I keep my travel books on the countries where Simon is posted. The volume on Turkey lies on the floor. Below it, an odd gap has appeared on the bottom shelf. Something's missing.

"Alli," I hear Simon call from the foyer. "Come here a sec."

My books on the Shroud. They're gone, along with my handwritten research for Ugo.

My heart knocks against my ribs. My very first instinct was right. The break-in and Ugo's murder must be connected. This surely has to do with Ugo's exhibit.

"Alex!" Simon repeats, louder now.

When I walk numbly back to the foyer, he's pointing at something on the floor. In his eyes is a new wariness. "I've been staring at it all morning," he says quietly. "But it just clicked."

"Simon," I murmur, "whoever did this must've known we helped Ugo on his exhibit."

But Simon is too distracted to process it. "Notice anything missing?" he says through his teeth.

I kneel beside him among the capsized toys and phone books.

He's pointing to my day planner. It's turned to yesterday's page. Not until I leaf forward do I understand.

Today and tomorrow have been torn out.

I'm frozen. It bubbles up in me like tar, what this means.

"What was on those pages?" Simon asks.

Everything. A cross-section of our lives. Fall term starts next week, so I had written down my teaching schedule. All our plans with Simon were there, too.

I murmur what Simon has already figured out. "He's still looking for us."

My brother begins to dial a number on his mobile phone. "I'm going to reserve a room at the Casa for you and Peter."

The Casa. Our Vatican hotel. Very private; very anonymous. It solidifies what this all means. Peter and I aren't safe anymore in our own home.

Even as Simon talks to the receptionist, a sharp knock comes at the door. Peter instantly comes running out of the bathroom in terror. With him pressed against the backs of my legs, I step forward and turn the knob.

It's a gendarme. The same one from last night.

"Officer," I say eagerly, "you caught someone?"

"Unfortunately, no, Father. I just need to take a few more notes."

I invite him inside, but he chooses to stand on the threshold, stooping to inspect the doorjamb.

Peter tugs at me, not wanting the policeman to be here. Maybe not wanting to be here himself.

The cop glances up. "Father, your nun told me the door was locked when the man entered."

"That's right. When I leave the apartment, I always lock it."

"Even last night?"

"I double-checked it before I left for Castel Gandolfo."

He stares at the doorjamb. One of his fingers runs up and down the wood. He tests the knob. It takes me a second to understand. There's no damage to the door or frame.

"I'm going to need to take some photos," he says. "I'll call you later to discuss some things."

PETER REFUSES TO STAY at the apartment while the policeman is there, so we pass an hour outdoors before our meeting with Uncle Lucio. Keeping to the well-guarded trails, we visit the fountains in the pope's gardens, which Simon and I know by unofficial names from our childhood. Fountain of the dead frog. Fountain of the unexplained eel. Fountain of the night Caterina Fiori drank too much and danced. Eventually we find ourselves at the little playground beside the Vatican tennis court, where Peter asks his uncle to stand behind the swing and push him higher and higher. From the arc of his flight, he cries out, "Simon! Do you know why the leaves change color? It's chlorophyll!"

His hobbyhorse of late.

Simon is staring elsewhere, into the distance. When he becomes aware of his silence, he says, "Why don't all trees change color?"

He was never a strong student, but after four years of college, and four years of seminary, and three more years of Academy, he has become an advertisement for our Church's constitutional obsession with schooling. John Paul holds a doctorate in theology and a doctorate in philosophy. We encourage Peter to learn anything and everything.

"Because," Peter shouts, "the chlorophyll just stays in their leaves!"

Simon and I trade a glance, deciding this sounds right. "Do you know," Simon says, "what *I've* been reading about?"

"Tigers?" Peter cries.

"Remember Doctor Nogara?"

I send him a high-voltage stare, but he ignores me.

"He let me feed the birds," Peter says.

For the briefest moment, Simon smiles. "A long time ago, near the city where Doctor Nogara and I met, there was a saint named Simeon Stylites. He sat on top of a pillar for almost forty years and never came down. He even died up there."

His voice seems to come from far away, as if he finds something entrancing about this detachment. About the thought of retreating into himself like a monk rather than embracing the world like a priest.

"So how did he go pee?" Peter asks.

The one, timeless question.

Simon laughs.

"Peter," I say, trying to muster a serious look, "do not repeat that at school."

He swings higher, grinning. There are few greater joys than to make his uncle happy.

Little by little, the hour slips by. We see nobody we know. We hear no news. There's a distinct impression, as we peer down over the Vatican walls, that nobody in Rome this morning is paying close attention to the facts of our lives.

When we've nearly reached the doorstep of Lucio's palace, Sister Helena calls to say she can't watch Peter later today. Then, sounding as if she's nearly in tears, she rushes to get off the phone. As we hang up, I wonder if there's something she didn't tell me. Something she may not even have realized until she got home last night. Sometimes she takes Peter to visit with neighbors in the building. She might've left the door unlocked.

THE GOVERNOR'S PALACE IS a young building by local standards—younger than John Paul. It dates to 1929, when Italy agreed to make the Vatican an independent country. The blueprint was for a seminary, but the pope, finding himself in need of a national government, converted it to an office building. Today it's where Vatican bureaucrats come and go, planning postage stamps of Michelangelo. We call it the Governor's Palace in remembrance of the days when a layman ran this town, but there are no more governors anymore. The new sheriff wears a collar. Lucio lives in a suite of private apartments on the top floor with his priest-secretary Don Diego, who answers the door when we arrive.

"Come in, Fathers," he says. "And son."

He bends down to welcome Peter, mainly so that he can avoid looking at Simon. They are the same age, two priests on the fast track, and to Diego this means competition. Behind him, gloomy classical music fills the air. Lucio was an accomplished pianist before the onset of arthritis, and he used to keep a framed newspaper article here describing a performance of Mozart he gave in his youth. Now the piano goes unplayed, and the soundtrack is macabre Russians and Scandinavians. This particular work by Grieg sounds like the theme music of Calvinism.

Diego ushers us into my uncle's private office. Instead of facing Saint Peter's, it has a northern exposure that keeps it clammy. One of Lucio's predecessors was a plain-talking American archbishop who kept a bearskin rug on the floor and Westerns playing on the television. *That* was an apartment Peter would've enjoyed visiting. But my uncle's taste runs to oriental rugs and claw-footed chairs because they're available free of charge from the Vatican warehouse, where the stockpile of baroque furniture grows each time another prelate dies.

"Forgive me," Lucio says, raising his arms, "for not being able to stand and welcome you."

This has been his greeting since he suffered a small stroke last year. In its aftermath he has given up wearing the scarlet skullcap and scarlet-trimmed cassock of a cardinal because his balance sometimes fails and his hands can't manage the buttons or sash. Instead he dresses in a loose-fitting priest suit, and a nun drapes a pectoral cross over his neck every morning. Simon and I come forward to clasp his outstretched hands, and Simon, as always, gets a longer squeeze than mine. The longest, however, is reserved for Peter.

"Come over here, my boy," Lucio says, tapping his desk eagerly.

The stroke paralyzed part of Lucio's face, but he worked hard at rehab so that his appearance wouldn't frighten Peter. While they embrace, I glance at the papers on the desk, looking for gendarme reports about Ugo or our apartment. But there are only the budget reports that are the oxygen of Lucio's existence. He is the mayor of a small city that always needs updated facilities and new parking lots; the minister of culture to the world's greatest collection of ancient and Renaissance art; the employer of more than a thousand workers who receive free health care, duty-free shopping, and subsidized food, without paying a penny in income tax; and the negotiator of a fragile relationship with secular Rome, to which our landlocked country owes all its petroleum shipments, garbage collection, and electricity. I try to remind myself, whenever I brood on the way Lucio neglected Simon and me, that he was busy honoring the promise he made to John Paul.

"Do you want a drink?" he says to Peter now, managing to make both halves of his mouth move. "We have orange juice."

Peter's face brightens. He almost leaps off my uncle's lap to follow Diego out of the room to fetch it.

"I trust," my uncle adds in a lower voice, "there were no other incidents last night?"

The question seems like a courtesy. Nothing happens in this country without his knowing.

"No," I say. "Nothing else."

But Simon jumps in. "The gendarmes don't have anything," he says with an edge. "Meanwhile Alex and Peter can't even sleep under their own roof."

His tone takes me by surprise.

Lucio gives him a long, unappreciative stare. "Alexander and Peter are welcome to stay under *this* roof. And you're mistaken: I received a call from the gendarmes twenty-five minutes ago saying they may have caught an image of a suspect on one of the security cameras."

"That's great news, Uncle," I say.

"How long before they have something definite?" Simon asks.

"I'm sure they're working as quickly as they can," Lucio says. "In the meantime, what can you tell me about all of this?"

I glance at Simon. "We found some things in my apartment this morning that suggest the two . . . incidents . . . were related."

Lucio adjusts the angle of a pen lying on his desk. "The gendarmes are examining that same possibility. It's obviously very concerning. You told them about these things you found?"

"Not yet."

"I'll ask them to contact you again." He turns to Simon. "Is there anything else I should be aware of?"

My brother shakes his head.

Lucio frowns. "Such as, what you were doing at Castel Gandolfo in the first place?"

"Ugo called me and asked for help."

"How did you get there?"

"A driver from the car service."

Lucio clicks his tongue. The car service reports to him, but ordinary priests aren't allowed to call for rides, and the boss's nephews are expected to stay above reproach.

"Uncle," I say, "have you ever heard of someone getting through the gates at Castel Gandolfo? Or here?"

"Certainly not."

"How would someone have known our apartment number?"

"I was going to ask you the same question."

Through the open door I watch Diego serve Peter the orange juice in a crystal glass. Peter recoils, remembering that he broke one of these last year. The nuns were on their knees for half an hour collecting shards. I glare at Diego for not remembering.

"Well, then," Lucio says, "there's another matter I called you here to discuss. Unfortunately, Nogara's exhibit needs to be changed."

Simon explodes. "*What?*"

"My curator is gone, Simon. I can't mount his exhibit without him. In some of the galleries it's not even clear what's to be hung where."

My brother rises from his seat. Almost hysterically he says, "You can't do that. He gave his *life* for this."

I murmur to Simon that after what happened last night, a change or postponement might be a good idea.

Lucio taps a bony forefinger on a budget sheet. "I have four hundred invitations out for opening night. Postponing is out of the question. And as of right now, since Nogara never finished setting up the last few galleries, it isn't really a matter of *changing* an exhibit so much as mounting one. Therefore I'd like to discuss the possibility—particularly with you, Alexander—of centering the exhibit around the manuscript rather than the Shroud."

Simon and I are agog.

"You mean the Diatessaron?" I ask.

"No," Simon says. "Absolutely not."

Lucio ignores him. For once, only my opinion counts.

"How would that even be possible?" I ask.

"The restorers are done with the book," Lucio says. "People want to see the book. We put the book in a case and show it to them. The details would be up to you."

"Uncle, you can't fill ten galleries with one manuscript."

Lucio snorts. "If we remove the binding, we can. Each page can be mounted separately. And we've already made some large photographic reproductions for the walls. How many pages in the book? Fifty? One hundred?"

"Uncle, that's probably the oldest intact binding on any gospel ever discovered."

Lucio makes a brushing motion with his hand. "The people in the manuscript laboratory know how to manage these things. They'll do whatever we need."

Before I can refuse, Simon slams a hand on Lucio's desk. "*No*," he says firmly.

Everything freezes. With a look, I urge Simon to sit. Lucio raises one great, snaking eyebrow.

"Uncle," Simon says, running a hand through his hair, "forgive me. I'm . . . grieving. But if you need help finishing the exhibit, I can tell you what you need to know. Ugo told me everything."

"Everything?"

"This is very important to me, Uncle."

There was a time when these unpredictable eruptions doomed

Simon in my uncle's eyes. They were a Greek trait, Lucio said, not a Roman one. But now he says this is what sets Simon apart. What will launch him places even my uncle has not been.

"I see," Lucio says. "I'm glad to hear that. Then you'll need to direct the other curators, because we have much to do in the next five days."

"Uncle," I interject, "you realize Simon and I are dealing with a situation of our own right now?"

He shuffles the pages on his desk. "I do. And I'm having Commander Falcone send an officer to guard you and Peter as a precaution." He turns to Simon. "As for you: you'll sleep here, under this roof, until the exhibit work is done. Agreed?"

Simon would sooner sleep on a street corner outside of Termini station. But this is the price of all this uncharacteristic pleading. He's shown Lucio who holds the cards.

Simon nods, and Lucio raps his knuckles twice on the desktop. We're done. Don Diego returns to see us to the elevator.

"Should I send someone for your bags?" Diego needles Simon.

They will be suitemates for the next five nights. Warden and prisoner. But there is momentary solace in the hollow of Simon's eyes. Relief. He won't take the bait. When the metal door slides open, Peter rushes inside, eager to push the elevator button. Before Diego can find another way to prod Simon, Peter and I are descending.

CHAPTER 8

IT WAS SHORTLY after my dinner at Ugo's apartment that I helped him break into the Vatican Library to see the Diatessaron. "Meet me at my apartment at four thirty," he'd said. "And bring a pair of gloves."

At four thirty I was at the apartment. Ugo arrived a quarter-hour later. In his hands were two plastic bags from the Annona, the Vatican grocery store. One of them bore the unmistakable contours of a bottle of alcohol.

"To calm the nerves," he said, winking. But his brow was damp and his eyes were uneasy.

Once we were inside his flat, he drank shot after shot of Grappa Julia. "Tell me something," he said. "Do you know how to find your way around down there?"

Down there: below his apartment, in the library.

"How could I?" I said testily. He'd given me the impression that he'd done this before. That I would just be following. After all, just to get in the front door of our library required an application with references from accredited scholars. To see a book required paperwork. To fetch it required a library employee, since no patron was ever allowed to enter the stacks.

"If we already know where the manuscript is," I asked, "then can't we just take it off the shelf and read it?"

His other supermarket bag contained a trove of equipment. Two flashlights, an electric camping lantern, a box of latex gloves, a loaf of bread, a bag of pine nuts, a pair of slippers, a notebook, and what appeared to be a loop of wire the size of a child's tennis racket. All of which he was proceeding to bury in a duffel bag.

"Oh, we can take it off the shelf," he said. "*That* isn't the problem." He checked his watch. "Now step lively, Father Alex. We need to hurry."

I pointed to his bag. "We won't get past the guards at the front desk carrying that."

He scoffed. "Don't be silly. There's a steam duct that vents through a window on the second floor. It's been out of commission for years."

I stared at him.

Ugo chuckled and gripped my arm. "Kidding, kidding. Now stop worrying and come on."

HE HAD A FRIEND on the inside. An old French priest whose office stood in a forgotten corner of the building. The library closed in ten minutes, but Ugo's apartment was so close that we reached his friend in under two.

Ugo stopped me outside the office and said, "Wait here a moment."

He went in alone but didn't shut the door completely.

"Ugolino," I heard the man say anxiously in his French accent, "they've found out about you."

"Doubtful," Ugo replied.

"Security went door-to-door today, warning us to report any unfamiliar persons."

Ugo didn't answer.

"The priest who came with them," continued the voice, "knew your name."

Ugo cleared his throat. "The new system is still being tested?"

"Yes."

"So the door's still open?"

"It is. But it's not a good idea for you to be down there alone anymore."

"Agreed." Ugo came to the door and admitted me. "Meet Father Alexander Andreou. He'll be joining me tonight."

The Frenchman was a silver fox of a priest. He had a bottle-brush beard that almost concealed the sharp downturn in his mouth at the sight of me.

"But Ugolino . . ." he began.

Ugo collected his friend's hat and umbrella from the coatrack. "You're wasting your breath. And they're going to notice if you don't leave at the usual time. We'll talk tomorrow."

The priest closed the blinds over the glazed office door. "This isn't wise. Every little sound travels in these halls. With *him* here, you're bound to talk. To draw attention."

But Ugo only nudged him toward the door. The clock over the door read twelve past five. In the reading rooms, scholars had already packed away their notebooks and laptops. They were returning to the main desk for keys to their lockers, and in a few minutes they would be gone. After that point, it would be impossible to explain why Ugo and I were here.

"What was he warning you about?" I asked when Ugo closed the door.

He peeked between the blinds. "Nothing."

"Then why are you looking into the hallway?"

"Because I wish your uncle would hire a few curators who look like Signorina de Santis next door!"

I slumped against the wall. In camaraderie, Ugo followed suit, retrieving the loaf of bread from his duffel bag. He smiled sadly. "You understand you won't be able to tell anyone what you see tonight. Not even your students."

Under the door, the hall lights began to go dark.

"I'm not doing this for my students," I said.

"Father Simon tells me your father trained both of you to read the New Testament in Greek."

I nodded.

"He also said you were the studious one, and he was the laggard."

"The gospels were my favorite subject in seminary."

For any gospel teacher—even one who taught altar boys in pre-seminary like I did—there was excitement in knowing that our understanding of the Bible was imperfect. That older, better, more-complete manuscripts of the gospels were always waiting to be discovered. Tonight was a chance to hold one of those manuscripts before it was locked away like the rest.

Ugo cleaned his glasses on his handkerchief. He peered at me with eyes that were surprisingly lucid. "And did we tell Father Simon what we were doing this evening?"

"No. I haven't been able to reach him for a couple days."

He sighed. "Neither have I. Your brother disappears sometimes. Glad to know it isn't personal." He checked his watch and stood up. "Now, there's something you need to know before we go. We mustn't leave a trail, because it seems someone's been following me."

Remembering his conversation with the French priest, I said, "Who?"

"I don't know. But after tonight I hope he won't have another opportunity." Ugo removed his shoes and changed into the slippers from his duffel bag. "Just follow me. Down we go."

THE HALLS WERE DARK, but Ugo knew his way. For a man of his size he was soundless even when we entered the first monstrous corridors of stacks.

I had expected old wooden bookcases piled high in vast frescoed arches. Instead there were low, industrial tunnels longer than ocean liners, veined with electrical conduit. On the cold metal decks my shoes made a slapping sound that echoed down the corridors, and I had to stoop to avoid hitting my head on the caged lightbulbs. But Ugo traveled deftly, as if the drinks had only limbered him up.

The steel stacks were on all sides of us now—left and right, above and below—floor upon floor connected by attic-like openings linked by narrow ship-ladders. Ugo relied on the flashlight he had brought because the overhead bulbs were on timers. Down we went, and down again. At last we came to an elevator.

"Where does it go?" I asked.

My voice, just as the French priest had warned, rebounded across the marble floors, shearing through the woolly darkness.

"To the very bottom," Ugo whispered.

The doors closed after us, and the car immediately went dark. The beam of Ugo's flashlight went straight to the control panel. Before I could even read the inscriptions there, he had launched us on a slow descent.

The doors reopened on an area with butter-colored walls and fluorescent lights. There were no shelves here, only the occasional crucifix and holy icon on the walls, separated by fire detectors and boxes of emergency lights. All of it had the unfamiliar, chemical odor of newness.

"Are we underground?" I whispered.

Ugo nodded and led me around the bend, murmuring, "Now to see if he was right."

Around the corner we came to an immense door built entirely of steel. The adjoining wall was mounted with a security keypad.

But instead of entering a passcode, Ugo reached his fingers behind the lip of the door and leaned backward.

The slab of steel quietly swung open. Beyond it lay darkness.

"Excellent," Ugo muttered. Then he turned and said, "Touch absolutely nothing until I explain why this door was left unlocked."

He reached inside to twist the timer on the electric lights. When they came on, my legs went numb.

Twenty years ago, John Paul had broken ground on a new project. The Vatican Library had run out of shelf space, so in a small courtyard north of the library, where employees once grew vegetables in wartime and where Uncle Lucio now ran a café to squeeze money from visiting scholars, John Paul dug a pit. Into it he poured the foundation of a bombproof concrete chamber, designed for his most prized possessions. Today, when scholars sipped drinks at Lucio's café, they stood on a thin layer of grass concealing the steel-reinforced crypt of John Paul's treasures.

As a child I had imagined the place. It was, in my daydreams, as large as a bank vault. But the room that now lay before me was the size of a small airfield. The main passage was half the length of a soccer field, with aisles on either side deep enough to park a tour bus.

"Behold," Ugo whispered, "the world's greatest collection of manuscripts."

There are two kinds of books in the world. Since the time of Gutenberg, printed books have been spawned by the millions, mass-produced by machines, blotting out the older species of book: manuscripts. An illiterate Renaissance businessman with a printing press could spew ten books faster than a team of educated monks could hand-make a single manuscript page. Considering how few manuscripts were produced, and how much mistreatment they endured over the centuries, it's a miracle any have survived. But since books were first invented, they have had a powerful friend: there has always been a Christian Church to make them, and a pope in Rome to collect them. Of all the great libraries in human history, only one still exists. And by the grace of God, into the heart of that library I now stepped.

"Take this," Ugo said, handing me the other flashlight. "The timer lasts only twenty minutes. Now let me show you what we're up against."

He synced the countdown to his digital watch, set it running, then removed the loop of wire from the grocery-store bag. For the first time I got a good look at it: an electronic handset connected to an oval of metal like an oven coil. When he turned it on, red letters flickered across the handset.

"They're installing a new inventory system," he said, "so they won't have to shut down the library for a month every year to do it by hand. Do you know what this is?"

It looked like the offspring of a TV antenna and a towel warmer.

"It's a radio frequency scanner," he said. "Tags have been implanted in the manuscript bindings, and this scanner can read fifty at a time, straight through the air."

He led me past the first stack, demonstrating as we passed. Lines of text scrolled down the screen faster than I could read them. Call numbers. Titles. Authors.

"Even with this wand," he said, "it took me two weeks of searching to realize the manuscript must be down here. Two weeks, and a bit of luck." He nodded in the direction of a white plastic box installed on the ceiling. "Those are the permanent scanners. For some reason, they interfere with the security system, so the steel door has to remain unlocked until the problem has been fixed." He glanced at me. "For us, that's good news. The bad news is that this RF technology makes the steel door irrelevant. My first visit to this vault, I made the mistake of taking a book to a different shelf across the aisle. The scanners saw it moving. In five minutes, a security guard was here."

"What did you do?"

"Hid and prayed. Fortunately, the guard thought the system was just on the fritz. From then on, I've followed two rules. One: I read in situ. And two: I wear *these*."

He produced the pairs of latex gloves from the bag.

"To avoid leaving fingerprints?" I said.

"Not the kind you're thinking of," he said with a glint in his eye. "Now follow me."

As we moved through the stacks, his precision increased. Leaving the duffel at the end of an aisle, he exhumed a vial of alcohol swabs and cleaned his hands before donning the gloves.

"Is this it?" I asked, seeing that the handset was now registering a fondo of manuscripts in Syriac, the ancient language of Edessa in the time of the Diatessaron. The language, also, closest to Jesus' Aramaic.

But Ugo shook his head and continued deeper into the aisle. "*This,*" he said, "is it."

On the screen, a strange notation had appeared. Where call numbers should have been, there was a Latin word. CORRUPTAE.

Damaged.

"This shelf," Ugo said, "is a backlog for the restoration workshop." He gestured at an entire stack, more than one hundred in all. "They don't even seem to realize it's here."

"How did you find the right manuscript?"

Ugo couldn't read Greek, and knowledge of Syriac was far rarer.

"Father Alex, I've been coming down here every night since I came back from Turkey. I sleep only during the days. What you see here has become my life. I'm *this* far"—he pinched his fingers in the air—"from proving that the Shroud was in Edessa in the second century. If I'd had to, I would've searched every manuscript in this palace by hand." He grinned. "Fortunately, all the manuscripts on this shelf still have indexes from the *old* inventory system—written in beautiful Latin."

Squinting, he peered up at the shelves and ran a gloved finger through the air, just a hairsbreadth from their spines. When he came to the one he wanted, he cocked his head and glanced back at the nearest scanner on the wall, as if estimating its tolerance for movement. Finally he said, "Put your gloves on."

The thrill of those words was more intense than I had expected. "Before I do," I asked, "could I touch it? Just for a second. I'll be very careful."

He didn't answer. Instead, with a practiced movement he notched the volume off the shelf, opened the gilded leather cover—and out slid something gnarled and awful looking. It was no bigger than a necklace case, with rust-colored scratches that webbed the black, pitted surface of its cover. The librarians had never removed the original binding to slip it inside the papal covers.

"There's something you need to know," Ugo said, "before you touch this. Something I was able to track down only after I discovered it. Three hundred years ago, the pope sent a family of priests to search for the oldest manuscripts in the world. One of them stumbled upon a library in the deserts of Nitrian Egypt, in the Monastery of the Syrians, where an abbot had assembled a collection of texts in the nine hundreds AD. Even in the abbot's day, these texts were extremely old. Today they're the most ancient books known to exist. The abbot printed a warning inside them: *He who removes these books from the monastery will be accursed of God.* The priest, Assemani, ignored this warning, and on his way back to Rome his boat capsized in the Nile. One of the monks was drowned. Assemani paid men to dredge up his manuscripts, but the books needed repair for water damage, which is one reason this book ended up on a forgotten shelf.

"The other reason is that when Assemani's cousin tried to make a catalog of these manuscripts, he died in the attempt. A third Assemani took over, only to have a fire break out in his apartment beside the library. The whole catalog was destroyed, and no one has ever completed it. That's why no record of these manuscripts exists, and nobody seems to know they're here."

"Ugo," I said, "why are you telling me this?"

"Because while I consider myself to be above superstition, and lucky to have found this book, you're entitled to decide for yourself."

"Don't be ridiculous." I was a teacher of modern gospel methods. The scientific, rational reading of the Bible. I didn't even hesitate.

He shifted the ancient text between his own gloves so that it sat in the palm of one hand while he raised the other for me to see. Where the manuscript had made contact with the glove, the latex was ruddy brown.

"The cover," he said, "leaves an almost indelible stain. It took me days to scrub it off my skin. Please, wear the gloves."

He waited until I had done it; then, tenderly, like the doctor who placed Peter in my arms, he handed the text over.

Never had I seen a book made that way. Like a prehistoric creature found living at the bottom of the sea, it bore only the faintest resemblance to its modern cousins. The manuscript's cover was made with a sheet of skin hanging off like a satchel flap, designed to wrap around the pages again and again, to protect them. A leather tail dangled from it, beltlike, looping around the book to cinch it closed.

I undid the straps as carefully as if I were arranging hairs on a baby's head. Inside, the pages were gray and soft. Flowing letters were penned in long, smooth strokes with no rounded edges: Syriac. Beside them, inked right there on the page, was a Latin index written by some long-dead Vatican librarian.

Formerly Book VIII among the Nitrian Syriac collection.

And then, very clearly:

Gospel Harmony of Tatian (Diatessaron).

A shudder went through me. Here in my hands was the creature invented by one of the giants of early Christianity. The canonical life of Jesus of Nazareth in a single book. Matthew, Mark, Luke, and John fused together to form the super-gospel of the ancient Syrian church.

There were no sounds down here except from the titanic earthworms of ductwork on the ceiling, ventilated by a faraway mechanical lung. But in my ears was the watery drumming of my blood.

"Dyed goatskin," Ugo said nervously under his breath, "over papyrus boards. Pages made of parchment."

With a type of tool I didn't recognize, he turned the first page.

I gasped. Everything inside was too water-stained to read. But on the next page, the stains became smaller. And on the third, handwriting became visible.

"You're right," I whispered. "It's a diglot."

There were two columns on the page: the left one in Syriac, the right one in Greek. And this time, when Ugo turned the leaf, it was as if the fog of damage had begun to roll off. There, in all capital letters, with no spaces in between, was a line of Greek I could transform into something familiar.

ΕΓΕΝΕΤΟΡΗΜΑΘΕΟΥΕΠΙΙΩΑΝΝΗΝΤΟΝΤΟΥΖΑΧΑΡΙΟΥ.

"*The word of God came to John the son of Zechariah*," I said. "That's from Luke."

Ugo glanced at me, then back at the page. In his eyes there was now fire, too.

"But look at the next line!" I said. "*He confessed, 'I am not the Christ.'* That verse is only in the gospel of John."

Ugo searched his pockets for something but didn't seem to find it. He dashed back to the duffel bag and returned, panting, with a notebook.

"Father Alex," he said, "this is the list. These are the Shroud references we need to check. The first one is Matthew 27:59. The parallel verses are Mark—"

Before I could scan the page, though, he frowned and stopped short. For a moment he turned and stared at the scanner.

"What's wrong?"

He cocked an ear. Distantly there was the faintest sound.

But he shook his head and said, "Air current. Carry on."

I wondered how he could be so focused on his small list of verses—or even on the Shroud—when an entire gospel lay before us. I would've stayed here a month, a year, until I had taught myself enough Syriac to read both columns together, every word.

Yet the muscles of Ugo's face were strained. All trace of jovial good humor had left. "Read, Father," he said. "Please."

There were eight verses on the list. I knew them by heart. Each of the four gospels—Matthew, Mark, Luke, and John—says that Jesus' dead body was wrapped in linen after the crucifixion. Two of the gospels—Luke and John—also say that disciples returned after the Resurrection and saw the linen lying by itself in the empty tomb. But the Diatessaron, by merging the gospels into a single story, distilled all these references to only two moments: the burial and the reopening of the tomb.

"Ugo, there's a problem," I said, finding the first of the quotations. "There's too much rot here. I can't make out some of the words."

Hazy black stains spotted the page, rendering words illegible. I had read about manuscripts destroyed by fungus but had never seen one firsthand.

Ugo collected himself. Then as calmly as he could, he said, "Very well, scrape it off."

I blinked at him. "I can't. That would damage the page."

Ugo reached over. "Then show me the word, and *I'll* do it."

I moved the book away from him.

His temper flashed. "Father, you know how important that one word is."

"What word?"

He shut his eyes and collected himself. "Three of the gospels say Jesus was buried in a linen *cloth*. Singular. But John says *cloths*. Plural."

"I don't understand."

He looked incredulous. "Singular means we have a burial shroud. Plural means we have something else. If John was right, then all of this has been a grand mistake, hasn't it? The man who wrote the Diatessaron had to choose. And if he really saw the Shroud in Edessa, then he would've chosen *cloth*, singular."

This newfound intensity repelled me. "You told me we were here to prove the Shroud was in Edessa when the Diatessaron was written."

He shook his list of Bible verses in the air. "*Eight* Shroud references. Eight. Four from Mark, Matthew, and Luke. Four from John." He pointed to the manuscript. "The fellow who wrote this book—"

"Tatian."

"—had to break the tie. He couldn't use *both* words, so which did he choose? The battle begins here, Father. So let's have it."

Yet no matter how I squinted, the rot was impenetrable. "I'll check the other reference," I suggested. "The empty tomb."

But there, too, the word was hidden by black splotches.

Ugo removed a plastic kit from his breast pocket. "I brought swabs and solvent. We'll begin with saliva. The enzymes may be enough."

I placed a hand on his arm. "Stop. No."

"*Father, I didn't bring you—*"

"Please, tell the Cardinal Librarian what you've found. The restorers will do this the right way. We don't have to risk damaging it."

He became incensed. "The *Cardinal Librarian*? You said I could trust you! You gave me your word!"

"Ugo, damage these pages and you'll have nothing. Neither will anyone else. Forever."

"I didn't come here to be lectured. Father Simon told me you had experience with—"

I lifted the manuscript up in the air.

"Stop!" he cried. "You'll set off the alarm!"

When the book was level with my eyes, I said, "Move the flashlight at an angle. Maybe I can see the indentations of the pen strokes."

He stared at me, then patted his pockets and produced a small magnifying glass. "Yes. Okay, good. Use this."

One hundred years ago, a lost book of Archimedes had turned up in a Greek Orthodox convent, hidden in plain sight. A medieval monk had erased the treatise by scraping the ink off the parchment and had written a liturgical text on the blank pages instead. But under the right light, from the right angle, it was still possible to see the old indentations, the tracks of that ancient pen.

"Stop," I said. "Keep the beam just like that."

"What do you see?"

I blinked and looked again.

"What is it?" he repeated.

"Ugo . . ."

"Speak! Please!"

"This isn't rot."

"Then what is it?"

I squinted. "These are brushstrokes."

"What?"

"These stains are *paint*. Someone already found this book. It's been censored."

THE BLOTS WERE EVERYWHERE. Swallowing up words, phrases, entire verses. The text beneath was impossible to read.

In shock, Ugo murmured, "You're saying someone got to this book before we did?"

"Not anytime recently. This paint looks very old."

I scanned the text, trying to understand what I was seeing.

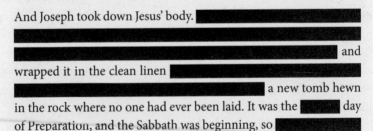

And Joseph took down Jesus' body. ███████████████
███
███████████████████████████████████ and
wrapped it in the clean linen ████████████████
███████████████████████ a new tomb hewn
in the rock where no one had ever been laid. It was the ████ day
of Preparation, and the Sabbath was beginning, so ████████
█████████ they laid him in it and rolled a great stone against the
door of the tomb, and departed.

"Who did it?" Ugo asked.

I closed my eyes. I knew these gospel verses by rote. Fusing together the testimony of all four gospels would yield:

And Joseph took down Jesus' body. <u>Nicodemus, who had at first come to him by night, came bringing a mixture of myrrh and aloes, about a hundred pounds' weight. They took the body of Jesus,</u> and wrapped it in the clean linen <u>cloth/cloths. Now in the place where he was crucified there was a garden, and in the garden</u> a new tomb hewn in the rock where no one had ever been laid. It was the <u>Jewish</u> day of Preparation, and the Sabbath was beginning, so <u>as the tomb was close at hand,</u> they laid him in it and rolled a great stone against the door of the tomb, and departed.

The censored parts were about the burial spices, the shroud, the man named Nicodemus, and—strangest of all—the word *Jewish*. The only unknown was whether the word for the burial linen would be singular or plural: three of the four gospels use the Greek word *sindon*, meaning "cloth" or "shroud"; the other uses *othonia*, meaning "cloths," plural.

I could think of just one thing that connected these censored words.

To be sure of it, I checked the rest of the column.

"Ugo," I whispered, "do you have any idea how old this manuscript is?"

"Fourth or fifth century, I estimate," he said.

I shook my head. "I think it's older than that."

A nervous smile crossed his face. "How much older?"

I tried to contain the trembling in my hands. "Nicodemus is mentioned only in the gospel of John. So are the burial spices. So is the word *Jewish* in this final sentence. Everything this censor cut out was from the gospel of John."

"What does that tell us?"

"There was a group of Christians called the Alogi. They wanted John's gospel rejected. I think they censored this manuscript."

"Is that a good thing or a bad thing?"

"The Alogi existed in the late *one hundreds* AD. This manuscript is probably the oldest complete gospel manuscript in the world."

He looked despondent. "So the word they censored must be *cloths.* That's the word John uses." Then he registered what I'd said. "Sorry, repeat that?"

"I said, *this is probably the oldest—*"

Only then, when he interrupted me, did I understand the depth of his obsession.

"No. Before that. You said these people wanted to reject the gospel of John. Why?"

"Because the Alogi knew the gospel of John wasn't like the other gospels. It's more theological. Less historical."

"What do you mean, less historical?"

"It's complicated, but Ugo—"

"John says *cloths*, but the other three gospels all say *cloth*. Are you telling me John can't be trusted?"

"Ugo, we have to tell the Cardinal Librarian about this book. It can't stay hidden down here."

"Answer me! If John is unreliable, then the whole gospel testimony about the Shroud would change. Correct?"

I hesitated. "It might, but it's not as simple as that. There are rules. Reading the gospels takes training."

"Fine. Then teach me the rules."

I raised a hand, trying to slow him down. "Tell me this manuscript is going to be safe."

He sighed. "Father, of course it's going to be safe. But *I* found this book. *I* need it. And I can't lose it to neurotic, overprotective librarians. You know they'll just—"

Suddenly he stopped. He cocked his head toward the steel door and stared at it in alarm.

"What is it?" I whispered.

But he was too rigid to speak. Only his eyes moved. They glanced at his watch, then peered down the far end of the aisle.

Finally I made out a faint mechanical whirr. A motor turning at a lower note than the drone of the distant ventilator.

The elevator.

"Did I set off the alarm?" I asked.

But he only stared at his watch as if it must be deceiving him.

"How do we get out?" I asked. "Is there another exit?"

"Don't move."

I peered through the open spaces between shelves. A moment later, my eyes caught it. Movement near the door.

Ugo stepped backward.

Where are you going? I mouthed.

Silently he refilled the duffel bag and lifted it onto his shoulder, eyes never leaving the main door.

An instant later, a voice rose in the vault.

"Doctor Nogara, please come out."

Ugo's hand gripped the duffel bag. He knelt and pointed at the scanner on the wall, reminding me not to move. Then he himself began to slink away.

"I mean you no harm," the voice said. "I was sent here by the Secretariat of State. I need to know what you're doing here."

The sound of it was drawing closer. Ugo raised three fingers in the air, but I couldn't understand the signal. Closing the manuscript, I prepared to slide it back on the shelf.

"We know you've been working in Turkey," the voice went on, only a few stacks away. "We know you've been helped by Father Andreou. I've followed him to Esenboğa Airport several times. He's supposed to work for us, so we have a right to know where he goes."

Ugo's eyes were wide with fear. He gestured wildly for me not to replace the book on the shelf. He lifted his hand in the air again but this time raised only two fingers.

Now I could see the man's silhouette. It passed across the mouth of the aisle with the shadowy sweep of a cassock.

I stepped toward the steel door, but Ugo waved me off. He glanced at his watch and extended a single finger in the air.

My fears got the better of me. Without waiting, I placed the Diatessaron on its shelf and made for the door.

As soon as Ugo saw me move, he turned back and darted toward the Diatessaron. "The book!" he rasped. "*The book!*"

The sound echoed through the vault. The silhouette turned. At that moment, the timer on Ugo's watch went off. Instantaneously, the lights on the timer went out. The vault went black.

"*Run!*" Ugo shouted into the pitch.

I sloped through the darkness, moving toward the sliver of emergency light beneath the steel door. Behind me, something lurched into motion. I could hear a tattoo of footfalls, then a piercing mechanical scream.

The alarm.

"*Go!*" Ugo shouted. "*I have it!*"

I swung into the hallway and ran for the elevator. As I frantically pressed the button, Ugo appeared, carrying the Diatessaron.

"Hurry!" Ugo cried. "He's coming!"

The doors opened, and we rushed inside. In the moments before they shut again, I stared out, frozen with surprise, waiting for a glimpse of the man's face.

But the vault remained silent. He never came.

As the elevator car rose, Ugo cradled the book in his hands and closed his eyes.

"Who was that?" I asked.

"I don't know."

"We need to tell my uncle."

But at the top of the elevator shaft, the gendarmes were waiting. Ugo and I were taken into custody. An hour later, Don Diego arrived to free us.

"You found *what* down there?" Uncle Lucio demanded when we returned to his palace.

Ugo's answer, in retrospect, probably saved his skin.

"Eminence," he said, placing the manuscript on Lucio's desk, "I've discovered the fifth gospel. And I'm going to use it to authenticate the Shroud of Turin."

Never had I seen my uncle forget his anger so quickly. "Tell me more," he said.

Only later would we piece together the second surprise of that night: that the gendarmes never found the other man in that crypt.

"Who was he?" I asked Ugo later.

"I wish I knew," he said. "I never saw his face."

"His voice, though. Did it sound familiar to you?"

Ugo frowned. "Odd. Now that you mention it, I had meant to ask you the same thing."

CHAPTER 9

ON THE ELEVATOR ride down from Lucio's penthouse, I can't stop thinking of the priest in the library vault. I wonder why my uncle can't finish Ugo's exhibit without help from Simon. I wonder why Ugo wanted to keep the finale a secret. There must be something he didn't want anyone finding out.

Peter tugs at my cassock. "When is Simon coming back?" he bleats.

"I don't know. He has to help Prozio Lucio right now. And we have to check in to the Casa."

"Why?"

I lower myself to his level. "Peter, we can't go home."

"Because the police are there?"

"Things are just going to be different for a few days. Okay?"

Different. He knows this word. A slinky synonym for *worse.*

CASA SANTA MARTA IS the only hotel on Vatican soil. It's where the Holy Father puts up his official visitors and where bishops stay during their required visits to see him every five years. It's also a home base for Secretariat priests in their comings and goings. Simon would be staying here if he had no family in town.

The building is almost Amish in its plainness, with six rows of identical windows, inside of which are a hundred-odd rooms slightly bigger than monastic cells. On one side, the view from the windows is of the

Vatican gas station. On the other side, guests can stare at the towering border wall that runs only an arm's length from the hotel. All of John Paul's building projects are this way. The only luxuries that interest a pope who was forced to shovel limestone in Nazi-occupied Poland are four walls and a roof.

The apologetic nun at the front desk says they can't give us our hotel room yet because the special part of the hotel reserved for us is still being cleaned. She seems not to have heard that keeping religious minorities in their own ghettoes went out of style while John Paul was shoveling limestone. We just want the first available room, I explain. But her response, after sizing up my cassock and beard, is, "Father, your Italian is very good!" I pull Peter out the front doors before I can say something I'll regret.

"Where are we going now?" he asks. "Can we get something to eat?"

I never fed him a proper breakfast. If he ate at all, it was whatever Sofia gave him back at Leo's apartment.

"Soon," I tell him. "But there's something important we need to do first."

IT'S BEEN WEEKS SINCE I came to Ugo's apartment. When we stand dumbly in front of the lintel, Peter stares at me, wondering why we don't knock. He can't see what I see. There are pry marks on the door.

Someone tried to break in. But Ugo kept two padlocks on this entrance. Unlike the door at our apartment, this one refused to give in.

I unlock it with the keys Ugo gave me so that I could watch over the place while he was in Turkey. Peter bursts inside, and I race after him, but there's no one here. The place looks just the way it did when I last saw it.

"Doctor Nogara?" Peter calls out in a singsong tone.

"He isn't here," I say. "We're just looking for something that belongs to him."

There will be time to explain later. I ask him to stay here, in the living room, until I return. I don't know what emotions I'm about to feel.

The modest space where Ugo Nogara slept is beyond a wall of oriental screens. The makeshift room is heavy with the kind of sadness that seems peculiar to this country. Priests are encouraged not to accumulate property, so even the most urbane cleric usually lives in a featureless room with borrowed furniture. For Roman priests, it's even worse. Photographs on walls have no wives or children to populate them. Floors are not littered with bath toys and fist-size shoes. Closets seem underfed with no colorful jackets and miniature umbrellas making their doors bulge open. Instead, Roman priests keep newspaper clippings and postcards of the landmarks they visit and the pilgrimages they make during their mandated weeks of vacation. It shouldn't have been this way with Ugo. He was a layman. But you would never know it, to see this room.

Bottles of Grappa Julia have piled up in the trash can. There isn't even a veneer of private joy in the pictures on the walls, just monuments in Edessa with no trace of Ugo standing in the foreground. The only sign that a vibrant, living force once slept here is the wreckage of books on his desktop, where the chair isn't even tucked in. It's as if, engrossed in his work, he stepped away to answer the door and could be back any minute. Beneath the desk I make out the canted edges of Ugo's iron safe. But before I kneel to open it, I close my eyes and feel the tidal pull of a familiar emotion. My father left behind a life like this, warm with unfinished business.

Opening my eyes again, I study the corkboard Ugo kept on his wall. Pinned to it is a diagram he made. It resembles a caduceus: two serpentine lines braided around each other. One is labeled GOOD SHEPHERD, the other LAMB OF GOD. Beside each loop are gospel quotations.

Those words carve a swath of emptiness in me. The first time Jesus appears in the gospel of John, he is called "the Lamb of God." No other gospel calls Jesus this, but the meaning is obvious. In the time of Moses, at the end of the ten plagues of Egypt, God protected the Jews from the Angel of Death by telling them to sacrifice a lamb and daub its blood on every door the angel should pass over. Now God was saving His people with a new Lamb: Jesus. Jesus saved us, spiritually, by his death. To this John adds a second metaphor: his Jesus says, "I am the Good Shepherd. A Good Shepherd lays down his life for the sheep." There is a shepherd in the other gospels, a symbolic figure who finds joy in saving lost sheep, but the Good Shepherd in John is different. He will save his flock *by dying*. This diagram is morbid. Chilling. The Lamb and the Shepherd meet in death. One man dies so the rest may live. It seems ominous that this idea would've preoccupied Ugo just before he was killed. It reminds me of the e-mail he sent me. Ugo asked for help. I failed him.

In the kitchen I hear Peter rummaging for food in the refrigerator. But I can't find the voice to tell him no. I remember, years ago, Mona returning home from the geriatric ward after an old man had died. She was in agony; for some reason, she blamed herself. A wrong medicine. A failed intervention. But no man ever died on my wife's watch because he begged her for help and she refused him.

I lower myself into Ugo's chair. Then suddenly I hear something. Peter, shouting.

"What's wrong?" I call out, rushing into the kitchen.

He's gone.

"*Peter!*" I roar. "*Where are you?*"

His head emerges beside a distant oriental screen. "Look!" he says.

I lumber toward him, disoriented. There, behind the screen, is one of the large west-facing windows that overlooks the library courtyard below. He's standing near it, holding one of Ugo's pieces of suet.

"Look at what?" I ask.

He points to the floor. There, pecking at the suet Peter took from the refrigerator, is a small bird. A starling.

"He just flew inside!" Peter says jubilantly.

But he's lying. The handle on the window is cocked at the wrong angle. He's been opening this window himself.

"Lock it," I tell him sternly, feeling the nearness of something awful, narrowly averted. "Never do that again."

It's thirty feet down to the stone courtyard. I'm shaking at the thought.

"I *didn't*," Peter says crossly. And he stands on his tiptoes, raising his arm to prove it. He is inches from reaching the handle.

Then I see it. There is shattered glass on the floor behind him. The pane behind the window handle is broken.

"Did the bird do that?" I ask.

But I already know the answer.

"No," Peter says angrily. "It was already broken."

The front door refused to budge. So someone entered this apartment through the window.

I peer down again at the courtyard below. Thirty feet. I don't even know how it could be done.

"Stay right here," I tell Peter. "Don't touch *anything*."

Back in Ugo's bedroom, I understand. Ugo didn't leave the mess on this desk. He didn't leave the chair pulled out.

When I kneel, I see the pry marks on the iron safe.

Against this safe, though, no crowbar had a prayer. It weighs as much as a man and has been bolted to the floor.

The combination is the Bible verse in which Jesus established the papacy: first gospel, sixteenth chapter, eighteenth verse. *You are Peter, and upon this rock I will build my Church, and the gates of hell shall not prevail against it.* Despite being battered, the mechanism is silky and the hinges make no sound. Ugo bought this safe to protect the manuscripts for his exhibit, and protect them it did.

Everything inside is familiar. Two months ago, when he was stranded in Turkey, Ugo told me to lock up the manuscripts he didn't need. The leftovers; the runts. But among them is one new jewel—a cheap, bonded-leather notebook that I've seen Ugo carry with him almost everywhere. I wonder if this is what the intruder came to find: the research diary containing Ugo's notes.

When I open it, a photo slips out. Seeing it, I feel my stomach clench. The man in the photo is lying on a tile floor. He appears to be dead.

A priest. A middle-aged Roman Catholic with fine, dark hair and one limpid green eye. His nose is broken. Where his left eye should be, there is a black bulge slotted like a coin purse. The jaw beneath it is covered with blood. Pinned under his body, as if he was pushed down on top of it, is a sign written in a language I don't understand. PRELUARE BAGAJE. Only some flicker of animation in his green eye suggests he isn't dead, just badly hurt. On the back of the photo, someone has written:

Be careful who you trust.

I feel dizzy. The air hums.

"Peter!" I shout.

I close the photo back into the diary. From the corkboard I take the diagram Ugo made.

"Peter, we're leaving!"

I shut the safe. Lock it. But the diary goes into my cassock. We won't be back here again.

Peter is waiting for me on the other side of the screen. "What's wrong, Babbo?" he says, still holding the suet in his hand.

I lift him in my arms and carry him out the door. I don't tell him about the picture. I don't tell him that I recognize the bloody priest.

AN UNFAMILIAR MAN IS talking to a gendarme in the hall. He glances up at the sound of Ugo's apartment door being locked, but we're already slipping down another staircase. The older wings of the palace are cork-screwed with these private passages.

"What are we doing?" Peter says.

He's too young to know these back ways, but he knows something's wrong.

"We'll be out soon," I say.

The spiral staircase is narrow and unlit. In the darkness, the image of the bloodied priest returns to me. I haven't seen his face in years. Michael Black, my father's former assistant. Another Secretariat man.

Peter murmurs something indistinct. I'm too lost in thought to ask him to repeat himself.

So Ugo was *not* the first to be attacked. I wonder if Michael survived.

Peter pushes impatiently at my chest.

"*What?*" I demand.

"I said, why is that man following us?"

I freeze. In the tight cylinder of the staircase, there are footsteps.

CHAPTER 10

I BEGIN DOUBLE-STEPPING, BUT the footsteps quicken. With a boy in my arms, there's no higher gear. I feel Peter clutching my neck, forcing his face into the crook of my throat.

Out of the murk, a shape descends. A silhouette nearly as tall as Simon. He's wearing layman's clothes.

"Who are you?" I ask, backing away.

In the dark, the man's eyes are splinters of silver.

"Father," he says in a gruff voice, "what were you doing up there?"

His face is completely unfamiliar.

"Why are you following us?" I demand.

"Because those are my orders."

I take one more step back. Another ten feet and we'll be in public view.

The man extends his arms so they press against the walls of the stairwell. He says, "Father Andreou?"

In my arms, Peter's body is tense. I don't respond.

The man reaches for something in his pocket. I begin to retreat. Then I see what it is: two metal laurels around a yellow-and-white Vatican flag.

A badge.

"I'm your security escort," he says.

"HOW LONG HAVE YOU been following us?" I say.

"Since you left the Casa."

"Why aren't you in uniform?"

"Because those are the orders that came down from His Eminence."

I wonder if Lucio did this for Peter's sake. To frighten him less.

"Tell me your name," I say.

"Agent Martelli."

"Agent Martelli, the next time you follow us, wear your uniform."

He grinds his teeth. "Yes, Father."

"Are you the one who's going to guard us overnight, too?"

"Someone else will work that shift, Father."

"Who?"

"I wouldn't know his name."

"Tell him to wear his uniform, too."

"Yes, Father."

He waits, as if I'm delaying his own question: why were Peter and I in Ugo's apartment? But priests don't answer to policemen inside these walls. Peter and I turn and descend toward the light.

OUR ROOM AT THE Casa is a fourth-floor suite. Peter, who has never stayed in a hotel before, says, "Where's the rest?" No kitchen, no living room, no toys. Boys in our building have told him that hotels are like heaven. But this can't be heaven. There's no television.

A plain cross hangs over the narrow metal bed frame. The parquet floor, polished like a Secretariat priest's shoes, reflects the featureless white walls. Other than a bedside table and a valet stand that seems designed for a Roman Catholic priest suit rather than any traditional robe, there's only a radiator beneath a window. The window, though, opens onto the small inner courtyard of this oddly shaped building, and below us are earthenware flower boxes and a potted tree with fantastic stalks of sharp fronds resembling towers of green Christmas stars. The air smells of lavender.

"Who was that man?" Peter asks, hopping onto the bed while still wearing his shoes, to test the lone pillow.

"A policeman," I say. "He's going to help keep us safe."

There's no longer any point avoiding it. The escort will be around us at all hours.

"We're safe here?" Peter asks, rifling the contents of the nightstand.

"The gendarme station is right next door. Agent Martelli is keeping watch in the hall. And everyone here takes special care of guests. We're *completely* safe."

He frowns at the Bible in the top drawer. It's the Vulgate, the fourth-century translation that Roman Catholics consider the gold standard. Written in Latin, it seems intended to suit men from all nations, just as this hotel is. But Peter sighs. He knows the evangelists wrote in Greek, the first universal language. The contribution of our people is always undervalued.

"I'm going to call Leo and ask him to bring up some food," I say. It will give us more privacy than the dining room, and I could use the company. "What do you want?"

"Pizza margherita from Ivo," he says.

"He's not getting takeout."

Peter shrugs. "Then anything."

Leaving him to peruse the Bible he can't read, I go to the small desk in the attached room. After phoning Leo, I brace myself. My next call is to Simon.

"Alex?" my brother says.

I start right in. "What happened to Michael Black?"

"What?"

"I found a photo in Ugo's office. Is he still alive?"

"Yes. Of course."

"What did they do to him?"

"You shouldn't have gone there, Alex. You need to stay safe."

"There was a warning written on the back of the photo. Why would someone have sent Ugo a warning? Because of his exhibit?"

"I don't know."

"He never mentioned this to you?"

"No."

"I don't think he was robbed last night, Simon. I think all of this is connected. What happened to Michael; what happened to Ugo; what happened at the apartment. How could you not tell me Michael was attacked?"

His silence is longer now.

"Last night at the cantina," I say, "when I showed you that e-mail from Ugo, you said it was nothing."

"Because it *is* nothing."

"Ugo was in trouble, Sy. He was scared."

Simon hesitates. "The reason I didn't tell you about Michael is that I'm under oath not to talk about it. And what happened at the apartment—I spent every minute of last night thinking about it, and I don't understand it. So please, I'm asking you to stay out of this. I don't want to get you involved."

Pressure builds behind my eyes. My hand pulls at my beard. "You knew he was in trouble?"

"Stop, Alex."

It's all I can do to keep from shouting. Instead, I decide to hang up.

An oath. He said nothing because of an oath.

IN ANGER, I DIAL the main number at the nunciature in Turkey. An expensive call, but I'll keep it short.

When the nun at the switchboard answers, I ask for Michael Black.

"He's on leave," she says.

"I'm calling from the Vatican on important business. Could you please give me his mobile number?"

She offers it without a hitch.

Before calling, I try to clear my mind. It's been over a decade since I spoke to Michael, and we're separated by a graveyard of hatchets. He turned his back on my father after the debacle of the Shroud's radiocarbon dating. He also reported Simon for going absent without leave at work. Yet there was a time when I knew him better than any priest but my father. When I trusted him above any other man. That's the Michael I try to think of as I dial.

"Pronto," comes the voice on the other line.

"Is this Michael?"

"Who's this?"

"Alex Andreou."

The silence is so long that I fear there will be nothing after it.

"Michael," I say, "there's something I need to talk to you about. In person, if possible. Where are you?"

"That's none of your business."

His voice is almost exactly the way I remember it. Dry and sharp and impatient. But the flat American accent that was once so prominent has been smoothed by a decade of practice, making it easier to hear the note of defensiveness behind his words. To hear him trying to piece together why I'm calling.

When I explain about the photo, he doesn't respond.

"Please," I say. "I need to know who attacked you."

"None. Of. Your. Business."

Finally I tell him a man was killed.

"What are you talking about?"

It's unexpectedly hard to talk about Ugo. I try to be concise—to say that he was a Vatican curator, that he had been working on the upcoming exhibit—but Michael must hear the emotion swelling in my voice. He waits.

"He was," I say, "my friend."

Just for an instant, Michael softens.

"Whoever did that," he says, "I hope to hell they catch him." Then the gruffness returns. "But I'm not going to talk about what happened to me. You got to ask someone else about that."

I'm not sure if there's an insinuation in it.

"I already asked my brother," I tell him. "Simon's under oath not to talk about it."

Michael makes a derisive sound. There must still be bad blood between them. Or else this is the residue of something older, of the way he left things with my father.

"Please," I say. "I don't care what happened before—"

He howls. "*You don't care?* I had my eye socket broken. I had to have my nose rebuilt."

"I mean whatever happened between you and Simon. Or my father. All I want to know is who did this."

"You people are unbelievable! I might as well be *talking* to your father. You Greeks, always the victims. *He's* the one who sent *my* career down in flames."

You people. You Greeks. I try to keep the anger out of my voice.

"Please. Just tell me what happened."

He's breathing heavily into the phone. "I can't. I'm under oath, too."

Something snaps inside me. "I've got a five-year-old son who can't sleep in his own bed because you took an *oath*?"

Oaths. A bureaucrat's best friend. How a desk-job bishop buries his mistakes: by swearing his priest-underlings to secrecy.

"You know what?" I say. "Forget it. Enjoy your vacation."

I'm about to hang up when he shouts, "You asshole, my nuncio ran me up the pole for not being able to answer his questions. I don't need it from you, too. If you want to know what happened, go ask the Holy Father."

I falter. "The Holy Father?"

"That's right. *He's* the one who ordered it."

I'm caught by surprise. So that's why Simon can't tell me. There are oaths, and then there are oaths.

But an uncomfortable feeling scrapes at me. John Paul would have no reason to silence something like this.

"Michael, I—"

Before I can speak another word, though, the line goes dead.

THE KNOCK COMES A moment later. Standing at the door is Leo, bearing a basket of food.

"Who's the stiff?" he murmurs, stepping inside. He nods in the direction of Agent Martelli, who hovers a few feet beside the door.

"The security detail my uncle got us."

Leo wants to say something disparaging—the Swiss Guards and gendarmes are old rivals—but he holds his tongue. Instead he lifts a ceramic dish from the basket and says, "From the wife."

I thought he would pick up food from downstairs. Instead, Sofia has cooked us a meal.

"How's Little P holding up?" he asks.

"Scared."

"Still? I thought kids were supposed to rebound fast."

Fatherhood has many surprises in store for him.

I enter the bedroom with Peter's food, only to find he has fallen asleep. I close the wooden shutters to dim the room almost to black. Though the autumn afternoon is warm, I pull the counterpane over him.

"Come on," Leo whispers, handing me a plate of food. "Let's talk."

But just as we sit down, my mobile phone begins to ring. The voice on the other end is gruff.

"Alex, it's Michael again. I've been thinking about what you said."

He sounds different. More on edge.

"I didn't know you had a kid," he goes on. "There are some things you deserve to hear."

"Then tell me."

"Go to the pay phone outside the walls, near the train station."

"We're safe. This is my mobile."

There is rampant fear in our country of talking on bugged lines. Some Secretariat men won't use phones at all, except to set up face-to-face meetings.

"I don't trust your idea of safe," he says. "Go to the phone on Via della Stazione Vaticana. It's near the billboard by the service station. I'll call you there in twenty minutes."

The place he is describing is almost immediately behind the Casa. I could be there in five. I turn to Leo and mouth, *Can you stay with Peter for a few minutes?*

When he nods, I say, "Fine. I'll be waiting."

THE SERVICE STATION IS a dump with spray-painted walls and metal grates behind its porthole windows. On the billboard, a woman with football-size breasts advertises phone service. The dumpster across the street gapes at her with a half-open lid. From here I can make out the rear of the Casa over the Vatican walls, and towering above it, the dome of Saint Peter's. What catches my eye, though, are the train tracks in the distance.

Simon and I used to love watching the freight trains come and go at the Vatican station. Instead of hoppers of coal or grain, they carried business suits for our department store, or marble for Lucio's construction projects, or vaccines for missionaries in far-off countries. When I was twelve, Guido Canali tried to steal a box of wristwatches from a train car and ended up tipping two stacks of crates on himself. FOR HIS HOLINESS ONLY, the crates said, so the other boys wouldn't touch them, not even to lift them from Guido's body. Only Simon would heave them off, a hundred pounds apiece. Blood oranges: that's what ended up down on the station platform, smashed like Easter eggs. Blood oranges sent to John Paul by some monastery in Sicily. That's what Guido had almost died for.

I wonder if the Simon of that night lives only in my imagination now. If the Secretariat has trained him out of existence. An oath is a weighty thing for any Catholic; there can be penalties under Church law for breaking one. But even Michael Black has the heart to make an exception.

Michael is the Judas of our family—in Simon's eyes, at least. Sixteen years ago, Michael and my father traveled together to Turin for the unveiling of the radiocarbon dating on the Shroud. My father left Turin shattered. By the time he died, eight weeks later, Michael had quit his job and written my family a letter saying that our idea of a reunion between the Churches was laughable. The Orthodox obviously wanted nothing from us but fodder for ancient hatreds, fresh reasons to blame us for everything. Michael demanded to know why my father would push for a reunion with three hundred million Orthodox who treated Eastern Catholics—many of us minorities in Orthodox countries—like heretics and turncoats. Soon after, Michael found a new job working for the Vatican's new second-in-command: Cardinal Boia.

Boia was just beginning to clamp down on John Paul's outreach to the Orthodox, and Michael fit into his plans as a type of priest known as a Quasimodo—a man sent out to frighten the villagers, to create ugly misunderstandings and ruin the clockwork of diplomacy. The Quasimodo is the valve of dissent in a bureaucracy where no one can outwardly defy the pope. Michael got into shouting matches with Orthodox bishops, uttered public slurs, made an art of the bombshell interview. To Simon, this was the deepest betrayal. My brother could never accept that faith sometimes lends itself to wild changes of heart, and that a man who turns his back on one thing will often repent by becoming its opposite. Get behind me, Satan.

The Michael I remember is different. In a world of uptight Roman priests in cassocks, he was a young American in a short-sleeved priest shirt with a cheap tab collar. He wore a digital watch and Nike hightops in priestly black. Two years before the radiocarbon fiasco, he brought Simon and me to the Spanish Steps for the opening of Rome's first McDonald's. He scandalized the Italians by drinking Coca-Cola at breakfast. I never understood, until I met Michael, the possibility of being successfully different. Of being happily and completely unassimilated. I am saddened to think that the Secretariat took that wonderful golem and shaped him into something worse than an ordinary bureaucrat. At the bottom of my father's sadness I always sensed the unanswered conviction that the world would someday budge. That it would meet him in the middle. I never knew why Michael had his change of heart, but I suspected it was my father's fault for infecting him with too much optimism. A Greek has twenty-five centuries of painful history to keep his dreams in check, but there's nothing more dangerous than to give an American hope.

The phone begins to ring, and I turn to grab it. Only then do I notice there's a man standing at the next street corner, watching me.

I step back. But the man raises a hand in the air.

Agent Martelli. I didn't even notice him follow me here from the Casa. Michael was right. My idea of safe isn't safe enough.

I pick up the receiver. "Michael?"

"Are you alone?"

I hesitate. "Yes."

"Before we do this, I need to be clear. If you tell anyone that I talked to you, these people will find me again."

I think of the photograph from Ugo's apartment. "I understand. I just want to keep my son safe."

He lowers his voice and drops a long breath into the receiver. "Hard to believe you got a kid of your own. You were seven when I started working with your father."

Not *with*, I think. *For.* But there's something touching about the way he says it. When my father took him home for the first time, to introduce him to the rest of us, Michael brought a gift for me, a Bible embossed with my name. He thought, mistakenly, that Greek Catholics celebrated first communion at age seven, as Romans do.

"You name him after your dad?" he asks.

"No, after Simon."

This strangles the warmth out of him. The conversation turns.

"Well, down to business," he says. "What I wanted to tell you is, I met that curator. The one who was killed."

I'm caught off guard. "Ugo?"

"He came to visit your brother at the nunciature. I only talked to him once or twice, but the people who broke my nose thought I knew him. They threatened me. They wanted to know what he was working on."

"That's . . . impossible."

The silence bristles, as if he mistakes this for skepticism.

I ask, "What did they say to you?"

"That he was working on an exhibit about the Holy Shroud. Is that true?"

"It is."

Michael goes quiet. Maybe he's surprised to hear that the Shroud really has been resurrected after so many years. Or maybe, like anyone reading the newspapers this summer, he imagined Ugo's exhibit was on the Diatessaron.

"What did they say about it?" I ask.

"That Nogara was hiding something he found, and they wanted to know what it was."

"He wasn't hiding anything. What did you tell them?"

"To ask your brother. He was the one who would know."

My teeth are clenched. "You told them about Simon?"

"He and Nogara were thick as thieves."

"Michael, I worked with Ugo myself. Simon doesn't know anything. Who were the people who did this to you?"

"Priests."

"*Priests?*"

It never seriously entered my mind that a cleric could've done this.

"Romans," he says, "not beards. Since I'm sure that'll be your next question. They must've followed me from the nunciature."

Everything is slipping through my fingers. The motive I've been trying to piece together. The logic of what happened at Castel Gandolfo. Even in Rome, almost no one knew what Ugo was planning. I don't know how this could've begun among priests one thousand miles away.

"Did they catch anyone?" I ask.

"The Secretariat did some kind of investigation, but it went nowhere."

I'd assumed the break-in and murder were committed by the same person, if they were related at all. Now I wonder if two or more people were working in coordination. The facts even hint at this, since so little time elapsed between the attacks.

"How could they have known where to find you?" I ask.

Michael hesitates. "Probably the same way they knew where to find *you*. By threatening someone until he told them where to look."

"What do you mean?"

In a dryer voice, he says, "I think you know what I mean."

A shadow passes over me. "*You told them where I live?*"

"Alex, look—"

"My son could've been killed!"

"*I* could've been killed!" he roars.

"So you let them hunt down Simon? You even told them where to find him?"

"Like hell. They already knew about your brother. His little weekend trips were how they got on Nogara's scent in the first place."

I feel sick. The logic of this conversation is clearer now. There's a reason Michael called back after hanging up on me the first time. He feels guilty. He was the one who reported Simon for missing work. Who created a paper trail that anyone could follow.

"Keep Simon out of this," I say, forcing my voice to stay level. My father always said Michael was prone to fits of emotion. "He was just helping Ugo."

It doesn't seem to occur to him that he probably brought this on himself. By ratting on Simon, he made himself a reference point for anyone trying to hunt down Ugo.

But Michael howls, "Helping Nogara? That's what Simon told you he was doing?" He gives a scornful laugh. "What a pro, that guy. He's got a real future. Alex, your brother's been lying to you. Lying to everyone. He's been doing some work on the side, inviting a few of his Eastern friends to Italy for the Shroud exhibit."

I'm taken aback. "That's not true. Why on earth would you think that?"

"Look," Michael grunts, clearing his throat, "I said more than I wanted to. Go talk to your brother. Get *him* to answer some questions."

I'm too unnerved to respond.

"And," he adds, "keep your son safe. My impression is, these people won't quit until they have what they want."

"Okay," I tell him. "Thanks. For calling me back."

"Yeah. Well. You have my number?"

"I do."

"If Simon tells you anything, drop a line. I'm owed some answers, too."

I say nothing.

"And hey. Call if you need anything."

He must truly believe Simon can't be counted on.

"Michael, we're going to be fine."

"Yeah," he says. "I hope so, too."

CHAPTER 11

THE FIRST THING Leo says when I get back to the Casa is, "Your uncle wasn't kidding around." He points toward the door. "They sent a replacement cop as soon as Martelli tailed you out."

In the hall, the two gendarmes are conferring with a nun from downstairs.

I step out. "Is something wrong?"

"Nothing," Martelli answers. "This is Agent Fontana. He'll be the night shift."

But the nun looks me up and down. "Father, we can't have every visitor bringing a pair of bodyguards. You're safe here without them."

"My situation isn't the same as the other guests'," I tell her.

"I've been told about the situation," she says. "We've taken every precaution."

I don't know what to say. But Martelli does.

"Take it up with our commander, Sister. We stay until our orders change."

BACK IN THE ROOM, Leo is hurriedly collecting the dishes he brought over.

"Sofia just texted," he says. "We've got the hospital walk-through in an hour. How'd your call go?"

"Fine."

"Anything you want to talk about?"

I want to tell him more. But I made Michael a promise. "Not right now."

"Then I'll be back in the morning," he says. "You need anything before that, just call."

I thank him, then lock the bolt after he leaves, padding into the bedroom to sit down beside Peter.

He sleeps like a furnace. His forehead is pink, bangs dark with sweat. His mouth is open in a tight oval, all his energy concentrated in the act of breathing. He's exhausted. I've underestimated how much this is affecting him.

I think of what Michael said on the phone: that the men who attacked him were priests. It seems absurd. Violence by clergy is always aimed at other denominations, other faiths. The Christmas brawl in Bethlehem last year was between Armenians and Greeks. Catholic priests in Turkey have been victims of brutality before, but always at the hands of Muslims.

And yet Catholic priests would've had much better odds of getting past security here and at Castel Gandolfo. Much better odds of entering my apartment building unnoticed. Turin priests, in particular, might've noticed the Shroud had been moved from its chapel and might've gone hunting for answers. The most revealing thing Michael said was that the priests who attacked him were looking for information about Ugo's exhibit, because they claimed Ugo was hiding something. There's a simple way to rule that out: Ugo's research journal.

The entries begin with something he taped inside the front cover. A letter sent to all Vatican Museums curators.

IN VIEW OF THE IMPORTANCE OF MUSEUM TICKET INCOME TO THE ECONOMY OF THE CITY-STATE, HIS EMINENCE REQUESTS THAT ALL CURATORIAL STAFF SUBMIT PROPOSALS FOR THREE NEW EXHIBITS, INCLUDING BUDGET REQUIREMENTS, TO THE OFFICE OF THE DIRECTOR, COPYING HIS EMINENCE, WITHIN SIXTY DAYS.

The letter is dated eighteen months ago. After it, Ugo's diary begins with a handwritten list titled "Exhibit Ideas." It mentions early medieval manuscripts. Late antique Christian graffiti. The evolution of Jesus portraiture in the Byzantine Empire. Nowhere does it mention the Holy Shroud. Only two weeks later does he come across an initial scientific study questioning the radiocarbon tests. His reaction is three underlined words at the bottom of the page: _Resurrect the Shroud?_

On the following page is the relic itself, quickly sketched but with the wounds circled and the corresponding gospel verses noted: beating, scourging, crown of thorns, spear wound. One week later, Ugo proposes the exhibit to Uncle Lucio in person. Their meeting seems to have a galvanic effect on Ugo's research. My uncle, the world's most inexperienced motivational speaker, has somehow inspired Ugo. Diary entries grow longer. More scientific. Then, overnight, something odd happens.

Without explanation, Ugo devotes two pages to titles of other books. _The Gospel of Thomas. The Gospel of Philip. The Secret Book of James._ These are noncanonical texts, not recognized as scripture by Christians. Though he gives no reason for their inclusion here, I can read between the lines. Just as my uncle is showing interest in Ugo's idea, the biblical gospels have brought him to a dead end. Their Shroud references lead nowhere. So Ugo is casting a wider net, trying to follow the Shroud out of Jerusalem in 33 AD by any road possible. For ten days, no entries follow. Then, in astonishment, I find this:

> _Today I was put in touch with an Orthodox scholar who claims to know where the Shroud was brought after the Crucifixion. He says there is an ancient tradition about a mystical, Shroudlike image in a Byzantine city called Edessa. Despite my skepticism, I am meeting tomorrow with the priest who put us in touch. Can't say no, since he's H.E.'s nephew._

His Eminence's nephew.

Simon.

My eyes rise from the pages. An unpleasant, antic feeling buzzes through me like a fly trapped on the inside of a window. Something is wrong.

There's an unmistakable description in the next entry.

> _He's the quintessential Secretariat priest: handsome, blue-eyed, elegant. Very tall and thin. He acts so solicitous about my exhibit_

that I know he has some private investment in it. He wants to have
dinner tomorrow. I see no way out of it.

The unlikely first meeting of two future friends.

Yet on my first visit to Ugo's apartment, he and Simon told the story
of how a Vatican curator collapsed in the Turkish desert and was saved
by a young embassy priest. The entry in this diary is nine months older
than that.

Ugo and Simon lied to me about how they met.

I put the book on my chest, feeling rattled. They had no reason to
hide anything from me.

And yet there was always something awkward about the story they
told me. Simon seemed to recoil from it even as Ugo told it. The details
were real enough—Ugo's sunburn, his broken glasses—but if their encounter in the desert really happened, it may not have been their first
meeting. So why the selective memory? What could they have felt they
needed to dance around?

I reopen the diary. In the next entry, the whole logic of Ugo's exhibit
surfaces for the first time.

The disciples discovered the Shroud and carried it to Edessa, whose
king had once invited Jesus to visit him.

Ugo, however, is full of doubts.

Don't these Orthodox recognize a medieval legend? They really
believe our most precious relic was kept for centuries in a second-
rate Byzantine border town?

The irony of this question seems to have escaped him. More than a
thousand years later, it was in a no-name French village that the Shroud
first surfaced in western Europe. Like its maker, the relic was never in a
hurry to visit the great cities.

But Ugo continues:

Had dinner again with Andreou. Confronted him with my suspicions.
No surprise: it's political. He didn't even bother to deny it. He doesn't

*care where the Shroud came from. Only how we got our hands on it.
If the relic's past can be brought to light, he says, it will be a rallying
cry for all Christians. A stepping-stone in our relations with other
Churches.*

I'm stung. These few sentences conjure the essence of Simon: the
familiar agenda; the lack of guile; the breathless assurance that the future of Christianity could be at stake. My brother comes off as utterly
candid—which makes it harder to understand how he and Ugo both
withheld this information from me for months. *A stepping-stone in our
relations with other Churches.* Surely Simon was referring to the Orthodox, in which case Michael may have been right. Simon might've found
it irresistible to finish the work our father left behind sixteen years ago
in Turin.

Then there's this:

*He doesn't care where the Shroud came from. Only how we got our
hands on it.*

Michael Black said the priests who attacked him believed Ugo had
found something. They wanted to know what it was. I fan the pages
forward, searching for entries from around the time of Ugo's final e-mail
to me.

They come near the end, where his notes are shorter and less personal. The Diatessaron seems to preoccupy him. Then, one week before
the e-mail, a familiar diagram appears. The caduceus of entwined gospel
verses. Below it is the disturbing hint I've been looking for.

*Fr. Simon must've told Fr. Alex the news. They both refuse to answer
me. I'm all alone now. I suppose they're happy to have the exhibit
end with the Crusades.*

Nothing is written in the diary after these words. The pages are
blank. But that final word—*Crusades*—is enough. In the context of the
Diatessaron, I can think of only one thing it might mean.

The Shroud appeared in western Europe for the first time right after
the Crusades, surfacing inexplicably in medieval France. Where had it

come from? The answer was right under Ugo's nose: Edessa. The city he believed, from the beginning, the Shroud and Diatessaron had both called home. For centuries, Eastern Christians and Muslims had battled over control of Edessa—but at the end of the First Crusade, something unprecedented happened: the city fell into the hands of Catholic knights from the West. Edessa became Christianity's first crusader state. The experiment lasted less than fifty years before Muslims retook it, but in the meantime those Catholic knights would've packed up everything valuable and sent it home—which means the Diatessaron and the Shroud might've been shipmates on the trip west. If Ugo found records of the Diatessaron's arrival in our library, then he might've found records of a relic that came west in the same shipment. In which case, the explanation for the Shroud's sudden appearance in medieval France would be tidy: it came back from Edessa during the Crusades.

Yet even as I feel the thrill of this possibility—an elegant solution to one of the cloth's most puzzling mysteries—something inside me rattles. A new and darker problem, which Ugo may not even have understood when he made his discovery.

If he was able to prove that the Shroud came west after the Crusades, then he was stepping onto an ancient religious battlefield. Catholics and Orthodox were united back when Muslims first took Edessa from Christendom—but by the Crusades we had split. This means we lost the Shroud together, but the knights who retook Edessa were Catholic, so the Shroud ended up in Catholic France. The Orthodox claim to ownership of the Shroud is just as strong as ours—yet the Orthodox ended up with nothing.

This is the first time since Ugo died that I feel the reason for his death might be devastatingly familiar. Relics are a flashpoint in Church relations. John Paul has tried to placate the Orthodox more than once by returning saints' bones that Catholics allegedly stole. But if I'm right about Ugo's discovery, then it could've created a custody battle around our greatest relic and fed the long-standing Orthodox grudge that Catholics are bullies, that we go where we don't belong and take what isn't ours. The missionaries who converted Orthodox into Eastern Catholics were only following in the footsteps of these Crusaders who brought home the Shroud and Diatessaron—all of them just tentacles of the great, hungry mouth that is Rome. Some Catholics would certainly have opposed publicizing a discovery like this. Especially mounting it in the pope's museums.

Maybe there was a reason Ugo told me a very different story: he claimed the Diatessaron came to the Vatican from a collection of cursed manuscripts in an Egyptian monastery. I wonder now if that tale—like the one about his first meeting with Simon in the desert—was meant to keep me at arm's length, off the scent of a difficult truth he wasn't sure I could accept.

I close Ugo's diary and fold it into my cassock. Down in the small hotel courtyard, an Eastern Catholic priest is sitting alone on a bench. Three Roman priests bustle past in conversation, paying him no more attention than the potted plants. I watch him for a moment, then close the window. Remembering the way Ugo's apartment was broken into, I lock the shutters. I turn on Radio Uno for the rebroadcast of yesterday's Supercoppa soccer match. Then, wedging myself into the toothpick of space Peter has left on one side of the bed, I close my eyes and listen, trying to drift away on the current of familiar voices and rhythms. Trying to pacify the feeling that everything is suddenly foreign. That, in my own home, I have become a stranger in a strange land.

■ ■ ■

IN THE BLACK OF night, I'm wakened by screaming.

Peter is rigid. Upright. Staring at something in the darkness.

"What?" I shout. "What's wrong?"

There's a noise. I don't understand what it is.

"He's here!" Peter screams. "He's here!"

I pull him to my chest for protection. I fling my other arm into the murk.

"Where?"

"I saw his face! I saw it!"

The sound is coming from beyond the door. From the outer room.

"Shhh," I whisper, drawing Peter to my shoulder.

The shutters are still locked. The door is still closed.

"Father!" comes the voice. "What's happening in there?"

"It's okay," I whisper. "Nightmare, Peter. Nightmare. Nobody's here."

But he shakes. The fear is so strong, his body is stiff.

"I'll show you," I say, turning on the bedside lamp.

The room is untouched. Agent Fontana beats on the main door again.

"Father! Open up!"

I stagger out to the door, Peter clinging to me. When I open it, Fontana makes a fluid movement: his hand, moving away from the holster at his hip.

"Nightmare," I say. "Just a nightmare."

But Fontana isn't looking at me. He's looking over my shoulder. He goes first to the bedroom, then checks his way back out. Only when the examination is done does he say something for Peter's benefit.

"Everything looks safe, Father. Very safe."

I kiss Peter on the forehead. When we close the door again, though, I hear Fontana say into the radio, "Send someone to double-check the courtyard."

It's half an hour before Peter gets back to sleep. He leans against me while I stroke his head. We keep the lights on. At home, there's a book we read to ward off nightmares. It's about a turtle who survives a thunderstorm. But the turtle isn't here, so I gently knead the bridge of his nose and sing him a song. As I do, I wonder if Michael Black was right.

"Maybe," I think out loud, "we should take a vacation."

He nods. "America," he says dreamily.

"How about Anzio?"

A beach town thirty miles south of Rome. I've saved enough money that two or three days won't break us. I've been considering a special trip anyway. My boy will be leaving for primary school soon.

"I want to go home," Peter says.

A flashlight down in the courtyard sends a beam strafing across the shutters. There's the faintest hiss of a gendarme radio.

"I know, Pete," I whisper. "I know."

CHAPTER 12

MY OWN DREAMS are uneasy. They're all of Ugo.

For a time, after the night he and I spent down in the Vatican Library, we worked together so closely that I mistook our acquaintance for friendship. The morning after our adventure in the library vault, we went together to explain his discovery to Uncle Lucio. The Cardinal Librarian was the man we should've told, but His Eminence would never have let Ugo keep his job, let alone keep his hands on the manuscript. All lay workers have to sign ninety-five moral conditions of employment, and librarians tend to be sticklers for the ones about papal property. Lucio, though, had a moneymaking exhibit on the line and could be counted on to protect the golden goose. What I hadn't predicted was what *else* he would do.

No public announcement was ever made about the Diatessaron, because Ugo lobbied hard against one. But forty-eight hours after our meeting with my uncle, an article appeared in a Rome paper: FIFTH GOSPEL DISCOVERED IN VATICAN LIBRARY. The following Friday, three dailies picked up the story. That weekend, our discovery ran above the fold in *La Repubblica*. That was when the TV networks started calling.

Priests underestimate the appetite of laymen for cheap thrills about Jesus. Most of us roll our eyes at the prospect of new gospels. Every cave in Israel seems to contain one, and most turn out to have been written centuries after Christ by little sects of Christian heretics, or else forged for the publicity. But the Diatessaron was different. Here was a headline the Church could get behind. A legitimate and famous text, discovered in an extremely ancient manuscript, preserved thanks to the popes' centuries-long devotion to books. Lucio had foreseen that it was a story everyone inside the walls would want to tell. So he made sure no one but Ugo could tell it.

Someone in John Paul's apartments must've rubber-stamped Lucio's decision to give custody of the Diatessaron to Ugo, because the whole arrangement made the Cardinal Librarian furious. Ugo hid the manuscript under lock and key in the restoration laboratory, where a team of conservationists under his command started removing the mysterious smudges. Thus the one book everyone wanted to know about, no one was allowed to see. Library staff went off the record with reporters to complain that the book might not even exist; the whole thing might be a stunt. Ugo, in retaliation, released a photo of the manuscript. Experts quickly studied the style of penmanship and declared it authentic. The major European dailies reprinted the photo, and now the questions intensified.

The attention scared Ugo. He knew the Diatessaron might be the keystone of his Shroud authentication, one of the pillars of his exhibit. But now it was threatening to *become* the exhibit. The Shroud had waited sixteen years for redemption and was now being overshadowed by its supporting cast. Wishing he had kept as mum about the Diatessaron as he had about the rest of his exhibit, Ugo decided to correct that mistake. From now on, he would stonewall. He would choke the flame. It must have seemed reasonable at the time, but he had forgotten that nothing fans a religious delirium quite like Vatican silence.

Peter and I, walking the streets of Rome over the summer, heard laymen discussing the Diatessaron. Was it right for the Vatican to withhold information? Didn't the patrimony of Christianity belong to all of us? What needed hiding, anyway? Headlines in leftist tabloids seized on the opportunity. They wheeled out the usual conspiracy theories in the guise of proposing what the Diatessaron's secret might be. Jesus was a married man. A gay man. A woman. One professor at a secular university was quoted as saying that the Diatessaron failed to report that Jesus was ever seen again after his death. Later the professor clarified that he was talking about the gospel of Mark, not the Diatessaron, since early manuscripts of Mark do indeed fail to report this.

Day by day the hubbub grew. Finally a panel of forty Bible scholars wrote an open letter to John Paul, calling for the manuscript to be studied. And so it came to pass that Uncle Lucio, having dealt the cards, now played his ace. In response to public pressure, he announced, the Diatessaron would be publicly displayed for the first time—at Ugo's exhibit. Overnight, advance ticket sales quadrupled.

Ugo was beside himself. I told him there was no shame in letting a new gospel share the pedestal with the Shroud—after all, they were ancient brothers, both leading us back to first-century Jerusalem. But I'd let my enthusiasm for the Diatessaron carry me away. Ugo was irate. He growled that the Diatessaron was not a new gospel and that I obviously didn't understand his exhibit's duty not just to redeem the Shroud but to show the world where it belonged in the pecking order of ancient Christian testimony. "The gospels weren't written by Jesus," he snapped. "They aren't Christ's testimony about Himself. Only the Shroud holds that honor. So if every church on earth has a copy of the gospels, then every church on earth should have an image of the Shroud, and that image should be revered *above* the gospels. I'm surprised at you, Father Alex. It's an insult to God to let a second-class gospel—a man-made thing—be celebrated on par with our Lord's gift."

I realized he was paralyzed by this idea. Horrified with himself for having allowed the Shroud to be betrayed. Not until then did I understand the fatherly protectiveness he felt toward it. And though I didn't feel the same way, I could identify with the strength of that emotion. Unfortunately, it squeezed something to the surface in Ugo that I'd never encountered before. In his eyes, my enthusiasm for the Diatessaron had revealed me as a traitor. So he approached me one day in the mess hall and grabbed me by the cassock.

"If you hadn't twisted my arm to tell your uncle about the manuscript," he growled, "none of this would be happening."

"We made the right choice," I told him.

But he turned his back to me and said, "I don't think we can work together anymore. I'll be finding someone else to teach me the gospels."

■ ■ ■

I RAN INTO THEM only by accident, teacher and pupil, huddled over a Bible in a private study room beside the manuscript workshop. Ugo's new instructor was an ancient priest named Popa who spoke with an accent and wore an Eastern cassock. I didn't recognize him; *Popa* is a Romanian name, and there are fifty thousand Romanians in Rome. I just assumed he was Eastern Catholic. But I was wrong. He was Orthodox. And in gospel scholarship that made all the difference in the world.

"Father, please," I overheard Ugo saying, "we need to get to the *burial*. The cloth. I know these early parts are important, but what interests me is the Shroud."

"Don't you see?" Popa answered. "The two are connected. The birth of Jesus anticipates his rebirth, his Resurrection. The liturgy and the Church Fathers agree th—"

"Respectfully, Father," Ugo said, "I don't need the liturgy or the Church Fathers. Just the hard facts of what happened in 33 AD."

Popa had a mystical, lovable way about him. His soft white beard looked jovial when he smiled. But neither he nor Ugo seemed to understand what was separating them.

"Remember, my son," Popa said, "the Bible didn't create the Church; the Church created the Bible. The liturgy is *older* than the gospels. Now, please, let's begin at the beginning. To understand the tomb, we need to understand the manger."

I couldn't help myself. "Ugo," I said, "Jesus wasn't born in a manger. Factually speaking."

Suddenly Popa looked a bit less jovial.

"We don't even know the city where Jesus was born," I continued. "Factually speaking."

"Father, that's not true," Popa protested. "The gospels agree it was Bethlehem."

"Show me two gospels that say so, and I'll show you two that don't."

Popa frowned. He said nothing more; he just waited for me to finish my business and leave.

But I had caught Ugo's attention. "Father Alex," he said, "please explain."

I lowered my stack of books onto his table. "Jesus grew up in Nazareth, not Bethlehem. All four gospels agree about that."

"The question is where he was born," Popa objected, "not where he grew up."

I held up a hand to quiet him. "Two gospels never say anything about where he was born. The other two tell different birth stories. Draw your own conclusions."

Ugo looked as surprised as most seminary students on their first day of scripture class. "You're saying those stories are fiction?"

"I'm saying read them carefully."

"I have."

"Then which one says Jesus was born in a manger?"

"Luke."

"And which one says Jesus was visited by three wise men?"

"Matthew."

"So why does Luke *not* mention the wise men, and Matthew *not* mention the manger?"

Ugo shrugged.

"Because they're both trying to explain how Jesus could've been born in Bethlehem even though he grew up in Nazareth. And they come up with completely different explanations. Matthew tells us about an evil king named Herod who wants to kill baby Jesus, but when the wise men won't tell him where Jesus is, Herod kills all the babies in that whole region. So Mary and Joseph flee, and that's how they end up in Nazareth. Luke, on the other hand, says Jesus' family *started* in Nazareth. But the Roman emperor declared a huge census, and for some reason everyone had to go back to their ancestral hometown to be counted. Mary and Joseph went to Bethlehem, because that's where Joseph's family came from, and *that's* why Jesus was born in a manger: because there was no room at the inn. The stories are completely different. And since there's no evidence Herod really killed those babies *or* Caesar Augustus really declared that census, it's likely that neither story actually happened."

Popa stared at me with a crawling sadness in his eyes. He said, as if Ugo weren't even in the room, "Is this really what you believe, Father? That the gospels don't agree? That they lie to us?"

"The gospels *don't* agree. And that doesn't mean they're lying." I picked up the stack of books again. "Ugo, I'll come back later sometime when—"

But all three of us knew, even before Ugo interrupted me, that it was done. Most Orthodox hew to the traditional way of reading the gospels: there are few new answers, mainly just faith in the old ones. Catholics used to share that belief, until we recognized the power of biblical science.

"Father Alex, wait," Ugo said. "Stay a moment. Please."

He didn't need to say another word. Popa and I knew which path he had chosen.

IT WAS AS IF Ugo's accusations in the mess hall had never been spoken. Our lessons were broad at first. Like most laymen, he had only a basic understanding of how the gospels should be read, and not enough confidence to apply it. So we began at the beginning.

But for me, unlike for Father Popa, that meant the hard evidence. The oldest unchanged facts. The books.

Before the Diatessaron, and before the Alogi, there were our four gospels, named after the men who were believed to be their authors: Matthew, Mark, Luke, and John. Matthew and John were disciples, Jesus' closest followers. Tradition says Mark took dictation from the chief disciple, Peter. And Luke tells us that he gathered his information from people who saw Jesus firsthand. This means our gospels, if they were really written by these four men, give us a portrait of Jesus' life based almost entirely on eyewitness testimony.

But it isn't so simple. Three of the four gospels are so similar that they seem less like independent accounts than like replicas of each other. Mark, Matthew, and Luke not only record Jesus' words almost identically, they *translate* those words almost identically from Jesus' Aramaic into gospel Greek. Their thumbnail sketches of many minor characters are verbatim duplicates, and at times all three gospels stop midstream, at the same point in the same sentence, to offer the same stage directions and asides:

MATTHEW 9:6:	MARK 2:10-11:	LUKE 5:24:
"But that you may know that the Son of man has authority on earth to forgive sins"—he then said to the paralytic— "Rise, take up your bed and go home."	"But that you may know that the Son of man has authority on earth to forgive sins"—he said to the paralytic— "I say to you, rise, take up your pallet and go home."	"But that you may know that the Son of man has authority on earth to forgive sins"—he said to the man who was paralyzed— "I say to you, rise, take up your bed and go home."

No wonder Tatian, the author of the Diatessaron, wanted to combine the gospels into a single text. In many passages the gospels already *share* a single text. But why? Forty percent of Mark's gospel appears wholesale in Matthew—the same words in the same order—which suggests that an eyewitness like Matthew copied a large part of his testimony from another source. Why?

Biblical science provides a surprising answer: he *didn't*, because the gospel attributed to Matthew was not really written by him. In fact, not one of our four gospels was written by an eyewitness.

Scholars have gathered together our oldest surviving gospel manuscripts and found that, in the most ancient texts, the four gospels are *not* attributed to Matthew, Mark, Luke, and John. They're anonymous. Only in later copies do the names of their would-be authors appear, as if tradition or guesswork has added them. A close comparison of the texts shows how they were really written. One of them—the one we call Mark's—is raw and unrefined, presenting a Jesus who sometimes becomes angry, sometimes performs magical incantations, and is considered by his own family to be out of his mind. Two of the other gospels—the ones we call Matthew's and Luke's—make these embarrassing details disappear. They also correct Mark's small lapses of grammar and vocabulary. Matthew and Luke borrow whole passages from Mark, word for word, yet they systematically fix his weaknesses. This leads strongly to the conclusion that Matthew and Luke aren't independent accounts. They are *edited versions of Mark.*

The gospel of Mark, in turn, is a patchwork of individual stories that seem to come from older, fragmentary sources. This is why most scholars believe—and most Catholic priests are taught in seminary—that our four gospels are not memoirs of the men whose names they now carry. They were assembled, decades after Jesus' ministry, from older documents that recorded an oral tradition of stories about Jesus. Only at that earliest, deepest level of testimony would it be possible to find the actual memories of the disciples.

This means the gospels *do* stretch back to Jesus' life—but not directly, and not without additions and subtractions. Understanding this editing process is crucial to anyone searching for the pure historical facts about Jesus' life. This is because the changes were often theological or spiritual: they reflected what Christians *believed* about the Messiah, rather than what they actually knew about Jesus the man. For instance, the gospels of Luke and Matthew disagree about the details of Jesus' birth, and there's reason to believe neither account reflects the facts. But the authors of both gospels—whoever those authors really were—believed Jesus was the Savior, so He *must've been* born in Bethlehem, as the Old Testament predicts.

This ability to separate theology from fact is crucial, especially in the last and strangest of the gospels—the one that would become the focus of Ugo's Diatessaron work: John.

"So the Alogi took issue with the gospel of John," Ugo said, pulling at his thinning hair.

"Yes. And *only* the gospel of John."

"They tried to snuff John out of the Diatessaron."

"Right."

"Why?"

I explained to him that John was the last of the gospels to be written—sixty years after the crucifixion, twice as long as Mark had been. It set out to answer new questions about the fledgling religion of Christianity, and in the process it revolutionized Jesus. Gone is the humble carpenter's son who heals the sick and exorcises the possessed, who speaks simple parables with a common touch but never says much about his own identity. In his place, John offers a new Jesus: a high-minded philosopher who never performs exorcisms, never speaks parables, and talks constantly about himself and his mission. Scholars today agree that the other three gospels trace their roots to an original layer of factual memories—historical events that were recorded at an early stage and edited over time. But the fourth gospel is different.

John paints a portrait of God rather than man, removing facts and replacing them with symbols. The gospel even leaves guideposts to teach its readers what it's doing: John says the bread we eat isn't true bread; Jesus is the true bread. The light we see isn't true light; Jesus is the true light. John's word *true* almost always means the invisible realm of the eternal. In other words, the fourth gospel is theological rather than historical. And for many readers, that theology comes as a shock. After reading three gospels rooted more strongly in history, it's perilously easy to read the fourth and fail to see how these facts have been transformed into symbols.

For that reason, John has always been the black sheep of the gospels. Only one Christian scholar before Tatian tried to write a gospel harmony like the Diatessaron, and he didn't use John at all. No group, however, made its opposition to John clearer than the Alogi.

"And you're telling me," Ugo said, "that for our purposes the Alogi were right. If all I care about is history—facts—then I should toss John out."

"It depends. There are rules."

"Father Alex, I'm a good Catholic. I'm not trying to take a pair of scissors to the Bible. But the other three gospels say Jesus was buried in a cloth. John says cloths. They can't both be right. So John is out?"

It was as if he didn't even want to see the words that his team of conservationists was uncovering from beneath the smudges of the Diatessaron. I should've sensed the pressure on him, the urgency he felt.

"Or," he said, "to take another example, John says Jesus was buried in a hundred pounds of myrrh and aloes. The other gospels say the burial spices weren't used because Jesus was buried in such a hurry."

"Why does that matter?"

"Because the chemical tests that disprove the radiocarbon dating also found no myrrh or aloe present on the Shroud. Which is exactly what we have if we remove John's testimony."

I rested my head in my hands. It wasn't that he was wrong. It was that he was moving too quickly. The creed of any Bible student is humility. Caution. Patience. Sixty years ago, the pope let a small team of men dig beneath Saint Peter's to look for Peter's bones. Today, gospel teachers are those men, entrusted with digging under the foundation of the Church, allowed to search where searching is most dangerous. Anything less than immense care is reckless.

"Ugo," I said, "if I gave you the impression we use these tools lightly, then I made a mistake."

He put a hand on my shoulder, as if to comfort me. "Father, don't you see? This is *good*. It's very good. Everyone who has ever studied the Shroud assumed the four gospels were all factual. The world has been making the same mistake as the Diatessaron without even realizing it: we weave together the four gospels even though John isn't historical. There must be a dozen aberrations in his version of the burial story alone: Jesus is buried by a different man, on a different day, in a different way. You've changed the future of the Shroud, Father Alex. You've found the skeleton key."

But instinct told me otherwise. It told me the tool I had placed in his hands wasn't a skeleton key but a battering ram. Having taught the gospels to hundreds of students of all ages, I had never come across a man so fearless about the truth. He felt a heroic, almost militant, compulsion to side with it. To explode the most cherished beliefs if they were mistaken. No doubt, this was what so attracted him to the defense of the Shroud in the first place, this rage against the injustice of error.

It worried me, though, for his sake. Sometimes I wondered if he would sooner make an enemy than assuage a friend so long as the smallest crumb of factual truth hung in the balance. He was relentless, ruthless, even with himself. He admitted to me once that it saddened him to relinquish the gospel stories he'd grown up believing to be historical; some childish part of his heart sank to know that the manger and wise men existed more in a little nativity scene than they ever had on that magical night two thousand years ago. But he smiled with pride and said, "If the pope's behind it, then so am I." And he insisted on beginning all our lessons by saying, "Time to put away childish things." He was eager to give up his manger and wise men if it meant winning back the Shroud for the world.

Deep in the marrow of our religion is the conviction that loss and sacrifice are noble. To surrender something beloved is the highest proof of Christian duty. I always admired this quality in Ugo. Yet I couldn't help feeling that his bravery contained an undercurrent of self-flagellation—and that this was an important insight into how he'd become such fast friends with my brother.

CHAPTER 13

PETER SLEEPS IN. He's usually up first, marching into the bedroom and rowing my limp arm like the oar of a Greek trireme. I'm out of practice sneaking out of bed, but I manage not to wake him. While ironing my cassock, I can't help cracking the front door just to be sure.

Fontana is still on duty.

An hour later, Peter and I have breakfast in the dining hall. As he enters the room, old bishops and cardinals look up from their plates and smile. There are more men here over the age of eighty than under the age of thirty. And all of them are Roman Catholics. Peter and I sit at a conspicuous table where any Eastern Catholics passing by might notice us and decide not to flee. But in vain.

Midway through the meal, my mobile phone starts beeping. Simon has left a message.

Alli, something's come up. Meet me at the exhibit hall as soon as you get this.

I set my napkin beside my plate and tell Peter to grab a last bite for the road.

IN PREPARATION FOR UGO'S exhibit, a whole wing of the museums has been closed. Work trucks idle outside the galleries like war elephants, making the air shimmer with their exhaust. Inside, a highway of carts and dollies carries paintings and display cases and raw lumber, all moving at the same speed like cars in a funeral caravan. Wooden frames are being raised, hiding ancient frescoes behind makeshift walls, turning gold corridors into empty white pipes. Art that hasn't been moved since Italy became a country is suddenly gone.

A service elevator opens. Two art restorers appear from downstairs. In the distance, workmen tape drywall seams. Electricians check lights. This many people, from this many departments, working together at short notice, gives the vague feeling of a state of emergency. This must be why Simon called. Ugo seems to have left a lot unfinished.

The deeper we get into the galleries, the more curious I become. On the wall is a billboard-size photo of the scientists who announced the radiocarbon results in 1988. Behind them in the photograph, written on a blackboard, is the official date range established by the carbon tests, punctuated by a snide exclamation mark: *1260–1390!* I don't understand why Ugo would've mounted this here, until I see a glass cabinet resembling a jeweler's case, padded with black satin. Hovering on gold armatures inside it is a row of ancient books, one of them sitting higher than the rest. A Hungarian Mass book, a placard says. It's opened to a black-ink illustration showing Jesus' dead body being prepared on its burial sheet.

The burial sheet is strikingly consistent with the Turin Shroud: it has the right dimensions, the right method of wrapping the corpse, the right posture of Jesus' body with his hands modestly crossed over his genitals. It even gets right a rare detail that Ugo once explained to me: no thumbs are visible. Modern medical examiners have found that a nail piercing a particular nerve near the hand causes the thumbs to retract involuntarily. Almost no painting in Western art gets this correct—but the Shroud and this little drawing both do. Most amazing of all, the cloth in the illustration has four dots in the shape of an L. These are the unexplained "poker holes" in the Holy Shroud, just below Jesus' elbow. The artist of this book must have studied the Turin Shroud up close. Yet the placard beside the illustrated Mass book says, in modest type:

MANUSCRIPT WRITTEN IN 1192 AD.

1192 AD. Sixty-eight years before the earliest possible radiocarbon date.

Scanning all the placards in the case, I suddenly understand. Ugo is making a point. The giant photo on one side of the gallery is facing off against the manuscripts on the other. We will pit our library against your lab. Your science is young and has no memory, but our Church is ancient and forgets nothing. These books virtually prove that the radiocarbon tests are wrong: every book in this case mentions a relic seemingly identical to the Shroud, and *all* of these books were written before the earliest possible radiocarbon date.

I stare at the strange, fanciful names of their authors. Ordericus Vitalis. Gervase of Tilbury. These manuscripts are starlight from an extinct universe. Original copies of Latin authors writing in the age of the Crusades. The schism between Catholics and Orthodox is usually dated to 1054, when an angry papal messenger in the Orthodox capital of Constantinople took it upon himself to excommunicate the patriarch. But it would never have happened if Westerners hadn't already become disconnected from the East and its Christian traditions. The Crusades, decades later, were what reopened the West's eyes—and the manuscripts I see here, written in the 1100s, capture that exact moment. My rusty Latin is just enough to make out the news trickling in from the Holy Land, the news that again and again seems to have captured the Catholic imagination: there is a city called Edessa, in which is kept an ancient cloth imprinted with a mystical image of Jesus.

I didn't realize the extent of the evidence Ugo had found. And the Diatessaron is yet to come, probably in the final gallery that lies ahead.

Suddenly Peter's hand breaks out of my grip. "Simon!" he cries.

I look up to find my brother moving toward us quickly, descending like a bird of prey—blade-thin, with his cassock feathered out behind him.

"What's wrong?" I say.

His blue eyes swirl with emotion. He sweeps up Peter in one arm and slips the other behind my back, ushering us back outside to the rear entrance to the museums. Then, in a low voice, he says, "Last night Lucio had a visitor at his apartment. A messenger from the Rota who had news about Ugo."

I hang on his next words. The Rota is the second-highest court of Catholicism.

"They're empaneling a tribunal," he says. Then he continues in Greek, to prevent Peter from understanding. "*To try Ugo's killer.*"

"Who did they arrest?"

Simon looks at me impatiently. "No one. They're making it a canonical trial."

Canon law. The code of the Church. But the Rota spends most of its time ruling on requests for marriage annulments. It never handles murders.

"That's impossible," I say. "Who decided that?"

The Vatican has a separate civil law. We can convict criminals and send them to Italian prisons. That's how Ugo's murder should be prosecuted. Not under Church law.

"I don't know," Simon whispers. "But Lucio has a friend coming over with more news tonight. I think you should be there."

I tug at my beard. Our criminal court is run by a layman, but our canonical courts are run by priests. Somewhere in this I hear an echo of Michael Black's warning. Someone in a collar has a hand in this and won't give up until he has what he wants.

"Okay," I tell Simon. "I'll be there."

But my brother's focus has been distracted by something else. The rear door to the museum is open. Standing at the threshold are Don Diego and Agent Martelli.

I raise a hand in the air and call out, "We're okay. I just need a minute with my brother."

But Diego says, "Father Simon, the curators need you."

So my brother puts Peter down and kneels to hug him. To me he murmurs, "Stay safe. I'll see you both in a few hours."

THE CASA HAS A small library for guests. When Peter and I arrive back at the hotel, I borrow the law book that applies to all Roman Catholics—Codex Iuris Canonici, the Code of Canon Law—and we go straight to our room.

The code and its built-in legal commentary are immense. They make the Bible look like beach reading. Here in my hands is the combined wisdom of two thousand years of solving the Church's day-to-day problems. How much can a priest be paid for performing a funeral? Is it okay to marry a Protestant? Can the pope retire? Canon law dictates who can teach at a Catholic school, or sell Church property, or lift an excommunication. But Ugo's case will revolve around canon 1397: *A person who commits a homicide or who kidnaps, detains, mutilates, or gravely wounds a person by force or fraud is to be punished.* Nowhere in the list of punishments, though, is there any mention of prison. This is the most obvious problem with trying Ugo's murder under Church law: the killer won't spend a day behind bars, because prison isn't a punishment under canon law. If the killer is a priest, though, a more harrowing punishment looms—dismissal from the clerical state.

It's hard for a layman to understand the gravity of being laicized. Saying that a priest is no longer a priest is paradoxical, like saying a mother is childless or a person is inhuman. What God gives a man at his ordination, no human power can remove. So while a laicized priest can still validly celebrate the sacraments, he's forbidden to. Any Mass he celebrates must be shunned by the Catholic laity. He may not give a homily or hear a confession except on a deathbed. He may not even work at a seminary or teach theology at any school, Catholic or not. This is what gives the sentence such power: it turns us into ghosts. It obligates the world to deny our existence. No secular court has this power over laymen. It's a verdict that pushes many priests to suicide. As I think about it now, this may be a clue to what's happening in Ugo's trial. Trying the case in a canonical court isn't just a way to let priests control the outcome. It's a peculiarly awful way to threaten a priest as well.

"Peter," I say, "can you get my pack of index cards from the suitcase?"

"Why?"

"There's something I need to figure out."

He groans. Though he's too young to know the meaning of these legal terms, he knows what it means when Babbo needs to figure something out. Bookwork.

At first, it's painstaking. The gaps in my education seem chasmic. Every priest takes a basic class on canon law in seminary, but nothing serious until fourth year, when men choose between theology and canon law for their graduate work. My choice of theology has never seemed so inconvenient.

"Write down this number," I tell Peter. "One-four-two-zero."

Canon 1420: *Each diocesan bishop is bound to appoint a judicial vicar . . . distinct from the vicar general.*

I know how a canonical trial starts. In theory, a bishop investigates an accusation. If it has merit, he summons a tribunal. But the reality is different. A bishop is a busy man, so his work is done by assistants. This is especially true of John Paul, who oversees not only the diocese of Rome but the universal Church. So which of John Paul's underlings is making this decision? The answer is in this canon: the special assistant in charge of legal matters, a priest known as the judicial vicar. Now that I know his title, I can use the Vatican yearbook to hunt down his name.

"Next," I say, "write one-four-two-five. And then a little squiggle with the number three."

Peter frowns. "Which way does three go again?"

I tousle his hair. "Like B, without the line."

Canon 1425 §3 says the judicial vicar also assigns the judges. The whole trial now seems to lie in the hands of this one man, whoever he is. It leaves me curious about who these judges will be. But I came here looking for something more: a back-door way to find out who stands accused of Ugo's murder.

Church trials are secretive. A parish may never find out that a crime was committed in its backyard, let alone that a Church court has rendered a verdict. Knowing the name of the judicial vicar will be helpful, but it isn't as if I can call his office and ask about his investigation. Fortunately, in our Church there is always—*always*—a paper trail. And canon law tells me what to look for.

"One-seven-two-one," I tell Peter. "Then add a star. And below it, one-five-zero-seven."

I repeat each number to him, digit by digit. The code, like the Bible, jumps forward and backward, each line referencing others hundreds of pages away. Canon 1721 says that when the bishop decides there's enough evidence for a trial, he asks a Church prosecutor to write a formal accusation, called the libellus, which includes the name and address of the accused. This invokes 1507, which says the libellus must be sent to all parties of the trial. In other words, the libellus is how word of the trial seeps beyond the bishop and his immediate contacts. If Lucio is receiving a visit from a friend with information about the trial, then I infer the libellus is in circulation. And if that's true, then I know where one copy of it must've been sent. The Holy Father's safety requires that the Swiss Guard be notified about any dangerous persons on Vatican soil.

"Peter," I say, "put a rubber band around those cards. I think we're done."

I'm already dialing the phone number.

"Alex?" Leo answers. "Is everything okay?"

I explain the situation. "Have you seen anything about a name?"

"No. Nothing."

"But did they tell you to keep an eye out for anyone?"

"No."

I'm taken aback. If the libellus is out, then whoever killed Ugo knows he's being prosecuted. Yet no one is even looking for him.

"I'll make some calls," Leo says to reassure me. "I'll double-check with the guards on palace duty. Maybe their orders were different."

But Leo is senior enough that I doubt orders go over his head. I'm about to dig back into the code when a sound in the hallway distracts me. The swish of something sliding under the door.

"Hold on, Leo," I say.

It's an envelope. My name is written on the front of it. The handwriting is somehow familiar.

When I open it, I find a single photograph. It shows the exterior of the Casa with an Eastern priest leaving the front doors.

My breath slips out.

"What's wrong?" Leo asks.

The Eastern priest is me.

This picture was taken yesterday. Whoever took it was standing just across the courtyard.

There's a note on the back, in the same handwriting.

Tell us what Nogara was hiding.

Below is a phone number.

I lurch toward the door and open it.

"Agent Martelli!"

Distantly I hear a sound. An elevator opening. When I turn to look, I see the tail of a black robe entering the car. A priest, leaving.

I turn back. *"Martelli!"*

But this end of the hall is empty. Martelli is gone.

A knot of Eastern priests stands by the elevator bank. They stare at me with concern.

I feel Peter behind me, tugging at my cassock. Without a word I lift him in my arms and run to the nearest stairwell.

"What's wrong?" he cries.

"Nothing. Everything's okay."

I pull the handle to the stairwell door, but it doesn't budge. The door is locked.

We return to the room and bolt the door. I call Simon's mobile, but there must be no reception at the museums. I dial gendarme headquarters instead.

"Pronto. Gendarmeria."

"Officer," I blurt, "this is Father Andreou. I was assigned a security escort, but he's disappeared. I need help."

"Yes, Father. Of course. One moment."

But when he returns to the line, he says, "I'm sorry. There's no escort under your name."

"That's a mistake. I—I need a way to find Agent Martelli."

"Martelli's right here. Please hold."

I'm stunned. The voice that comes on the line is unmistakable. "This is Martelli."

"Agent," I fumble, "it's Father Andreou. Where are you?"

"At my desk," he says gruffly. "Your escort was canceled."

"I don't understand. Something's happening. We need your help. Please come back to the Casa."

"Sorry, Father. You'll have to call security there like all the other guests do."

Then the line goes dead.

PETER WATCHES IN A frantic state as I gather our belongings.

"Babbo, where are we going?"

"To Prozio Lucio."

I've called Lucio's apartments. Don Diego is on his way. He will escort us back to the penthouse of my uncle's palace.

"What's wrong?" Peter asks, clutching my arm.

"I don't know. Just help me finish packing."

Ten long minutes later, the knock comes. Glancing through the peephole, I see Diego standing beside an unfamiliar Swiss Guard. I unbolt the door.

"Father Alex," Diego says, "this is Captain Furrer."

"Father, what happened?" Furrer asks.

"Someone left this message under my door."

He shakes his head. "Impossible. Access to this floor is restricted."

I show him the envelope, but he disregards it.

"The stairwells are secured," he says, "and the elevator attendants won't bring anyone to this floor without a room key."

So this is what the nun meant yesterday about the precautions the sisters have taken.

"I saw a priest in a cassock getting into the elevator," I say.

"There must be another explanation," Furrer says. "We'll straighten it out downstairs."

Diego extends his hands, offering to take our bags. Peter, misunderstanding the gesture, runs into his arms for a hug. Over his shoulder, Diego gives me a quizzical look, asking where our gendarme escort is. Down the hall, the Eastern priests continue to stare.

THE NUN AT THE front desk is wearing a black habit.

"*I* brought up the envelope," she says. "What's the matter?"

"Where did it come from?" I demand.

"It was with the incoming mail."

But there's no postage or address on it. Someone dropped it here by hand. I wonder if that was after they tried delivering it themselves.

I notice the lobby is dead. The dining hall has closed early, and a sign says the rear chapel is closed, too. Cordons block the way.

"What's happening?" I ask the nun at the desk.

"Repairs," she says.

Another sign announces that the top floor, where Peter and I were staying, can be reached only by the secondary elevator.

"Sister, did you tell anyone where we were staying?" I ask.

The nun looks concerned. "Of course not. We're under strictest orders. There must be a misunderstanding."

But I reach into my cassock and fish out our room key. The Casa's initials are raised on the fob, and engraved beside them, our room number. I wonder if this was my mistake. If someone saw this key. It's an advertisement of where Peter and I have been staying.

"Will you be checking out, Father?" the nun asks, offering to take back the key.

"No," I say, slipping it back into my cassock. I doubt we're coming back, but there's no need to advertise that, too.

Diego takes our bags and gestures toward the door. "Your sedan is waiting," he says.

Our sedan. It would take five minutes to walk to Lucio's palace. Yet never in my life have I been more grateful to take a car.

ONLY THE NUNS ARE home when we arrive.

"His Eminence and your brother are still working on the exhibit," Diego explains. He shakes his head as if a new circle of hell is being excavated down at the museums. "So what happened?"

I hand him the photo in the envelope. When he reads the message on the back, he frowns. "And your escort?"

"The gendarme agent said it was called off."

Diego growls. "We'll see about that."

Before he can reach for the phone on his desk, I say, "Diego, do you know anything about that?" I point to the message on the photo. "A discovery Ugo made?"

"The Diatessaron?"

"No. Something more than that."

He turns the photo over. "That's what this is about?"

"Michael Black mentioned something like it, too."

He frowns, not recognizing Michael's name. Few clerics below the grade of bishop can get their business onto my uncle's desk. "First I've heard of it. But I'll see what the chief of gendarmes says."

I wave him off. "Let me talk to Simon and my uncle first."

"You're sure?"

I'm not sure I can trust the gendarmes now.

Diego looks me squarely in the eye. "Alex, you're safe here. That's a promise."

"I appreciate that."

Peter says, "Can I have a fruit punch, Diego?"

Diego smiles. "Three fruit punches, coming up," he says, winking at me. He makes a good Negroni.

But just for a second, he hesitates. Under his breath he adds, "I ought to tell you that we have a visitor coming tonight."

"I know."

"Will you be joining us?"

"Yes."

Something about the idea makes him frown again. But he continues on toward the kitchen.

WHEN PETER HAS HAD time to settle in, I tell him I need to unpack our bags. Diego takes the hint and distracts Peter so I can be alone in the bedroom.

Sliding the photo out of the envelope again, I look at the phone number on the back. It's a landline somewhere inside these walls. Vatican numbers have the same area code as Rome but begin with 698. For a few euros, the owner of this number could've bought a nearly anonymous SIM card in Rome. Doing this instead sends a message.

I dial the switchboard and ask the nun to do a reverse lookup.

"Father," she says politely, "we have a policy against that."

I thank her for her time and hang up. There are a dozen nuns at the switchboard, so I know I won't get the same one twice. When I call back, I explain that I'm an electrician in the maintenance department. Someone has called for a repair, but all I have is this callback number, no name or address.

"It's an unregistered line," she says helpfully. "In the Palazzo di Niccolò III. Third floor. That's all it says here."

"Thank you, Sister."

I close my eyes. The papal palace is a heap of smaller palaces built one on top of another by successive popes centuries ago. The Palace of Pope Nicholas III is its nucleus, more than seven hundred years old. It contains the most powerful organism in the Holy See. The Secretariat of State.

My stomach churns. The Secretariat is faceless. Its men come and go. They are recruited, sent abroad, replaced. There's only one way to know whose phone this is.

When I dial the number, the line rings and rings. Finally an answering machine picks up. But there's no voice. No message. Just silence, followed by a beep.

I haven't prepared anything to say. But it comes out.

"Whatever you want from me, I don't have it. I don't know anything. Nogara never told me any secret. Please. Leave me and my son alone."

I hesitate, then hang up. In the adjacent room, through the crack in the door, I see Peter playing a game on Diego's computer. Fishing. I watch him cast his line and wait. Cast his line and wait.

THE AFTERNOON FADES AWAY. From the windows of the penthouse I can see everything that happens in this country. Anyone coming from any direction will be visible; nothing can take us by surprise. This helps the panic to drain, replacing it with weary vigilance. Diego finds a deck of cards and introduces Peter to scopa, the game I played with Mona in the hospital after he was born. It's just past six when Lucio and Simon return from the exhibit. My uncle immediately demands to know what happened, why Peter and I no longer have our security escort. Rather than belabor everything in front of Peter, I let the topic go. The nuns have finished preparing dinner and setting the places, so with a sense of expedition I don't quite understand, we all sit down to eat. Lucio begins the blessing from the head of the table. We all say it together, four priests and a boy. To the extent that we've ever felt like a normal family, we feel like one now.

After dinner comes a lull. Peter watches the evening news with Diego. I find the Vatican yearbook. Almost thirteen hundred pages go by before I find a page titled VICARIATE OF THE VATICAN CITY-STATE—the special administrative unit devoted to our tiny country. The name of the judicial vicar will be here.

To my surprise, the post is empty. All decisions are made by our vicar general, a cardinal named Galuppo. And the first words of Cardinal Galuppo's profile ring alarm bells.

Born in the archdiocese of Turin.

The man controlling Ugo's trial is from the Shroud's city. I wonder if this can possibly be a coincidence. The other Turin cardinal I know of is Simon's boss, the Cardinal Secretary of State, and he, too, is touched by the shadow of Ugo's death: the phone number on the back of the photo I was sent at the Casa rings a Secretariat phone, and Michael said he suspected Secretariat priests beat him up.

Hometown networks are important in this city, and cardinals are their hubs. John Paul couldn't have removed the Shroud from its chapel without the knowledge of Cardinal Poletto, the archbishop of Turin, and I imagine the first men Poletto might've contacted were his fellow cardinals from the archdiocese.

I wonder if Ugo's death can really boil down to something so petty. The feelings of a few powerful men about the transfer of a relic from their birth city. As the sun sets, the trees below are black with roosting birds and loud with their evening chatter. At half past seven the telephone rings. I hear Diego say, "Send him up."

Lucio emerges from his bedroom looking grim. He shuffles forward on his four-legged cane as the nuns bring a pitcher of iced water to a table in the next room, then make themselves scarce.

A sharp knock comes at the door. Diego steps forward to answer it, and I see Simon close his eyes and breathe.

The man who enters is an old Roman priest I don't recognize.

"Monsignor," Diego says, "please come in."

The old man greets Simon by name, then turns to me and says, "Are you Father Alexander Andreou? Your brother mentioned you would be here."

He offers a handshake, then spots Lucio down the hall and begins to plod toward him. I glance at Simon, wondering if the monsignor is a Secretariat friend, but he gives no sign.

Lucio sits in his private library, at a long table with a red felt top and a red silk skirt. A poor man's version of the furnishings in the papal palace. At Lucio's invitation, the monsignor takes a chair and puts his briefcase on the table. Simon and I follow him in.

"Diego," my uncle says, "that will be all. Hold my calls."

Without a word from me, Diego brings Peter out with him. Now the four of us are alone.

"Alexander," Lucio says, "this is Monsignor Mignatto, an old friend of mine from seminary. He works at the Rota now. Last night we received some important news, and I've asked him to advise the family about what happens next."

Mignatto bows his head slightly. My uncle is constantly surrounded by old priests trying to make themselves useful to our family in the hope that Lucio will be their meal ticket. Already I wonder about this man's motives. The title *monsignor* is an honorary promotion only halfway up from priest. In most dioceses it's a badge of pride, but around here, for a man of Mignatto's age, it's a sign of not really having made it. A consolation prize for not having reached bishop. Simon will make monsignor next year, the standard promotion after five years of Secretariat work.

With a hint of lawyerly self-importance, Mignatto places three sheets of paper on the table, one at a time. Then he clicks the briefcase shut. A Rotal advocate ranks far below a cardinal, but Mignatto's cassock is still expensive-looking and tailored, nothing like the ones in the clerical supply catalogs I shop from. Monsignors of his grade have the honor of wearing purple buttons and sashes instead of black, to set them apart from ordinary priests. Though Eastern Catholics consider this finicky—there's no biblical basis for the title of monsignor, let alone for the color of their buttons—it's still daunting to be the only Greek priest in a room of successful Romans.

"Father Andreou," he says, turning to me, "let's begin with *your* situation."

I stare at him. "What situation?"

"Don Diego says you lost your police escort today. Would you like to know why?"

He has my full attention.

Mignatto slides a sheet toward me. It looks like a police report.

"They examined your apartment twice," he says. "And they found no signs of forced entry."

"I don't understand."

"They think your housekeeper lied. They think the break-in never happened."

"*What?*"

Mignatto's eyes never leave mine. "They believe the damage to your apartment was staged."

I turn to Simon, but he's wearing his diplomat face, trained to register no surprise. Uncle Lucio lifts a finger in the air, asking me to contain my disbelief.

"This," Mignatto says, "is important in Nogara's murder trial because the prosecution pivots on what happened at your apartment. If there was a break-in, then you and your brother are victims, and we have more than one crime. Without the break-in, we have only what happened at Castel Gandolfo."

"Why," I say, trying to sound calm, "would they think she lied about something like this?"

"Because your brother told her to do it."

I swallow back my incredulity. "I'm sorry?"

"They think she staged the break-in to distract attention from what happened at Castel Gandolfo."

I glance at Simon again. He's staring at his hands. For the first time, I sense that this is not the meeting I thought it was.

"Simon," I say, "what do they think happened at Castel Gandolfo?"

He drags a knuckle across his lips. "Alli," he says, "I wanted to tell you at the museums. But Peter was there."

"You wanted to tell me what?"

He straightens himself up. At his full height, even seated in a chair, he seems majestic. This majesty is only deepened by the sadness in his eyes.

"The trial," he says, "is mine. They're accusing me of killing Ugo."

CHAPTER 14

I AM COLD. GUTTED. It feels as if there's an opening at the bottom of me into which everything else is sliding. Into which I can't stop myself from falling, too.

They're staring at me. Waiting for me to say something. But I look to Simon. My hands are flat on the tabletop. I feel my weight pressing on them, needing to be steadied.

Simon doesn't speak. Instead, Mignatto says, "I'm sure this comes as a shock."

Everything moves more slowly. My vision flexes, making them all seem more distant. Mignatto is looking at me with a polite, muted pity that belongs to some other situation, some alien world. I feel myself scrabbling for traction, like a rat trying to escape a trap. All three of them knew. All three of them have accepted this.

"No," I murmur. "Uncle, you've got to stop them."

The first clear thoughts penetrate the fog of shock. The people who attacked Michael, who killed Ugo, who threatened me: this must be their way of reaching Simon.

"Cardinal Galuppo," I blurt. "He did this."

Mignatto squints at me.

"Galuppo," I repeat. "From Turin."

"Alexander," Lucio says, "just listen."

Mignatto removes another document from his briefcase. "Father Andreou," he says to Simon, "this is the libellus. A copy of it was sent to your Ankara address before the court messenger confirmed your whereabouts last night. To prepare you to read this document, I need to make sure you remember your rights in this process."

"I don't need a reminder," Simon says.

So that's what this is: a strategy session. An acceptance of the inevitability of a trial.

"Father," Mignatto says gently, "everyone in your position needs a reminder." He checks his shirt cuffs, then says, "These proceedings won't resemble an Italian trial. The Church follows the older, inquisitorial system."

Now I see Mignatto for what he really is. Not the bearer of bad news, but the family attorney. The Rotal messenger who came to Lucio's apartment last night must've notified Simon he was being charged. Now my uncle has hired Mignatto to be Simon's defense lawyer.

I stare at Lucio. His otherworldly calm begins to seem comforting. A reassurance that we can prepare ourselves for whatever Simon is about to endure.

"In *our* system," Mignatto says, "a trial does not consist of the prosecution and defense offering competing views of what took place. It is the judges who call the witnesses, ask the questions, and decide which experts will testify. The defense and prosecution may make suggestions, but the judges are empowered to decline them. This means we will not be able to pose questions in court. We will not be able to force the tribunal to consider a particular line of inquiry. We will only be able help the judges seek the truth on their own. As a result, you won't have some of the rights you may be expecting."

"I understand," my brother says.

"I must also warn you that a guilty verdict in this canonical trial would result, to a moral certainty, in your being handed over to the civil authorities for a state homicide trial."

No change registers in Simon's face. Here are the reserves of strength our parents could never fathom. He is even more placid than Lucio. And yet his peace seems anchored in sadness. I want to comfort him. But if I reach out, I know my hand will shake.

Mignatto slides the libellus toward him. When Simon picks it up, though, he only taps the pages on the table to level them, then returns them.

"Please," Mignatto clarifies. "You can examine it now."

But when he offers the document again, Simon says, with a serene look on his face, "Monsignor, I appreciate your help. But I don't need to see the libellus."

There's a short silence before he speaks again. And in that pause, a pang of fear sinks through me like a depth charge. I feel an old, familiar undertow. I pray that I'm wrong, that my brother is no longer the man he once was. And yet I have a clear premonition of what he's about to say.

Simon stands. "I've decided that I won't defend myself against the murder charge."

"Simon!" I cry.

An awful expression crawls across Mignatto's face. A strange, disbelieving smile. My heart feels cavernous, echoing with a pain I prayed I would never feel again.

"What are you saying?" the monsignor asks. "You confess to the murder of Ugolino Nogara?"

Simon answers emphatically: "No."

"Then explain yourself, please."

"I won't mount a defense."

"Simon," I urge him, "please don't do this."

"Under canon law," Mignatto says gravely, "you're *required* to mount a defense."

The words of a reasonable man. An ordinary, reasonable man. Who doesn't understand my brother at all. I grab Simon's arm and try to make him meet my eyes.

Lucio hisses, "Simon, what is this nonsense?"

But my brother ignores him and turns to me. His stare is almost vacant. He has prepared himself for this moment. I know, already, that nothing I say will be able to reach him.

"I shouldn't have involved you in this, Alex," he says. "I'm sorry. From this point forward, please stay out of it."

"Simon, you can't do th—"

"Don't be a fool!" Lucio barks. "You'll lose everything!"

But before he can say more, Diego appears in the doorway. In a tense voice he says, "Eminence, there's a visitor waiting outside."

Simon glances at his watch. He steps away from the table, in the direction of the door Diego has opened, and trades a look with the stranger in the entryway.

"What are you doing?" I say.

"Sit down!" Lucio barks. Hysteria circles in his voice.

But Simon tucks in his chair and bows slightly.

My body is numb with grief. With mourning. Here he is again, returned from the dead. The Simon no one has ever been able to change, who can still shed the world in a heartbeat.

"Uncle," he says, "I've been asked to accept house arrest. And I've agreed."

"That's absurd!" My uncle points at the stranger just visible through the doorway. "Who is that man? Send him away!"

But there's a grandeur to Simon's deafness. He turns and begins to walk away. Nothing can reach him now.

Almost nothing. From beside Diego's desk, Peter comes running up. "Is your meeting done now?"

Simon, nearly at the door now, stops.

My son's expression is angelic. "Can you read me a story?"

His eyes are so innocent, so hopeful. He is standing before his hero, the world-record holder in his life for always saying yes.

"I'm sorry," Simon whispers. "I have to go."

"Where?"

My brother kneels. His arms, as endless as albatross wings, enfold Peter. He says, "Don't worry about that. Will you do something for me?"

Peter nods.

"No matter what you hear people say, believe in me. All right?" He presses his face against Peter's, so that my son can't see the emotion in his eyes. "And remember. I love you."

■ ■ ■

THE MAN IN THE doorway says nothing. Does not shake Simon's hand. Does not acknowledge the rest of us. Just waits for a signal from my brother, then leads him away.

Lucio has risen to his feet. "Come back!" he wheezes.

His breathing is shallow. Diego tries to ease him back into his seat, but Lucio stumbles toward the entryway and throws open the door.

The elevator in the distance is closing.

"Eminence," Diego says, "I can call down and have the guards stop them."

But Lucio only leans on the wall and croaks, "What is this? What does he think he's doing?"

I hurry toward him and say, "Uncle, I think I might know what's happening."

I begin to explain about Ugo's exhibit, about Turin and the threats. But Lucio only stares at the door my brother left by.

"That man who came for Simon," I continue, "may have been sent by Cardinal Galuppo. He's John Paul's vicar. And he's from Turin."

But from the other room, Mignatto says, "No. The vicar would've issued a written order. There was no order. That man was probably a plainclothes gendarme."

"If Cardinal Galuppo is trying to threaten Simon," I continue, "he wouldn't leave a paper trail."

Lucio is still breathing hard. "If someone were trying to threaten your brother," he says, "then Simon wouldn't have gone willingly."

Mignatto approaches us. "I can resolve this very quickly," he says. Producing a phone from his briefcase, he dials a number and says, "Ciao, Eminence. Sorry to interrupt your dinner. Did you just send a man to pick up Andreou?" He waits. Then: "Thank you much."

After hanging up, he turns back to us. "Cardinal Galuppo has no idea who that man was. And I should add that His Eminence has been my friend for twenty years, so I find your accusation absurd."

I turn to him. "Monsignor, a Secretariat priest was attacked. My apartment was broken into. Someone sent me a threat this afternoon at my hotel room. They're going after everyone who knew about the exhibit."

Lucio's breathing has grown even shallower. "No," he pants. "This has nothing to do with Galuppo."

"How do you know?"

He has just enough strength to give me a withering look. "The people of Turin didn't go murdering each other after the radiocarbon tests, so they're not doing it now." He takes a gasping breath. "Find your brother. I want answers."

He gestures at Diego for help, then hobbles into the darkness of his bedroom. The door closes after him.

Diego murmurs to me, "What the hell is this about?"

I whisper, "They think Simon killed Ugo."

"I know that. Where were they taking him?"

"Into house arrest."

"In whose house?"

I hadn't even registered this point. Simon has no house, no home. He lives in a Muslim country a thousand miles away.

"I don't know," I begin to say. But Diego has already followed my uncle into the darkness.

"COME," MIGNATTO SAYS TO me, stepping back toward the negotiating table and closing the door. He lifts the libellus and says, in a low voice, "You really think this is another threat?"

"Yes."

He clears his throat. "Then I'm willing to discuss it. But to do that, there's a bit of procedure we need to get out of the way. Will you agree to be your brother's procurator?"

"His what?"

"The procurator receives court documents and acts in the defendant's interest." Mignatto gestures at the papers on the table. "It entitles you to see the libellus, which I otherwise can't show you."

How strange the world of canon law is. *Procurator* is the title Pontius Pilate had in the gospels. The title of the man who signed Jesus' death warrant. Only lawyers would resurrect a word like that.

"My brother should make those decisions," I say.

"To judge from what we just heard, your brother isn't interested in making decisions."

Mignatto rummages in his briefcase and finds a pack of cigarettes. Here, in the home of the Cardinal President, in the world's first country to outlaw smoking, he lights up. "What's your answer, Father?" he says.

I lift the page. "I'll do it."

"Good. Now look carefully at the judges listed there, and tell me if any of them are familiar."

Morbid fascination pushes my eyes through the text.

August 22, 2004

Rev. Simon Andreou
c/o Secretariat of State
Vatican City 00120

DECREE OF CITATION

Dear Rev. Andreou:
This letter is to inform you that a formal ecclesiastical penal process has begun against you in the Diocese of Rome. You are requested to identify an advocate who will represent you in this process. Your immediate response is required to the charge established in the enclosed document.

Sincerely,
Bruno Card. Galuppo
Vicar for Vatican City
Diocese of Rome

cc: Presiding Judge: Rev. Msgr. Antonio Passaro, J.C.D.
cc: Associate Judge: Rev. Msgr. Gabriele Stradella, J.C.D.
cc: Associate Judge: Rev. Msgr. Sergio Gagliardo, J.C.D.
cc: Promoter of Justice: Rev. Niccolò Paladino, J.C.D.
cc: Notary: Rev. Carlo Tarli

My pulse quickens. "I know the first judge. And the third one. Passaro and Gagliardo. Stradella is the only one I don't recognize."

Mignatto nods as if he expected this. "All three have been Rotal judges for almost twenty years, so it's not surprising you might have crossed their paths in Rome. It's *very* surprising, however, that a penal case against a priest would be tried by Rotal judges. Only a bishop or legate is supposed to receive that treatment unless the Holy Father approves otherwise. So the question arises: would you say Passaro and Gagliardo are hostile toward your brother?"

Now I understand. He's saying this is the form the threat would take. Cardinal Galuppo would stack the bench against Simon.

"No," I tell him. "Passaro taught Simon at the Academy, and Gagliardo is a friend of my uncle's. They're both friendly."

Mignatto smiles. "Monsignor Gagliardo was two years behind me in seminary. Your uncle was his tutor. Sadly, both will have to recuse themselves. But if Cardinal Galuppo were threatening your brother, are these really the judges he would've chosen?"

I hesitate. "Maybe Galuppo knows they'll recuse themselves. Maybe the bad ones will replace them."

Mignatto shuffles the pages in his hands. "Then this may convince you otherwise."

When he offers me another paper, I'm mesmerized. It's the final sheet of the accusation. The libellus itself.

Before The Reverend Father Lord John PASSARO,
Presiding Justice

VATICAN

Penal Case

Promoter of Justice v. Rev. Andreou

Prot. N. 92.004

-LIBELLUS-

I, Niccolò Paladino, the Promoter of Justice at this Apostolic Court, hereby accuse the Reverend Simon Andreou, a priest incardinated in the Diocese of Rome, of the delict of homicide against the person of Ugolino Nogara, in violation of Canon 1397 of the Code of Canon Law. The accusation is that, on August 21, 2004, at or about five o'clock in the evening, Fr. Andreou deliberately shot to death Dr. Nogara in the gardens of the Pontifical Villas of Castel Gandolfo. The following evidence is adduced:

As witnesses: Mr. Guido Canali, employee of the pontifical farm at Castel Gandolfo; Dr. Andreas Bachmeier, curator of medieval and Byzantine art for the Vatican Museums; and Inspector General Eugenio Falcone, chief of the Vatican gendarmerie.

As documentary evidence: Fr. Andreou's personnel file at the Secretariat of State; a voice message left by Dr. Nogara at the Apostolic Nunciature in Ankara, Turkey; and video footage from security camera B-E-9 of the Pontifical Villas of Castel Gandolfo.

I ask the Court to find him guilty and, thereupon, to impose the following penalty: dismissal of Father Andreou from the clerical state.

On this 22ⁿᵈ *day of August, in the Year of Our Lord, 2004,*

Reverend Niccolò Paladino
Promoter of Justice

I hang on the threatened punishment. The court has the power to throw Simon out of the Secretariat and even banish him from Rome. But the libellus asks for the heaviest penalty of all: to laicize my brother. I knew this was possible, but it casts a pall to see the prosecutor beg such a thing.

"Look at the evidence," Mignatto says. "Anything familiar?"

"Guido Canali," I say sickly, pointing to his name on the libellus. "The night Ugo was killed, he opened the gates and drove me down to see Simon."

Mignatto makes a note. "What did he see?"

I'm at a loss. "I made him drop me off before we got close enough to see anything."

"And this?"

He points to a line of text. Simon's personnel file at the Secretariat.

"I don't know. Simon was cited for missing work this summer, but I don't see how that's relevant."

"Why was he cited?"

"For visiting Ugo in the desert."

But it returns to me now that Michael said Simon was doing something else.

Mignatto glances up. "Should I know anything about their relationship? Your brother and Nogara?"

He doesn't even try to disguise his meaning.

"No," I say sharply. "Simon was just trying to help him."

Mignatto leans back. "Then, with the exception of the security-camera footage, I see no direct evidence here. It's a circumstantial case, which needs a motive. And if the motive isn't your brother's relationship with Nogara, what is it?"

"Simon had no motive."

Mignatto lays his pen at the leading edge of the page. A boundary separating us. "Father Andreou, why do you think they're prosecuting him under canon law instead of criminal law?"

"You already know what I think."

"In two decades of service at the Rota, I've never seen a murder trial. Not one. But I can tell you why I think they're doing it. Because in a canonical trial, the proceedings are secret, the records are classified, and the sentencing is private. At every level there's confidentiality to protect against uncomfortable things coming to light."

There is the gentlest lilt in his voice, offering me an opportunity to reveal any information I might have.

"I know nothing about it," I say.

"And yet," he continues, "in two decades of service at the Rota, I've also never seen a man refuse to defend himself. Which suggests to me that my client already knows what the uncomfortable something is."

I nod. "I told you. They think Ugo had a secret, and they think Simon knows what it is."

"What I'm asking you is: are they wrong?"

"It doesn't matter. You're agreeing that this trial is a way to threaten Simon."

"You misunderstand. This trial is a way to *prosecute* him while guarding against the contingency that something confidential might come up in the proceedings."

"My brother didn't hurt Ugo."

"Then let's start at the beginning. Why was he at Castel Gandolfo the night Doctor Nogara was killed?"

"Ugo called him and told him he was in trouble."

"Did they have some kind of exchange on that afternoon, prior to the murder?"

"I don't think so. Simon said he got there too late to save Ugo."

Mignatto points to the section of the libellus detailing the evidence. His finger hovers beneath the words *video footage from security camera*. "Then what is this going to show?"

"I have no idea."

He grimaces and writes a few short notes on his pad.

"Would you explain something?" he says, looking up. "I overheard you talking to your uncle about Doctor Nogara's exhibit. Why did you think Cardinal Galuppo would threaten your brother over an exhibit on the Turin Shroud, when the Shroud has been proven to be medieval?"

"Ugo was going to prove that the tests were mistaken."

Mignatto's eyes widen slightly.

"He was also going to prove," I continue, "how the Shroud got here. How it ended up in Catholic hands."

Mignatto begins writing notes again. "Go on."

"It used to be in Orthodox territory, in Turkey, where my brother works. And Simon may have invited Orthodox clergy to the exhibit without permission from the Secretariat."

Mignatto taps the pen on the page. "Which is important why?"

"Because the message of Ugo's exhibit may be that the Shroud isn't ours. It belongs to the Orthodox, too. We owned it together when we were a single Church, before the schism of 1054."

How it came to the West, I don't know for sure, but no matter how it came, the implications remain the same.

"Is this a controversial thing to suggest?" Mignatto asks.

"Of course. It could open to the door to a custody battle. Especially if we were to say it at the pope's own museum."

Mignatto begins writing again. "And in that battle, you think Turin stands to lose."

"Turin stands to lose no matter what. Without the custody battle, Ugo told me the Shroud might be moved into a reliquary at Saint Peter's. It's not going back to Turin."

"So your theory," Mignatto says, "is that the enemies of Nogara's research wanted to stop the whole exhibit."

"Yes."

He looks up. "Which means Nogara was killed in the hopes of silencing him."

I haven't admitted this to myself so frontally. "I guess so."

"Yet you said people are being threatened—*you* are being threatened—because someone believes Nogara had a secret and wants to know what that secret is."

"Yes."

He stops. Rolls the pen between his palms. Modulates his voice so that it sounds both kind and firm. "I'm afraid I don't understand, Father Andreou. Someone wants to stop the exhibit, to silence it. Yet you're being threatened to reveal what it's about."

"If you don't believe me, I can show you the message that came to my hotel room."

Grudgingly he agrees. For the first time, though, it occurs to me that he's deciding how far to trust me.

When I return to the bedroom, I find Peter passed out on the bed. After tucking him in, I come back to Mignatto with the envelope. He studies the text on the back but remains silent for a long while. Finally he says, "I need time. May I take this back with me tonight?"

"Yes."

"I also need to think about everything you've just told me." He checks his watch. "Would you meet me in the morning at my office?"

"Of course."

He hands me a business card and writes *10 AM* on the back. "I'll have more questions for you about Nogara's exhibit, so please come prepared to answer them. In the meantime, I expect to find out shortly where your brother is. If *you* find out, please contact me immediately."

When I nod, he rises and packs the libellus back into his briefcase.

"One last thing," Mignatto says, clicking the locks. "You need to speak to your housekeeper about the break-in."

"She didn't lie about what happened."

He lowers his voice. "Father, you're asking me to believe a theory of this murder that I consider almost impossible. In return I need you to do the same. Speak to your housekeeper. I have to know why the gendarmes came to the conclusion they did."

CHAPTER 15

For a while after Mignatto leaves, I sit alone at the meeting table. I stare at the chair where Simon sat. At the place on the red baize where he placed the libellus after refusing to look at it. With Mignatto gone, the reckoning comes. He has done it. My brother has finally cut his own throat.

We are a religion of captains hoping to go down with the ship. Though we teach our children that the worst thing Judas ever did—worse even than betraying Jesus—was committing suicide, the truth is that what moves the lifeblood of our faith is a thumping impulse toward self-destruction. *Greater love has no one than this*, Jesus says in the gospel of John. *To lay down one's life for one's friends*. I wonder why Simon is doing this. For Ugo? For the memory of our father?

Or for me?

A few months after our father died, when Simon was seventeen, he went to a bar with some of our Swiss Guard friends and found a pack of gendarmes running arm-wrestling matches. Nothing organized, just policemen letting off steam. Simon wasn't even old enough to drive, but he had grown to be the tallest man in our country. Since our father's death, he'd also spent every day developing an interest in punching the speed bag in the Swiss Guard gym. So by the time he walked into that bar, his forearms were thicker than his biceps, and when the gendarmes got a look at them dangling from the bottoms of his rolled-up sleeves, they wanted to see what he could do.

The guards felt protective of my brother. He and I were already slipping into the dark pit that our father's death left behind. No one understood our loneliness better than those boys from the faraway cantons. That day at the bar, they pulled Simon away and started to lead him out the door—when their own Guard officer ordered them to wait. He wanted to see what would happen.

Simon lost the first match. He lifted his elbow off the table, a foul, and the gendarme smashed him into the wood. But they reset the table, and Simon got some coaching from the Swiss Guard officer. This time he won, nearly breaking the man's arm. That was how it started.

The same night, the officer took Simon to the deck of his apartment in the Swiss barracks. He posed two questions: Was it true Simon wanted to be a priest? And would he consider another kind of service to the Holy Father?

Simon listened as the officer explained there was a military tradition in our Church, which moved hand-in-hand with the priesthood. Five centuries ago, the Jesuits were founded on military discipline, by a soldier, and now the time had come to rekindle that spirit: to recruit men, train them, and enlist them in a military order to serve a troubled world. For a man like Simon, it would capitalize on physical gifts the priesthood would never use. So the next night, Simon followed the man into Rome for what the officer described as a demonstration of what he meant. And the officer encouraged my brother to keep an open mind.

I discovered later that the place they went was a dogfighting pit. The Rome police had shut it down a month before, but it had found new life running street-boxing matches instead. Most of the fighters were homeless people and immigrants, and the purse was big enough that the fights were bloody.

The officer showed Simon that there were children in the crowd. Boys and girls, eight and ten and twelve years old, greasy like rats, shouting for their favorite fighters. *Those kids don't come to Mass*, the officer said. *If we want to reach them, this is where we have to do it.*

Later, Simon would tell me about the things he saw that night. The children were stretching out their arms to touch the fighters who passed by, grabbing the hems of their shorts as if they were a disease they wanted to catch. Everyone old enough to gamble was in the front of the crowd, putting money on the fights. But the children were in back. That was when the officer spoke the words Simon never forgot: *Tell me you've ever seen a kid look at his priest that way.* And he pointed to a boy in the ringside stands, pressed between gamblers, watching the fight with upturned eyes. Simon said it was like a saint being martyred in a painting.

"Sir," Simon said, "I don't fight."

"But if I trained you," the officer told him, "you could. And when you win, these boys will follow you. Even to Mass."

Simon said nothing. So the officer explained: "It's a dance. Two men agreeing not to turn the other cheek. Not sinful. I would train you for a couple of months, then we would get you in the ring."

"A couple of months," my brother said.

"Son, you're already good on the speed bag. If we work the heavy bag and some blocking, you could be ready in ten weeks."

And Simon, never taking his eyes off that boy in the crowd, said, "If this place is still standing in ten weeks, I'll burn it down."

"Don't fool yourself. They'll find another place. They have no parents, no priests. But you: the arms on you, the strength. You could lead them."

"I thought you wanted to create military priests. These are just boys."

"Not them, son. *You.* Your strength is a gift. What do you say?"

And I know what Simon must have thought, hearing that officer call him *son, son, son.* Father was dead. The doctors hadn't found cancer in our mother yet, but it was there, spreading its wings. And Simon, who had always been a year ahead in school, was a college man now, swimming in the general population, pulling friends out of fistfights and watching them drink until they didn't bother getting out of bed to relieve themselves, just urinated like beasts on themselves and the girls they brought home, who looked more inconvenienced than degraded. I never asked Simon why he said yes to those fights. But I imagined him staring at that boy in the crowd and thinking of me.

So the guards trained him. They brought him down to the dojo in their barracks, where neither of us been allowed before, and Simon learned the jab, the hook, the cross. Not the uppercut, because he drew the line at a punch you always aimed at a man's head. But with strength like Simon's, it was enough.

Nine weeks later, he had his first fight. I heard about it afterward, the way I heard about everything until that final bout. He fought a hairy Algerian whose day job, people said, was drinking fig liquor when he should've been unloading bags at the airport. What people said about Simon, I never knew.

It was ugly. Simon danced and jabbed until the Algerian got impatient; then, when the man leaned in for something big, Simon tattooed him with body blows. Late in the third round, it registered on the man's face that this oversize boy was wearing him down. That those meaty forearms were throwing fire. But the boys in the back seats hated Simon's style. The bobbing and weaving, the bloodlessness. They sympathized with the Algerian, who thought there might've been some hitting in the ring. But after the match, Simon went to them and told them he wasn't a fighter, just a kid hoping to become a priest someday. He was fighting for *them*, for *his boys*. And he repeated this, match after match, until it sank in. He talked to them about how it felt to be scared by the men he fought. How he prayed before each fight, and how he prayed after. Soon he discovered how cheaply the affection of lonely kids can be bought. Before long they were bleeding their lungs for him, waiting for Simon's signature punches each night, for the way my brother could turn a man's aggression against him, eye for an eye, dialing up hooks and crosses like fire and brimstone.

That was when, after Simon's sixth or seventh fight, my friend Gianni Nardi heard about the fights. Not about Simon, but about the street-boxing ring. So we went.

I must've known Simon had been elsewhere all that time. Most weekends, until the night he arm-wrestled at that bar, he'd come home from college to check on Mamma and take me to American movies at the Pasquino. Now it was every other weekend or less, and he was bringing me gifts from the city as if he felt guilty.

But I was thirteen and full of appetites I couldn't fathom. Full of emptiness I couldn't fill. I was getting so used to my family's piecemeal extinction that Simon's disappearance was just one more. I had living of my own to do. Gianni's dad was a sampietrino, a custodian of Saint Peter's, with keys to the toolsheds on the basilica roof, so Gianni and I would sneak up there and host picnics for our girlfriends, drinking wine and staring down at Rome like kings. He was seeing a girl named Bella Costa, and I had Andrea Nofri, then Cristina Salvani, then Pia Tizzoni, whose body was so far outside the curve of fourteen years old that I expected the statues on the basilica roof to turn around and stare. I never gave a thought to what Simon was up to. Even if I had known, I wouldn't have believed. Back then, *I* was the fighter in our family. Simon had a Roman body—the letter-opener silhouette, the fan belts for muscles—but I had Father's Greek genes, the pack-dog neck and unbreakable back. I fought other boys for the joy of it. So when Gianni heard there was street boxing at the old dogfighting pit, *I* dragged *him* there. Because a bare-knuckle fight was something I needed to see.

The first fight was two bums off the streets, playing for laughs. They managed six rounds before the crowd became restless, then the barker called a second bout in which a short Turk laid out a jiggling man in overalls. Finally came bout three. And with no explanation, the crowd of boys on all sides of us stood up and grew quiet.

Down into the pit crawled a pale white fighter, glistening like soap. He scratched his soles on the dirt as if they were new Sunday shoes. And at the sight of him, every boy in that house screamed as if he were pierced with nails. Eyes-shut, bloodthirsty wailing. The fighter kept his back to us, but when he pulled off his shirt—stripped it off like a skin of glue—I felt my throat tighten. Because I knew those muscles. I knew the way they strained around that backbone like wings.

"Oh," I heard Gianni say. "No shit. Get outta here." He grabbed my shirt. "Alex, that's your brother down there."

But I was already pushing my way into the crowd. The kids were chanting now. Slapping their legs.

Pa-a-a-a-dre, Pa-dre, Padre.

Men in the front rows threw money into piles for bets. A second fighter jumped in. He was pink-skinned and hunchbacked. A Russian, people murmured. And for the first time in my life, my big brother looked like just a boy. A kid in a sandbox. He was nine or ten inches taller than the Russian, with forearms like cement mixers, but the rest of him was so thready that God seemed to have stretched him from chewing gum.

Someone hit a wrench on an overhead pipe, and Simon came off his corner first. I shouted his name, but it vanished in the rush of noise.

I pushed myself toward the edge of the pit, and then—I don't know why—I just stood there. I watched. Because what I wanted, desperately, was to see this happen. To see Simon hurt this man.

Our parents had always hidden us from places like this. When I fought at school, my father strapped me. *But now that we're alone, Sy,* I thought, *you can show me. Because I have this in me, too. So tonight, do this for me. Put your fist through this man's jaw.*

Each step Simon took in that pit, I tracked with my own legs. The rhythm of his feet, the instinct that told him how long to dance and when to stop, was in me, too. The Russian had meaty hands, fists that must've left craters in heavy bags, but they were slow. And by the time they reached Simon, we were gone. We came with straight rights that cracked like bones breaking. And back he went, still swinging. He was bleeding from the face now, black around the ribs. And still he came back for more. So more is what we gave.

The kids were roaring. I split the skin around my mouth, screaming so loud.

Come on, Sy! I shouted. *Hit him!*

But the words that came out were:

"Come on, Sy! Kill him!"

And all of a sudden, down there in the pit, Simon stopped. Flat-footed—dead in his paces—he stared into the crowd.

The Russian scraped along the back wall, buying space.

I felt a shadow fall over me, so dark that Simon couldn't have seen me if Rome was burning.

But he could feel me there. I wanted to run, but his stare closed in.

The Russian was coming now, barreling down on my brother. All I could do was point.

Simon turned just in time; the Russian caught the hairs on his chest. But for some reason, Simon staggered. He stared at me, and the rhythm fell out of him. Even the kids up above saw it.

"Padre!" a boy in the crowd yelled.

But Simon never took his eyes off me.

I will never come here again, Sy. I swear to you. But this one time, for me, finish this. Even if they have to piece this man together in the hospital, show me you understand.

And from the look on Simon's face, hanging from the blacks of his eyes, I knew he did understand. He turned back and tilted his hands, inviting the Russian back.

Just for an instant, the Russian looked for me in the crowd.

Not him, Simon mouthed, waving him in. *Me.*

The crowd came back to life, people shouting like cannibals. The Russian stepped up, jabbed and pulled back.

Simon bobbed. But nothing more.

The Russian came one-two this time—and Simon let the punches slap him so loudly, it shut those kids up.

"Come on," he said, opening his hands. But this time, his hands didn't fist up; they stayed open.

So the Russian drove a blow into Simon's ribs, and Simon barely stayed on his feet. He winced as he straightened up.

Now the Russian came with a one-two-three: a jab that almost missed Simon's shoulder, except that it came with a cross rolling behind it like a freight train. That cross knocked Simon out of his stance, bending him over.

My brother's hands shot up instinctively, to protect his head. But he forced them down. And now a smile broke over the Russian's face when he brought the left hook to finish. Because if this kid was going to take a beating—if he was going to dangle his head there like a bobber—then this would be no left hook to the body.

No fighter I ever saw, before or after, wound up for a punch like that. The Russian dropped his right hand to the bottom of the ocean, not even bothering to keep up his guard, and threw a left hook that crushed Simon's cheek as if he'd been hit by a bolt from a cattle gun. My brother's head almost jumped off his neck, but instead his body popped up in the air. Then he lay there, dead in the dirt.

I jumped over the pit wall, wailing, screaming, not knowing what I did; but there were hands on me, grabbing my shoulders and pulling me back. I threw punches, but Simon was already moving on the ground, pulling himself up. He turned in my direction and stared. Fat parachutes of blood fell from his mouth, but he locked me in, like there was no one in this seminary but us brothers, trying to get our thick heads around this lesson.

And the Russian just waited there, holding his punches, because he knew what was coming.

Above us, in the high seats, the kids were coming unglued. *Stop!* they were shouting. And *No!* And *Why won't he fight?* I shook my head at Simon, the spit hanging from my mouth, and I screamed, *Don't do this. Please.*

But he wiped an arm across his bleeding mouth, tapped the sides of his head, and stepped back into that fight.

The Russian sent an uppercut through his chin that would've split a tree in half. It shattered what was left of Simon's jaw, and when his head snapped back, everything was done. Before he ever hit the ground, my brother was gone.

And then.

My God. Those kids, how they loved him. They burst from on high like water from a broken dam. An army couldn't have stopped them. While I sat there, hogtied in the first row, wave after wave of them came into the pit, surrounding Simon's body, not letting the Russian take another step. What the men in that pit would've done with my brother—left him out on the street, carted him to the next rione to keep police off the scent—I never knew, because those kids swarmed Simon like the whole future of their race depended on it. They carried him on their knobby backs through the crowd and out the door. I watched them take a collection right there, hands in pockets, to find cab fare to the hospital. Half of them looking like they hadn't eaten in a week, pulling lint off their last coins.

When I finally caught up to them, Gianni was explaining who we were, how we would take Simon home, where we had doctors. And they stared at us like we had come down in a chariot of fire. Because they had heard that one word, that one magical word, that parted seas and brought dead men back to life.

Vatican.

"Save him," one said to me. "Don't let him die."

Another said: "Take him to Il Papa."

Il Papa: John Paul.

The last thing I ever saw of that place, before the taxi pulled away into the night, was those kids huddled together, watching Simon leave. Watching my brother vanish from their streets. And praying while they watched.

———

IT'S A GOOD CHRISTIAN thing my brother does now, I think to myself, as I sit alone at the table where he refused to mount a defense. He believes in his heart that he does this for the good of someone else. I don't know who. I don't know why.

But I know I have to stop him.

CHAPTER 16

I CHECK ON PETER before I leave. He was watching cartoons, but the TV is now off. The open toiletry bag on the dresser, speckled with water drops, tells me he brushed his teeth. He has even plugged in the nightlight. I kiss his forehead and move his sleeping body away from the edge of the bed, wondering if he will grow up to be as inhumanly self-reliant as his uncle. Wondering if he will someday break my heart, too.

On a sheet of Lucio's stationery by the main telephone, I write:

> Diego—
>   *Running an errand for Mignatto. Be back in an hour or two.*
>   *Please call my mobile if Peter wakes up.*
>   —*Alex*

Then I call Leo and ask him to join me on a walk to Sister Helena's.

THE CONVENT IS UP the flanks of Vatican Hill, a dead zone at night. Below us, in Rome, the world is powdered with electric light, but here in the gardens the darkness is so thick it seems liquid. Leo and I navigate by memory.

He doesn't ask why we're here. He doesn't say a thing. When the silence begins to feel heavy, I decide to tell him.

"They're charging Simon with the murder. They think he killed Ugo Nogara."

Leo stops. I can't see his expression in the dark.

"What?" he says. "What the hell did Simon do?"

"I don't even know. He's refusing to defend himself."

"What do you mean, *refusing*?"

There is no possible answer. "It's just . . . Simon."

"He'll spend the rest of his life in a cell at Rebibbia."

"No. You've got to keep this secret, but they're trying him in a Church court."

He is a long time chewing on it. "Why would they do that?"

"I don't know."

"He won't talk to you?"

"He's under house arrest."

More silence.

"If you can figure out where they took him," I say, "that would give me someplace to start."

The Guard has sentries all over the papal palace.

"Of course," he says. "I'll find him." But his voice drifts in uncertainty. Quietly he adds, "Simon didn't do it, though. Right?"

My brother at his strangest, at his most inscrutable. Even to a friend, Simon seems capable of anything. God knows what a panel of three judges will think.

FINALLY, FLOATING OVERHEAD, WE see lights burning on the hilltop. We've reached the old medieval tower that has a new Vatican Radio antenna rising from its roof. Connected to it by a wall covered with satellite dishes is another of John Paul's construction projects: a convent for our tiny community of Benedictine nuns.

"I'll stay back," Leo says.

He doesn't ask what we're doing. He knows Helena lives here.

I ring the convent bell. No one answers. A light is on in one of the windows, but there are no sounds inside. Still, I wait. Every Benedictine house in the world, for the past sixteen hundred years, has obeyed a rule that guests must be greeted as if they're Christ.

At last the door opens. Before me is a round-faced woman with plain eyeglasses in a white wimple. Everything else—black veil, black tunic, black cincture, black scapular—blends into the darkness.

"Sister, I'm Father Alex Andreou," I say. "My son is the boy Sister Helena watches. Would it be possible for me to speak to her?"

She studies me in silence. Only seven nuns live in this priory—it isn't even large enough to qualify as an abbey—so the women all know each other's business. I wonder how much they know about me.

"Would you wait in the chapel, Father," she says, "while I fetch her?"

But in the chapel the other sisters might overhear us. "If it's the same to you," I tell her, "I'll wait in the garden."

She unlocks the gate and acts as if I have every right to be here, even though the sisters do the sowing and harvesting, and the pope gets the produce. There are no Benedictines in my church—Greeks have an older tradition of monasticism—but I admire these women and their unselfishness.

While I wait, I pace the garden rows. Every Vatican boy steals fruit from these trees, and every pope turns a blind eye. Finally a sound comes from the gate: the faintest swish of a habit. When I turn, Prioress Maria Teresa hovers before me.

"Father," she says with a small gesture of deference. "Welcome. May I help you?"

She has a gentle face, younger than its age, darkened only by the pockets of loose skin beneath her eyes. But her expression is solemn. I've come during the Great Silence, the hours after compline prayers when Benedictines don't speak. Only the rule of hospitality trumps the Silence.

"Actually, I'd hoped to speak to Sister Helena," I say.

"Yes. And she'll speak to you, briefly, in a moment."

I assume the prioress has come down as a courtesy, since Uncle Lucio is the cardinal-protector of her branch of Benedictines, the man who represents their collective interest at the Vatican. And yet there's no deference in her voice when she continues, "This will be the only time I allow Sister Helena to involve herself, or our community, in this matter. I hope you understand."

She must know about Simon.

"Whatever you've heard," I tell her, "it's not true."

Her hands are hidden behind her scapular, making even her body language impossible to discern. "Father," she says, "those are my wishes. Please finish your affairs with Sister Helena as briefly as possible. Good night."

She bows slightly, then drifts back to the door. A familiar silhouette waits there, lowering her head as the prioress passes. Then she comes gliding toward me in the dark.

The wrinkles of Helena's face are a web of sadness. She doesn't even make eye contact. "Father Alex," she whispers, "I'm so sorry."

"You heard about Simon?"

She looks up. "What about him?"

I'm relieved. News of Ugo's death and the break-in may have gotten out, but not news of the charges against Simon.

"I need to ask you about what happened at the apartment," I say.

She nods, unsurprised.

"Before it happened," I continue, "did Simon say anything to you?"

The lids of her eyes pinch closed. "*Before* it happened? My memory must be playing tricks." She sighs in frustration. "I spoke to Father Simon before it happened?"

But her memory doesn't play tricks.

"Did you?" I ask.

Now when she looks at me, the sadness is gone, swept away by a sharp inquisitiveness. "Father, what's happening? What are they saying? A policeman came to the convent a few hours ago, but he was sent away before he could ask any questions."

"Please. Did you talk to Simon beforehand?"

"No."

"Not in any way?"

"Father Alexander," she says, "I haven't traded words with your brother since I cooked him dinner at your apartment the *last* time."

"Months ago."

"At Christmas."

Behind her, at the convent door, the prioress calls out, "Sister Helena, please finish your visit."

Quickly Helena says, "Tell me the truth. Is someone in trouble?"

"The gendarmes think there was no break-in."

She growls. "And I suppose the furniture just threw itself on the floor?"

I steer clear of what the gendarmes think. "They didn't find any signs of forced entry."

She winces as if stung. "That is true. There was shouting and banging, then the door just seemed to open."

"But I locked it when I left."

"Yes, I remember."

"And you didn't take Peter anywhere? Not to Brother Samuel's apartment for dessert?"

"No."

"There's no other way the door could've been unlocked?"

"None." She seems flustered. The memory is returning. "I grabbed Peter as quickly as I could, but the man was already inside by the time Peter and I locked ourselves in the bedroom."

The prioress calls, "*Sister Helena . . .*"

Helena places a hand on her cheek in dismay.

"You did everything you could," I assure her. "Let me take it from here."

Behind her, Maria Teresa is descending on us. I step away, but Sister Helena grabs my wrist and whispers, "She won't let me watch Peter anymore."

"Why not?"

"It scandalized her to have a gendarme come here. I'm trying to change her mind, but I'm so sorry, Father."

Before I can answer, she is backing away. The prioress gives me a heavy look, then guides Sister Helena to the door. Six silhouettes peep down at me from convent windows as I return to Leo on the unlit road.

He veers down the path toward Lucio's palace, asking me with a glance what Helena told me. But I motion him in the other direction.

"Where are we going?" Leo says.

"To my apartment."

THE WINDOWS OF THE Belvedere Palace are still shot with light. Televisions flicker. The Argentine woman who married Signor Serra on the second floor is dancing in her kitchen. Before Leo and I reach the door, two teenagers loitering in a corner release from an embrace. I feel a spontaneous burst of happiness to be back here.

Home.

Inside the back door we find one of my neighbors sitting like a porter. "Father!" he cries, leaping to his feet.

"What are you doing here?" I ask.

Ambrosio is the all-hours computer repairman for the Holy See Internet Office.

He lowers his voice. "After the gendarmes stopped guarding the building, a few of us began taking turns."

I give him a grateful clap on the arm. At least *they* believe Sister Helena.

Ambrosio asks if I've heard any more news, but I tell him no and quickly mount the stairs, not wanting to attract more notice. At the top floor, someone has replaced a broken lightbulb on the way to my apartment. More vigilance. When we reach my door, I kneel and inspect it. The strike plate looks untouched. There are no signs of damage to the door frame. I have the key, but I turn to Leo and say, "Know how to pick a lock?"

He smiles. "Better than you."

We give it a crack, but the mechanism is old and scratchy. The pins don't like to move.

"Embarrassing," he says. "I used to be good at that."

I step down the hall to the next apartment, where the brothers of the pharmacy live. This is what I've been afraid of.

"Where are you going?" Leo says.

I pull up the doormat.

"Damn," he whispers, seeing it.

Since my parents first moved into the Belvedere Palace, this is where we've kept the spare key. Ours beneath the brothers' mat, theirs beneath ours. But not anymore.

I turn and lift my own mat. The brothers' key is still there. I rub my temples.

"How could someone know that?" Leo asks.

"Michael," I murmur.

"What?"

"Michael Black told them."

He told them where I live and how to get inside. Father was always forgetting his keys. Michael knew about the spare.

"I thought he was a friend of your family's," Leo says.

"Someone threatened him."

Leo sneers. "Coward."

Hearing a distant sound on the staircase, I drift back to my apartment door and unlock it. Then a thought comes to me. Someone still has our key, which means someone may have been coming and going from this apartment for two days. Or may even be inside.

"Your neighbors have been guarding the building," Leo reassures me when I tell him as much. "Whoever broke in wouldn't come back."

"Right."

Inside, nothing has changed. Leo reaches for the lights, but I nudge his hand away and point to the windows. "In case someone's watching."

Not liking the sound of that, he says, "Then what's the plan?"

The moon gives the furniture an eerie glow. Without touching anything, I try to visualize what Sister Helena told me about the chronology of that night. She was sitting at the table when she heard a banging at the door. A voice calling for Simon and me. With my eyes I follow the path she took, carrying Peter toward the bedroom. The door opened before she got inside. That distance is less than twenty feet.

A breath slips out of me.

"Leo . . ."

He turns his eyes to the staircase, thinking I must've heard something. He doesn't understand.

"Peter saw him," I say.

"What?"

"Last night he woke up from a nightmare. He was screaming, *I can see his face, I can see his face.*"

"No. He would've said something, Al."

"Sister Helena carried him. That's what she told me: she carried him to the bedroom."

She has always carried him the same way: pressed against her, with his head looking back over her shoulder.

"You really think?" Leo asks.

The telephone begins to ring, but I say, "When the gendarmes were here, he was too upset to talk. I didn't bring it up after that. I didn't want to worry him."

I won't wake him tonight. But I will have to find pictures for him to look at. Faces he might recognize.

The answering machine plays its message, but there's no voice on the other end. Only a strange sound that resembles a door closing.

"Come on," I say. "Let's go."

But suddenly I feel Leo's hand on me. Pushing me back. He's staring at something in the apartment doorway. The hulking silhouette of a man.

"*Who are you?*" Leo demands. "*Identify yourself!*"

I back up.

The shape doesn't make a sound. It only extends an arm.

The lights go on.

An old man shuffles into the room. The pupils of his eyes flex. He has raised an arm in the air to shield himself from the light, or perhaps to stop Leo from attacking. It's Brother Samuel, one of the pharmacists from next door.

"Father Alex," he says. "You're back."

"What are you doing here, Brother?"

"I tried calling."

"What's wrong?"

He's tense. His voice has a queer note of rehearsal. Of delivering a message that isn't his own.

"Someone came looking for you."

"When?"

"This morning. There was a sound in the hall. I came out to see what it was."

"What happened?"

He fidgets mightily. "Father Alex, I don't want to be in the middle of this. The arrangement was that if I saw you again, I would make a phone call."

"What are you talking about, Samuel?"

"I made the phone call, Alex."

I'm about to respond, when Leo murmurs something unintelligible. He's staring down the outer hallway at something I can't see. His face is paralyzed. Finally the sounds from his mouth resolve into words.

"My God."

Samuel backs away. He slips into his apartment. I hear the door click shut.

I step out.

A human form stands at the end of the hall. It hovers near the stairs, dressed entirely in black. When I recognize it, my skin tightens.

"*Alex.*"

That single word comes echoing down the hallway. And the sound of her voice splits my heart like an ax.

She takes a small, hesitant step forward. "Alex, I'm so sorry."

I can't even blink. I'm too afraid she will be gone when I reopen my eyes.

"I heard," she says, "about Simon."

I say the only word my mouth will form. The only one that is etched on every particle of me like gospels on grains of rice.

"Mona."

It is the first word I have spoken to my wife since her baby learned to walk.

CHAPTER 17

LEO MAKES HIMSELF invisible. They glance at each other in passing, my friend seeing himself out, my wife seeing herself in. Memories detonate in my thoughts. I'm standing at this door with her, holding groceries, holding furniture, holding our newborn son. Neighbors have come out to coo and pay compliments. Brother Samuel has hung so many balloons on our door that we can't even climb inside.

At the threshold, she waits. She needs to be invited into her own home.

"Come in," I say.

Just the smell of her, passing in front of me, restores electricity to the oldest districts of my heart. I know this scent. The soap she always bought at the pharmacy. A fragrance I've tracked down in every nook of her body.

I make sure we don't touch as she enters. Yet the air vibrates. My body's reaction is violent. But my mind is already registering the differences. Her hair is shorter. She doesn't keep it drawn back anymore; it hangs down just past her chin. There are the first hints of wrinkles beneath her eyes, but her neck and arms are leaner than I remember, her lines tighter. Covering her body is the same sleeveless black dress, plain but flattering, that used to be her favorite: the rare garment that was both traditional and modern, respectful and liberating. Around her shoulders is the thin black sweater she used to wear when women were required to cover their arms. I wonder what message this outfit is supposed to send.

"May I sit?" she says.

I gesture to a chair and offer her something to drink.

"Water would be nice."

As she glances around the room, there is a twinge in her expression. Nothing has changed, not even the photos in the picture frames. I kept it this way in the spirit of honoring her memory, of awaiting her return. Like all good Romans, Peter and I have built our roads around our ruins.

"Thank you," she says when I return with the glasses. Again I make sure our hands don't touch.

She waits for me to take the seat across from her, then she composes herself and forces her eyes to meet mine. When she begins to speak, the words come out rigidly, as if no amount of practicing has prepared her, as if she sees now that her husband is not just an audience of one. All the lost hours and days, the lonely weeks and months and years, crowd around me and stare across at her, waiting at my back to hear what answer there will be. What possibly can be said. The unrequited moments stretch so far into the distance that she realizes some of them can never be reached by words.

"Alex," she begins, "I know you must have so many questions about what happened. About where I've been. And I will try to answer anything you want to ask. But first there's something I need to say."

She swallows. Her eyes seem desperate to look away.

"When I left," she continues, "I truly thought I was doing the right thing for you and Peter. I was scared of what would happen if I stayed. My mind was so full of awful thoughts. But for a while, I've been feeling like myself again. I'm better now. And I've wanted to call, or come see you both, except that I was afraid. My doctor says the risk of a relapse is low, but even if it were one chance in a thousand, I couldn't put you and Peter through that again."

I begin to interrupt, but she raises a hand from the tabletop, asking me to let her finish while she still can. Her mouth is pinched. For a second she seems gaunt, every muscle in her neck tense, the hollows in her cheeks darkening as she clenches her jaw. In that second, it looks as if the years away have wasted her, as if the regrets have devoured her from the inside. In the sludge of my emotions, the portion that is anger weakens. I cannot forget how Peter and I suffered without her. But I see now we weren't the only ones to suffer.

"I begged my family," she continues, "to find out how you and Peter were doing. They asked around and heard you were doing okay. Doing *well*. So it didn't seem fair to turn your lives upside down just because the time was right for me."

For the first time, she lets her eyes fall.

"But then I heard about Simon." She hesitates. "And I know how much you love him. How hard this must be for you. So I told myself that since things had already been turned upside down, maybe now you might need some help."

These last words end feebly, almost as a question. As if this is a hope she isn't sure she has the right to harbor. Mona swallows. She places both hands back on the table and looks at me again, bracing herself. She is done.

Faintly I ask, "You heard about Simon? How?"

Relief crosses her face. It is far less painful to answer this than so many other questions that remain.

"Elena's new boyfriend works in the vicar's office," she says. "He saw the paperwork."

Elena. Mona's cousin. I wonder how far from that one office the news about Simon has already spread.

"And who," I ask, "told you about Peter and me?"

Relief fades. When she forces herself to look me in the eye again, I prepare myself for difficult news.

"My parents," she says. "I got back in touch with them last year."

This is a blow. For a year those miserable people have hidden her from me.

"I made them swear they wouldn't tell you," she says, putting her hands in a praying posture, asking me not to blame them.

My anger subsides. But only because I see, on her upturned finger, the ring I gave her. She still wears it. Or at least, she wears it tonight.

"And where have you been living?" I ask.

"An apartment in Viterbo. I work at a hospital there."

Viterbo. Two hours from here. The last stop on the train line heading north. She went as far away as she could without leaving entirely, to be sure we would never run into each other.

And yet she didn't escape to the beach or the mountains. Viterbo is an austere medieval town. Its biggest landmark is a palace where the popes used to come to escape Rome, and it towers over the land like Saint Peter's. She did this for a reason, I tell myself. To torture herself into remembering.

Her eyes have found the pictures of Peter. As she stares, the corners of her mouth sag. She fights to raise a wall in front of her emotions, but suddenly she blinks. Tears hop from her eyelashes to her cheeks like water dancing in a hot pan. She refuses to give herself up to it, though. Merciless control is all that keeps her balanced on this wire.

My hands want to stretch forward and hold hers. But I'm on the wire, too. So I open my wallet and pull out a picture of Peter. I slide it to the middle of the table.

She picks it up. And seeing the boy our baby became, she says in a choked voice, "He looks just like you."

The first lie of our reencounter. He doesn't look just like me. The softness in his features is hers. The dark lashes. The expressive mouth. But maybe she isn't referring to the picture in front of her. Her voice is haunted, her stare distant. She's venting some preconception of what Peter really is. He looks like me because I'm the one who clothes him, who cuts his hair each month and brushes it every morning. Even in the signed watercolor paintings taped to the walls, there's a faint resemblance between his poor autograph and mine. Peter is the duet that Mona and I wrote together. The music sounds like me, though, because I have performed it alone.

"Mona."

She is looking at me, but her eyes are vacant. She is retreating. Her body language now is a plea for going slow. She is strong, but this is harder than she imagined.

I've waited years to ask this one question, and it rages inside me. She owes me this answer. And yet I can't ask. Not when I see her this way.

Her eyes close. "I know," she says, "how you must feel." She sweeps a hand through the air, gesturing at the pictures of herself in frames. "I don't understand any of this." Her body is racked by a sudden, heaving breath. "I had hoped—I know this doesn't make sense, but I'd hoped you'd moved on."

Such darkness swims at the bottom of those words. As if she can see no happiness in this refusal to forget. As if she can even imagine an alternative.

"Mona," I say quietly, "did you find someone else?"

She shakes her head in agony, as if I am making this so hard.

"Then why did you never—"

She waves her hands in front of her head. No more. Not right now.

We are strangers. We share nothing but wreckage. Maybe this is as far as we can come in one night.

"So," she says in a choked voice, "is Simon okay?"

I glance away. For years she and her family have kept secrets from me. Now she asks this about mine.

"He didn't kill anyone," I say.

She nods forcefully, to convey that this is self-evident. The brother-in-law she once considered so inscrutable, so unpredictable, now a clockwork saint.

"I don't know why they're attacking him," I say.

For a second her expression is so tender. As if my loyalty to Simon is a beautiful thing to be reacquainted with, full of new meaning after these years of separation.

"How can I help?" she says.

I try to keep all emotion from my voice. "I don't know. I have to think about what's best for Peter."

She collects herself. "Alex, I would give anything to see him."

It comes out quickly, before I can let myself second-guess: "Then I want you to meet him."

"Okay," she says, suddenly sitting taller. "I would love that."

She keeps glancing at Peter's radio-controlled car on the floor. A red Maserati with a broken axle from a joyride into a medieval wall. Peter has written his name on the door. Mona can't take her eyes off those scrawled letters.

"I would," she repeats more faintly, "*really* love it."

The discovery of how much those words mean to me is a warning that I need to step back. If hope comes this easily, so will disappointment.

"I can't let that happen until Peter's ready," I say. "And I need time to get him ready. So you can't just come knocking at our door again."

She looks decimated. Trapped in her silence.

Finally I stand and say, "Peter's at my uncle's place right now. I need to get back to him."

"Of course."

She rises. On her feet again, she seems stronger. She tightens the sweater around her, then tucks in the chair. At the door, she makes a point of not moving, of letting me shepherd the parting. But the thought of her departure fills me with a premonition of vast loneliness. If in the morning she has gone back to Viterbo, I will have to hide my emotions from Peter. I will have to never let him know tonight happened.

As my hesitation deepens, she lifts a hand in the air and, as if touching a wall of glass, lets it linger.

"Here's my number," she says. It's already written on a piece of paper in her hand. "Call me when you and Peter are ready."

WHEN SHE'S GONE, LEO slowly drifts back. He doesn't speak. We've returned to the oldest terrain of our friendship. In silence he walks me back to Lucio's.

At the palace door he gives me a tap on the arm and a meaningful look. Making the sign of a telephone with his hand, he says, "If you want to talk about it."

But I don't want to talk about it.

Peter is asleep. His body is misaligned on the bed, feet nearly touching the pillow. I move him, and his eyes open. "Babbo," he says lucidly, then tumbles back into the abyss. I kiss him on the forehead and stroke his arm.

Mothers in the neighborhood ask how a single father does it. They see me at playdates, at the meet-ups where rising students are supposed to become friendly before primary school starts, and they say how lucky Peter is to have me. Never do they suspect that I am a ghost. A sunken ship dragged back to the surface by the little boy hanging from the monkey bars. God took Mona but left me Peter. Now she is only one phone call away. And yet I wonder if I can bear to dial those numbers.

I say a prayer for Simon, then decide to sleep on the floor. My little boy deserves a bed of his own. But before I crawl out, I whisper in his ear.

"*Peter, she came home.*"

CHAPTER 18

Peter wakes at dawn. Lucio and Diego are still in their beds, but we find nuns in the kitchen preparing the last of the summer produce, peeling the carrots and rinsing the lettuce. They don't seem to mind sharing their hour of peace with a little Napoleon who marches into the middle of them, pushing aside their habits like a showman forcing his way through theater curtains, and says, "Where are the cereals? What kind do you have?" No self-respecting Italian would eat cereal for breakfast, but Michael Black introduced me to American breakfast when I was a boy, just as he would later introduce Simon to American cigarettes. I think of what Mona would say, to find that her son has inherited the habit.

She is everywhere in this raking daylight. Ever since she left us, I've felt Mona's presence mostly in the early hours, in the silence that blankets the world, where dreams linger in the borderlands of the night.

"Honey Smacks, please," Peter says, rummaging in the drawer of utensils for a spoon and then plopping down in a chair to await service.

I get it myself. There were never foods like this in the palace until Peter was born. At his age, I remember asking Lucio for a slice of panettone for breakfast on the second day of Christmas and being told that it had all been thrown away. While I sip my espresso, I stare at the carton of milk beside Peter's bowl. Fresh from the papal pastures at Castel Gandolfo. The first pangs of reality are returning. I wonder if Leo has tracked down Simon. The distant sound of church bells means it's half past seven. Two and a half hours until our meeting with Mignatto.

"Can I go kick with the boys?" Peter asks when he finishes his bowl and buses it to the nuns for rinsing.

The pre-seminary boys normally let him join their games of pickup soccer, a perk of being the teacher's son, but Peter doesn't seem to realize how early it is.

"There's somewhere we need to go," I say. "We can kick the ball together on the way."

BELOW THE PALACE, IN the flower beds shaped like John Paul's coat of arms, teams of papal landscapers are at work early, trying to finish before the midday sun. The head gardener, who has kids himself, smiles to see us dribble down the steep paths. It's a cruel place to teach a boy soccer. The grade is so steep that on stormy days the stairs that connect the paths become waterfalls. Learning to control a ball here is like learning to swim by treading upstream in the Tiber. But Peter is stubborn, and like his uncle he seems to prefer his foes implacable. After months of losing the war against gravity, and chasing runaway balls down to the foot of the basilica, he is now able to hop down the slope on one foot, tapping the ball with the other to slow its momentum. His facility makes another gardener give a hand gesture meaning "excellent." Soccer is the other thing we all have in common here.

"Where are we going?" Peter asks, buoyant.

But when I point at the building, he groans.

The museums don't open until nine, but since Vatican offices open at eight in order to close for the day by one, I have only half an hour to see the exhibit in private before the curators show up. I need that time to prepare myself for Mignatto's questions.

The main doors are locked. So are the doors from the curators' quarters, which are also guarded. But Ugo showed me a convoluted back way, down to the art restorers' underground laboratories, around a bend, then back up through a service elevator. Soon Peter and I are traveling down a line of galleries I didn't see yesterday. He's immediately mesmerized by the sight of an empty boom lift that has been used to hang a giant painting of the Deposition. Nearby is an even bigger canvas, wide enough to block a highway underpass, showing the disciples staring at

Jesus' shroud in an empty burial cave. Gospel verses are stenciled on the wall here, parts of them in bold, and something catches my eye.

Mark 15:46: Joseph **bought a linen shroud**, and taking Jesus down, **wrapped him in the linen shroud**.

Matthew 27:59: Joseph took the body, and wrapped it in **a clean linen shroud**.

Luke 23:53: Joseph took the body of Jesus down and wrapped it in **a linen shroud**.

Then an extraordinary finale. The sight of it stops me midstep. This is surely the first time any such idea has ever been advanced in the pope's museums. Across the gallery is a huge reproduction from the Diatessaron page describing Jesus' death and burial. The smudges have been removed, so the full Greek text is visible, but a haze remains, showing that the Alogi censored John's version of events. It is here, far from the other gospel citations, that John's text is stenciled on the wall. Ugo has separated the black sheep of the gospels from the other three. And to drive home the point, he has bolded very different words:

John 19:38–40: So Joseph came and took away Jesus' body. **Nicodemus also**, who had at first come to him by night, came bringing **a mixture of myrrh and aloes, about a hundred pounds' weight**. They took the body of Jesus, and bound it in **linen cloths** with the spices, as is the burial custom of the Jews.

I'm caught by surprise. Ugo has taken our gospel lessons and mounted them for the world to see. Everything he highlighted in John's version shows how John is different from the other gospels. How the other three speak in unison while John is hard to square with the rest. Ugo has also made a brazen point by mounting this page from the Diatessaron: he seems to be saying that even nineteen centuries ago, in the time of the Alogi, Christians knew John was not quite writing history.

This makes me deeply uncomfortable. Ugo was supposed to be working on the history of the Shroud. I thought our gospel lessons were building toward something else, some theory of how the Shroud left Jerusalem for Edessa. What I see here is far more controversial. The Church believes that some minds aren't ready to be exposed to some ideas. What's good for the shepherd may not be good for the flock. Lay Catholics, lacking scriptural training, may leave this gallery with the impression that John is a second-class gospel or should be thrown out entirely for changing the facts. Everything Ugo has mounted here is technically correct, but he's taken a huge risk by displaying it so publicly and leaving the viewer to draw his own inference.

I lead Peter quickly through the galleries we saw yesterday. We have only twenty minutes to see what else Ugo has in store.

Finally we reach an area almost at the end of the museums, where the galleries feed into the Sistine Chapel. Before us hangs a sheet of black plastic, thick as canvas, covering the next entryway. Peter hugs his soccer ball defensively. He peers into the darkness beyond the curtain as if it's the closet where he huddled with Sister Helena.

I pull back the sheet. The air has a claylike smell. Long sets of make-shift walls have been raised in front of the windows, blocking the natural light. The floor is white with dust. Something's wrong. The exhibit opens in three days, but the preparations seem to stop right here.

All around us are ornate display cases that seem to have been treated no better than sawhorses. The glass tops are floured with particles of drywall mud. Electrical cords are coiled on them. I swipe my hand across the surface and see a manuscript by Evagrius Scholasticus, a Christian historian who lived two hundred years before Charlemagne. The page in front of me tells how Edessa was attacked by a Persian army but was saved by its miraculous image of Jesus. Beside him is Bishop Eusebius, the father of Church history, writing in 300 AD, who says he's been to the archives of Edessa himself and has seen the letters Jesus traded with the city's king. Peter, noticing that the texts are in Greek, lights up. "Those words are *long!*" he says.

Each page looks like an endless string of letters because these manu-scripts were written before the invention of spaces between words. They are mystical, mystifying documents, so old that the world reflected in them is unlike ours and reminiscent of the world of the gospels instead. Mysterious things seem commonplace. The boundaries of history, fan-tasy, and hearsay are muddy. But Ugo's point is clear: by a very early date, intellectuals across the Christian East had heard of a powerful relic in Edessa that originated in Jesus himself.

I look around for some sign of what happened here. Of why nothing's been finished. The net impression is that the exhibit underwent a sudden change. The individual parts are familiar, but the thrust is different and strange.

"Come on," I say, waving Peter toward the next hall, hoping to find it in better shape.

But a display case has been pushed into the entryway, as if the workmen were unsure which gallery it was meant for. Inside the case is a small, unimpressive manuscript that records a sermon given a thousand years ago. The occasion for the sermon is a miraculous rescue: a Byzantine army marched to the gates of Edessa, seized the mystical image of Christ from Muslim hands, and carried it eight hundred miles across the Turkish highlands and desert before leading it triumphantly into the Orthodox capital of Constantinople.

I pause and look more carefully. This isn't what I thought Ugo had discovered. This sermon was given in 944 AD, long before the Crusades. Which means we Catholics didn't rescue the Shroud from Edessa. Before the first Catholic knight ever went crusading, the Orthodox had already rescued it and moved it out of Edessa. So then, how did *we* get it?

The next gallery is the end of the line. The walls are painted dark gray, but as my eyes adjust, I notice shapes. Glossy silhouettes of ships and armies, domes and steeples. An ancient city skyline at night, painted in a dozen shades of black. There's nothing else but a single, small display case, and behind it a pair of doors that lead to the next corridor. When Peter rushes forward to test the doors, he finds them locked. Perhaps the Diatessaron is being kept back there. I turn back toward the display case. Inside is a solitary sheet of parchment, written in Greek, with a regal-looking red seal. It is dated 1205 AD.

A knot forms in my stomach. This is out of sequence. Ugo's Latin manuscripts, two galleries earlier, were older than this parchment. The Greek manuscripts I just saw were *far* older. 1205 reverses direction. Ugo must be introducing something new. A different line of argument. And 1205 hovers uncomfortably close to an event in Eastern history that this exhibit must never, ever invoke.

The placard beside the parchment says I'm looking at a document from the Vatican Secret Archives. A letter sent to the pope by the Byzantine imperial family.

An ache travels through my body. There's only one reason the Eastern emperor would've written the pope in 1205.

Words flit by under my eyes. *Thieves. Relics. Unforgivable.* I'm filled by a leaden sensation that makes it impossible to turn away. This can't be.

Finally my eyes find the lines that must've thrilled Ugo when he first discovered this letter, and horrified him when Simon explained what they meant.

> *They stole the most sacred relic of all. The linen cloth in which our Lord Jesus was wrapped after his death.*

I recognize the image on the wall now. I understand why Ugo had it painted black. *This* is why Ugo was concerned about the Crusades. *This* is how we got the Shroud. We didn't rescue it from Edessa. We stole it from Constantinople.

1204 IS THE DARKEST year in the history between the Catholic and Orthodox Churches. Far darker than the year of our schism, a century and a half earlier. In 1204, Catholic knights sailed for the Holy Land, bound for the Fourth Crusade. But they stopped first, on their way, in Constantinople. Their intention was to combine forces with the Christian armies of the East, to join their Orthodox brethren in the greatest of all religious wars. But what they found in the Orthodox capital was unlike anything they had seen in the Catholic West. Constantinople was then the stronghold of Christendom. Ever since the fall of Rome it had been the protector of all Europe. Not once had its walls been conquered by barbarian invaders, so within those walls lay a thousand years of unspoiled wealth. Treasures from the ancient world, side by side with the greatest collection of Christian relics that has ever existed on earth.

In the West, meantime, it had been eight centuries since the fall of ancient Rome, eight centuries of barbarian invasions and foreign overlords and chaos. We Catholics were poor. We were hungry. We were weary. We owed money on the ships we sailed in and couldn't afford the contract on our own holy war. Seeing the riches of the Orthodox capital,

Catholic knights made the greatest mistake in the thousand-year schism between our Churches.

Instead of sailing to the Holy Land, they attacked Constantinople. They raped Orthodox women and killed Orthodox priests. They put fellow Christians to the sword and burned whole swaths of the city, erasing the magnificent library of Constantinople off the face of the earth. In Hagia Sophia, the Saint Peter's of the East, Catholics put a prostitute on the throne. And when the emperor couldn't pay the huge ransom we demanded as the price of his city's freedom—not even by melting his gold—we broke into Orthodox churches and looted his city's relics.

The combined treasures of all Western churches today are only a pale reflection of what lay in those reliquaries. For centuries the oldest Christian cities of the East had sent their most precious objects to Constantinople for protection from our enemies. Imperial armies safeguarded them and patriarchs called on God to protect them. Byzantine civilization itself became a life-support system for the massive religious treasury at its heart. Which we Catholics now proceeded to pillage.

That is the skyline on this gallery wall. Constantinople in the endless darkness of 1204.

Western Catholics today don't understand the permanence of this wound. But another moment in history illustrates it well. Two and a half centuries later, long after Catholics had come and gone from Constantinople, Muslim armies arrived in their place. Orthodox bishops, faced with the extinction of their civilization, were forced to ask for help. They traveled west and negotiated a humiliating pact with the pope. But when they returned home, their own flock threw them out. The ordinary men and women of the Orthodox Church had made their choice. They would rather die at the hands of Muslims than owe their lives to Catholics.

So Constantinople fell. Istanbul was born. And to this day, if you asked an Orthodox what sealed the split between our two Churches, he would grit his teeth and say, with the knife still jiggling in his back: 1204.

The letter before my eyes resurrects the horror of that year. Ugo has discovered the most damning fact I can imagine. It's no longer a mystery how the Shroud arrived in medieval France. It's no longer a mystery why it seemed to have no past. We Catholics had every reason to forget where it came from. Because we stole it from the Orthodox.

I am speechless that Ugo had the audacity to mount such a thing on these walls, under the pope's own roof. It is a shocking confession of Catholic sin. Though no one can be more familiar than I am with Ugo's allegiance to the truth, and his insistence on presenting the facts at any cost, even I am stunned. If ever there was time to paper over a discovery and hew to a respectful silence, surely it was now. I wish that I could be moved by Ugo's bravery. Instead I am shocked by his indifference to the cost.

A single thought bubbles up from my emotions. I have misunderstood everything. The Secretariat wouldn't have tried to silence a discovery like this. The Secretariat would've encouraged it. If Simon invited Orthodox priests into this hall, the same way my father invited Orthodox to Turin sixteen years ago, it would only accomplish what Cardinal Boia has tried to do since becoming Secretary of State: set back our relations with the Orthodox Church by half a century. Thousands of Christians have lost their lives over the hatreds born in 1204. Now Ugo makes one more.

So this is why Simon refuses to talk. Here is the secret he values more than his own priesthood. The unfinished galleries tell the story. No wonder Ugo's work came to a halt. No wonder he didn't give Lucio his final notes to finish the exhibit. Yet Lucio gave Simon the power to finish Ugo's exhibit, the power to change what was mounted in these halls, and I found him working in an entirely different branch of the museum. How could he have let this remain?

I feel Peter tugging at my cassock. But I can't speak. Instead I kneel and hold him and try to collect myself.

"Is it time?" he says. "Can we go?"

I nod and whisper, "Yes. It's time."

He reaches down and grabs my hand. He tugs and tugs, pulling me up. "What are we going to do now?"

I don't know. I simply do not know.

CHAPTER 19

MIGNATTO'S OFFICE LIES across the Tiber River, at Via di Monserrato 149. We pass a dozen churches, a pontifical seminary, and a handful of Renaissance buildings marked with plaques identifying the former homes of saints. The apartments here are owned by the Church and rented cheap to papal employees, so that even by Roman standards, Mignatto's neighborhood is a virtual extension of the Vatican.

We are early, but I don't know where else to go. Peter and I sit on the steps of a church and try calling Simon's mobile, but he doesn't answer. If the phone is on, the battery will die by tonight. If it's off, Simon has already made his choice. His silence is total.

"I want to go home," Peter says.

Home. What home?

I lift him into my lap and say, "Peter, I'm sorry."

He nods.

"This is going to be a hard time," I tell him. "But we're going to get through it."

Ugo's discovery must be part of the case against Simon. Any Orthodox priests he invited to the exhibit will be aghast and outraged, so no one stands to be more humiliated than my brother. The half-finished exhibit halls even lend themselves to the idea that Ugo was killed to stop the secret from coming out. The threats Michael and I received contain an echo of this, too.

Tell us what Nogara was hiding.

Strange feelings skate through me. Thoughts of Mona. Pangs of loss with no object or cause, as if the experience of losing my wife has been reattached to the dread of losing my brother.

"Monsignor Mignatto can help us," I say. "Let's go find him."

Peter counteroffers, "Can we see Simon instead?"

"Maybe tomorrow, Pete."

He rolls the soccer ball ahead of him on the cobblestone street and practices his Marseille turn, the dribbling move he imagined Simon would help him perfect. "Okay," he says. He practices the move again and again. "Maybe tomorrow," he repeats.

There is a trace of disappointment in his voice. But only a trace. Life has taught this boy to string nets beneath his hopes.

WHEN WE REACH 149, Peter pushes the button, and Mignatto buzzes us to the top floor. "You're early, Father," he begins. Then he sees Peter in tow, and with the slightest hitch he says, "But please. Both of you. Come in."

The office turns out to be a room in his small apartment. There's no money in canon law, and men in his position often moonlight as professors at pontifical universities or editors of Church journals, finding dignity in the priestly middle class.

The office itself is spare but handsome. The oriental carpet, though thinning, shows signs of its former elegance. Most of the atmosphere is supplied by shelves of legal texts and by Mignatto's desk, a burl-wood table with rococo legs that may be a bona fide antique. It holds the compulsory photo of Mignatto with John Paul. Both are much younger men.

"Is there a room where Peter could play while we talk?" I ask.

The edges of Mignatto's cheeks flush. "Of course," he says.

When he leads Peter across the hall, I realize how I've embarrassed him. The kitchen isn't large enough for a table and chair, and the only other room is his bedroom. Its furnishings are stark: a crucifix over the bed, and a tiny TV on a narrow table with a single placemat.

"May he watch the television?" Mignatto asks.

"How many channels do you get?" Peter asks innocently.

The monsignor hands him the remote control and says, "Only the ones that come over the antenna."

WHEN WE'RE ALONE IN his office, I say, "Monsignor, I was just at the museums. There's something you need to know about Ugo's exhibit."

I explain everything—the unfinished galleries and the discovery that's about to upend the whole question of who owns the Shroud.

"I was wrong," I tell him. "The Secretariat can't be trying to stop the exhibit. If anything, they'd be trying to make the show go on."

Darkly, Mignatto says, "Then we've found your brother's motive."

"No. He would never have killed Ugo."

The monsignor weaves his head back and forth, balancing facts on either side. "His Eminence," he says, meaning Lucio, "has informed me that Orthodox relations are your brother's fixation."

"But Ugo would've done anything for my brother. All Simon had to do was ask."

Now that I say it, I wonder if that's exactly what happened. Ugo tried to contact me about what he'd found. But he would've gone to Simon first. And if Simon begged him to keep quiet, then the result might've been the galleries he left unfinished and the Secretariat's sudden interest in the reason for his change of heart.

Mignatto makes a long note, then slips it into a folder. "We'll need to return to this later," he says. "First I need to ask you some important questions. Above all, I haven't heard a word about your brother's location. Have you?"

"No. But I have someone working on it. How long do we have?"

"If this were an ordinary trial we would have weeks, months. But this is developing with astonishing speed. I hope we'll have at least a week." To my surprise, he smiles. "Since there have been some *developments* since last night."

He pauses to reach into a stack of papers, and I hang on his words. I'm eager for good news but anxious that what appeared as such yesterday is already proving otherwise.

Mignatto hands me an open envelope. "Your brother's Secretariat file is mentioned in the libellus, but I never received a copy with my *acta causae*, so I petitioned for one. An hour ago, this came by courier." He waves me on. "Go ahead and look. As procurator, you may see it."

Inside is a single sheet of stationery.

Reverend and Dear Monsignor Mignatto,

It is my pleasure to confirm receipt of your request for the personnel file of Rev. Simon Andreou. At this time, however, the information you requested cannot be found in the general records of the Secretariat of State, and is therefore unavailable.

With every good wish, I remain,
Yours devotedly in the Lord,

+ Stefano Annibale

I turn the page over for something more. "I don't understand."

"The file is missing."

"How is that possible?"

"It's not. Someone doesn't want it to be seen."

I slam the paper on his desk. "How are we supposed to make a defense without seeing the evidence?"

Mignatto lifts a finger of caution. "If the file's gone, the judges can't see it either."

"But what if the personnel file could help Simon?"

Mignatto rolls an old fountain pen across his lips. "I asked myself the same question. Until I received a phone call twenty minutes ago from the tribunal clerk. It seems your brother's file isn't the only piece of evidence that's gone missing."

His eyes sparkle as he slides a copy of the libellus toward me. His middle finger is glued to one line in the list of evidence.

"You're kidding," I say.

With a flourish of his other hand, Mignatto says, "No more surveillance video."

My eyes hang on the printed words. A giddy feeling stirs inside me.

"I can't tell you how concerned I've been about that video," the monsignor continues. "Any detail contradicting your brother's testimony would be damning."

"So where's the footage?"

"They're looking for it, of course. Somewhere between Castel Gandolfo and here it took a detour." His eyebrows rise, as if waiting for my reaction.

"This is good news, right?" I say tentatively.

He chuckles. "Oh, I would say so."

Then the smile dims. His eyes sharpen.

"Father, I want to suggest something to you. And I need to know your honest reaction."

"Of course."

"I think your brother has a friend on high. A guardian angel. He's being protected by someone who has access to the evidence."

"Who?"

"You tell me. It's extremely important that I know who our friends are."

"I don't even know who could *do* something like this."

Mignatto tugs at his earlobe, waiting.

"You think my uncle did it?"

"Did he?"

I'm speechless.

"Don't the groundskeepers at Castel Gandolfo report to him?" Mignatto prods.

"Maybe. But he couldn't make a file disappear from the Secretariat. And you saw the condition he was in last night."

The monsignor shrugs, as if my uncle is a clever man. "Food for thought."

I glance at the libellus. With the video footage gone and the personnel file missing, the case against Simon has shrunk dramatically. Two-thirds of the direct evidence has evaporated.

"Is there still grounds for a trial?" I ask.

Mignatto becomes more solemn. "Unfortunately, not all the developments since last night are positive. You probably remember that the libellus mentions a voice message left at the nunciature by Nogara. I haven't heard the message yet, but the promoter of justice—the prosecutor—feels it's an important part of the evidence against your brother."

"Why haven't you heard it yet?"

"Because I've petitioned the court for forensic verification that it was really left by Nogara."

"What does that mean?"

"It means I'm trying to win us a few more days of preparation time. The message probably *was* left by Nogara, but—"

"If the message is really from Ugo, then there's nothing to worry about. Ugo and Simon were close friends."

Mignatto frowns. "Father, there's something irregular about this piece of evidence that suggests to me a certain attitude of caution."

"What is it?"

The monsignor runs his thumbs along the inner edge of the desk surface. For a second, his eyes leave mine. "Nogara left your brother the voice mail on his bedroom phone at the embassy. Somehow a recording of the voice mail was made. It appears someone was tapping your brother's phone."

I feel myself go hot. "Monsignor . . ."

"I realize," Mignatto continues quickly, "this might strengthen your feeling that your brother was somehow targeted. But I want to warn you against premature conclusions. I don't pretend to understand how the Secretariat operates, but recordings like this may be routine. We both know that in practice Secretariat priests rarely talk over an open line and seem to have little expectation of privacy. There's no reason to worry ourselves over this until we have more information."

"Monsignor, you have to make the judges throw out the voice mail. There has to be a rule against stolen evidence."

"It may not have been stolen. Secretariat phones are property of the nunciature, as may have been the voice mail system or answering machine where the message was left. Regardless, the fact is that the judges have already ruled on this. They will accept the message."

I'm taken aback. "Why?"

Mignatto presses his hands downward through the air, asking for a détente. "Please," he says, "try to remember that this isn't civil law. In our inquisitorial system, the highest good is not protection of the accused's rights but pursuit of truth. Information with probative value, even if illegally obtained, must be considered by the tribunal."

"So then," I fume, "what else can they do to Simon? Anything they want? You still think all of this is fair and normal?"

"It *is* fair. And no murder trial in a canonical court is normal."

"Then who made the recording?"

"I assure you I'm trying to find out."

Michael said that before he was beaten up, he was followed to the airport by priests who had come from the nunciature. Too many threads lead back to the Secretariat.

"Please," Mignatto says, pushing forward, "leave this to me. For now, there's one other point we need to discuss. As I mentioned to you last night, the defense may suggest deponents, even though the tribunal isn't required to hear their testimony. Since your brother's priesthood is at risk, I hope to convince the judges that they should accept character witnesses. It would help me if you could provide a list of candidates. The more impressive, the better."

Immediately I say, "Michael Black."

He brandishes a pen. "Say again?"

"Father Michael Black."

"My advice is that these witnesses should be at least bishops."

"He's not a character witness. He was threatened by the same people. They beat him up." I slip the photo out of my wallet and hand it to him.

Mignatto studies the picture gravely. "Where is this man now? I need to speak to him."

"He works at the same nunciature as Simon, but he's laying low."

"How do I reach him?"

I have Michael's mobile number, but if Mignatto calls him directly, Michael will take it as a breach of trust.

"Let me talk to him first," I say.

He told his attackers where to find my spare key. He owes me much more than a call on a pay phone.

"If Black's going to be deposed, we need him in Rome as soon as possible."

"I'll make it happen."

He nods, and his acquiescence soothes my nerves. The sight of Michael's injuries seems to have made him less hostile to my concerns. We run through a short list of character witnesses whom Mignatto appears to have been sent by Diego, but my mind remains on Michael. With testimony from him, the gendarmes might reevaluate the break-in. In which case, one more piece of proof might be all the court needs.

"Monsignor," I say, "there's something else I need to tell you. I think Peter saw the man who broke into our apartment."

His expression changes. The last of his cheer fades. "You talked to him about it?"

There is the faintest innuendo, almost a warning, about Peter's having remembered such a convenient thing.

"I haven't said a word to him," I say. "You asked me to talk to my housekeeper, and it came up."

Mignatto frowns. "Your son is just a boy. We shouldn't make him dredge up the whole thing." He tries to smile benevolently. "The defense is coming together well enough for now, but I appreciate your mentioning this."

I suddenly feel awkward. Silence falls.

Mignatto shuffles his papers. "Well," he says, "keep working on tracking down your brother. Call me right away when you hear something."

I'm caught off guard. He's already coming around the desk to see me off.

"I will, Monsignor. Thank you."

As I go to collect Peter, I feel Mignatto watching me. Sizing me up somehow. Then at the door, he says something no human being has ever said to me before.

"Your uncle was the cleverest man in seminary. And you remind me very much of him."

"I do?"

He clasps my hand between his. "But listen to me. Please. From now on, both of you must leave the work to me."

CHAPTER 20

I TAKE PETER TO the park so he can distract himself while I try to process the news. I wonder if Mignatto understands how important Ugo's discovery is. How much it will damage our affairs with the Orthodox. I think back to the first conversation Simon and I had with Lucio after Ugo died—and for the life of me I can't understand my brother's behavior. He insisted that the exhibit not be changed. That the Diatessaron not replace the Shroud as the main event. Yet an exhibit on the Diatessaron would've solved all his problems. It would've hidden the truth about 1204 and made it possible to drag a horde of Orthodox priests through the galleries without offending anyone. Not even when Lucio gave Simon the power to finish the exhibit did my brother dismantle the last gallery. All it would've taken was a few display cases moved and a little whitewashing of the walls. The whole finale could've been erased.

I watch Peter climb a tree. He perches in the crook of a limb and sits back. When he sees that I'm watching, he smiles and waves. I wonder what inspired Mignatto to say that I resembled my uncle. Whether it was my willingness to ask Peter to identify the man who terrorized him.

We take a roundabout way back to Lucio's palace, stopping by the pre-seminary to let Peter play with the boys stranded there during the dead week between summer and fall terms. While they start a game of pickup soccer in the dirt outside their dorm, I leave a note for Father Vitari, the pre-seminary rector, explaining that a family situation may affect my availability. I have a good rapport with the boys, so the administrators will indulge me.

Just as I return, one of the boys steps forward. It looks like he's been waiting for me.

"Father," he says, "we have a question to ask you."

The teachers call him Giorgio the Vain. His curly black hair droops around his ears like bunches of wet grapes. He's related to a Vatican bishop, so he puts himself above the rest of his classmates.

"Yes?" I say.

The other boys have tensed up. Some are looking at their shoes. One of them elbows Giorgio, but he ignores it.

"Is it true, Father Andreou?" Giorgio asks. "About your brother?"

I clench my teeth. My skin suddenly tingles. "Where did you hear about that?"

Giorgio makes pistols out of his hands and waves them, gesturing at the whole group of students. "Everyone's heard. We want to know if it's true."

Peter glances around, wondering what the silence means. I have to contain this before it spreads. With a look, I beg them not to say more. Peter's heart is in their hands.

The biggest boy, a gentle brute named Scipio, leans forward and casts a shadow over Giorgio. The other boys glance at each other and seem to consent to keep quiet. But their eyes are eager. Giorgio wasn't lying. They want to know.

I have a covenant with my pupils. I teach hard truths about sacred texts, and I don't sugarcoat or water down. Honesty is our currency here.

But they are children. I can't talk to them about Simon.

"I'm sorry. This isn't something we can discuss."

Yet they wait. I'm the priest they talk to about video games and girlfriends. About the older sister who almost died in a car accident this spring and the little cousin who has been dying of birth defects. If they're allowed to ask if Jesus really walked on water, if the pope is really infallible, then surely they can ask this.

"It's very personal," I say. "Not appropriate."

Giorgio snorts, "So then it must be true."

I realize the crossroads we've come to. These boys come from all over Italy to live inside the Vatican walls, to serve Mass in the pope's basilica.

But what I say right now, in the dirt beside this dormitory, may be what they remember best.

"Sit down," I say to Giorgio.

Giorgio hesitates.

"Please," I say.

He lowers himself to the ground.

"All of you," I say. "Sit."

My thoughts race forward, raising a frame in my mind. The shape of what I will say. I know the message. I ache to say it. The question is how.

"A man is on trial," I start. "He's accused of something terrible. There are witnesses who say he did it, but the man won't say a word. Won't lift a finger to defend himself. So his closest friends lose faith. They abandon him."

I let the words settle.

"You all know that story," I say. "It's the story of Jesus' trial."

A few nod.

"The man in that trial," I say. "Was he innocent?"

"Yes," the boys all respond.

"And no matter what anyone tells me about that man, I know the truth. I know how I feel about him. And nothing can ever change that, no matter what kind of evidence people say they have."

This is my most naked answer. I will believe in Simon always. To the end, against all proofs and verdicts.

But I have an obligation to these boys. Telling them what *I* believe isn't enough.

"Is that why your parents sent you to this pre-seminary, though?" I say. "To find out what *I* think? Or was it to learn how to think for yourselves?"

Deep feelings push up from the bottom of my throat.

"If you're going to believe what other people tell you," I say, "then don't become priests. Nobody needs priests like that. *You* have to be the judge. People lie. People disagree. People make mistakes. To find out the truth, you have to know how to search for it."

My shaky delivery, my barely disguised emotion, has captivated them. They're really listening now. I know what direction I need to take. It's been hovering in my thoughts for days. But not until this moment has it seemed so clear.

"A long time ago," I say, "our Church used to have a fifth gospel. The Diatessaron. Its title is Greek for 'made of four,' because that's how it was written. The author wove together the four gospels into one story. And because of that, the Diatessaron has one great weakness. Do you know what it is?"

I can feel Ugo beside me now. We are staring at the pages of the ancient manuscript.

"Its weakness," I say, "is that the four gospels don't always agree. Matthew tells us that Jesus did ten mighty deeds. Ten miracles in a row. But Mark says Jesus didn't do those ten things in a row; Jesus did them at different times, in different places. So which gospel do we believe?"

No boy dares raise his hand.

"I want you to stop and think for yourself," I say. "I want *you* to answer this. But I'll help you get there. Name one other famous Jewish leader who did ten miracles in a row."

A boy in front—Bruno, who will make a great priest someday—murmurs, "Moses did the ten plagues."

"Correct. Now, what does Moses have to do with Jesus? Why would the gospel of Matthew change the order of the facts so that Jesus reminds us of Moses?"

There are no takers. They can't feel it yet, but the momentum is building.

"Then remember," I say, "that one of Jesus' ten miracles was to calm a storm at sea. And that his disciples asked, 'What sort of man is this, who even the winds and sea obey?' Remind you of anything Moses did?"

"Parting the Red Sea," says Giorgio, not to be outdone by Bruno.

"Now we're getting somewhere. Now we're getting past *what* Matthew says and asking ourselves *why* Matthew says it. I'll give you another clue. Matthew also says that when Jesus was a baby, a king named Herod tried to kill him by slaughtering all the infants in Bethlehem. Now, where have we heard a story like that before? A king murdering all the Jewish babies?"

The connection is starting to form in their minds. As it dawns on them, they find the courage to make eye contact with me.

"Pharaoh did that," says a new boy, "in the Moses story."

I nod. "So once again, we have Matthew making Jesus' life sound like Moses' life. Does any other gospel agree with Matthew about these things? No. But Matthew wants to teach us something. Think of who Moses was: a special Jewish leader who saw God face-to-face on Mount Sinai and came back down with the Ten Commandments. The man who gave us the tablets of the law."

With that, the dam breaks. At the same time, two or three boys make the leap. "Moses brought the *old* law," one says. "Jesus brought the *new* law."

"This is one of the most important things Matthew teaches us about Jesus: that Jesus is the new Moses, the even-greater-than-Moses. When Jesus delivers the new law, where does it happen? Where does Jesus say, 'Blessed are the meek,' 'Blessed are the merciful,' 'Blessed are the peacemakers'? Where does he say, 'Turn the other cheek,' and 'Love your enemies,' and 'I have come not to abolish the law but to fulfill it'? It all happens in one sermon, which we know as the Sermon on the Mount because Matthew tells us Jesus gave it on a mountain. *The same place God gave the tablets of the old law to Moses.* No other gospel agrees with Matthew. Luke says Jesus gave that same sermon in a plain. But Matthew had his reasons. Every single one of the gospels has its reasons.

"Which brings us back to the problem we started with. What would you do if you were writing the Diatessaron? If you had to combine all four gospels into one narrative, which gospel version of the story would you choose? Would you say Jesus really performed those ten miracles in a row? Or at different times, in different places? Would you say he delivered his sermon on a mountain or in a plain?"

Their eyes seem to shimmer with the newness of these ideas. I am, for this brief moment, a magician. But we will put that to the test.

"That's why," I continue, "the Diatessaron failed: because when we weave the four gospels together, we create something different. We lose the truth that exists separately in each gospel's account. In other words, witnesses have their own ideas. Their own motives. And not everything you hear or read is really fact. The Church has something to say about this, too. Under Church law, can you guess what a judge is supposed to do when the witnesses disagree? Do you think he's supposed to mix their testimony together?"

The boys, swept up in the logic, all shake their heads without thinking.

"Of course not," I say. "That would obviously be a mistake. So what does canon law tell the judge to do? Take each piece of information on its own merits and use good judgment to figure out where the truth is. You mustn't take everything you hear at face value." I do my best not to glare at Giorgio. "And you must never believe rumors that assume the worst about a good person. Because as the gospels teach us, we might condemn an innocent man."

I punctuate this sentence with a meaningful look. There may be some younger boys who don't understand what I'm talking about, but the older boys know. Some look chastened. Others nod as if they accept the point. Then, suddenly, Peter begins to cry.

Giorgio is sitting beside him, and my first instinct is that Giorgio has said something upsetting.

As Peter rushes toward me, bawling, I pick him up and say, "What did he tell you? What's wrong?"

But just as I prepare to turn on Giorgio, I see something in the distance. Far off, down the path, is a lone figure. Motionless, almost hidden behind a statue in the garden. She's watching us.

I freeze. As I hold Peter in my arms, I watch her cover her mouth with her hands.

She followed us here. She couldn't help herself. Finally being so close, she needed a glimpse of her son.

In a thin voice I say, "That's enough, boys. Please, go back to your rooms right now."

Some of them turn to look, wondering what's caught my attention. But Bruno marshals them away. One by one they retreat back to the dorm.

I'm trying to understand what Mona has done. How she made Peter cry. I'm stunned that she broke the agreement we made.

Peter's eyes are wide and glassy. He whispers something in my ear. At first I can't make sense of it.

"What's wrong?" I say. "What happened?"

He's breathing hard. The words are ragged.

"Giorgio said Simon is in jail."

I look up. Giorgio is already gone.

"That's not true," I say to Peter. I squeeze him, as if I can force the poison out. "Giorgio doesn't know what he's talking about."

But Peter cries into my ear, *"Giorgio says Simon is a killer."*

"He's lying, Peter," I say. "You know that isn't true."

Mona drifts closer to us as the boys disappear. Her face is anguished. She can see that Peter's crying.

I wave her away, but she's already stopped. She knows.

"Ignore Giorgio," I whisper to Peter. "He was just trying to upset you."

"I want to see Simon."

I nuzzle him with my forehead. "We can't."

"Why not?"

"Do you remember what he said before he left? What you promised him?"

Peter nods, but he's miserable.

Even as I hold him, I imagine my altar boys back in their dorm, spreading the news. I wonder how many people in this country have heard.

Mona is a hundred feet off, still watching. I should be angry with her. She shouldn't be here; we made that decision together. But I understand the compulsion that brought her here. For a moment we stare at each other over Peter's shoulder. She hovers on the hilltop like a vision. But then she raises a hand in the air, telling me that she's leaving.

I prop Peter up and offer to take him for an Orange Fanta. It's safer to go somewhere outside the walls than to risk staying here. Anyone we run into might know about Simon.

But Peter says, "Prozio has Orange Fanta. I want to go back to the palace."

Lucio's apartments. At his age, the place I dreaded most.

"You're sure? You don't want to go somewhere else?"

He shakes his head. "I want to play cards with Diego."

He wraps his arms around my hips and squeezes.

"All right. Then that's where we'll go."

He collects his soccer ball from under a bush to bring it home. Like all his toys, he has written his name all over it, for fear of losing it. He has no idea the confusion I feel. The inversion of everything I've known for so long. Mona so close by, and Simon so far.

"Let's go," I say, pointing to Lucio's palace on the hill. "I'll race you there."

CHAPTER 21

THE WONDERS OF a child's mind. Once Peter is engrossed in a game of scopa with Diego, Giorgio becomes a distant memory.

"Where is Simon really, Babbo?" he asks, just once, never moving his eyes from his cards.

"Talking to some people about Mister Nogara's exhibit," I say.

Peter nods as if this sounds important. "Diego," he says, "can you deal again?"

While they play, I call Leo to see if he's heard anything about Simon. There's something in his voice when he answers, "Give me an hour. I think we're onto something." While I wait, an idea comes to me. I decide to slip inside Simon's bedroom and see what he left behind.

The room is almost bare. The dresser and desktop are empty. His wallet and mobile phone were probably on him when he was taken away. Father's old garment bag hangs alone in the closet. A note pinned to it in Diego's hand tells Simon that he left it in the car-service sedan that drove him from the airport. My brother doesn't seem to have touched it, but in one of the small outer pockets of the bag, I find a little brown booklet with a golden emblem of the papal tiara and keys. Below are the words PASSEPORT DIPLOMATIQUE. I open the cover.

On the right-hand page is a passport photo of Simon in his cassock. Stamped in red are the words SEGRETERIA DI STATO—RAPPORTI CON GLI STATI. *Secretariat of State—Relations with States.* My eyes skip to the handwritten calligraphy in Latin.

*The Reverend Simon Andreou, Secretary Second Class, Secretariat of
State. This passport is valid for five years until the day June 1, 2005.*

The bottom is signed by the Secretary of State: *D. Card. Boia.*

I fan the pages forward to the visa section, the entry and exit stamps.
No surprises here. Bulgaria, Turkey, and Italy. Nowhere else. Even the
dates match up to visits I recall.

I keep fishing. Zipped into one of the inner plastic pockets of the
garment bag is Simon's day planner. Tucked inside it is an envelope addressed to Simon in familiar handwriting. The postmark is three weeks
ago. Ugo mailed this to Simon at the nunciature just a few days before
he wrote his final e-mail to me.

The letter is written on a sheet of homily paper—stationery with
an empty column on the left side, where a priest can record the gospel
passages he's preaching on. I gave Ugo a sheaf of this paper as a tool for
comparing verses, and this particular sheet appears to have been used
for that purpose, leaving the impression that Ugo was writing in a rush
and grabbed the first thing at hand. I wonder why.

3 August 2004

Dear Simon,

Mark 14:44–46	*You've been telling me for several weeks now that*
John 18:4–6	*this meeting wouldn't be postponed—not even if*
Matthew 27:32	*you were away on business. Now I realize you were*
John 19:17	*serious. I could tell you I'm ready for it, but I'd be*
Luke 19:35	*lying. For more than a month you've been stealing*
John 12:14–15	*away on these trips—which I know has been hard*
	on you—but you need to understand that I've had
	burdens too. I've been scrambling around to mount
Matthew 26:17	*my exhibit. Changing everything so that you can*
John 19:14	*now pull off this meeting at the Casina will be*
	difficult for me. Yes, I still want to give the keynote.
	But I also feel that doing it compels me to
Mark 15:40–41	*make some grand personal gesture toward the*
	Orthodox. For the past two years I've given

John 19:25–27   *my life to this exhibit. Now you've taken my*
work and given it a much larger audience—which
is wonderful, of course—and yet it gives this
keynote a heavy significance. This will be the
moment when I officially hand my baby over. The
moment when, with a great flourish, I sign my
Matthew 27:48   *life away.*

So, then, I need to share with you what I've
been doing while you were out of town. I hope it
John 19:28–29   *agrees with your agenda for the meeting. First, I've*
taken my gospel lessons from Alex very seriously. I
study scripture morning and night. I've also kept up
my work with the Diatessaron. These two avenues
of investigation, together, have repaid me richly.
Brace yourself, because I'm about to use a word
that, at this late stage in the process, probably
Mark 15:45–46   *horrifies you. I've made a discovery. Yes. What*
I've found erases everything I thought I knew
about the Turin Shroud. It demolishes what we
both expected to be the central message of my
John 19:38–40   *keynote. It might come as a surprise—or even*
as a shock—to the guests you're inviting to the
Luke 24:36–40   *exhibit. For it proves that the Turin Shroud*
John 20:19–20   *has a dark past. The radiocarbon verdict killed*
serious scholarship on the Shroud's history before
1300 AD, but now, as that past comes to light, I
think a small minority of our audience may find the
truth harder to accept than the old idea that the Shroud
Luke 23:46–47   *is a fake. Studying the Diatessaron has taught me what*
a gross misreading we've been guilty of. The same
gross misreading, in fact, that reveals the truth about
the Shroud.

My discovery is outlined in the proof
enclosed here. Please read it carefully, as this is

> what I'll be telling your friends at the Casina. In the
> meantime, I send my best to Michael, who I know
> has become your close follower.

John 19:34   *In friendship,*
              Ugo

The echo of Ugo's voice leaves a dull throb at the bottom of my throat. He's alive in this letter. Excitable; eager; full of anticipation. The final e-mail he sent me was full of urgency and worry, but almost none of that is present here. Simon seems to have removed the proof Ugo mentioned, but what he left behind is enough.

So it's true: Ugo made a dramatic discovery. Oddly, this letter credits it to a combination of my lessons with him and the work Ugo did on the Diatessaron, even though I never knew of any discovery arising from either. Surely what he found was our theft of the Shroud in 1204— though I can't imagine how he ever stumbled across that by comparing gospel verses on sheets of homily paper. Nor does Ugo seem to realize how devastating 1204 would be to his audience, how his enthusiasm for proving the Shroud to be older than the carbon-dating range was coming at the cost of resurrecting a poisonous ancient hatred. I don't have to guess how my brother would've reacted to the news. No wonder Ugo's proof isn't in this envelope anymore. In Simon's shoes I might've been tempted to dispose of it, too. Maybe this is why Ugo sounded so upset in his final e-mail to me, sent only four days later: Simon had just explained to him what a bombshell 1204 was and what a storm it would create if he mounted his discovery. Maybe Ugo wanted a second opinion from an Eastern priest like me.

There are bigger surprises in this letter, too. Michael Black was right: Simon has been inviting Orthodox clergy to Rome. Ugo seems to have been very aware of it—he refers to the trips Simon was taking and the gesture that should be made toward the Orthodox at an upcoming meeting. Strangest of all, there's even a hint in the final lines that he and Simon were joined by Michael in the work they did together. The only contributor to Ugo's exhibit who seems not to have known of these other arrangements was me.

I open the bedroom door and ask Diego if he can look up something for me.

"Daily schedules from the past few weeks," I say. "For the Casina."

The Casina, mentioned in this letter, where Ugo was preparing to deliver a keynote to visiting Orthodox, is a summer house in the middle of the Vatican gardens, a ten-minute walk from my apartment. It was built in the Renaissance as a papal retreat from the Vatican palace, but John Paul rarely uses it, and the building stays vacant other than the occasional meetings of the Pontifical Academy of Sciences. That connection may be a clue about the meeting Ugo is discussing here. The Pontifical Academy is a group of eighty international researchers and theoreticians, including dozens of Nobel laureates, whose stamp of approval on Ugo's exhibit might erase the radiocarbon stigma for good. No one would be better qualified to send the message that today's science has overthrown yesterday's. I could envision Simon inviting Orthodox priests to a meeting of the academy just as reassurance that my father's Turin fiasco was not about to be repeated.

While I wait for Diego to return, I riffle through Simon's day planner. Most of what I see is familiar. Simon's trips to Rome are marked off with black Xs, over which he's written *Alex and Peter!* in red. Michael emphasized Simon's habit of disappearing over the weekends, and sure enough there are weekend meetings penciled here. But the notations tell me nothing. Written slapdash in pencil on the third Saturday in July is *RM—10 AM*. I presume *RM* means "Reverendissimo"—archbishop. But there's no name, no location. The next weekend says *SER 8:45 AM*, which probably means "Sua Eccellenza Reverendissima"—a bishop—but again, no name or place.

Still, one thing gives me pause. At the beginning of the planner, in the directory of my brother's contacts, I find a listing for the nameless archbishop: *RM* it says again. His phone number is odd. It has too many digits to be Turkish. It looks more like an international line.

I punch it into my mobile and wait for someone to answer.

"Bună ziua," comes a man's voice. "Palatul Patriarhiei."

I've spoken to many Turks on the phone. This is not Turkish.

"Parla Italiano?" I say.

No answer.

"Do you speak English?"

"Small. Little."

"What country am I calling right now? Can you tell me where you're located?"

He pauses, and seems about to hang up, when I say, *"Where are you?"*

"București."

"Thank you," I fumble.

I stare at the letters Simon has written in the book: *RM*. They don't mean "Reverendissimo." They mean "Romania." My brother has been doing business with someone in Bucharest.

So *SER* can't be "Sua Eccellenza Reverendissima." It must be—

"Belgrade," says the man who answers the second number I call. *Serbia.*

I can't believe my ears. Romania and Serbia are Orthodox countries. Simon has been reaching out to Orthodox clergy on a scale I didn't imagine. From Turkey and Bulgaria to Romania and Serbia, he has paved a wide path toward Italy that travels through half of Orthodox Eastern Europe. If he has invited a few priests from each of these countries, then he has begun to create a symbolic bridge between the capital cities of our two Churches.

I pull out my wallet and stare at the photo of bloody Michael Black. Just visible behind him is the airport sign I noticed before. PRELUARE BAGAJE. I wonder.

Calling the main offices of Vatican Radio, I ask for a translator on the Slavic Languages desk. An ancient-sounding Jesuit answers. When I explain the situation, he chuckles. "Those words are Romanian, Father. They mean 'baggage claim.'"

So Michael was in Romania. It seems impossible that he could've been helping Simon, and yet the casual way Ugo invokes his name in the final lines—*send my best to Michael*—suggests the three of them were closer than I imagined. *Your close follower,* Ugo called him. I was never able to do more than guess at the reasons for Michael's first change of heart. I wonder if Ugo's research on the Shroud was enough to propel him into another.

I find his number in my call log, but when I dial it, no one answers.

"Michael," I say excitedly into his voice mail. "It's Alex Andreou. Please call me. I need to talk to you about Romania." Remembering what Mignatto asked me, I add, "Simon's in trouble. We need your help. Please, call as soon as you can."

I leave him my number but don't mention that I need him to fly to Rome. It's too soon for that; this is more delicate than I realized. If Michael was working amicably with my brother only weeks ago, then what happened in the airport must've changed everything. Michael seemed so hostile toward Simon on the phone, so quick to point out Simon's responsibility for what the rest of us have suffered since.

Diego returns, holding his laptop like an open book between his hands. "Calendar's up."

I scan the screen. "This is everything? You're sure?"

He nods.

Strange: the Casina has been vacant all summer.

"When's the next meeting of the Pontifical Academy?" I ask.

"A working group is coming next month to discuss international water conflicts," Diego says.

That's long after opening night of Ugo's exhibit.

To be sure, I say, "Do you have the list of attendees?"

"I can get it by tomorrow."

"Thanks, Diego."

Just as he leaves, my phone rings.

Michael, I think.

But the number is local.

"Father Andreou?" says the voice.

Mignatto. He sounds shaken.

"Is everything okay?" I ask.

"I just got word. They're opening the trial tomorrow."

"*What?*"

"I don't know where these orders are coming from. But I need you to find your brother immediately."

CHAPTER 22

Diego agrees to watch Peter while I hurry down to the Swiss Guard barracks. But Leo and I almost run into each other on the stairs of Lucio's palace.

"Come on," he says. "I've got something for you. Follow me."

Outside, late afternoon has struck. The angry heat of the Roman summer bakes my outer cassock. I don't understand how Leo ran here in full uniform, beret in hand, eight pounds of ribbons tied to his body with straps and cords. Yet he only urges me to move faster. "Shifts are changing," he says. "We need to get there before he's gone."

"Who?" I say.

"Just come on."

We cross half the country until we're nearly at Saint Anne's Gate, the border entry from Rome that employees and residents use. Here the papal palace reaches its eastern terminus in the hulking tower of the Vatican Bank, which casts a long shadow at this hour. Just before reaching it, we stop.

Here in the immense defensive wall is one of the strangest spots in our country. Just across the wall is a part of the palace so private that even villagers never see it. Up there, in a private wing, lives John Paul. Any vehicle trying to reach his apartments must enter a guarded gate one-eighth of a mile west of here, pass through tunnels and checkpoints, cross the patrolled cortile of the Secretariat, and enter a private courtyard across from where Leo and I now stand, which is kept be-hind locked wooden doors. From there, I don't know the rest of the procedure, since I've never even seen the inside of that courtyard. And yet one hundred years ago, part of the Vatican near the palace exit was occupied by enemy soldiers, so Pope Pius X cut a hole right through that courtyard wall, straight down to where Leo and I now stand. Whether he did it to give his palace employees a route home to the village or to give himself a back door into his gardens, I've never known, but today that hole is the biggest weakness in the pope's security bubble. An iron gate has been built inside the tunnel, and pickets of Swiss Guards keep watch there around the clock. It must be one of those guards we've come to see.

"This way," Leo says, waving me up into the tunnel.

It's dark and cool inside. I peer up the staircase. Silhouettes of four men impress themselves against the grid of the iron gate. Leo reaches out his hand to stop me from taking another step. We wait in the darkness.

Above us, the two pairs of guards are switching places. Second shift is beginning. As the replaced men descend, Leo says, "A word, Corporal Egger?"

Both silhouettes stop. "About what?" says the first sharply.

"This is Father Andreou," Leo tells him.

A flashlight clicks on. Its beam plays over my face. The silhouette I take to be Corporal Egger turns to Leo and says, "No it's not."

In the reflection of the flashlight, I briefly see his face. Now the name registers with me. I realize why Leo has brought me along.

"You're thinking of my brother," I say. "Simon. I'm Alex Andreou."

There's a long hesitation. "Simon's your brother?"

Six years ago, when a guard committed suicide in the barracks with his service weapon, Simon volunteered to counsel any other men con-sidered at risk. Egger's CO identified him. My brother worked with him for more than a year, and according to Leo, Simon is now the only man in this country other than John Paul whom Egger would lift a finger to defend.

"Okay," Egger says.

His voice is deadpan. The other guards have a clipped, military way of speaking. Egger just sounds vacant.

"Last night," Leo begins, "a gendarme at the railway service post saw Father Andreou enter a car outside the Governor's Palace. He says the car drove down toward the basilica. It didn't turn right toward the gate, so he thinks it went left toward Piazza del Forno."

This must be the car that drove Simon to house arrest. Leo has been tracking where it took him.

"Captain Lustenberger tells me," Leo continues, "that you were stationed at first gate last night. Is that right?"

Egger scratches a lump at the corner of his lip and nods.

Leo clears his throat. "So if the car came through Piazza del Forno, and you were at first gate, then it would've driven right in front of you."

Egger turns to me. "I don't know you. And I didn't see Father Simon in any car."

"Hey," Leo says, tapping him on the chest. "I'm *telling* you he was in that vehicle. So did you see it or not? This would've been about . . ." He draws a scrap of paper from his pocket and plays his own flashlight over it. "Eight ten PM."

"There was a car at eight oh seven," Egger says.

Leo glances at me. "Okay, so where did it stop?"

I know what Leo's thinking, so I just say it. "Was it going to the old jail?"

When the Vatican became its own country, the pope built a three-cell jail in the courtyard Leo mentioned. It used to hold the occasional thief or Nazi prisoner of war, but these days it's used as a storage warehouse. No one looking for Simon would search for him there.

"Maybe you should just look at the sheet," Egger says.

Leo grits his teeth. "I did, Egger. And since you didn't record a sedan passing *through* the gate, we're asking if the car stopped in the courtyard beside the jail."

"Corporal," I say, "Simon helped you. Please help him." I try to lock eyes with Egger, staring into the black zeroes. Simon always chooses the lost sheep.

"The car didn't stop in the courtyard," Egger murmurs. "It came through the gate."

"Into the *palace*?" Leo's anger flashes. "Then why the hell is there no record on the sheet?"

Egger's head slowly pivots. "Because I was doing what I was told."

Leo grabs Egger's uniform, but I pull him back and whisper, "That means there'll be records of it on the other sheets, right?"

Leo never takes his eyes off Egger. "Wrong. I checked all the sheets for last night, and there's no car on any of them. So what are you telling us, Corporal?"

I can see it in Egger's eyes, though. The spell is broken. He's done helping us.

"Leo," I whisper, "I believe him."

But Leo clamps a hand on Egger's jaw and says, "Tell me how it's possible for a car to go past three checkpoints and not get recorded once."

For the first time, Egger's partner speaks up. "You're out of line, Corporal Keller." He breaks Leo's grip and pulls his partner away. Leo stands in their way, blocking the end of the tunnel, but I sense we're not going to get more information than this. We may have hit on something bigger than Egger.

"Let them go," I whisper to Leo. "You got me what I needed. I'll take it from here."

AFTER DROPPING LEO AT his post beside Saint Peter's Square, I weave down a route I've known since I was a boy. Between the square and the Vatican village is a narrow no-man's-land where walls have been built and torn down for centuries as the borders between public and private have changed. In the untraveled darkness beyond Bernini's colonnade there are small gaps where the walls meet. I slip back into our village and head for a forgotten place.

For years it's been Uncle Lucio's job to quietly demolish historic sites inside our walls. Our country of five hundred people hosts fifteen hundred commuters and ten thousand tourists a day, so the sad fact is that we need parking spaces more than we need ancient ruins. The first place to receive the treatment was the Belvedere Courtyard. Where Renaissance popes once held jousts and bullfights, palace employees now park their Fiats and Vespas. Next came a Roman temple beside our oldest church, which Lucio converted to underground parking for two hundred fifty. More recently he excavated a second-century villa to fit another eight hundred cars and a hundred tour buses. When people saw garbage trucks leaving our land with ancient mosaics heaped up like shavings of Parmesan, there was an uproar. But the granddaddy of them all is the garage I'm headed to now.

In the 1950s, a strip of land between the Vatican Museums and my apartment building was excavated to build a covered lot for the pope's own cars. A few feet down, workmen discovered the corpse of a Roman emperor's secretary with his pen and inkpot. His grave became our autopark, home to the Vatican car mechanics and papal car service. The place is constructed like a bomb shelter, dark and low-slung, with plantings of trees on its roof. The only way inside is through hangar doors that are unlocked for a few seconds when a car comes in or out. The sun hasn't set, but the street is so sunken that the landscape is shadowy. Motor oil bleeds out from under the door, shining like chrome under an electric light.

"Help you, Father?" says the man who answers my knock at the door.

He wears the uniform of a Vatican driver: black trousers, white shirt, black tie.

"I'm looking for Signor Nardi," I say.

He rubs the back of his neck as if I've caught him at a busy time. As if the prelates who call for rides in these cars aren't all heading to bed now as late afternoon slips into evening. The night shift here seems to exist only for the morbid emergencies of clerical old age.

"Sorry, Father," he says. "Could you come back later?"

"It's important. Please ask him to come out."

He glances over his shoulder. I wonder if he has a visitor. Girlfriends sometimes visit these drivers on the night shift.

"Hold tight. I'll see if he's here."

A moment passes. The door reopens, and out comes Gianni Nardi.

"Alex?"

The last time I saw Gianni was more than a year ago. My old friend has gained weight. His shirt is wrinkled and his hair is too long. We clamp hands on each other and trade kisses on the cheek, holding on longer than we should, because as the distance has grown, so has the enthusiasm of our greetings. Someday we will be the greatest of strangers.

"What's the occasion?" he says, looking around as if to locate the parade on the streets. *Alex Andreou, coming to see _me_.* He has always made this kind of thing funny.

"Can we talk somewhere private?" I say.

"You got it. Follow me."

And when he doesn't even ask why, I already have my first answer. Gianni must've heard about Simon.

We climb a set of stairs to the tree-lined terrace of the autopark roof.

"Listen," he says before I can get a word in, "I'm sorry, Alex. I should've called. How are you and Peter holding up?"

"Fine. How'd you hear the news?"

"Are you kidding? The gendarmes won't leave us alone." He points a finger downward, indicating the cavernous parking lot underneath us. "I've got three of them in my garage right now asking questions."

So that's why I wasn't allowed inside. "Questions about what?"

"About some Alfa they towed back from Castel Gandolfo. It's in their impound lot."

Ugo drove an Alfa Romeo.

"Gianni," I say, "I need your help."

WE WERE BEST FRIENDS growing up. This building is where we cemented our friendship. One summer we heard a rumor that when the autopark was built, the workmen discovered a whole necropolis under there, tunnel upon tunnel of ancient Roman tombs. This meant we villagers were living on top of a cemetery, over the dead bodies of the pagans who once vowed Christians would never replace them. Gianni and I needed to see it with our own eyes.

Getting down to those tunnels wasn't hard. A sewer will take you almost anywhere. But one night we shimmied through a whole maze of stone passageways until we found ourselves at a new metal grate. The grate led to a utility closet. And the utility closet opened inside the autopark, right next to the papal limousine.

Driving age in Italy was eighteen years old. We were thirteen. And the keys to eighty luxury automobiles were hanging from a board on the wall. One year earlier, my father had taught Simon how to drive in our old Fiat 500. That summer, I taught myself in an armored Mercedes 500 custom-fitted with a papal throne in the backseat.

Right off, I wanted to invite girls down with us. Gianni said no. I wanted to hide in a car trunk and hitch a ride with John Paul. Gianni said no. *Don't get greedy,* he said when I wanted to drive a limo into the gardens. *You always want too much.* That was my first taste of the real Gianni. For years afterward, he would end up making a religion of not getting greedy. Of not wanting too much. After graduation, I went off to college, but Gianni said he was going to become a surfer. He went to

Santa Marinella the way the blind go to Lourdes. A year later, his father found him work as a sampietrino. But there are a lot of inches in Saint Peter's, and the sampietrini have to clean all of them. So when Gianni lost interest in scraping gum off walls and buffing marble floors with the riding machine, he thought hard about what he really wanted in life. And he decided to become a driver for the car service.

It couldn't have been an accident that he ended up here. When he thought back to a time when life had really felt big, I doubt there was anything that came close to our summer in the autopark. And ever since he made that choice, just the sight of Gianni has made me wonder if any of us Vatican boys, other than Simon, has really ever had the guts to experience the world outside these walls.

"They took Simon into house arrest," I tell him. "The Swiss Guards saw his car enter the palace complex. I need to find out where it went."

The Swiss may not know. But the driver of that car can tell me.

"Alex," Gianni says, "we're under orders not to talk about that."

This is what I was afraid of. Egger was telling us the same thing: he was under a gag order.

"Can you tell me anything?" I say.

Gianni lowers his voice. "It's been pretty weird around here since that man was killed. We're not supposed to talk about *anything*." He smiles that old mischievous smile. "So all of this stays between us."

I nod.

"Last night, a call came down for a pickup. I don't know who the request came from, but our dispatcher sent my friend Mario to cover it. Mario ended up driving to your uncle's palace to pick up Simon."

"Where did he drop my brother off?"

"At the elevator."

"What elevator?"

"*The* elevator."

The papal palace is so old that it has few modern amenities. Gianni must mean the ancient elevator in the courtyard of the Secretariat, originally built to operate on water power. This is the one presidents and prime ministers use when they visit.

But when I ask, he shakes his head. On the dust of the ground, he draws a large square with the toe of his shoe. "Damasus Courtyard."

He means the courtyard in front of the Secretariat. I nod.

He adds a smaller square, just beside the first. "Palace of Nicholas the Fifth."

This is the final branch of the palace, the one that famously overlooks Saint Peter's Square.

He scrapes a line to connect the boxes. "Between them is an opening. An archway through the ground floor here. In the archway is a hidden door leading to the private elevator. That's where Mario's car dropped Simon off. Do you understand now?"

I do. This explains everything. I wonder how Simon can ever have allowed himself to be put under house arrest there. I wonder if he even knew where they were going to take him.

"What's wrong?" Gianni asks.

The Palace of Nicholas V has four floors. The ground floor, as in many Renaissance palaces, was designed for servants or horses. The top two floors belong to the Holy Father, who would've had no reason to cover his tracks if he'd wanted Simon under house arrest. The only remaining floor is the private residence of the Cardinal Secretary of State.

"Gian," I murmur, putting my head in my hands, "they took him to Boia's apartments."

THIS IS A GIANT setback. No one will be able to reach Simon there. Not even Lucio. When Simon submitted to house arrest, surely he assumed the order came from the vicar's office, not from his own boss.

"What about afterward?" I say. "Has Mario taken Simon anywhere else?"

He shakes his head slowly. "Al, as far as I know, no driver's seen Simon since. If he went anywhere else, it was on foot."

But that part of the palace is crawling with Swiss Guards. If Simon was escorted elsewhere, Leo would've heard about it.

"I don't get it," Gianni says, half to himself. "Why would they take him there?"

I tell him I don't know. But I can imagine an answer. House arrest would be the perfect pretext for ensuring that Simon couldn't return to the museum to erase the damning part of Ugo's exhibit: 1204.

"Any other strange calls?" I ask.

Gianni smiles thinly. "How long do you have?" He lowers his voice. "The day that man was killed—I've never seen anything like it. Five o'clock in the morning, I get a call at home. They want me to work a new shift, noon to eight. I tell them I've got a doctor's appointment at two o'clock. Heck, I just got off my last shift five hours ago. They tell me to cancel the appointment. Lo and behold, when I arrive, we're *all* there. Every single one of us got the same call."

"Why?"

"The dispatcher only tells us that someone at the palace needs cars running shuttles. According to the schedule, we're supposed to be doing short trips to an event in the gardens. But suddenly there's a change of venue. Now two junior guys will stay back to cover the regular calls, while the rest of us run pickups to Castel Gandolfo completely off the books."

"What do you mean by that?"

"No clocking in or out. No pickup logs. On paper they wanted this to look like any other day."

The sky looms, vertiginously high. This sounds like what Corporal Egger said about the Swiss Guard's checkpoint sheets—cars coming and going with no paper trail. The unknowns are beginning to grow.

"It gets stranger," he says. "They tell us we can't step out of our cars except to open doors for our pickups. We can't greet anyone by name. And we're supposed to drive them forty-five minutes each way without saying a word."

"Why?"

"Because these guys apparently don't speak Italian, don't know Rome, and don't like small talk."

"Who were they?"

He pulls at an imaginary beard on his chin, then points to me. "Priests. Like you."

My pulse quickens. The Orthodox priests Simon invited to the exhibit.

"How many of them?"

"I don't know. Twenty? Thirty?"

I can only stare at him. My father invited nine Orthodox priests to Turin for the radiocarbon announcement. Four came.

Gianni nods.

"Can you tell me exactly how they were dressed? Were they wearing crosses?"

The details could pinpoint where they came from. The family tree of Orthodoxy splits between Greeks and Slavs. Slavic priests wear crosses around their necks, but Greeks aren't allowed to.

"My pickup definitely wore a cross," Gianni says.

That suggests a priest from the Slavic tradition, including Serbia and Romania.

Gianni adds, "On his hat."

I'm taken by surprise. "Are you sure?"

Gianni squeezes his fingers together. "Just a small thing. Fingernail size."

This is the sign of a decorated Slavic bishop. Or even a metropolitan, the second-highest of all Eastern ranks. These are Orthodox royalty, outranked only by the ancient brother-bishops of the pope, the patriarchs.

"Did some of them wear chains around their necks?" I ask. "With little paintings in them?"

Gianni nods. "Like an amulet with the Madonna in it? Sure, one of my pickups wore that."

Then he was right about the little crosses. These medallions are another sign of an Orthodox bishop. I try to hide my amazement. For a bishop to have accepted Simon's invitation is a coup. I can't believe my brother was able to broker this.

And yet the more successful his diplomacy was, the more devastating it makes Ugo's discovery about 1204. I fear I'm beginning to see the outlines of the prosecution's case.

"Go back," I say. "You said they relocated the meeting to Castel Gandolfo. Where was it originally supposed to be?"

"In the gardens."

"Where in the gardens?"

If I'm right, then everything is starting to converge.

"The Casina," he says.

This is it. Ugo's letter was about a meeting at the Casina. They must be the same: the meeting at Castel Gandolfo was the one Ugo and Simon had discussed weeks earlier, in which Ugo was slated to deliver the keynote address about his discovery. The site may have been changed at the last minute, but the gathering had been planned long in advance.

"Were all the passengers who rode to Castel Gandolfo priests?" I ask.

Gianni nods.

So Diego's calendar was right: this had nothing to do with a meeting of the Pontifical Academy of Sciences. The academy's scientists would've been laymen. This event seems to have revolved entirely around the Orthodox.

Still, that doesn't explain why the location was changed.

"Can't the Casina hold twenty or thirty people?" I say.

"Definitely."

So the size of the crowd can't have been the reason. And in a country overrun with grand meeting halls, why choose a new location forty-five minutes away? The only advantage of Castel Gandolfo was the privacy.

"Why were you told not to keep records?" I ask. "Was someone in particular not supposed to find out about this?"

This strikes me as an extreme precaution. Almost no one would've known those records existed, let alone would've had the power to flush them out to track down the location of the meeting.

Gianni slices a hand through the air over his head. The answer is above his pay grade. But the timeline nags at me. As I try to arrange the dates in my mind, it seems to me that Michael was attacked around the same time Ugo wrote that letter. And everything since then—the secret transport of the Shroud, the furtive change of meeting place, the total silence Simon adopted even before he was accused of Ugo's murder—could be a reaction to Michael's attack. What happened to Michael might've been a warning sign that word of Simon's outreach was leaking. And in that vein, I can't help remembering that Mignatto said Simon's phone was tapped. If there was a leak, I wonder if it started there: Ugo and Simon discussing the Casina meeting too openly.

My silence seems to make Gianni nervous. "So," he says, popping a mint, "is Simon going to be okay?"

He catches me unprepared. "Of course. You know he didn't murder anyone."

He nods. "Not in a thousand years. I told the other drivers he would've put himself in the way of that bullet if he could've."

I'm relieved to hear him say it. At least someone in this country remembers the real Simon. We both watched my brother fight in the boxing pit, so Gianni knows what he's capable of, but also knows where he draws his lines.

"So," I say, steering the conversation away from Simon, "tell me about the Alfa they brought back from Castel Gandolfo."

"Something must've happened out there. The gendarmes were asking the mechanics about some problem with the driver's seat."

Mignatto wouldn't approve of what I'm about to say, but I say it anyway. "Could you go down and have a look? Anything you can find out would help."

"The Alfa's not here. It's in another garage that they turned into an impound lot."

Even Ugo's car is being hidden away. I'm beginning to feel that Castel Gandolfo is a black box. Fighting the accusations against Simon will be impossible without knowing what happened on that hillside.

"I'll ask around," Gianni volunteers. "I'm sure one of the other drivers has been in that lot since they put the Alfa there."

But I can't afford to have Gianni ask around. And I can't settle for seeing things through other men's eyes.

"Gian," I say, "I need to ask an even bigger favor. I've got to see it myself."

He stares as if I must be kidding.

"Please," I say.

"It could get me canned."

I look him in the eye. "I know."

I wait for him to ask for something. A favor. A promise. A handout from Uncle Lucio.

But I've misjudged him. He empties his last mint into his palm and stares at it. "Damn," he says. "Simon could lose his collar, and here I'm worried about my bullshit job." He hurls the mint into the darkness, then rises and tucks in his shirt. "Stay here. When you see me pull up, get in."

CHAPTER 23

WHEN HE'S OUT of sight, I hurriedly call Mignatto.

"Monsignor, I found out where Simon is. They took him to Boia's apartments."

"Damn it," he growls. "They're closing ranks. Cardinal Boia's secretary called me an hour ago to say we won't be getting Father Black's personnel file."

"Father Black's?"

"To see what the Secretariat concluded about the attack against him."

As I scan the darkness for a sign of Gianni and his car, I hear Mignatto breathing into the phone. I wonder again why Simon accepted house arrest. Whether it was to protect the secrecy of his Castel Gandolfo meeting or to protect Peter and me. Maybe, after what happened to Michael, he wouldn't have made a distinction between the two.

"Your brother is on the list to testify tomorrow morning," Mignatto says finally, "after the character witnesses."

"Can you file a protest with the court to get him released?"

"It wouldn't change anything."

"So what do we do?"

He makes a long, inarticulate sound, then says, "We wait and see how powerful your brother's guardian angel is." He thinks a moment longer, then adds, "Very well, be at the Palace of the Tribunal at eight o'clock tomorrow."

I hesitate. "Am I testifying?"

"Father, you're procurator. You're sitting beside me at the defense table."

Below me I hear the autopark doors open. Instinctively I crouch, in case another driver's sedan rounds the bend. But it's Gianni rumbling toward the foot of the stairs. And I can't believe my eyes.

"Monsignor," I say, "I've got to go."

"If you find out anything else," he says, "at any hour—"

"I'll call you."

I hang up and slink down the terrace steps, trying to suppress the nervous urge to laugh. Gianni's car is a Fiat Campagnola, the white military jeep that the rest of the world knows as the popemobile.

"Get in," Gianni says anxiously. "Before anyone sees you."

I know the vehicle well. When we were thirteen, Gianni and I spent a whole night searching for dots of John Paul's blood in the bed, because it was in the back of this truck that he was shot by a gunman in Saint Peter's Square.

"Get in *where*?" I say.

There's no room in back, where an armchair has been installed for John Paul. The passenger seat is stacked with a removable plastic tarp that covers the Holy Father when it rains.

Gianni moves the plastic. "Under there."

It takes me a moment to understand. He wants me to crawl into the foot well.

"And no matter what happens," he adds in a voice that hums with uncertainty, "don't say a word. Okay? There's a gendarme outside the door, but once we get past him, the garage should be empty. I think I can buy you five or ten minutes inside."

I do what he says, and Gianni piles the plastic tarp back over the foot well. Then the jeep starts to move.

The ride is rough. The popemobile is almost as old as I am. John Paul received it as a gift a quarter-century ago when he visited Turin, Fiat's headquarters, on a trip to venerate the Shroud. Thirteen months later, on the day he was shot in it, a team of Shroud scientists was in Saint Peter's Square, waiting to deliver their preliminary findings. One of the mysteries of living inside these walls is that there are no loose ends to our lives.

"Stay quiet," Gianni says. "We're close."

There's a jarring thud as we cross the raised barrier into the industrial quarter of town, a grimy area of workshops and warehouses. I see only the flash of electric lights as we plunge through it. Then the jeep slows, and I hear the first voice.

"Signore! No farther!"

Gianni brings the Fiat to a halt. He scrapes his foot toward me as a warning.

"No access here tonight," the gendarme says.

He's approaching. Voice growing louder.

Gianni says, "I have orders from Father Antoni."

The village nickname of Archbishop Nowak.

"What orders?"

I hope Gianni knows what he's doing. When John Paul travels in this jeep, he always has a gendarme escort. One call to the station could disprove anything Gianni says.

But he thumps the pile of plastic with his hand and says, "Chance of rain tomorrow."

The gendarme says, "All right. How long will it take?"

"Ten minutes. I have to check the spare tarp."

Now I understand his plan. Tomorrow is Wednesday, the day of John Paul's weekly audience. The only time this open-topped Campagnola is used anymore.

"It's been a dead zone out here tonight," the gendarme says. "I'll give you a hand in there."

Gianni tenses up. His foot makes the engine idle at higher RPM. But before he can refuse, I hear the gendarme opening the steel door on its metal rollers. Gianni turns the jeep around and reverses slowly into the bay.

"Whose Alfa is that?" I hear him say.

We've found Ugo's car.

"Not your business," the gendarme says sharply. "Where's the thing you need?"

Gianni hesitates. My pulse is thready. He's never been a good liar.

"Inside one of the boxes back there," he says.

He takes the keys out of the ignition and reaches down as if to pick up something he dropped. When his hand is in front of my face, he jabs a finger toward the door, pointing. Something must be on the other side of the jeep.

Then he's gone. The two voices fade away.

Carefully I raise my head over the low doors of the popemobile. The garage is long and narrow, just wide enough for two cars abreast. Gianni has parked right beside the Alfa Romeo, which has its doors propped open, as if someone's been inspecting the interior.

Now I see why the gendarmes brought it here. The driver's window is shattered. A crinkled eggshell of glass surrounds a hole larger than a man's head. There are pebbles of glass on the seat.

My heart begins to hammer. I can't climb out of the Fiat without the gendarme seeing me. Instead I lower the hinged windshield, push it flat, and silently slide down the hood.

Ugo's car is waterlogged. It smells of mildew. In the foot well, the gendarmes have left a plastic red marker in the shape of an arrow. It points backward, under the driver's seat. But there's nothing down there, just a rectangular impression on the upholstery, as if something *was* there. I need a closer look.

Behind me, Gianni and the gendarme have started building the rain shield. My five or ten minutes have begun.

I lower myself onto Ugo's seat and scan the underside with my keychain flashlight. Gianni said the gendarmes were asking questions about the driver's seat. The seat is attached to the car body with metal sleds, and one part of the sleds is rubbed away. Whatever was on the floor must've been attached here.

I play the flashlight beam around, and something glints. Jutting out from the floor mat is a sliver of metal, no bigger than the white of a fingernail. I reach down to pick it up, then remember to be careful about fingerprints. In a prison outreach group I belong to, an inmate in our Bible class was caught hiding a used syringe, so the whole group had its fingerprints and blood taken. I roll my hand under the fabric of my cassock before picking up the bronze-colored arc.

Its outer edge seems smooth, but the inside is jagged and bent. Something about it seems familiar, yet I can't think why.

There's a noise in the distance. Gianni, warning me. I put the sliver of metal into my pocket and start crawling back toward the popemobile.

On the way out, though, I pass a utility cart. On top of it, in plastic bags, are the objects that must've been removed from Ugo's car. A car charger for a mobile phone. A flask engraved with Ugo's initials. A scrap of stationery. There are several others below. I stop.

The plastic bags have red seals that say EVIDENCE. Their backs are embossed with boxes for the time and place of collection, the case number, the chain of custody. It seems odd that these would still be here, rather than entered as exhibits at the trial. A loose sheet of paper atop the utility cart says HOLD FOR FURTHER INSTRUCTION. I wonder if Mignatto knows any of this was found.

There's something else. No object here matches the impression under the driver's seat. Nothing the size of a small laptop computer, nothing that could've been tied around the metal sleds of the seat. Maybe that's why the window was broken: to steal whatever was down there.

I start to reach for the bags at the bottom of the heap, whose contents I can't see—when my eyes focus on the scrap of stationery.

A number is written on it. A phone number.

I look closer, and the breath catches in my lungs.

My phone number. The landline at my apartment.

Another sharp clang comes from the back of the garage—Gianni knocking over the rain frame, warning me that time's running out.

I scurry to the Fiat.

Gianni doesn't even check that I'm in the foot well. He turns the ignition and shifts the jeep into first. The drive is short. In the same dark corner of the autopark where we started, he stops to let me off.

I want to thank him, but his eyes are wide and anxious, glancing behind him in the mirror. Distractedly he says, "So did you find anything useful?"

"Yes," I say.

His head bobs. "Good. That's good."

I step away from the jeep. He's panting. "If you need anything else . . ." he says.

"You've done plenty," I say, thinking only of the phone number on that scrap of paper. "I really appreciate it, Gian."

He offers a small wave and makes the sign of a telephone, as if I should call if I need anything else. He's trembling. The Fiat drives away toward the autopark doors.

I think to myself how often I've seen Ugo's handwriting. How many sheets of his homily paper scrawled with gospel verses I've corrected when he insisted on giving himself homework after our lessons. I would recognize his penmanship anywhere. But the writing on that scrap of stationery was not his.

The contents of those evidence bags shouldn't still be locked in the impound garage. If the gendarmes are waiting for someone to collect them, then that someone seems to have decided to keep them out of sight.

Gianni's final gesture lingers with me. The sign of the telephone. It gives me an idea.

CHAPTER 24

Behind the autopark is the Belvedere Palace. I jog up the stairs to my apartment. Before entering, I listen for sounds on the other side of the door. Until the locks are changed, this will have to be a part of my visits here. But I see that Leo has left something behind from our last visit: the flap of a matchbook, stuffed between the frame and the door. It's a trick he uses in the barracks to make sure cadets don't sneak into Rome. Paper on the floor means someone's come and gone. Paper in the door means the seal is unbroken. I'm relieved.

I let myself in and go to the telephone in the kitchen. It seems strange that Ugo would've wanted the number for this landline. Whenever we exchanged calls about the Diatessaron, he dialed my mobile. Maybe this time he was trying to reach Simon, not me. The question is, when?

I scroll through the caller ID list of incoming calls, and there isn't a trace of Ugo's number. There are only three calls from an unfamiliar phone—a Vatican number—all within forty minutes of each other on the night before Ugo died. Peter and I were away that whole evening, seeing a movie. I never knew about these calls.

Loose sparks float through my thoughts. I check the date on the calls again, just to be sure. It's as if someone was checking to make sure we were gone. Casing the apartment before the break-in. Yet the following night—when the break-in actually happened—there's not a single un-recognized call.

Losing patience, I scroll back to the unfamiliar number and punch it into my phone. It barely rings before a woman picks up.

"Pronto. Casa Santa Marta. How may I help you?"

A nun. At the front desk of the Casa.

"Hello," I say. "I'm trying to reach someone who called me from a hotel line. Can you connect me?"

"The name, sir?"

"I don't have the name. Just a phone number."

"For the privacy of our guests, sir, we can't honor that request."

"It's important, Sister. Please."

"I'm very sorry."

Thinking quickly, I say, "Ugolino Nogara, then. Can you look for a room under the name Ugolino Nogara?"

Ugo had no reason to stay at the Casa. He would've stayed in his apartment over the museums. But I'm fishing for anything.

I hear her typing on the computer. "No guest under that name, sir. Are you sure he hasn't checked out? We remove guests from the system when they return their keys."

Their keys. Suddenly it comes to me. The sliver of metal I found under Ugo's car mat.

"Thank you, Sister," I say. Then I hang up the phone and reach into both pockets of my cassock. Out of one I take the metal crescent from Ugo's car. Out of the other I take my room key from the Casa.

Attached to the Casa key is an oval fob engraved with the room number. Color and thickness match perfectly. The sliver is a snapped-off edge of a Casa fob.

Looking closer, I can see the stress marks. It must've been used to pry something up. Whatever the job was, it failed.

I sit at the kitchen table, trying to arrange all this information into a pattern I can grasp. The phone calls to my apartment trace back to the Casa. The robbery of Ugo's car does, too. This may be the first hint that the break-in and the murder really are connected. But I'm also haunted by the thought that Peter and I were at the Casa, sleeping under the same roof as the man who did this.

I rub the metal sliver in my palm. The Casa. It was built for out-of-town visitors, but it's also where Secretariat priests stay when they're passing through. On the phone, Mignatto said Cardinal Boia doesn't want us to know who beat Michael up. He refuses to release that information. Boia, since the time of my father's death, has been the enemy of a Catholic-Orthodox reunion. The man who has used the Secretariat as a tool to kill John Paul's goodwill gestures toward our sister Church.

Simon must've known he was tempting fate by inviting Orthodox clergy to the exhibit. He must've tried to stay off Boia's radar as long as he could. That would explain why his diplomatic passport has no hint of trips to Serbia or Romania. He could've applied for a regular Italian passport to hide what he was doing. But once an Orthodox bishop—or a metropolitan—agreed to come to Rome, the game was over. Bishops are public figures. They travel with entourages; their plans appear in announcements and diocesan calendars. Boia was guaranteed to find out.

Around that time, though, Simon must've had an even nastier shock. It was in the thick of my brother's negotiations with the Orthodox that Ugo discovered the Shroud had been stolen from Constantinople.

That discovery must've set the rest of this in motion. Michael was attacked by men who wanted to know what Ugo had discovered. The same threat was written on the back of the photo I was sent. Cardinal Boia seems to know Ugo uncovered *something*, but not what it is. Maybe this is what he hopes to squeeze out of Simon by putting him under house arrest.

Ironically, though, all he needs to do is walk through Ugo's exhibit. Even though the galleries are unfinished, the answers are in plain sight. If His Eminence would learn a few words of Greek, he would realize the truth is painted on the walls.

I stand and wade through the darkness back to my bedroom. My brother may put this exhibit above his own career, but I don't. Simon was made for greater things than inviting some Orthodox clergy to Rome. When he testifies tomorrow, the judges need to hear what's really at stake.

I look in my dresser but don't find what I'm looking for. So I cross the imaginary line between my side of the room and Mona's and open the jewelry box her father made her after our engagement. She disappeared without anything but a carry-on bag of clothes, and since a priest's wife rarely wears jewelry anyway, it's all still here: the diamond stud earrings, the nostalgic teenage rings, the gold necklace with the Latin cross on it, superseded by the Greek cross she would've been wearing the day she left. I open the small lower compartment. Inside is a key. I loop it onto my chain.

On my way to the door, I stop and open the credenza that was overturned during the break-in. Inside it is the plastic bag where Peter and I keep our rat's nest of extra wires and cables and adapters. Anything I see that might charge a mobile phone, I roll up and stuff in my cassock.

Then, before going downstairs again, I try to brace myself for what I'm about to see.

ON THE BOTTOM FLOOR of our apartment building is Vatican Health Services. When Simon and I were boys, American priests would fly back to New York for their checkups rather than risk a trip to the Vatican doctors. Horror stories have followed every pope for half a century. Fifty years ago, Pius XII came down with recurring hiccups, so his doctor prescribed injections of ground lamb brains. Another papal doctor sold Pius' medical records to newspapers and embalmed his dead body using an experimental technique that made the pope's corpse bubble and fart like a tar pit while pilgrims queued up to view it. Ten years later, Paul VI needed his prostate removed, so Vatican doctors decided to perform the operation in his library. His successor, John Paul I, died thirty-three days into his papacy because our doctors didn't yet know he took pills for a blood condition. So you might think our Vatican morticians would be world-class, considering all the practice they get. But there's no such thing as a Vatican mortician and no such place as a Vatican morgue. Popes are embalmed in their apartments by volunteer undertakers from the city, and the rest of us settle for the back room at Health Services. That room is where I'm headed now.

There are two doors to the clinic, one for bishops and one for everyone else. Even now, I use the door appropriate to my rank. Mona's key opens the lock without a hitch. Before Peter was born, she worked here pro bono, like all our medical staff, in addition to her real job in the city.

I haven't stood in this waiting room since the day of my father's heart attack. The windows look out onto the autopark and the museums beyond, so I don't dare turn on the lights. But I don't need them to remember how this place looks. The white floors and walls, the white slats of the plastic window shades. The white-coated doctors and nurses who moved so slowly when we carried Father inside, as if they'd already decided this would be his doorstep to heaven. When Mona volunteered here, not once did I come down to meet her after work, and not once did she have to ask me why.

I walk down the hall, opening the waiting rooms one by one. As expected, the one I want is at the very end. Even before I open the door, I smell the embalming fluid. Inside the room there's no reclining bed dressed with sanitary paper, just a steel table draped with a white sheet. Under the sheet is the hump of a body.

I look away from Ugo, feeling as if I've invaded his privacy. This was a man who kept two dead bolts on his door and a safe bolted to his office floor. A man who in all the time we worked together never showed me a picture of his family, if he even had any to speak of. Maybe that's why his body is still here, three days later, languishing in a back room with no vigil or word of a burial Mass.

"Ugo," I say aloud, "I'm so sorry."

For being here. For interrupting your peace. For ignoring you when you came to me for help.

I look away and scan the wheeled cart in front of me, searching for his belongings. Instead I find a manila folder labeled NOGARA, UGO-LINO L. The first page is a diagram of a man's skull covered with handwritten notes. Mindful of my fingerprints, I pull a pair of latex gloves from the dispenser on the wall before touching it.

A black hole is drawn on the right side of the diagram's skull. Measurements are beside it. An exit wound is drawn on the left side, likewise measured. On the next page is a full-body silhouette listing the scars and discolorations on Ugo's skin. At a glance I see the word *jaundice*, followed by a reference to page eleven in the patient history.

I skim forward. The file has mostly been compiled during the past eighteen months, beginning just before Ugo's first trip to Edessa, when he was vaccinated for typhoid and tetanus. This spring, he tested positive for liver disease. Then failed a vision test. After that, the entries become more frequent. Ugo seems to have visited the doctor every time he was back in town. Page eleven, referenced in the autopsy report, was made less than a month ago.

Patient exhibits secondary delusions consistent with alcohol dependency. Fears losing job. Fears being followed, harmed. Evidence of possible confabulation. Tested for Korsakoff, but no evidence of amnesia. Retest for memory loss in six months. Prescribed thiamine; referred to specialist.

The date of this visit is shortly before he sent me his final e-mail. The doctors, seeing that he was an alcoholic, ignored everything else. I feel a second wave of guilt.

Returning to the autopsy report, I finally find the inventory of personal effects. It mentions the absence of wallet and watch. It says nothing about a Casa key—with or without a nick taken out of the fob. This strengthens my suspicion that the scrap I found under his floor mat wasn't his.

The inventory also says the pockets of Ugo's pants, shirt, and suit jacket were empty. But my suspicion was right. In the inner breast pocket of his raincoat, the examiner found Ugo's mobile phone.

No mobile phone was ever listed in an inventory of evidence Mignatto mentioned to me. I begin to search the metal trays for another red-sealed evidence bag, when my eyes catch one last line in the notes.

Staining of both hands.

I stop, and look again. Then I rifle through the pages for another reference. Beside the full-body diagram, a line item mentions the gunshot residue found on Ugo's shielding hand, the one he defended himself with. But that isn't what the notation said. It said staining of *both* hands.

Thinking back, I remember what the Swiss Guard said about Ugo's body to Simon and me in the cantina just hours after he died.

I heard there was something wrong with it. Something about his hands or feet.

I stare at the hump under the sheet on the metal table. And I dread what I need to do now.

■ ■ ■

ONLY SIMON WAS ALLOWED to see Father's body in this room. Two days afterward, when I leaned over the open casket to kiss the holy icon on his chest, I smelled the cologne the mortician had put on him, and I knew my father was gone. The body before me had become a stranger. No Greek priest wears cologne. But that smell has stayed with me, folded among the buried memories in the corners of my own skull. It returns now as I step toward the table.

I stare at the white sheet. At the bulging landscape of Ugo's corpse. Then I don the priest's familiar armor against death. There's nothing to fear here. The soul doesn't die. As surely as Ugo lived before, he still lives, just dislocated from his body.

And yet there's something haunting about the facelessness of his covered corpse. It feels as if all death resides here. I'm separated from it by nothing but this thin sheet. For some reason I think of Ugo at his dinner table, showing me his replica of the Shroud. His hand hovered respectfully over the cloth, never touching it.

The sheet feels powdery when I pull it up, just far enough to find Ugo's arm.

The stain on his hand is thick rust-brown. It spreads across the skin in a familiar pattern, darker on the fingertips and thumb, almost nothing in the palm.

My heart is thrumming now, sending a shiver of blood through my arms.

I lower the sheet and step to the other side of the table. An identical stain is on his left hand. Ugo was holding the Diatessaron not long before he died. But why? The restorers should've been done with it long ago. Huge enlargements of the Diatessaron's pages are already mounted in the galleries. I assumed the last gallery door—the one Peter and I couldn't open—was locked because the Diatessaron was already in place, elaborately mounted in that final room. Ugo had no reason to move it.

Unless he brought it to Castel Gandolfo. Unless he showed it to the Orthodox for some reason. In which case, the Diatessaron might be what was stolen from his car. The dimensions are very close to the impression I saw under Ugo's car seat.

Impatiently I search the metal trays. Finally, under a small pile of paperwork, I find a plain plastic bag with no seal and no gendarme markings at all. Inside it is Ugo's mobile phone. The battery is dead after three days in standby, so I pull the charging cords from my cassock and find one that powers it on. Then I begin working through the lists of calls.

The last four calls made to this phone were from Simon. At 3:26, 3:53, and 4:12, Ugo didn't answer. Then more than half an hour passed with no contact. Finally, at 4:46, my brother called Ugo for the last time. They connected for ninety seconds. Less than ninety minutes later, Ugo was dead, since Simon called my apartment shortly after six to ask me to find him at Castel Gandolfo.

I dial Ugo's voice mail. Sure enough, Simon has left messages. The automated voice says, "Three twenty-six PM." Then:

> Ugo, it's me. Just wanted to run through the script. A few reminders: Italian won't be their first language, so speak slowly. I'll introduce you, and you only have to talk for twenty minutes, so don't worry. Just please don't mention what we talked about.

Then a pause.

> Also, I wanted to let you know that the turnout is better than expected. We talked about a small group, but the Holy Father has been very supportive, so don't be surprised. That's another reason it's important for us to follow the script. We don't want to let him down.

A final pause.

> I know this is hard for you. But you can do it. If you're tempted to have a drink, stay strong. I'll be with you every step.

I save the message. Then seven minutes until four o'clock, Simon leaves a second one. This time, his voice is more strained.

> Where are you? The porter said you went for a smoke. We're supposed to start in a few minutes. I really need you back here.

Twenty minutes later, the last voice mail message.

> I can't keep them waiting. I'll have to give the talk myself. Ugo, if you're drinking, don't bother coming. I'll call you when I'm done.

There's nothing more. The automated voice returns. The final call—around quarter of five, when Simon and Ugo at last made contact—has left no message.

I feel the bitterest relief. Simon didn't know where Ugo had gone. He was giving a talk to a room of Orthodox priests while Ugo was alone in the gardens. Possibly even as Ugo was being attacked.

The judges need to hear these messages. They need to draw their own conclusions about why this evidence has never been collected. Mignatto will be furious at what I've done, but I unplug the phone and put it in my pocket. Then I check the room for anything I might've left behind, bless Ugo's body one last time, and return to the lobby.

Outside, in the small parking lot between here and the autopark, a car pulls up. Its lights strafe the vertical blinds, but it's only one of my neighbors who emerges, yawning, on his way home for the night. I wait for him to disappear inside, then I pad out and lock the door with Mona's key.

It's midnight. I consider calling Mignatto but decide it can wait until morning. We will meet at the courtroom in eight hours. He can rage at me then for what I've done. Once the anger passes, he'll see how much easier his job has become.

CHAPTER 25

I'M WOKEN AT half past five by a phone call from Michael Black.

"Where are you?" he says.

"Michael," I say groggily, "it's not even dawn here. I'm not running to a pay phone."

"Your message said you needed to talk to me?"

"I need you to get on a plane," I say. "We need you to testify."

"Come again?"

"The Secretariat won't release your personnel file. We have no other way to prove you were attacked."

Already his tone is changing. "You want me to stick out my neck for your brother?"

"Michael—"

"What would I even say? He never told me anything."

I sit up in bed and turn on the lamp. I press the sand out of my eyes. My mind is turning at half speed, but I know I need to be careful. *He never told me anything*: surely untrue. Ugo's letter referred to Michael as Simon's "follower," and when Michael was beaten up at the airport in Romania, it seems to have been because he was helping Simon invite Orthodox to Ugo's exhibit. That he won't admit as much to me in private tells me it will be hard convincing him to testify in court.

And yet he called. Some part of him is still willing to help.

"As soon as you get to Rome," I say, "I'll tell you everything I know. But I don't want to do this over the phone."

"You know what? I don't owe you anything."

"Michael," I say in a harder voice, "you *do* owe me. You didn't just tell those people where to find my apartment. You told them where to find my spare key."

Silence.

"The police won't help us," I say, "because they don't think anyone really broke in."

"I apologized for that."

"I don't want your apologies! I want you to get on the next plane to Rome. Call me when you're here."

Before he can say another word, I hang up. And I pray it was enough.

TWO HOURS LATER, I arrange an impromptu playdate for Peter with Allegra Costa, the six-year-old granddaughter of two Vatican villagers. At her doorstep, Peter and I take longer than usual to say our see-you-laters. We have a ritual of never saying good-bye to each other, another residue of Mona's disappearance. She is always there, turning up in the field of our lives like the potsherds Roman farmers find when they plow. For Peter's sake, I need to call her back soon. But the thought flees when I glance at my wristwatch. Everything tightens inside me. There's another place I need to be.

The Palace of the Tribunal sits catercorner to the Casa, sharing views of the Vatican gas station, but with the additional insult of being directly behind the tailpipes of the cars, which has contributed a sfumato of petroleum gray to the chipped Vatican beige of the building's exterior. The Rota normally operates out of a historic Renaissance palace across the river, closer to Mignatto's office, but today three of its judges have been forced to come here. In the old days, our canonical trials were held outside the Vatican walls, and this palace was reserved for civil trials. But John Paul, the only pope ever to revise both codes of canon law—one for Western Catholics, one for Eastern Catholics—decided to change the venue as well.

This palace often seems permeated with an air of languid underemployment. Judges loiter outside, leaning against the walls with wigs in their hands, whiling away time between cases. Like our Vatican doctors and nurses, our civil magistrates are volunteers imported from the outer world, part-time lawmen whose real jobs are in Rome. Today's judges, though, will be different. The ancient tribunal of the Sacred Roman Rota is the second-highest judicial authority in the Church. On the merits of a case, they can be overruled by no one but the pope. The Rota is the final appeals court for every Catholic diocese on earth, and each year its justices try hundreds of cases, annulling a Catholic marriage almost every workday. This endless churn takes its toll. I've known monsignors from the Rota who aged faster than dogs. The job made them grim, methodical, impatient. In this courtroom, there won't be any lackadaisical Italian-style justice.

Mignatto is waiting outside the courtroom when I arrive. He looks especially elegant, his monsignor's cassock tied around his waist with a sash that ends in two knotted pompoms that dangle just so, calling to mind the censers that priests and deacons swing on chains to spread the smoke of incense. Tassels like these were outlawed thirty years ago when the pope simplified the dress code for Roman priests, but either Mignatto was grandfathered in, or else there's a subtle nod to traditionalism here that he thinks will curry favor with someone in the court. As a Greek priest, I'm an outsider to these nuances.

"Is Simon coming?" I ask.

His tone is strictly professional, expressing no emotion at all. "He's on the list. Whether Cardinal Boia lets him go is another matter."

"There isn't anything we can do?"

"I'm doing everything I can think of. In the meantime, please explain your uncle's decision to me."

"What decision?"

Mignatto waits, as if he expects the answer to come to me. Finally he says, "His Eminence is already inside the courtroom. He informed me an hour ago that he'll be sitting at the table today as procurator."

I glare at the courtroom doors and bite my tongue.

Mignatto is doing his best not to look aggravated. His impression of our family is not improving. "I thought he might've spoken to you about it. In any case, I submitted a mandate to make him locum tenens. In your absence, I'm afraid."

Locum tenens. Latin for "substitute."

"I can't come inside?"

"Not today."

"Why's he doing this?"

Mignatto lowers his voice. "He told me it was to embolden your brother to testify. He thinks two nights of house arrest may have changed his attitude."

I'm angry at Lucio for making me look like a fool. But if he thinks he can make Simon talk, then he must have a reason. And his decision gives me the opening I needed.

I reach into my cassock for Ugo's mobile phone and say, "There's something I have to tell you before you go inside."

When I explain, Mignatto goes white. "But I specifically asked you," he says, "not to do anything like this. Not to interfere."

"You also told me the judges would accept evidence no matter where it came from or how it was gotten."

"What are you talking about?"

"They bugged Simon's phone to steal his voice mail."

He glares at me. "What I told you was that the judges are entitled to form impressions based on anything probative. Which includes our *conduct*. So when the Secretariat withholds evidence, or eavesdrops on its own employees, it makes an impression that works in your brother's favor. And when the defense *steals* evidence, it makes an impression that can only hurt him."

"Monsignor, you don't understand. The gendarmes have found things that could help Simon, but nobody's doing anything with the evidence. Nobody's even collecting it."

"What on earth are you referring to?"

I want to tell him about the phone calls to my apartment on the night before the break-in, about the scrap of paper in Ugo's car that had my phone number written on it. But it would mean telling Mignatto what I did last night, and he's too upset to take the news in perspective.

Instead I say, "Why haven't the judges seen this phone? Why was it never entered into evidence in the trial? The voice mail messages show that Simon didn't know where Ugo was at Castel Gandolfo. This should've been one of the first things the prosecution had to turn over."

A pink mottle creeps up the monsignor's neck. "I remind you again," he says, "that this is *not* a criminal trial under civil law. The gendarmes do *not* work hand-in-glove with the prosecutor. They perform their own investigation. If the court requests it, they supply it. So the problem here is not some nefarious, invisible cabal against your brother. It's that no one involved in these proceedings—not the judges, not the promoter of justice, not the defense, not even the vicar who performed the initial investigation—has ever tried a murder in a canonical court. We aren't accustomed to requesting police homicide reports. We don't know what sorts of reports are available. And though we're making every effort to overcome these deficits, it's extremely difficult when a trial is moving this quickly."

"Then why," I say, "is the court being asked to do something it can't do? The pressure's coming from *somewhere*."

Mignatto grimaces. "Father, someone obviously believes Nogara's death is a scandal threatening the arrangements for this exhibit. The best hope for resolving that problem, in someone's mind, is a quick trial. I see nothing to suggest there's more to it."

The courtroom doors are opening. Arguing is getting us nowhere. Before Mignatto leaves, I need to make sure he understands the significance of Ugo's phone.

"When Simon's testifying," I say, "please just ask him about the calls he made to Ugo. And if he won't answer, play the messages on Ugo's voice mail."

Mignatto clenches his teeth. He takes the phone and turns his back on me. The last thing I hear him say as he leaves is, "Father, you aren't listening to me. I don't ask the questions. Only the judges do."

I'M TOO ANXIOUS TO leave, so I decide to stay outside the courtroom. Minutes later, the first witness comes walking up on foot.

It's old Bishop Pacomio, former rector of Simon's seminary, the Capranica. He's an overweight, balding man with a broad, wise forehead and serious eyes. Though he wears a plain priest suit, the thick gold pectoral cross on his chest says he's more than a priest: for almost a decade he's been a bishop in the Archdiocese of Turin. To the judges he will also be a minor celebrity—author of books and broadcaster of TV programs. Mignatto is opening with a bang: Bishop Pacomio has traveled four hundred miles to put in a good word for my brother.

As the gendarmes open the courtroom door for him, I get a peek inside. The three judges sit at the bench with expressions like pallbearers. Behind them is a wooden façade like a mausoleum entrance, overhung by a black iron crucifix.

Then the door closes, and I'm blind again. The waiting begins. For the next fifty minutes I pace the dusty courtyard, unsure how else to help. Then Bishop Pacomio resurfaces, looking placid. I want to ask how it went, but he wouldn't be allowed to answer me. The oaths of court forbid it. So I watch him trot away, and I check my phone for any message from Mignatto.

Nothing.

Soon after, a lowly Volkswagen Golf pulls up with its windows rolled down. It disgorges a man I haven't seen in a decade: Father Stransky, who worked with my father in the Christian Unity office back when it was nothing but a Vatican-owned apartment with a bathtub for its filing cabinet. Time has bleached his hair and lengthened his face, but he stops in front of me, stares quizzically, then makes the connection. "My heavens," he says. "It's little Alex Andreou!"

"Father Tom."

He embraces me as if I were a son, and I wonder how Mignatto could possibly have tracked him down. Last I heard, he was the rector of an institute in Jerusalem.

"Just happened to be in Rome," he says with a wink. "Fortuity, I guess."

Lucio. Only Lucio could have flushed these men out of the woodwork. I wonder if he paid to fly them here overnight.

Father Tom lowers his voice. "So what did your brother get himself into?"

"Father, he didn't do anything wrong. He just won't tell the judges he's innocent."

Stransky shakes his head. Simon in a nutshell. He points to the door and says, "Join me?"

When I explain that I can't, he smiles and says, "Well, let's pray I don't make an ass of myself. Haven't dusted off ye olde canon law in a decade."

Modest words from a living legend. Working with two cardinals, Father Tom drafted a historic Church document on the future of our relations with non-Christians. Though he can't testify to anything except Simon's behavior as a young man, Mignatto's strategy seems clear: to dazzle the judges with my brother's character witnesses.

An hour passes. Father Tom leaves. The third witness arrives—and he's a showstopper.

Archbishop Collaço is the former nuncio at Simon's first posting in Bulgaria. Born in India, trained in Rome, Collaço is one of the most senior of all Vatican diplomats, the embodiment of Secretariat service. In his quarter-century career he's been nuncio to a dozen countries. Today he wears a pure white cassock with purple sash, the attire worn by priests in the tropics, which lends even more dignity to his arrival. I have no trouble understanding the reason he's here. Mignatto and Lucio are sending an important message: the Secretariat stands behind Simon even if its leader doesn't.

A final hour passes. Then, at two o'clock, Archbishop Collaço is followed by the last of the defense's character witnesses. This time, I can't believe my eyes.

Even Lucio must've been hard-pressed to pull strings this high. Cardinal Tauran is a Secretariat giant. There was a time when people said he would become the new Cardinal Secretary, replacing Boia and revolutionizing our relations with the Orthodox. Then Tauran was diagnosed with Parkinson's disease, just like John Paul, so out of concern for his health he was transferred to the less demanding job of Librarian of the Holy Roman Church. But not before getting to know Simon in a diplomacy class His Eminence taught at the Academy. The papal librarian is about to finger my brother as one of his favorite pupils.

Tauran slips by discreetly, lowering his head and smiling self-consciously. With that, the pieces of the defense are assembled. I wish I could be inside to see the judges' faces as they witness this conveyor belt of Church celebrities. No wonder Lucio wanted to watch it for himself.

At three o'clock, Tauran exits. The stage is now set for Simon. Since most Vatican offices close at one o'clock, and workers are given at least an afternoon break during longer shifts, I expect the judges to declare a recess first. So I wait by the door for Mignatto, preparing to celebrate with him about a triumphant opening.

But no one comes. The longer the silence stretches, the more I feel unease spreading behind my ribs. They're waiting for Simon. And Simon isn't coming.

Twenty minutes later, a sedan pulls up. The driver exits, opens the rear door, and waits. The courtroom doors swing open. My uncle descends in a huff.

"What's happening?" I say.

But Lucio walks straight past me and into the waiting car. A moment later, it pulls away. I turn back to find Mignatto standing behind me.

"Did something go wrong?" I say.

"No word from Cardinal Boia," Mignatto growls.

"How can they treat Simon this way?"

The monsignor doesn't answer.

"Is my uncle coming back?"

"No."

I clear my throat. "So I can come inside the courtroom?"

He wheels on me. "You need to understand something. I can't properly defend your brother if your family continues to take matters into its own hands."

"Monsignor, I'm sorry. But Ugo's phone will—"

"I know what the phone will do. If you can't agree to what I'm asking, then I can't agree to represent your brother."

"I understand."

"Everything else you consider doing, you come to me first."

"Okay. Agreed."

My acquiescence seems to calm him. "Very well," he says. "The final deposition is in an hour. Get some lunch and meet me back here in fifty minutes."

I'm supposed to pick up Peter in an hour, but that will have to wait. "Who's testifying?"

"Doctor Bachmeier."

Ugo's assistant curator. This must be how the judges will learn about the exhibit.

"I'll be here," I tell him.

AT FOUR THIRTY, THE doors open. Mignatto leads me to a table on the right side of the courtroom. I see an identical table on the left for the prosecution, led by a priest with the ancient title of promoter of justice. Flanking him is the all-important notary, without whom the proceedings are void. Then comes the gallery behind us, rows upon rows of vacant chairs. Finally, a third small table with a microphone stands between the defense and prosecution. On the table are a pitcher of water and a glass. I don't have to guess who'll sit there.

Mignatto whispers, "It is not our place to ask questions. If you hear things you disagree with, write them down. If I consider the questions useful, I can submit them to the judges."

"Please be seated," says the presiding judge.

Then the gendarmes admit Dr. Bachmeier, a tweedy layman with a thatchy beard and poorly combed hair. I met him twice when Ugo and I were working together, and I know Ugo kept him in the dark. I doubt he really knows much about the exhibit.

The notary rises to swear him in. There are two oaths: an oath of secrecy and an oath of truthfulness. Bachmeier looks slightly cowed as he agrees to both.

"Please identify yourself," says the presiding judge. He's a gentle-faced monsignor with an old-fashioned appearance, his eyeglasses large and black-framed, his full head of graying hair combed back with tonic into a shiny little pompadour. I don't recognize him, or either of the other two monsignors on the bench, so Mignatto must've been right: any judge who knew Simon has had to recuse himself. Instead this monsignor's accent is Polish, which would make him one of the judges appointed to the Rota during the beginning of John Paul's pontificate. But for having that much experience, he still seems uncomfortable on the bench. His voice is unimposing, his body language tentative. When the time comes for the judges to meet in private and vote on sentencing, it's hard to imagine this man bending others to his will.

To his left is a much younger judge, still in his late forties, a friendly-looking man with tightly cropped hair. He has the air of a new student, eager to please. The last of the three is a grizzled bulldog with a clifflike brow and accusing eyes. He's older than the others and wears his irritation plainly. Instinct tells me he's the one this case will rest on.

"My name is Andreas Bachmeier. I am curator of medieval and Byzantine art at the Vatican Museums."

"You may sit," says the presiding judge. "Doctor Bachmeier, we're here to establish why Doctor Ugolino Nogara might have been killed. You worked with Doctor Nogara?"

"To an extent."

"Tell us what you know about his exhibit."

Bachmeier plucks at his bushy eyebrows in a sour, querulous way. He seems to find the question open-ended. "Ugolino wasn't very forthcoming about his work," he says.

"Nevertheless," says the lead judge.

Bachmeier looks down at the tip of his nose, gathering his thoughts. Finally he says, "The exhibit shows that the radiocarbon tests on the Shroud of Turin were wrong. The Shroud existed in the Christian East for most of the first millennium as a mystical relic called the Image of Edessa."

The judges glance at each other. One of them murmurs something inaudible. My muscles are tense as I wait to see if Bachmeier can establish the groundwork the prosecution needs. Only one motive can possibly be pinned on Simon for killing Ugo: that Ugo was about to reveal our theft of the Shroud from Constantinople in 1204. If Bachmeier doesn't know about 1204, then today has been a triumph for the defense.

The young judge says, "All of that comes as surprising and wonderful news. But how much of it was Father Andreou aware of?"

"I don't know. I met him only a few times and never asked him. But he was very close to Ugolino, so I'm sure he knew much more about the exhibit than I do."

"And can you think of a reason," the lead judge says, "why the defendant would've been motivated to kill Doctor Nogara because of what he knew?"

Even before Bachmeier answers, I'm thrilled. This is asking him for more information than he can possibly provide. Even if he knows about 1204, almost nobody is aware that Simon invited Orthodox clergy to attend. I glance at Mignatto and notice a certain gleam in his eye. Maybe this question came from a list of suggestions he gave the judges.

Bachmeier, though, takes us both by surprise.

"Yes," he says. "I can imagine a reason. We recently discovered that one of the most important parts of the exhibit has disappeared. Someone took the Diatessaron manuscript from a locked display case."

I launch from my seat in disbelief. Before I can speak, Mignatto's hand is on my arm, pulling me back. The promoter of justice stares at us from the prosecution table.

"You're suggesting Father Andreou stole the book?" asks the presiding judge.

"All I know," Bachmeier says, "is that the day after Ugolino was killed, Father Andreou came into the museum and made a change to the exhibit. He removed a photographic enlargement showing a page from the Diatessaron, and when I asked him about it, he offered no explanation."

I hastily scribble a note to Mignatto.

He doesn't know what he's talking about. There are still Diatessaron photos on the walls.

Mignatto mouths, *You're sure?*

When I nod, he rises and says to the judges, "Permission to approach?"

They wave him forward. A hushed parley follows. Then Mignatto returns to our table, looking stiff.

The young judge says, "Doctor Bachmeier, did Father Andreou remove *all* the photographic enlargements?"

"After I questioned him about the first one, he didn't touch the others."

Mignatto frowns. This isn't the impression he wanted to leave the judges with. But it's a dead end. I'm more concerned about the Diatessaron. I wonder what the stains on Ugo's hands mean. Whether it's possible he brought the manuscript to Castel Gandolfo, and now it has vanished.

"Doctor Bachmeier," the lead judge says, "can you think of a reason why—"

But the question is interrupted by the opening of the door at the rear of the courtroom. Its sound perforates the quiet hum of the proceedings. I turn.

A tall, doughy-faced man enters. He has downcast eyes and wears a plain black cassock. Soundlessly he sits on the last bench in the courtroom, trying not to attract attention. No gendarme stops him. And almost immediately his presence makes a stir. Even the judges are staring.

"Please," the soft-faced man says in Polish-inflected Italian. "Continue."

He has lived inside these walls for twenty-six years but has never shed his accent.

"Your Grace," the presiding bishop says, "may we help you?"

"No, no," says Archbishop Nowak, sounding contrite about the commotion. "I am here only to observe."

The judges are unsettled. It's one thing to be observed. It's another thing to be observed by the eyes and ears of the pope.

"Doctor Bachmeier," the presiding judge repeats, "can you think of any reason why the accused would want to steal the manuscript?"

I find these questions absurd. There's no evidence to suggest Simon ever laid a finger on the book.

"Pardon," comes a voice from behind us. Nowak again. "What is this question?"

The judge explains what Bachmeier has revealed about the theft of the Diatessaron.

"My apologies," Nowak says. "You may ask another question, please."

The judge tries to parse what the archbishop means. Looking uncertain, he decides to repeat his question to Bachmeier.

But Nowak interrupts, "My apologies. No more about this, please. The topic is now outside the dubium."

Two of the judges glance at each other. I whisper to Mignatto, "What's the dubium?"

Mignatto doesn't answer. He stares at Archbishop Nowak in what seems to be shock.

The presiding judge riffles through the papers before him, then holds one in the air to read from it. "Your Grace," he says, "I have the joinder in front of me, and it says the dubium is whether Father—"

Nowak raises a hand in the air and says in a mild voice, "His Holiness commands a change in the dubium. No more on this topic, please."

Mignatto scribbles something blindly on the pad between us.

Dubium: what is to be proved. The scope of the trial.

The presiding judge is so surprised that he says something to Archbishop Nowak in Polish. The older judge asks, "Which topic is His Holiness referring to, Grace?"

"The exhibit of Doctor Nogara," Nowak says.

Mignatto seems frozen. His eyes never leave Nowak. But under the table he clamps his hand on my forearm and squeezes. If the tribunal can't hear about the exhibit, then Simon has no possible motive. The trial is all but over.

"Are you sure, Your Grace?" the presiding judge asks.

Across the courtroom, the promoter of justice is agog.

Archbishop Nowak nods. "You may continue, if you wish, with another topic."

At the witness table, Bachmeier clears his throat. He isn't competent to speak on any other topic.

The judges confer. Finally the presiding judge says, "Doctor Bachmeier, you are excused. The tribunal will adjourn until tomorrow."

Nowak rises. The gendarmes open the doors for him, and he quietly shuffles out.

Mignatto calmly opens his briefcase. He places the legal pad inside, then seems to remember something and jots a note on it. The promoter of justice is already buzzing nearby, hovering between the defense table and the bench, waiting to confer.

"I'll call you later," Mignatto says to me. Before closing the briefcase, he tears off the top sheet, folds it over, and hands it to me. Then he joins the promoter on his way to meet with the judges.

Archbishop Nowak is already gone when I reach the courtyard outside. I sit on a bench by the gas station and close my eyes to collect myself. Few times in my life have I felt more acutely that my prayers have been answered. Then I open the sheet of legal paper. On it, Mignatto has written a single line:

I think we just found out who your brother's guardian angel is.

CHAPTER 26

As I walk back to the village to pick up Peter, I look at the papal palace in the distance and wonder about what I've just seen. Boia is trying to force Simon to talk. Nowak is trying to keep the exhibit a secret. Battle lines seem to crisscross the palace. If John Paul supports the exhibit—if he supports Simon—then none of this should be happening. He has the power to stop the trial; he has the power to bring Cardinal Boia to heel. But when a pope nears death, he sometimes finds that old friends are wolves in priests' clothing. Archbishop Nowak has been forced to play the role of illusionist, creating the mirage of a strong pope to stave off a power vacuum. That mirage can last only so long.

What puzzles me most is the disappearance of the Diatessaron and where it might be now. Why would Ugo have taken it from the museum? To distract the Orthodox at Castel Gandolfo from the news about 1204? Or to prove something to them? The last time Ugo and I worked on the Diatessaron, he proposed a theory that could've sealed the final gap in his research. If true, it would've proven that the Shroud came to Edessa in the hands of one of Jesus' disciples. And it would've located that proof in the Bible itself.

LEARNING THE GOSPELS BECAME Ugo's mania in the final weeks we worked together. He studied them the same way he drank. I would be reading in bed after Peter had gone to sleep, and my mobile phone would ring: Ugo, asking whether Jesus really turned water into wine, since John is the only gospel to claim he did. Knocks on the door during breakfast: Ugo, wondering if Jesus really raised Lazarus from the dead, since John is the only gospel to claim he did. A message left at the pre-seminary: Ugo, trying to understand why John left out twenty of Jesus' healing miracles and all seven of Jesus' exorcisms.

To buy myself respite, I gave Ugo a sheaf of Simon's old homily paper—the same stationery on which he would later write the letter I found in Simon's bag—and we invented an exercise for him to do: chapter by chapter, he began writing out parallel verses from the gospels, comparing them word by word, and crossing out the sections that must've been added or changed by the gospel writers. This thrilled Ugo, who believed that by weeding out theology he was coming closer to the historical facts of Jesus' life. And though it saddened me to see him return each day with a new handful of pages in which whole phrases and lines from the gospels, especially John, had been crossed out, his command of scripture was becoming so strong, and his errors were becoming so rare, that I decided to let him continue until he reached the end.

Meantime, the manuscript restorers told me they thought Ugo sometimes spent the night in the lab. They resented the way he refused to let the Diatessaron out of his sight, as if he didn't trust them. Their concerns reassured me about Ugo's true intentions. He didn't really believe that by whittling the gospels down to their factual core he would reveal something new about how the Shroud had left Jerusalem. Instead, all our work together was preparation for reading the Diatessaron—and his hopes for *that* gospel were well-founded.

The man who wrote the Diatessaron, Tatian, belonged to a Christian sect called the Encratites. *Encratite* is Greek for "self-disciplined," and they earned the title: they were teetotalers and vegetarians who also outlawed marriage. Since one of Jesus' first miracles was to turn water into wine at a wedding, it's tempting to ask how well the Encratites knew their gospels. But Tatian knew them cold.

It's a daring feat to weave Matthew, Mark, Luke, and John into a single gospel. But Tatian made it even harder on himself. His goal was to create a definitive version of Jesus' life, to disprove the pagans who said the Christian holy books contradicted themselves. A century earlier, the gospel of Mark had been edited to create the gospels of Matthew and

Luke. Now Tatian set out to edit *all* the gospels. One God, one truth, one gospel. And for anyone trying to prove the Shroud was in Edessa, his editorial changes were gold.

In merging the gospels, he left behind a trail of clues about himself and the world he lived in. For instance, the gospel of Matthew says Jesus was baptized by a man known as John the Baptist, who lived on a diet of locusts and honey. But Tatian, being an Encratite, was a vegetarian, and he happened to classify locusts as a kind of meat. So he changed the gospel text: in the Diatessaron, John the Baptist survives on *milk* and honey.

In the same way, it would take only a single word to prove that Tatian had seen the Shroud, or that the Shroud was in Edessa. The clue might be obvious, or it might be almost invisible. If *anywhere* in the Diatessaron Tatian described Jesus' physical appearance, it could be the lead we were hoping for. The four gospels never say what Jesus looked like, so a description in the Diatessaron would suggest Tatian had seen an image he considered authentic. Thus every page of the Diatessaron became pregnant. Ugo and I hung on what the restorers were recovering from under the smudges each day.

It was slow going. I convinced Ugo not to let the technicians remove the Diatessaron's binding, even though it would let them work faster. The pope's oldest Bible, Codex Vaticanus, was now just a collection of loose sheets under glass because someone had let the restorers disassemble it that way. But with the Diatessaron still bound, the conservators could restore only two pages at a time. So Ugo forced them to start on the pages that interested him most—the ones that described Jesus' death—and one morning a technician sidled up to us and said, "Doctor, the section you asked about is ready."

THE WORKROOM OF THE manuscript restoration lab was filled with wonderful contraptions. There were anvil-like things with hand-wheels as big as bicycle tires. Clotheslines sagged from the ceiling, draped with what looked like giant napkins. The conservators worked with vials of chemicals and huddled around the tiny manuscript with what appeared to be doll-size tweezers and brushes. Removing the smudges was painstaking work, and the manuscript had to be set open in an apparatus to recover overnight. Now, as the technician presented his work, Ugo stared. He had begun taking Greek lessons at a pontifical university, but he was too impatient to use that knowledge now.

"Father," he whispered, "tell me what I'm looking at."

Hazy clouds dotted the page where the restorers had removed the smudges of censorship. Before our eyes was the verse that had vexed Ugo most. The one he had been dying to uncover.

"It says *cloth*," I said. "Singular."

"Ha! That supports the Shroud!"

He was excited but not jubilant. He'd had enough lessons by then to understand that Tatian could've chosen that word for other reasons. In fact, the word Tatian used—οθονίο, or "strip of cloth"—was John's word, which Tatian had changed from plural to singular rather than using the completely different word found in the other gospels. Confronted by this discrepancy in the gospel testimony, Tatian had split the difference, and the Alogi had dutifully smudged it out. This proved nothing.

But there was more here.

"Look," I said, pointing to a word on the page.

According to Mark and Matthew, Jesus was offered a mixture of wine and gall to numb the pain of crucifixion. But Tatian was a teetotaler. He didn't want the Messiah drinking wine. So the page before us had changed the word from *wine* to *vinegar*.

"It's happening again," I said. "He's changing the text."

Ugo signaled to a conservator and called, "Bring me the photos of the other pages in this section."

I scoured the pictures for other examples.

ΚΑΙΠΛΕΞΑΝΤΕΣΣΤΕΦΑΝΟΝΕΞΑΚΑΝΘΩΝΕΠΕΘΗΚΑΝΕΠΙΤ ΗΝΚΕΦΑΛΗΝ.

"*And plaiting a crown of thorns*," I said, "*they put it on his head.*"

Ugo watched but said nothing.

ΚΑΙΕΤΥΠΤΟΝΑΥΤΟΥΤΗΝΚΕΦΑΛΗΝΚΑΛΑΜΩΙ.

"*They struck his head with a reed.*"

ΚΑΙΠΑΡΕΔΩΚΕΝΤΟΝΙΗΣΟΥΝΦΡΑΓΕΛΛΩΣΑΣΙΝΑΣΤΑΥΡ ΩΘΗ.

"*And having scourged Jesus, he delivered him to be crucified.*"

"What are you looking for?" Ugo asked.

These were the injuries that produced visible marks on the Shroud. So if Tatian had seen the Shroud, then he might've been tempted to enrich these verses with his own knowledge, just as he'd done elsewhere. The gospels don't say how often Jesus was scourged or how badly his wounds bled. They don't mention which side of him was stabbed by a spear or where each nail of the crucifixion pierced him. Only the Shroud maps this gore. And to Tatian, who wrote the Diatessaron at a time when Christians were suffering bloody persecution across the Roman Empire, it might have seemed important to make the gospels fully express the horror of Jesus' torture.

"I'm looking for anything different," I said. "Added or taken away."

"Get a Bible for Father Alex," Ugo called out.

But I waved him off. "I don't need it. I know these verses."

Yet there seemed to be nothing changed. Not a word.

"What do you see?" Ugo asked.

"Nothing."

"Are you sure? Look again."

But there was no need to look again. From the first torture until the last mention of the burial cloth, the account given in the gospels is scarcely a thousand words. I knew those words by heart.

"Maybe we're not looking in the right places," I suggested.

Ugo ran an anxious hand through his hair.

"There are dozens of pages left to be restored," I said. "It could be anywhere. We'll just have to be patient."

But Ugo ran a finger under his nose, considering something, then whispered, "Maybe not. Come with me. There's something I want you to see."

I FOLLOWED HIM BACK to his apartment.

"This is confidential," he said, wringing his hands with eagerness. "Do you understand?"

I nodded. Not since our initial meeting here, when he first described his exhibit, had I seen him so carried away.

"I've always proposed that the Shroud," he said, "was brought to Edessa after the Crucifixion. Around 33 AD, do we agree?"

I nodded.

"We don't have to be exact," he continued, "since the Diatessaron wasn't written until 180 AD. The point is: Shroud first, Diatessaron second. When the book was written in Edessa, the cloth was already there."

"Okay."

"But," he said with a glint in his eye, "what happens if we apply the same logic to *John*?"

"What do you mean?"

"The gospel of John was written around 90 AD. So the same idea applies. Shroud first, book second. The cloth was in Edessa before John was written."

"But Ugo—"

"Hear me out. Since you've shown me that John adds and subtracts material as he sees fit, what if John tells us something new about the Shroud in his gospel?"

I lifted a hand to stop him. "Ugo, you can't make that leap. There's a geography problem. Tatian was writing in Edessa. If the Shroud was there, he would've seen it. But John wasn't writing in Edessa. So how would he have seen it?"

Before answering, Ugo stepped back toward a bookcase and unraveled a map that was waiting there in a scroll. It showed ancient Syria, from the coast of the Mediterranean to the Euphrates and Tigris in the east. His index finger stabbed at a familiar point.

"The city of Antioch," he said. "One of the likeliest places John was written." His thumb moved an inch inland. "The city of Edessa. Where the Shroud was." He glanced up at me. "Sister cities. If the Shroud arrived in Edessa around 30 AD, news would've reached Antioch long before 90."

I shook my head. "Ugo, I think this assumes too much."

"Why? We have plenty of historical records showing that news traveled between the cities."

I fidgeted in my seat, feeling flustered. It was true that John had incorporated new material into the gospel corpus—hints of gnostic ideas and pagan philosophies and new Christian attitudes toward Jews—but Ugo was proposing something different. Something worse: that John's gospel was as tainted by personal prejudice and local color as the Diatessaron. The real problem wasn't geography. It was personality. Tatian was a brilliant but eccentric loner, a man who drifted further and further from mainline Christianity. He changed the gospels to agree with his sectarian beliefs. The author of John, whoever he might have been, was a philosophical genius who set his sights on something different and much higher. Something essential to all Christians. The invisible truth about God.

Yet Ugo said, "Please understand, I don't suggest this lightly. Try to stand apart from your emotions. It's a testable hypothesis: the authors of both John and the Diatessaron *knew* a disciple had brought the Shroud to Edessa and indicated this in their writings."

"Then let's test the hypothesis," I said. "Does John say the burial cloth had an image on it? No. Does the Diatessaron say that? No. Does John or the Diatessaron say the Shroud was brought from Jerusalem to Edessa? No. The hypothesis fails."

"Father," Ugo chided, "you know that isn't reasonable. These writers weren't trying to persuade *us*, two thousand years later, of something they considered obvious. It would be ludicrous for them to make a big fuss about the Shroud if everyone knew it was in Edessa. As ludicrous as if you or I made a big fuss about the existence of Saint Peter's Basilica."

"Then what are you saying?"

"I'm saying we have to look for an allusion. A few details feathered in to make the gospels acknowledge what everyone in Edessa and Antioch already knew."

"So where are those allusions?"

"Before I answer, tell me this: after the disciples found the Shroud, who do you suppose was allowed to keep it?"

"I don't know. It would've become communal property, I guess."

"But the disciples fanned out across the world to spread the Gospel. Which of them got to keep the Shroud?"

"I would be speculating. The gospels don't say."

"Don't they? I would suggest to you that John gives us a hint."

He waited, as if I might guess.

"How well do you remember the story," he said, "of Doubting Thomas?"

I recited, "Thomas, called Didymus, was not with the other disciples when Jesus came. So they said, 'We have seen the Lord,' but he replied, 'Unless I see the nail marks in his hands and put my hand into the wound in his side, I will not believe.' A week later Jesus came and stood in their midst, saying, 'Peace be with you.' Then he said to Thomas, 'See my hands. Put your hand into my side. Do not be unbelieving, but believe.' Thomas answered, 'My Lord and my God!' Jesus replied, 'Have you come to believe because you have seen me? Blessed are those who have not seen and have believed.'"

"Excellent," Ugo said. "Now, I ask you: does any other gospel give us the story of Doubting Thomas?"

"No. There's a similar story in Luke, but the details are different."

"Correct. Luke says Jesus appeared after his death and the disciples were all afraid. But he never mentions Thomas. Nor does he focus on this peculiar thing Jesus does, proving his identity by showing the nail marks and the spear wound. So why would John add those details? It's almost as if he took Luke's story and then specifically added Thomas and the wounds."

Here was the monster I had created. A man who now could dissect the gospels like a priest and test them like a scientist. These were exactly the right questions: How are the gospel accounts different? What do the differences mean? If a story isn't factual, then why is it there? But rather than encourage Ugo, I said, "I don't know."

Ugo leaned in. "Remember the question I asked you before? About which disciple received the Shroud? I think this story is our answer."

"You think Thomas got the Shroud?"

He rose and pointed to a map of ancient Edessa on the wall. "This building," he said, tapping a dot beneath the glass, "was the most famous church in Edessa. Built to house the bones of Saint Thomas after he died. Thomas was *there*, Father Alex. Later records suggest he sent the image to the king. All I'm suggesting is that the gospel of John agrees. Its author knew the story and added it to the gospel."

I squinted. "Ugo, there are other reasons John could've put Thomas in that story."

"True. But recite the beginning of the Doubting Thomas story one more time."

"Thomas, called Didymus, was not—"

"Stop!" Ugo said. "That's it, right there. *Thomas, called Didymus.* Let's remind ourselves what that means."

"*Didymus* is Greek for 'twin.'"

"Yes. And why?"

"They called him the Twin. It was his nickname."

"Whose twin was he?"

"The gospels don't say."

"Yet the gospel of John always identifies this man as 'Thomas, called Didymus.' Isn't it odd to keep calling someone 'Twin' without ever explaining whose twin he is?"

I shrugged. Jesus gave many nicknames. Simon became Peter, "the Rock." John and James became Boanerges, "Sons of Thunder."

"But the story gets stranger," Ugo continued. "As I'm sure you know, the nickname *Didymus* isn't the only odd thing about Thomas. The name *Thomas* itself is just as strange."

"It means 'twin,' too," I said.

Ugo lit up. "Yes! *T'oma* is Aramaic for 'twin,' just as *Didymus* is Greek for 'twin.' So 'Thomas called Didymus' actually means 'Twin called Twin'! Don't you find that bizarre? Why would John call him that?"

I smiled to myself. If Ugo hadn't been a museum curator, he would've made a very popular pre-seminary teacher. "Sometimes John gives us the Aramaic and then its Greek gloss. It doesn't necessarily mean—"

"Father, the other times John repeats himself like this, he's referring to Jesus. 'The Messiah, the Anointed.' 'Rabbi, Teacher.' So why is he doing it this time for Thomas?"

"Why don't you tell me?"

"Do you know," Ugo said, "who this man's twin was *alleged* to be?"

"I do. The legend says it was Jesus."

Ugo smiled.

"But that's *just* a legend," I added.

The gospel of Mark says Jesus had brothers and sisters. Inevitably, some readers imagined that the mysterious "twin" nicknamed Thomas might've been one of these siblings.

Ugo ignored me. "*A twin of Jesus.* A facsimile. A spitting image." He lowered his voice. "What does that remind you of?"

Finally I understood. "You think people associated Thomas with the Shroud. You think that's how he got his nickname."

"No. Even more than that: I think 'Thomas' and 'Didymus' *are* the Shroud. I think the disciples had never seen anything like it before, so they called the image what it seemed to be: reflection, duplicate, twin. Only later did the name attach to the man who brought the Shroud out of Jerusalem. By the time the first gospel was written, most Christians spoke Greek or Latin, so they had no idea what *Thomas* meant in Aramaic. They might've thought it was the man's actual name. That's why the gospel of John reminds them by adding the *Greek* word for twin: *Didymus.*"

I sat back, not knowing what to say. In the hundreds of books I had read on the life of Jesus, I had never encountered anything like this idea. There are other reasons John might've created the Thomas story—and yet, there was something magnetic about Ugo's idea. Something simple and elegant and grounded. For a moment, the author of John stopped being an unapproachable philosopher. He became an ordinary Christian trying to keep our greatest relic from slipping out of the memory of our religion.

"I suppose it's possible," I said. "Stranger things have been true."

"Then we agree!"

"But Ugo, it's not strong enough to make a convincing case unless we find corroborating evidence in the Diatessaron."

He opened his research diary to a page where his pen lay tucked like a bookmark. "Which brings me to our plan of attack. There are three passages in John that mention Thomas: 11:16, 14:5, and the Doubting Thomas story at 20:24. I've told the conservators to restore those verses next before they do anything else."

I took the pen from him and uncapped it. "There's a fourth reference in the other gospels. Thomas appears in their lists of the twelve disciples."

"Where?"

"Mark 3:14. Which Matthew copies at 10:2 and Luke copies at 6:13. All three versions mention Thomas, so the Diatessaron should have Thomas, too. If we find anything more than his name there—an adjective, another nickname, anything at all—it could be the corroboration you want."

"Excellent." Ugo clapped his hands together. "Now, one more thing. While we wait for the restorers, what's the best book on Doubting Thomas?"

I wrote a title in his diary. *Symbolism in John's Passion Narrative.*

"Do you own a copy yourself?" he asked sheepishly. "I'd rather not look in the library."

"Why not?"

"They've put those new scanners in the ordinary stacks. They can probably track what we take off the shelves."

"My library is at your disposal," I said. "I'll bring the book over tomorrow."

He smiled. "Father Alex, we're getting close. Very close. I hope you can feel it, too."

I went home that afternoon feeling as giddy as Ugo must've been. In my prayers that night I asked God for wisdom, for insight. The next morning I pulled out *Symbolism in John*, slipped a note inside for Ugo, and left it in his office mailbox before I went off to teach. That day I dreamed of Thomas. Of the Twin. Never did I suspect that Ugo and I had spoken to each other for the last time as friends.

OVERNIGHT, HE CHANGED. ONE morning he was invited to an important meeting—he never said with whom—and after that meeting, he was never the same.

In retrospect, I know what happened. Two weeks earlier, Simon had surfaced in Rome for the last time that summer. He stayed just one night. In the afternoon, he went into the city for a haircut and shave. Before bed, he rolled the lint off his best cassock. Next morning he vanished before dawn and reappeared a few hours later with a white rosary of plastic pearls for Peter. Those rosaries are given as gifts by offices throughout the Holy See. Not just by the Holy Father. But no Vatican office hands out invitations to seven thirty AM meetings—and no Secretariat man would fly across a continent to accept one. Simon had Mass with the pope. He never bragged about it, never even mentioned it. But there was no other explanation. And if John Paul reached out to Simon, then he must've done the same for Ugo.

The day after Ugo's meeting, he suspended work at the conservation lab until further notice. He put a lock on the door, as if he suddenly knew that he could get away with it. That he was supported from on high. Then he called me.

"Father, we need to talk. Face-to-face. Meet me for breakfast at Bar Jona."

Bar Jona. The nickname of the café Lucio had just opened on the rooftop of Saint Peter's. A public place. Looking back, it had all the trappings of a breakup.

When I arrived, Ugo was waiting with a cup in one hand and a brief-case in the other. A good way to prevent any handshakes or friendly embraces.

"What happened at your meeting?" I asked.

Nobody could've overheard me—there was a coffee grinder whirring, an air-conditioning unit moaning on the wall—but he led me away from the coffee bar as if we were trading secrets now.

Bar Jona is a play on words: Saint Peter's last name in Hebrew. But the place, like all of Lucio's creations, was humorless. Posters taped to walls, trash cans half-filled with soda cups. The all-important Vatican mailbox standing by the door like an alms box beckoned tourists to write postcards and cover them with lucrative Vatican stamps.

"I know," Ugo said, lowering his head toward me and bringing his voice down to a whisper, "what you've been doing. And I can't tell you how betrayed I feel."

I blinked in confusion.

"How could you do this?" he added. "How could you abuse my trust?"

"Ugo, what on earth are you talking about?"

He glared. "You *knew* your brother had been to visit the Holy Father. You *knew* it was because of my work."

I nodded. "So?"

"I won't have my work stolen away. This is *my* exhibit, Father Alex. Not your brother's. Not yours. How dare you transform it into some cheap negotiating chip behind my back? You know I don't give a damn about your Eastern politics. This is over. You and I are finished."

I was cold in my own skin. "I don't know what you're talking about."

"Go to hell."

"What did the Holy Father say to you?"

Ugo rose from the table. "The Holy Father? Ha! Thank God *he* isn't the only one who cares about my work."

I never made enough of those words. In retrospect, they told me everything I needed to know about who he'd really met with. Instead, the words that lingered in my memory were the ones that hurt most:

"Alex, don't say another word. I don't want to hear your lies. Respect my wishes and stay away from my exhibit. Good-bye."

———

I CALLED HIM A dozen times that afternoon. A dozen more in the week that followed. He never answered my messages. I stopped by the restoration lab, but the guards kept me out. So I waited outside the museum one night and confronted Ugo when he emerged from the door. No matter where I followed him, though, he refused to speak. I never understood, and he never explained. We never spoke again.

The morning after our meeting at Bar Jona, I phoned Simon at the nunciature in Turkey. He was away on business and took three nights to get back to me. When I told him the news, he was as upset as I had been. Now, though, my own feelings had turned to anger.

"He didn't tell you anything more?" Simon asked. "He didn't say what they'd told him?"

"Nothing."

"Is he still in Rome? Can you try to talk to him about it?"

"I did try, Simon."

"Alex, please. It matters a lot. He's . . . a very important person to me."

"I'm sorry. It's done."

I don't know why Ugo's silence hurt me so deeply. Maybe because his final accusation rang true. I had claimed ownership of work that wasn't mine. I had flattered myself that his exhibit was *our* exhibit, and he had seen through me.

But there was another reason. The work I did with Ugo made me feel, briefly, that I was a partner in something meaningful. The most thrilling thing about it wasn't that I found our work so urgent and heartfelt, but that *we* found it so urgent and heartfelt. I never envied Simon his travels and negotiations. To be a father and a teacher always suited me fine. But to have a partner in life who sits in a booster seat and only recently graduated from a bib is to crave a daily chance for adult companionship, to feel a pathetic gratitude for a short conversation with a bank teller or the man at the butcher counter. Walking into that restoration lab with Ugo each morning and wondering what the manuscript held in store—or sharing phone calls at the end of the day, with no purpose except to vent the day's frustrations and marvel at the little book that owned us—was the closest experience I'd had in years to walking into Peter's bedroom with Mona and wondering what the baby was about to teach us about being parents. Without realizing it, I'd let Ugo enter my life through the open door she left behind. And when he abandoned me, with no explanation, all of it returned. The old dreams. The weird pangs of solitude in the middle of walking to work, or dialing a phone number, or reading alone after Peter's bedtime. The sensation of having an anchor hung around my neck, dangling into an emptiness that seemed to have no bottom.

Worse, Ugo's disappearance felt as if it confirmed the verdict of Mona's disappearance: that the fault was somehow in me. Life had given me a parole hearing and found me still wanting. The last I ever heard from Ugolino Nogara was that e-mail. And I thought, because I ignored it, that I had finally learned my lesson.

CHAPTER 27

W HEN I PICK Peter up from the Costa apartment, the first thing he says is, "I don't want to go back to Prozio's palace. I want to go home."

"Did Allegra say something to you?" I ask.

"I just want to play with my cars."

"We can pick up some of your toys, but I don't think we're going to stay."

"Can I go to the bathroom, too? I don't like Prozio's bathrooms."

His insistence seems less odd now. "I'll give you a piggyback ride. We'll get there faster."

HOME. WHEN I WAS seven, Simon and I counted the number of stairs to our floor and the number of steps to our apartment. The steps have diminished over the years, but not the habit of counting them. Peter and I do it out loud. He says he will climb the stairs faster than I do when he comes back to live here someday as a world-famous soccer player.

Inside, the plants are wilting. The hake that Sister Helena made for Simon's arrival is developing smells on a lonely platter in the refrigerator.

While Peter is in the bathroom, I clean up what remains of the mess. The place looks like home again.

"I'm hungry," Peter announces on his return.

I pull down a box of cereal, the single father's standby. While I wait for him to finish, I call maintenance.

"Mario, it's Father Alex up on four. I need to change my lock. Do you have parts for that?"

Mario isn't known for promptness, but we went to school together, so I know I can trust him.

"Father, I'm glad to hear you're back," he says. "Coming right up."

By the time Peter's done with his second bowl, we have a shiny new knob and key. Mario has even insisted on installing them himself.

"Anything else you need," he says, "you call me."

He musses Peter's hair. He must know about Simon, but this is his reaction to the news. I miss this place. I didn't appreciate enough what a family we are in this building.

When he's gone, Peter brings his bowl to the sink and goes to play with the new knob. "I've been praying for Simon," he says, apropos of nothing.

I try to look unsurprised.

"Me too, buddy," I say.

"When it's for Simon, who do you pray to?"

He told me once that praying is like being a soccer coach and calling saints off the bench.

"The Theotokos," I say.

Mary, the mother of God. The highest power of intercession.

He nods solemnly. "Me, too." He picks up one of his toy cars and flies it through the air, making artillery sounds.

"Why do you ask?"

He scrunches up his face. "I don't know. But I think this car is out of batteries."

He opens the battery drawer beside the phone and decides to tap the button on the answering machine.

"Simon's going to be fine, Pet—" I start to say.

But when I hear the words coming out of the answering machine, I rush to cut it off.

Alex, it's me. I'm sorry. I shouldn't have come to see Peter at the class you were giving. Please call m—

I manage to stop the message before it can finish.

"Who was that?" Peter says.

It breaks my heart to say the word. "Nobody."

But he knows women rarely call this phone. He reaches onto the counter and scrolls through the list of incoming calls.

"Who's Vi-ter-bo?" he asks.

I stare at him. "Don't be nosy."

He grunts unappreciatively and starts rummaging through the batteries.

So this is how it's going to feel, every time the phone rings. This is how my heart will be crimped every time someone knocks on the door.

"When is Sister Helena coming back?" he says.

"I don't know." I feel tired of all the white lies. "Not anytime soon."

He gives up looking for batteries and, with a sigh, flies the car back through the air toward his bedroom.

"Peter," I say.

He returns with an old stuffed rabbit he used to sleep with, inspecting it as if for the first time. There were once teddy bears and blankets where there are now trading cards and soccer posters. I'm going to miss my baby boy. He's making his very final lap.

"Eh, Babbo?" he says, coming toward me.

The cartoon bear on TV says something like this. Maybe he's already forgetting the voice on the machine.

But I'm not. Until we finish this, I'm going to hear that voice in every silence.

I open my arms and lift him into my lap. I want to remember this moment.

Running my fingers through his hair, I say, "Peter, there's something I want to tell you."

He stops strafing the rabbit's ears against each other. "Good news or bad news?"

How I wish I knew. Every particle of hope says good. Every ounce of experience says bad.

"Good," I tell him.

And then the words he's been waiting to hear almost since he was born.

"That woman on the phone," I say, "was Mamma."

He stops. Confusion sets in his eyes.

"She came back two nights ago," I say. "While you were at Prozio's palace."

He shakes his head. At first he doubts. Then he recoils. I've kept this from him. This miracle, this divine visitation.

"She's here?" he asks, glancing toward the bedrooms.

"Not in the apartment. But we could call her if you wanted."

His perplexity is supreme. "When?"

"Anytime we want, I think."

He stares expectantly at the phone on the table. But there's a distance we need to travel first.

"You and I have waited a long time for this," I begin.

He nods. "A super-long time."

Since before he could form a memory of her.

"How do you feel about it?" I ask.

His hand is tapping the table. Feet kicking underneath. "Great," he says. But what he means is: *Hurry up, please.*

"Do you remember," I ask, "the story of when Jesus came back?"

It's the only way I can think to explain this. By returning to the story we know best.

"Yes."

"What happened when he came back? Did the disciples recognize him?"

Peter shakes his head.

It's one of the most mysterious, poignant moments of the gospels.

"*Two men were traveling on the road to Emmaus,*" I recite, "*and Christ drew near to them, and walked with them. But they did not recognize him.*"

I used to imagine the two men as brothers, one taller and one shorter. Now I picture a father and son.

"When Mamma comes back," I say, "she may be different. She won't look exactly like our pictures of her. She may not act like our stories about her. We may not quite recognize her at first. But she'll still be Mamma, right?"

He nods, but this is starting to fill him with anxiety.

"And what else did Jesus do," I continue, "after he came back?"

What a poor teacher I am. A thousand possible answers to this question, and I expect him to intuit the right one.

Somehow, though, Peter knows. It's taken him a moment to find my wavelength, to align our minds, but we have always understood each other.

"After Jesus came back," he says with a hint of desperation, "he left again."

I push forward. "And if Mamma leaves again, we'll be sad, but we'll understand, won't we?"

He turns his head away violently and slips out of my lap. He wipes away tears with lashing strokes of his hand, wanting me to see how upset he is.

"Peter." I kneel beside him. If I were to make him dread Mona's arrival, I would be sharing the very worst of myself. The part that is incapable of hope. My own heart drowns in these worries for his sake, but for his sake I have to do better. "Peter, I believe she's *not* going to leave. I believe she wouldn't have come back if she were going to do that. Your mamma loves you. And no matter what happens, she'll always love you. She would never want to hurt you. Not for anything in the world."

He nods. His lashes are dewed with tears, but his eyes are drying. This is what he wants to hear.

I place my hands on his sides. His ribs are thinner than my fingers. "When she meets you, she's going to feel something amazing. There's no love in the world like a mamma's love for her little boy."

The verdict of our whole religion. Between mother and child is the purest love in creation.

And yet I don't want to ply him with false hope. Neither of us knows Mona's motives. I don't even know my own. We've created a delicate life here, and the upheaval she could create is total. Right now, our energy needs to be focused on Simon. But I can't deny Peter this moment. He's waited so long.

"Can she come over?" he says, reaching for the phone. *"Please?"*

This last word is so bottomless that it guts me.

"We can call her," I say. "Okay?"

His finger is on the button. He itches to press it.

"Wait," I say. "Have you thought what you would say to her?"

Without even hesitating, he nods.

My heart cracks. I never guessed he had a script for this conversation. "All right, then," I say. "Go ahead."

But to my surprise, he hands the phone back. "Can we do it together?"

So with my finger over his, we press Dial.

I whisper, "Ready?"

He can't answer. He's fixated on the ring tone.

Mona answers almost immediately. It's as if we've called on the emergency frequency reserved for superheroes. Peter is entranced.

"Alex?" she says.

My son's blue eyes are as wide as the sky. I put the handset on speakerphone. Now I'm just a witness.

"Hello?" she says.

Peter is startled. He doesn't recognize her voice. Somewhere deep inside him, he's discovering the cement is still wet.

His lips form a smile. In a small voice he says, "Mamma?"

I wish I could see her face.

A sound comes out of the speaker. Peter stares in alarm. He doesn't recognize the sound of his mother crying.

"*Peter*," she says.

He looks at me again. Not for reassurance this time, but for material. I realize there was never any script for this conversation.

"Peter," Mona says, "I'm so happy you called me."

She's searching for words, too. In this most fundamental act of my daily life, speaking to our child, she is inexperienced.

"I—did you—what did you do today? Did you have fun with Babbo?"

Her voice is slow and full of sunny overabundance, as if she's talking to a child half his age. But Peter's already recovered. Without answering her question, he locks in his agenda: "Can you come over to our house?"

We're both caught by surprise. Mona says, "Well. I don't know if—"

"You can come right now. We're having cereal for dinner."

She responds with a pop of laughter that takes Peter aback. He didn't know his mother contained such noises.

"Peter," she says, still laughing, "sweetheart, we would need to talk to your father about that."

O naïve woman. Like a fish in his net.

Peter shoves the phone across the table. "Okay," he says. "My father's right here."

SHE ARRIVES TWENTY MINUTES later. I could've stopped her. But I've never seen Peter so lost in joy. I'd sooner have blown out candles in a church.

He rushes to answer the door, and it's like watching a train careen into a dark tunnel. God bless him, he doesn't even hesitate.

Mona is dressed in an outfit I've never seen before. No conservative summer sweater tonight, but an indigo sundress with bare shoulders. She is beautiful. And yet as she lowers herself to her knees, offering an embrace she isn't sure Peter will accept, the smile is plastered on her face. Sensing her terror, he is suddenly full of ambivalence, too, and lurches forward weirdly to take the hug. Neither says a word.

I'm relieved. Peter's too young to understand regret, but my body vibrates with the awareness that we're now playing with those dark materials.

Mona reaches into a plastic bag on the floor by her feet and says, "I brought dinner."

Tupperware. Her answer to our pathetic dinner of cereal.

"A gift," she clarifies, "from Nonna."

Peter's maternal grandmother. I recoil.

Peter looks at the Tupperware and says, as if there's still time to change his order, "My favorite pizza is margherita."

"I'm sorry," Mona says, crestfallen. "All I brought is some cacio e pepe."

Tonnarelli with cheese sauce. The devil inside me smiles. Her mother's version of the dish will be too peppery for Peter. A fitting introduction to the mother-in-law I always found to be an acquired taste.

"We already had cereal," Peter explains. But he takes her by the hand and leads her inside. "How long can you stay? Can you spend the night?"

Mona glances at me for help.

"Peter," I say, stroking his hair, "not tonight."

He frowns. If this is a preview of the new chain of command, he doesn't like it.

"Why?" he says.

Surprisingly, this is the moment when Mona chooses to assert herself.

"Peter, we aren't ready for that yet. You have to be patient with us."

The anger that blooms on his face is beautifully pure. What hypocrites we are. Grant us love, but not yet.

"I brought something for you, though," she says, reaching into the bag.

Peter waits expectantly, only to receive a picture in a frame. It shows the two of us watching soccer on TV. I'm holding his arms in the air to celebrate a goal. I have to guard myself against the emotion that comes with realizing she's kept this picture for years. But Peter pulls the frame out of her palm and says, "Okay, thanks," and plunks it on the nearest table.

I offer my wife a hand. "Let me put the pasta in the fridge."

And for the first time, as we make the exchange, our fingers touch.

THE HOUR WE SPEND together is bruising, in part because it's so obvious how wonderful Peter finds it. Mona is awkward with him, but for Peter there's no transition at all, no slow warm-up to the presence of an unfamiliar adult. He takes her to his bedroom and sits down on the floor, offering her the spot beside him. He tells belabored stories about other boys she doesn't know, whose escapades she can't possibly understand, especially in his stream-of-consciousness Italian. "Tino, downstairs? It was Thursday, but not this Thursday? He told Giada that his allowance, if she would show her underpants to him, he would give her all of it. And she said no, but he tried anyway, *and she broke his fingers.*" All the while he's playing with toy cars or showing her the new soccer cleats Simon scrimped to buy him. A lifetime of catching up might just be possible before sunset.

The fury of his mind is painful to watch. It reveals a kind of double existence, as if he hasn't just been living his life but curating it, preparing the museum of himself for his mother's return. Even sadder is his insistence on giving the whole tour tonight, as if he's not convinced he'll have another chance. Simon disappeared on him two nights ago. The possibility of loss is fresh. When this performance is over, I wonder how he'll sleep tonight. How he'll be able to think of anything except whether there will be a next time.

But for now, he's effusive. Determined to empty himself to the last drop. Keeping up with him exhausts Mona, who tries to follow everything he says until, deep into the visit, she finally capitulates and just enjoys this time for what it is.

At last, when Peter finishes his second discourse on tadpoles, I'm forced to say, "Peter, it's going to be bedtime soon."

I hadn't intended for us to stay here tonight. But we have a new lock on the door and the vigilance of neighbors who love us. Most of all, we have a chance to replace bad memories with good.

"*No,*" Peter cries.

Mona intervenes. "Could I read him a story?"

He launches himself into bed with expectation. This is the room where he hid with Sister Helena in fear while a stranger tore through our home, yet he seems oblivious to anything but his mother.

"Pajamas?" I suggest. "And brushing our teeth?"

Peter drags Mona to the bathroom, where an old hairbrush and two stray toothpaste caps lie on the countertop. There are no cups, because we rinse our mouths from the sink. Our toothbrushes are at Lucio's, so Peter intrepidly rinses off an old one from a drawer. This evidence of our manly state inspires a wry smile from Mona.

"Needs a certain touch," she says.

An hour with our son has loosened her up.

"Toothpaste," Peter says in the voice of a surgeon asking for a scalpel.

"Toothpaste," Mona replies, presenting the tube.

My eyes linger on Simon's knickknacks, scattered on the countertop from the night Ugo died, when he took a hasty shower here. He is the ghost of this visit. The shadow of our family's happiness. Seeing my son smile, I remember that my brother is alone tonight.

Mona and Peter read a few chapters of *Pinocchio*. Then I announce it's time for prayers. He lowers himself to the edge of the bed, clasping his hands, while Mona glances at me, wondering. Asking.

"Sure," I say quietly. "Together."

The world hushes. The night leans in. *For where two or three are gathered in my name, there I am, among them.*

"Almighty and merciful God," I say, "we thank You for bringing us together in this home tonight. With this blessing You remind us that all things are possible in You. Though we cannot know our future, or change our past, we humbly ask You to guide us toward Your will, and to watch over our beloved Simon. Amen."

To which I silently add:

Lord, remember my brother who is alone tonight. He doesn't need Your mercy. Only Your justice. Please, Lord, give him justice.

At the door, before Mona leaves, she says to me, "Thank you."

I nod. "It meant the world to him."

I can't let myself say more.

Mona has fewer inhibitions. "I'd love to come back and see you both again. Do you want me to bring over some dinner tomorrow?"

Tomorrow. So soon. I have to be at the courtroom in the morning. I have to be prepared for whatever Mignatto might ask of me at any hour of the day.

I begin to answer, but she sees my expression and waves me off. "It doesn't have to be tomorrow. You call me when you're ready. I want to help, Alex, not get in the way." She hesitates. "I could even stay with him if you're going to—"

"Tomorrow's fine," I say. "Let's do dinner tomorrow."

She smiles. "Call me if you feel the same way in the morning."

I wait. If she kisses me, I'll know we came too far, too fast. I'll have to second-guess what happened tonight.

But she places her hand on my arm and gives it a squeeze. That's all. Her fingers slip away, touching mine as they drop. She lifts them in the air, saying good night.

Tomorrow, I think.

So soon.

CHAPTER 28

AT SEVEN THIRTY in the morning, I arrive outside the tribunal palace. Brother Samuel and the other pharmacists are watching Peter because Mignatto summoned me for an early meeting. He's already here, waiting on a bench in the courtyard as I arrive, holding a paper that turns out to be a list of today's deponents. Wordlessly he shows it to me. First will be Guido Canali, then two men I don't recognize. The last name on the list is Simon's.

"Is he really coming?" I ask.

"I don't know. But this may be the tribunal's last chance." Mignatto turns to me, as if this is the reason for the meeting. "Father, it's possible the trial will end today."

"What do you mean?"

"When Archbishop Nowak disallowed testimony about the exhibit, it became impossible for the judges to establish motive. And without the security-camera footage, it may be impossible for them to establish opportunity."

"You're saying Simon could go free?"

"The judges are giving the promoter of justice latitude to propose new witnesses, but if nothing changes, the tribunal could find insufficient grounds to continue. The charge would be dropped."

"That's fantastic."

He places a hand on my arm. "The reason I'm telling you this is that

I decided to submit Nogara's phone into evidence. The tribunal needed a voice sample for forensic comparison with the message left on your brother's answering machine at the embassy, and the voice mail greeting on Nogara's phone gave me a window to introduce it. My hope is that the judges decided to listen to the messages your brother left Nogara at Castel Gandolfo. Still, I have to condemn in the strongest terms your development of evidence this way. We're fortunate the law forbids procurators to testify, or else you'd have to answer very difficult questions. I don't know who gave the phone to you, but I need to emphasize again that, for your brother's sake, you must not let this be repeated if the trial continues beyond today."

"Yes, Monsignor."

He relaxes. "I've filed a petition to have Father Simon placed in your uncle's custody. I don't know whether they'll honor it. In any case, I don't see how his testimony can do the prosecution much good, since he refuses to speak."

Mignatto takes back the list and fidgets with the locks on his brief-case before slipping the paper inside.

I put an arm around him and say, "Monsignor, thank you."

He gives me a careful pat on the back. "Don't thank me. Thank *him*."

In the distance, approaching the Palace of the Tribunal, is Arch-bishop Nowak. We watch in silence as the gendarmes admit him, then close the doors again.

JUST BEFORE EIGHT, THE courtroom opens again to admit the rest of us. On the hour, the judges enter together from the side door of their chambers. Without ado, one says, "Officer, please call the first witness."

Guido is admitted into the aula. He arrives in a black suit with a gray shirt and silver necktie, a bulging gold watch on his wrist. Only his leathery skin reveals him as a farmhand. The notary rises so that Guido can take both oaths before identifying himself as Guido Fran-cesco Andreo Donato Canali, the only man in Rome with more names than the pope.

"You were present at Castel Gandolfo," the presiding judge asks, "on the night Ugolino Nogara was killed?"

"Correct."

"Please tell us what you saw."

"While I was on my shift, I got a phone call from Father Alex Andreou, brother of the accused. He asked me to open the gates for him."

The old judge leans forward. Guido's delivery has none of the usual roughness or swagger. He doesn't even point a finger when he mentions my name.

"I drove him down in my truck," Guido continues. "We got almost to—"

The judge thumps his hand on the bench. "Stop! You're saying you opened the gates because a friend asked you to?"

Guido shrinks. "Monsignor, it was the wrong thing to do. I know that now. I apologize."

The presiding judge growls, "And where exactly did you chauffeur your friend, the accused's brother?"

"There's only one main road down from the gates. We headed that way. Then Father Alex got out when he saw his brother."

Mignatto lifts a hand.

The younger judge anticipates the objection. "Signor Canali, did you see the accused? Do you know that his brother saw him?"

Guido sips some water. He jiggles his wrist to shift the weight of his watch. "I know where Nogara's body was found. It's right near where Father Alex got off my truck. So."

The presiding judge lifts his hands in the air. "About the chronology: the defendant's brother contacted you at what time?"

"About fifteen minutes before he showed up at the gate. I checked my phone. Six forty-two."

"And where was he calling from?"

"A parking lot at the bottom of the cliff, he said."

The judge writes something down. "How long is the drive from here to Castel Gandolfo?"

"Seventeen miles. Three-quarters of an hour."

"You're sure?"

"I drive it every Sunday to visit my mother."

The judge writes another note. "But it rained on the night Doctor Nogara was killed?"

"As if sent by God."

"So the drive would've taken longer?"

Guido shrugs. "A little weather gets people off the roads. Less traffic. It depends."

I begin to see where the judge is going. He realizes Guido saw nothing at Castel Gandolfo, but he's calculating when Simon called me. Re-creating the timeline of Ugo's death. I notice that Mignatto looks concerned.

The presiding judge nods. "Thank you, signore."

He seems poised to release Guido, but Mignatto makes a signal to him, and the judge motions him forward. Everyone in the courtroom watches as Mignatto slips a sheet of paper to the presiding judge, who reads it silently and then nods.

"One last thing," he says.

For the first time, Guido glances at me. His eyes are full of hatred. I realize he's terrified. He just wants to go home.

"Sure," he says.

"Why did you open the gates for the accused's brother?"

I sense what Mignatto's doing, and for a second I pity Guido. The point has already been made. But if this is what it takes to free Simon, then so be it.

Guido brightens. He misunderstands. "I did it because Father Alex and I grew up together. We're old friends."

The presiding judge says drily, "Did you ask him for a bribe? Two tickets to Doctor Nogara's exhibit?"

The old judge peers cruelly down. Guido squirms like a hurt puppy.

"Well . . . I mean . . ." Guido Canali actually turns to me, as if for help. "It wasn't like that. I just said . . ."

Mignatto jots a note on his legal pad. It's pure gibberish. He just doesn't want to be seen gloating.

"Signor Canali," says the presiding judge with disgust, "you're excused. This tribunal is done hearing your testimony."

Guido lifts himself from his chair. He adjusts his belt and smooths his necktie on his belly with a stunned look. He leaves without a sound.

"OFFICER, THE NEXT WITNESS." The judge looks at the roster in front of him. "Please call Signor Pei."

This is one of the two unfamiliar deponents from Mignatto's list.

Who's that? I write on the pad between us.

Mignatto ignores me.

The man identifies himself as Gino Pei, driver in the pontifical car service. I take him to be a previously unscheduled witness, since Gianni never mentioned a driver being called to testify. Mignatto watches attentively.

"Signore," the lead judge asks once the oaths are finished, "it says here that your job is shift coordinator. What does that mean?"

"It's not a job, Monsignor, just a perk of seniority. It means I'm the driver who assigns pickups to my coworkers as the requests come in."

"In other words, you're familiar with all the incoming requests."

"On my shift. Correct."

"And how long have you been a driver in the service?"

"Twelve years."

"How many passengers have you driven in twelve years?"

"Hundreds. Thousands."

"So if we were to ask you about a specific passenger, how well could we expect you to remember him?"

"Monsignor, I don't need to remember. We keep records of everything. Time in, time out, pickups, locations."

The judge scans a sheet of questions that must have come from the prosecutor, the promoter of justice. "Very well. I'd like to ask you about the day of Ugolino Nogara's death."

I wonder if anyone else realizes this line of questioning is about to hit a roadblock.

"I'm sorry, Monsignor," Gino says in a nervous voice. He gestures at the promoter. "But like I told him last night, I can't answer that question."

"Why not?"

"There aren't any records from that day."

"What do you mean?"

"We were ordered not to keep any logs."

"Ordered by whom?" the old judge grumbles.

Gino Pei hesitates. "Monsignors, I can't answer that."

The promoter of justice watches the judges. He seems to be weighing the tribunal's reaction.

The presiding judge is the first to realize what the court has just encountered. "Are you under a prior oath not to discuss this?"

"That's correct."

The monsignor removes his dark-framed glasses and rubs the bridge of his nose. The promoter of justice is tense in his seat. Judges have no power to undo oaths. The pool of available questions has just evaporated.

"What's this nonsense?" the old one hisses. "Who swears *drivers* to secrecy?"

The promoter of justice bobs his head, as if this is exactly the right question. I glance at Mignatto. He's watching the promoter tensely.

"Is there anything you *are* able to tell us about the accused?" says the presiding judge.

"No," Gino says.

"Then can you tell us about what you saw at Castel Gandolfo?"

"Monsignor, I can't."

The silence is filled only by the typing of the notary.

The judges confer for a moment on the bench. Then the presiding judge says, "Enough. You're excused. The tribunal will hear the next witness."

AS PEI LEAVES, I glance at Mignatto excitedly, feeling the trial inch nearer to Simon's exoneration. The atmosphere in the courtroom has changed. The judges look impatient. One rubs a pen between his hands, back and forth, back and forth.

A sleepy-looking layman strides in. He has purses of skin under his sad eyes, and a drumstick of a nose. He bows to the judges before taking the oaths, then identifies himself as Vincenzo Corvi, forensic analyst with the Rome police. Mignatto, hearing that title, frowns.

The young judge says, "Signor Corvi, your office was consulted by our Vatican police in this case. Why?"

"For professional analysis of two items found at the scene, and verification of one voice recording."

"Could you identify these pieces of evidence?"

"The two items from the crime scene are a spent 6.35-millimeter bullet and a human hair. The recording is a voice mail message."

"Let's begin with the evidence from Castel Gandolfo. Were the bullet and the human hair found together?"

"No. Found separately."

"Would you explain your findings to the tribunal?"

Corvi produces a pair of glasses and glances at a report. "The bullet was located near the body of the deceased and has deformations consistent with the entry and exit wounds in the deceased's skull."

"You're saying this was the gunshot that killed Doctor Nogara?"

"Almost certainly. It's the same caliber fired by the weapon in question, a Beretta 950."

Mignatto's eyes widen. He looks from Corvi to the judges to the promoter of justice. Then he rises to his feet. "The defense wasn't aware that the murder weapon had been discovered."

The judges seem equally surprised. "The tribunal," one says sternly, "wasn't either."

Corvi avoids their glances, shuffling papers and pretending to search for something. He looks mortified. No good Catholic wants to disappoint a Church court inside these walls.

The lead judge adjusts his tone. "Signore," he says peaceably, "if our gendarmes are withholding information from us, we would appreciate knowing what it is."

The words thrill me. If the gendarmes' version of events is in doubt, then we're even closer to Simon's freedom.

For almost a minute, Corvi says nothing. He keeps studying the pages before him. During that entire silence, Mignatto stares at the promoter of justice.

Finally Corvi pulls a sheet from the pile. "Ah," he says. "Here it is. Yes, I was right. The weapon was a Beretta 950."

From the bench comes a sound of disbelief.

"When did the gendarmes find it?" the lead judge asks.

Corvi looks up. "As far as I know, they didn't. This isn't an evidence inventory; it's a firearm registration." He lifts the paper in the air. "A Beretta 950 was the weapon Ugolino Nogara registered with the state."

Mignatto turns to me breathlessly. "*Nogara had a gun?*"

I falter. "Not that I know of."

"Signore," the old judge says hoarsely, "you're telling us the man was shot with his own rifle?"

"Not a rifle," Corvi says. "A handgun."

"You mean a military pistol?"

Corvi shuffles his papers again and raises a manufacturer's stock photograph. It shows a small black weapon in a man's outstretched hand. The Beretta is shorter than the man's palm and fingers combined.

"How is that possible?" the presiding judge asks.

Very few Italians own guns like these.

"Italian permits are overwhelmingly for hunting weapons," Corvi says, lifting a second page. "Nogara's permit was for a self-defense hand-gun. That's another reason the identification is fairly sure."

I think of the notation in Ugo's medical file. *Fears being followed, harmed.* I jot a note on the legal pad in front of Mignatto: *Can you ask when he applied for the permit?*

Before Mignatto can respond, the lead judge reads my mind.

"The date on the application," Corvi replies, "is July twenty-fifth."

Michael was beaten up in the airport only one week earlier. Ugo must've decided to arm himself after finding the photo of Michael in his mailbox.

"So you're suggesting," the young judge says, "that someone took Nogara's handgun, killed him with it, and then did what with the weapon?"

Corvi raises his hands in the air. "That's for your police to establish. All I can tell you is the forensic analysis and the database results."

Mignatto is moving sheets of paper across the defense table. When he finds the list of deponents, he scans the column of names again, as if to reassure himself that no gendarmes will be called today.

"You mentioned a second piece of evidence you were called to analyze," the lead judge says, glancing down at his own notes. "What was it?"

Corvi nods. "Your police found a human hair in the deceased's car. They sent it to us for identification."

Mignatto begins to object. Simon was in Ugo's car many times. The hair proves nothing. But for once, the judges ignore him. The car tugs at their imaginations. Ugo wouldn't have carried a gun into a meeting of priests at Castel Gandolfo, so the car's broken window looms larger.

"Where was the hair found?" the judge asks.

"By the driver's seat."

This is odd. Ugo didn't let anyone else drive his car.

"The hair was Father Andreou's?" the judge asks.

"It was."

Yet there's an odd hitch in the way he says it. And in that hitch, a dark intuition slips through me. I have made an immense mistake.

Corvi stares at the lab report. "We were able to match it to a blood sample given at Rebibbia Prison three years ago."

Dread falls over me like a shadow.

"The name on the blood sample," Corvi says, "is Alexander Andreou."

Mignatto's brow pinches. He looks up, registering what he believes is an error. Then he turns on me, ashen.

I'm mute. The judges are staring.

"A recess," Mignatto coughs out. He turns to the judges. "Please, Monsignors. I need a brief recess."

IN THE COURTYARD, MIGNATTO paces silently. Glaring down from the niches of Saint Peter's are marble saints taller than two-story buildings.

"Monsignor, I needed to see the car," I say. "I didn't know—"

"You broke into the impound garage?" he says, still pacing.

"Yes."

"Alone?"

I won't drag Gianni into this. "Yes."

Mignatto chops the air with his hand, dividing each moment into particles of time. "When you were there, you took Nogara's phone from his car?"

"No."

He stops. "Then where did it come from?"

"Health Services."

He's nearly speechless. "What have you done?"

"I thought—"

"You thought what? That no one would notice?"

"I was trying to help Simon."

"Enough! Was this your plan all along? You and your uncle? To decide the outcome of this trial yourselves?"

"Of course not."

He steps closer. "Do you understand what the promoter of justice is doing to us in there?"

I don't know what he means. The prosecution got nothing out of Guido and Gino Pei.

When I say as much, though, Mignatto explodes.

"Don't be naïve! He got exactly he wanted out of Canali. And what he did with the driver was ingenious."

"What are you talking about?"

"*Who ordered the drivers not to keep their logs? Who would've put drivers under oath?* Well, who else? The car service reports to your uncle."

"You're reading too much into this."

"Then tell me: what was the point of Guido Canali's testimony? Canali saw nothing. He never laid eyes on your brother or Nogara or the crime scene. So why call him as a witness?"

"I don't know."

"Because he saw *you*, Father. Because he could testify that your brother's first reaction wasn't to call the police but to call his family. The incident report says the gendarmes thought you *both* called for help, because you arrived before they did. You bribed Canali using tickets from your uncle. Don't you see the scenario the promoter has begun to paint?"

I'm speechless.

"What's the only question the judges are asking themselves? The security footage is missing. The carpool logs are gone. Witnesses are under oath not to speak. The salient fact of the trial is the *silence*. The judges want to know where the pressure is coming from, and that's exactly what the promoter of justice is answering for them. Your brother called you for help. Your hair in the car suggests you helped him clean it out. Your uncle swore all his drivers to secrecy, then let your brother edit Nogara's exhibit as he saw fit. The exhibit is no longer permissible as a topic of testimony. Where do the silences point, Father? What does it say when your brother refuses to testify? Our possession of Nogara's mobile phone only confirms everything the prosecution is hinting at."

"Monsignor . . . I'm sorry."

He extends an arm in the air. "Enough. Go."

"Go where?"

"Do you really think," he snaps, "that I'm going to let you sit beside me while the tribunal considers the evidence of your own complicity? You've put me in the position of having to tell the court, in bad faith, that the hair is probably from some other time you drove with Nogara in his car. I have to invent excuses for the phone call, the bribe, the exhibit, the mobile phone. Get out of my sight! The only reason I'm letting you stay on as procurator is that I can't risk having you testify."

"Monsignor, I don't know what to say. I—"

But he swings his briefcase up and gives me his back as he walks away.

In the doorway to the palace stands the promoter of justice. He's too far away to have overheard anything, but he sizes me up. Mignatto passes him, and they exchange no words. But the prosecutor continues to stare.

CHAPTER 29

I WAIT. LONG AFTER Mignatto and the promoter have returned inside the palace, I stay in the courtyard. Pacing. Hovering in sight of the courtroom doors. No one comes out. I don't expect them to. But the illusion that I'm waiting for something is all that keeps this reckless feeling in check. This angry, anxious tension that shouts for me to *do* something.

I start making calls. Michael Black doesn't answer. So I try again, then a third time. He's ignoring me, but I'll wear him down.

On the sixth try I leave a rambling message.

"Michael, pick up your phone. *Pick up your phone.* If you're too scared to come to Rome, then you need to talk to Simon's lawyer. He has to know what happened in that airport."

As I talk, I stare down the road to the papal palace, looking for Simon. In vain.

Twenty minutes later, Corvi, the forensic analyst, emerges. A gendarme escorts him to the border and out the gate into Rome. Still no sign of Simon.

Then a sedan with tinted windows pulls up in front of the courthouse. I jump to my feet. When the driver gets out to open the rear door, I hurry over.

The back seat is empty. The driver motions me away, but I sidestep him to look into the passenger seat. Empty, too.

A moment later, the courthouse doors open. Archbishop Nowak exits the palace and shuffles to the open car door. I step back.

Nowak's eyes are downcast. He doesn't even look at my face. But he extends an arm in front of him to let me pass by first. "Please," he says.

"Your Grace."

He repeats the gesture with his arm, waiting for me to pass.

"Your Grace, may I speak to you?"

He's a large, stooped man, several inches taller than I am. His cassock is untailored. In his face is a faraway sadness, an abstraction that prevents him from looking up and recognizing me as a familiar face from the courtroom. People say that his father, a police officer in Poland, was killed by an oncoming truck at a traffic stop when he was a boy. Now he's driving home to a second dying father in John Paul. It seems impossible to bring up Simon's plight with a man who considers suffering a fact of life, but I have to do something.

"Please, Your Grace," I say. "It's important."

Nowak doesn't move. He says, "Yes, I know, Father Andreou." And one last time, he makes the gesture, extending his arm.

Finally I understand. He's inviting me into his car.

MY HEART DRUMS AS I crawl inside. My cassock is unwieldy. I pull it tight around me and slide to the far edge of the back seat to leave room for His Grace. The driver offers him a hand. I remember when my father would grab me by the shoulder and point out Nowak as he passed us on the village streets. The archbishop was almost as young then as Simon is today. Now he is sixty-five. His body has the same leaden heaviness as John Paul's, the barrel-like neck and cumbrous volume about the face, the eyes that haven't surrendered but have somehow retreated. He still smiles, but there's a sadness even in those smiles.

He says nothing as the driver closes the door after him. Nothing as the car gets under way. Just for an instant I see Mignatto leaving the courtroom. His eyes meet mine through the windshield as the sedan pulls away, and I see his mouth open.

"I remember you," Nowak says at last, in a fatherly voice. "As a boy."

I try my best not to be awed, not to feel like a child again.

"Thank you, Your Grace."

"I remember your brother, too."

"Why are you helping him?"

He leans over slightly, lessening the distance between us. His drooping eyes follow mine as I speak, showing me that he is listening.

"Your brother did something extraordinary," Archbishop Nowak says, inflecting this last word, this un-Polish word, with his accent. "The Holy Father is grateful."

So Nowak knows about the exhibit. About the Orthodox.

"Your Grace, do you know where my brother's being held?"

This is a more emotional question than I mean to ask. But he seems so solicitous, so invested in what I feel.

"Yes," Nowak says with a downturn of his eyes, acknowledging that this must be a painful subject for me.

"Can't you set him free? Can't you stop the trial?"

As we pass through the first entrance of the papal palace, the Swiss Guards stand and salute.

"The trial has a purpose," Nowak says. "To find the truth."

"But you *know* the truth. You know he invited Orthodox here, and you know why. The trial is just Cardinal Boia's way of pressuring Simon for answers about the exhibit."

One by one we slip past the security checkpoints. The sedan never slows.

"Father," Nowak says quietly, "before the exhibit opens tomorrow, it is important that we know the truth about why Doctor Nogara was killed."

As if to underscore the importance of this question, he asks the driver to stop the car. The final branch of the palace—John Paul's and Boia's—is before us. We are idling in the courtyard of the Secretariat.

"My brother didn't kill anyone, Your Grace."

"You know this for certain, because you were at Castel Gandolfo?"

"I just know my brother."

A pair of Swiss Guards marches up, sensing something amiss, but the driver waves them off.

"If I could set him free from house arrest," Archbishop Nowak says, "would you tell me the reason Doctor Nogara was killed?"

I understand now. He forbade discussion of the exhibit because he doesn't want Boia finding out about the visiting Orthodox—but without that testimony, Nowak has no idea why Ugo was killed either and can only guess who had a reason to kill him. Simon has kept everyone in the dark about 1204. Even the man who signed the papers bringing the Shroud here from Turin.

"Your Grace," I say, "Ugo Nogara discovered that Catholic knights stole the Shroud from Constantinople during the Fourth Crusade. The Shroud doesn't belong to us. It belongs to the Orthodox."

Nowak studies me. A pinch of something registers in his eyes. Surprise. Maybe disappointment.

"Yes," he says. "That is correct."

"You already knew?"

"But there is something more?" he says. "Something in addition to this?"

"No. Of course not."

The archbishop reaches out and takes my hand. "You are very unlike your brother."

Never taking his eyes off me, he taps the seat twice with his hand. The driver opens his door and steps out of the car. A moment later, the door beside me opens.

"I don't understand," I say. "Are you going to make Cardinal Boia let Simon go?"

I feel the driver's hand on my shoulder, instructing me to step out.

"Father, I am sorry," Nowak says. "It is not as simple as you believe. Your brother has not told you the whole truth."

He reaches out and squeezes my hand, the way John Paul used to do in Saint Peter's Square when comforting perfect strangers. As if I've come all this way for something I don't really understand.

A Swiss Guard behind me says, "Father." Nothing more.

Nowak's hand lets go of mine as I slide out. Even then, he continues to watch me.

■ ■ ■

THERE ARE ALREADY THREE messages on my phone from Mignatto, urgently commanding me to return to the Palace of the Tribunal. I ignore them.

I walk up to the Swiss Guard on duty at the eastern door. He saw me get out of Archbishop Nowak's car.

"It's David?" I say.

"Denis, Father."

"Denis, I need to see my brother."

Cardinal Boia's apartments are overhead. Simon is right up there.

"I'll call up for you," he says.

"No, I'll see myself up."

I step toward the door, but he blocks my way. "Father, I'll need to call first."

I push him aside. "Tell Cardinal Boia that Simon Andreou's brother is coming to see him."

A second guard materializes from thin air.

"Loris," I say, recognizing him, "I need to get through."

He puts an arm around me and guides me down the steps. At the bottom he says, "Father, what's wrong?"

I pull away. "I'm going to see Simon."

"You know you're not allowed to do that."

"He's up there."

"I know."

I stop short. "You've seen him?"

"We're not allowed inside the apartments."

"Tell me the truth."

He hesitates. "Once," he says.

The emotion feels like a fist against my throat.

"Is he okay?"

"I don't know."

"Let me inside."

"You should go home now."

I feel his hand on me again. I shake it off. The other Swiss Guard, seeing this, calls into his radio for backup.

"Father," Loris says, "go. Now."

I back away. At the top of my lungs I shout at the windows on the second floor, "Cardinal Boia!"

Two more Swiss Guards come running from the direction of the Secretariat.

I take another step back and shout, "Your Eminence, I want to see my brother!"

Their hands are on me. They begin forcing me toward the exit of the courtyard.

"Whatever you want to know, I'll tell you!" I shout. "Just let me see my brother!"

I fight to get my arms free, but they drag me across the cobblestones.

"*Please*," I beg them. "*I have to see him.*"

But when we reach the perimeter of the courtyard, the two Swiss posted there close a metal gate.

"Leave, Father," Loris says, pointing down the path that leads back out of the palace complex. "While you still can."

I stagger back, numb on my own legs.

Your brother has not told you the whole truth.

I stare through the bars of the iron gate, feeling myself crumple. And there, across the courtyard, I see something. Up in a second-floor window, the curtains have parted. Between them, just for an instant, is Cardinal Boia.

■ ■ ■

I MOVE NUMBLY AWAY. When I reach the outer palace gate, Mignatto is waiting. Seeing the look in my eyes, he loops an arm through mine and tells the guards, "I'll take him from here."

We walk in silence back to the tribunal. I don't know if he heard me shouting. I don't care.

Beside the courtroom is an office. Mignatto carries out an errand without a word to me. An archival aide hands him a folder of papers to sign. More new evidence. More new witnesses.

"Still no surveillance footage?" he asks her.

She shakes her head.

I wonder how he can keep this up. How he can pretend this isn't a travesty.

"These are the ones I requested?" he asks, pointing to a series of photos.

She flips through the pictures, trying to confirm. I see images of familiar evidence bags. The items from Ugo's car. Mignatto dressed me down for breaking into the impound lot, yet now he has requested the evidence I discovered there. I glare at him. He still says nothing to me.

"That's correct, Monsignor," the aide says.

"Thank you, signora."

His hand is at my back again, leading me out. Finally he turns.

"Have dinner with me, Father."

Afternoon has peaked and waned. He holds up a hand as a visor.

"No," I say.

"Peter is welcome to join us. And it's important that we discuss the voice mail message Nogara left for your brother at the nunciature. The tribunal admitted it."

"No."

He takes the visor away, stares at his feet. "I understand what you're feeling, but Father, perhaps it's best for you to take a break from the trial."

"I'm going to do what I need to do."

Mignatto squints. "What exactly did Archbishop Nowak say to you?"

"That my brother's been lying to me."

"About what?"

I don't know. If the reason is good enough, it could be anything.

"Father Andreou, tell me."

But at that moment, my phone rings. And I recognize the number.

"Michael?" I say, answering immediately.

"Alex, I was on an airplane. That's why I couldn't pick up."

"What?"

"I'm at the airport now."

"Which airport?"

"Timbuktu. What do you think? I'll be downtown in an hour. If Simon's lawyer wants to talk, he'd better be ready to talk."

Is that him? Mignatto mouths.

I nod.

"Let me speak to him."

I hand over the phone.

"Father Black?" Mignatto asks.

He pulls a pen from the French cuff of his cassock and flips back the evidence folder to write inside the cover. Behind him, trucks come and go from the museums. I think again of what Archbishop Nowak said. Opening night. Just twenty-four hours away.

"Will you testify?" Mignatto is saying. "How soon can you be ready?"

I stare at the folder in his hand. At the photos he was asking the clerk about. In one of them is Ugo's phone charger. In another, the scrap of stationery scrawled with my phone number.

"We need to discuss what happened to you. Can we meet at my office tonight?"

Beside them are the evidence bags I couldn't examine before Gianni hurried me out of the impound garage. A pack of cigarettes. The sun-faded Vatican ID Ugo probably flashed to the Swiss Guards every time he drove into the country. A key chain. Nothing big enough to match the impression under the driver's seat of Ugo's car.

"He can't be present when we meet. That's not part of the procurator's job."

My jaw goes slack. The fob of the key chain: it's oval, engraved with three letters and three numbers. DSM 328.

I pull the folder out of Mignatto's hand. He bobbles the phone and glowers at me.

DSM. Domus Sanctae Marthae. The Latin name of the Casa. The three digits are the room number. A sliver is missing from the metal fob.

This can't be Ugo's key. He didn't need a hotel room. So this must belong to whoever broke into the Alfa.

"I didn't hear that. You're breaking up. Say again?"

I close my eyes. I'm deceiving myself. The killer wouldn't have left behind his own key. So whose is it?

Mignatto takes back the folder to write more information on its cover. I wonder why Michael is being so forthcoming. It's unlike him.

The answer comes a moment later, when Mignatto hands back the phone and says, "Father Black wants to speak to you again."

"Listen up," Michael says. "The lawyer tells me you can't be at our little meeting tonight, so there's something you and I need to talk about in private. Meet me at Saint Peter's afterward."

"In the square?"

"No, in the right transept. I'll leave the north door open. You know the one I mean?"

Mignatto is trying to overhear. I step away.

"What time?" I say.

"Let's make it eight. And if I'm not there, you need to find yourself a new witness tomorrow."

"Tomorrow?"

"Eight o'clock. Got it?"

When I hang up, Mignatto says, "You're not to meet with him. Understood? Not outside my presence."

I ignore the question. "Good night, Monsignor," I say. "I'll see you in the morning."

■ ■ ■

I CALL BROTHER SAMUEL'S apartment and ask him to babysit Peter a while longer. Then I call Mona.

"I can't make it tonight after all," I say.

She must hear something in my voice. "Is everything all right? Do you want to talk about it?"

I don't. But the words trickle out.

"I'm angry. Simon lied to me."

Now the silence. The silence that reveals how, in her heart, she still doubts him.

"Lied about what?" she says finally.

"Never mind."

More silence.

At last she says, "I'm at my parents' place. I can meet you anywhere you want, just tell me where."

"I can't. Just . . . talk to me."

"How's Peter?" she asks.

I close my eyes. "I've been at the courthouse all day. Brother Samuel says he's fine."

"Alex, you don't sound good. Let me help you."

I'm sitting on the bench in the tribunal courtyard. The last commuters are queued at the gas station. Over the roofs of their cars I stare at the Casa.

"I just need some time to think," I say. "I'll call you tomorrow." I hesitate. "I'm sorry about tonight."

Before she can answer, I hang up. The ache that has been building for hours is now painful. When Simon and I used to feel this way after Mamma died, we would run cross-country and back. The hills. The steps. The shadows of the walls. We would run until we were buckled over, heaving on the ground, cooling ourselves in the overspray of the fountains. I close my eyes. *Give him back to me, Lord. I need my brother.*

I count the Casa windows. I know which room is 328. It's only a floor beneath where Peter and I were staying, but along the far side of the building. By my count, a corner room. I'm staring at its west-facing windows right now.

Maybe tomorrow will be the day. Maybe that's Boia's plan. To keep Simon until the exhibit is over.

The west-facing windows have their shutters closed. Other rooms have their drapes opened, but the occupant in that one room wants no air at all. Wants no view of the Roman afternoon. I open my phone and dial the front desk.

"Sister, please connect me to three twenty-eight."

"Just a moment."

The phone rings without stop. Whoever's up there doesn't want to talk, either.

I hang up. The last car drives off from the gas station. The air becomes quiet again. A breeze snaps the Vatican flag on the pole above the Casa entrance.

I stand. With a feathery feeling in my chest I begin walking toward those doors.

■ ■ ■

AT THE DESK, THE nun surprises me.

"Welcome, Father. How are you?"

She says the words in Greek.

Instinct tells me to respond in the same tongue. "Very well, Sister. Thank you."

"Are you enjoying your stay in our country?"

"Very much."

"How may I help you?"

"Just returning to my room." I flash my old room key and walk on.

But the security has been heightened since I left. A notice in the lobby says that each elevator will now serve only a specific floor of the building. I overhear the elevator operators asking passengers to show their keys before boarding the car.

I take the stairs instead. But just as I'm about to open the door to the third floor, a voice comes from overhead.

"Father, you've got the wrong floor. Up here."

A Swiss Guard comes double-stepping down from the fourth-floor landing. Fortunately, we don't know each other.

"May I see your key?" he says.

He seems to have been posted just outside the fire door.

When I show him, he nods. The key to the room Peter and I shared says 435.

"Follow me, Father," he says in slow Italian. And with an exaggerated wave of the hand, he leads me upstairs.

THE FOURTH FLOOR BRIMS with activity. There are priests everywhere. I'm astonished. Every single one is dressed in Eastern attire. These must be Simon's Orthodox. I count eleven of them standing in the hall. A twelfth priest opens his door, says something to a colleague outside, then turns back. His language is unfamiliar to me. *Serbian?* I wonder. *Bulgarian?*

Then it hits me: at least a few of these other priests must be Greek. The nun at the front desk, without knowing which country I came from, welcomed me in Greek. So Simon must've traveled there, too. He must've spread his invitations in the fatherland.

I wonder how many countries he visited in all. How many priests, from how many nations, are staying on this hall. Nothing like this has ever been attempted before.

I glance back at the Swiss Guard outside the fire door. Another thought settles over me. Only the pope controls the Swiss. Only John Paul and Nowak could've sent these soldiers here. They must know the scope of what Simon has done.

For a moment, all I can do is watch. The groups of priests form and re-form. Orthodox have no central power, no pope as Catholics do. The patriarch of Constantinople is their honorary leader, but really the Orthodox Church is a federation of national churches, many with patriarchs of their own. The mere idea of this kind of clerical democracy, with no bishop taking orders from any other, is a Catholic's nightmare, a recipe for chaos. Yet for two thousand years, the bonds of tradition and communion have made Orthodox priests from every corner of Christendom into brothers. Even in the nervous atmosphere of this hallway, with its air of expectation, men cross boundaries and greet each other. They speak, sometimes fluently, sometimes haltingly, in one another's languages. There are almost as many smiles as beards. I feel as if I'm witnessing the ancient Church, the world the apostles left behind. I feel strangely, deeply at home.

Some of them come toward me en masse. I realize I'm standing in front of the elevator. The doors open, and I step aside. Three of them filter in, speaking a language I don't recognize. I think I overhear the word for evening prayer, which must be why they're going downstairs. But one of them, in Italian, instructs the operator to hold the door. More are coming.

Now a room opens down the hall. A young priest comes out. His beard is thin. He idles by the doorway, staring back into it. And in my gut I feel a thrill. I know what this means. He's waiting for his boss.

I try not to stare as the bishop—fifty or sixty years old, with an impressive belly and a handsome loose cassock—comes striding out. Just as Gianni said, he wears the Orthodox stovepipe hat. The remaining priests in the hallway make room for him as he walks toward the elevator. The operator reaches for his key—but the bishop shakes his head. Another priest in the car says, "Wait, please. More coming."

I peer down the corridor. From the same open door, another bishop has appeared, this one wearing a gold chain with a painted portrait of the Theotokos, the Virgin Mary. Even at a distance I can see the glitter of something on his stovepipe hat: the tiny cross that signifies a high-ranking bishop or metropolitan. This bishop is more senior, surely at least seventy years old. He walks with a stoop. His aides travel on either side of him, minding that his cassock doesn't catch under his feet.

Yet even now, the door behind him doesn't shut. And suddenly, there's a commotion. For some reason, the priests in the hallway begin murmuring. Some of them gather outside the open door, stealing looks inside. The rest of them separate to the far walls of the corridor. They are parting like the sea, because someone else is beginning to emerge.

A man in white.

CHAPTER 30

A SHIVER GOES THROUGH me. All through the hallway, priests bow. My eyes must be playing tricks.

As the man approaches, he comes into focus. It isn't John Paul. It's someone even more ancient. His eyes are black smudges. And he has a beard.

The beard encircles his long, drawn face like a wreath of white fog. It extends down to the middle of his chest, where he carries something in his hand: a white stovepipe hat with a small jeweled cross. As he passes the other priests, he lifts a hand in blessing.

I'm frozen. I know who this is.

In poor, accented Italian, the man says to me, "God bless you."

"And you," I fumble as two priests exit the elevator to make sure he has room to enter it.

Simon has done the impossible. The tradition of Romanian Orthodoxy is that its highest leader may wear white. Before my eyes is one of the nine patriarchs of the Orthodox Church.

I begin hurrying down the stairs. The elevator must be going to the ground floor, to the private chapel attached to the Casa.

And then I realize: I can't follow them there. I would barely be able to communicate with these men. They might mistake me for a brother since my cassock and beard look Orthodox, but because of our schism, the Orthodox Church forbids me—a Catholic—from receiving the

Eucharist with them. Even joining them for evening prayer without revealing who I am would be an act of bad faith.

Instead, I take the stairs no farther than the third-floor landing and slip inside. My nerves are ringing. I lean against the wall, wondering how this could've gone so wrong. How something so beautiful, so historic, could've cost Ugo his life. How Simon could lose his priesthood over it.

Here on the third floor, a door opens. A Roman Catholic priest steps out of his room. He walks toward the elevator. As he presses the button, he takes a second look at me.

I know this look too well. Though I have more in common with him than I have with any Orthodox upstairs—I'm a Catholic; I follow the pope; this priest and I can receive the Eucharist in each other's churches—he seems to think I'm out of place.

"Good evening, Father," I say in Italian to assuage his concern. Or maybe, in some dark way, to assuage mine. Then I continue on toward room 328.

At the door, I calm myself by repeating the Jesus Prayer.

Lord Jesus Christ, Son of God, have mercy on me, the sinner.

Lord Jesus Christ, Son of God, have mercy on me, the sinner.

Nothing can happen to me here. This hall, this building, is full of men who would come running at the first shout for help. Whoever's inside, I'll invite him out to talk. Out; not back into his room.

I knock.

No answer.

I stare at the peephole, wondering if I'm being watched. Stepping forward, I knock again.

Still no answer.

I pull out my phone and call the front desk. "Sister, could you connect me to three twenty-eight?"

I hear the phone ring on the other side of the door. Standing in front of the peephole, I hold my phone in the air and point to it. We can talk this way, too. It makes no difference to me.

But no one responds.

Outside, through the large window at the end of the hall, the sun is setting. Something occurs to me. I glance down.

There's no light beneath the door. That's why the shutters are closed. Nobody's home.

I call the lobby again and say, "Sister, I'm coming down to meet a visitor in the dining hall. Could someone tidy my room while I'm gone? It's three twenty-eight."

"Father, I believe your visitor just rang up. I'll send the housekeeper right away. I'd say the tidying is a bit overdue."

I thank her, then wait near the elevator until the nun with the cleaning cart arrives. When she unlocks the room, I follow her inside.

"What in heavens?" says the nun in alarm.

For an instant, it's dark. From the outer courtyard comes a pale miasma of electric light, glowing through the shutter slats. Then the nun turns on the lights.

No one else is here.

"Sister," I murmur absently, surveying the room, "don't mind me. I left something behind."

It's almost identical to the room Peter and I shared. A narrow bed with a simple camelback headboard. A nightstand. A crucifix.

I sit at the desk and pretend to make notations, waiting for her to leave. She closes the closet and gathers up a pair of sheets lying on the ground beside the bed. The priest in this room might be a floor-sleeper like Simon. But the bed looks slept-in, too.

There must be two of them staying here. And there must be a reason the room is overdue for cleaning.

As the housekeeper makes the bed and empties the trash cans, I scan the floor. By the lamp is an old piece of luggage with no name tag visible. On the nightstand are a bag of toiletries, a camera, a softcover book. The nun stares at a pile of papers under the toiletry bag, then glances back at the closet.

"Father," she says, "who's staying in this room with you?"

"Just a colleague," I improvise.

Something catches my attention. The softcover book on the nightstand. It's about the Shroud.

I feel a nervous pinch in my chest. I've read that book. I own that same edition. It was stolen from my apartment during the break-in.

My eyes shift across the room anxiously. There's a glass bottle in the wastebasket the nun is emptying. Grappa Julia. Ugo's favorite drink. But there are no glass tumblers in sight, no sign that this was drunk here. Bottles like this were piled in the trash can at Ugo's apartment. The apartment someone had broken into. I wonder what else in this room was stolen from his home or mine.

The nun looks again at the pile of papers on the nightstand, and for some reason she seems in a hurry to finish now.

As she tidies the bathroom, I step over to look at the papers. Then I freeze.

The wheels of the nun's cart whine. The last thing I hear her say, before she closes the door behind her, is, "Father, I'm going to have to send someone up here. I don't think this is really your room."

It isn't a pile of papers after all. It's a pile of photographs.

Photographs of me.

MY HAND SHAKES AS I pick up the camera. I scroll through the backlog of pictures. Me, walking in the gardens. Me, standing outside the Palace of the Tribunal. Me, holding hands with Peter in the courtyard below. Near the end, I find it. Me, exiting the Casa. The same photo that was slipped under my door with the threat written on the back.

I try to think. But the fear is spilling through me.

A name. A face. I need something.

I throw open the closet. From the hanger dangles a black, buttoned robe. A Roman Catholic cassock. The nun must've known it couldn't be mine.

I check the tag. In a country of identically dressed men, we write our names in our clothing. But there's nothing here, just the faded insignia of a tailor shop near the Pantheon. On the next hanger is a ferraiolone, the long cape that Roman priests wear to black-tie events. Finally it clicks. I'm looking at a priest's best cassock and formalwear. This man is preparing for Ugo's exhibit tomorrow night.

I need a way to identify him. I lay the cassock on the bed and open the penknife on my key chain. Just below the back of the collar, I make a cut through the fabric. It's almost invisible. But when the cassock is stretched over a man's shoulders, it'll pucker, and I'll be able to see his white shirt from behind.

I hear a sound in the hallway. I rehang the cassock and start to leave—when a thought comes to me.

I backtrack to the desk, checking the drawers. It must be here somewhere. I find a lunch receipt, and what appears to be a parking ticket.

I stash them in my cassock. Then, on the nightstand, I see it. Under a loose sheet of paper is the pad of Casa stationery. I open the shutters and lift the pad in front of the slanting light of sunset. Just faintly, I see the impression of handwriting. The five digits of my phone number.

This is where the scrap from Ugo's car came from. This must be the room that called me three times on the night before Ugo died.

Two priests have been sleeping here. One of them broke into my apartment while the other was breaking into Ugo's car at Castel Gandolfo. Everything converges here, in this room. If only I had stopped the maid before she threw away that basket of trash. There must've been more inside it than an empty bottle of Grappa Julia.

Suddenly the door opens. A nun steps inside. Behind her is the housekeeper.

"Father! Explain yourself."

I step back.

"You don't belong here," she exclaims. "Come with me this instant."

I make no move.

Behind her appears a Swiss Guard. The same one I saw in the stairwell.

"Do what she says, Father," he commands.

An idea comes to me.

"Den katalavaino italika," I say to the guard. "Eimai Ellinas."

I don't understand Italian. I'm Greek.

He frowns. Then it dawns on him. "He's one of them from upstairs," the guard says. "He keeps going to the wrong floor."

I blink as if I don't understand. The nun clicks her tongue and waves at me to follow her. In relief, I obey.

Then the housekeeper speaks up. "No," she says. "He's lying. I talked to him in Italian."

I'M BROUGHT TO THE lobby. A gendarme is waiting there. He takes me across the courtyard to the gendarme station inside the Palace of the Tribunal. There's a holding cell inside. Instead of putting me in it, he instructs me to sit on a bench by the front desk and empty my pockets.

Out comes the lunch receipt. The parking ticket. My phone. The contents of my wallet.

He looks twice when he sees a Vatican ID. When he notices the name on it, he turns back to me and says, "I remember you."

I remember him, too. He was one of the gendarmes at Castel Gandolfo on the night of Ugo's murder.

"What the hell were you doing in the Casa, Father?"

The profanity is a sign that I have lost his respect. That I'm no longer worthy of being treated like a priest.

"I want to make a phone call," I say.

I'm staring at the parking ticket, trying to memorize the license plate on it.

He thinks it over, then shakes his head. "I need to talk to my captain."

To hell with his captain. "My uncle is Cardinal Ciferri," I say. "Give me the phone."

He flinches when he hears Uncle Lucio's name. But my surname is different from Lucio's, so he feels confident enough to doubt.

"Stay put, Father," he says. "I'll be back."

THE CAPTAIN SETS HIM straight. Twenty minutes later, Don Diego arrives to pick me up. I expect Diego to be furious. And he is. But not with me.

"You're lucky you don't lose your job for this," he tells the gendarme. "Don't ever humiliate a member of this family again."

And perhaps it says something about our country that the policeman, knowing he's in the right, still looks afraid.

The sun is low on the horizon as we walk up the path toward Lucio's palace. Diego doesn't say a word. His silence conveys that I'm in a kind of trouble that it would be above his pay grade to describe. But I find it impossible to focus on him. All I see in my mind's eye is Cardinal Boia staring back at me from between those curtains.

At the door to the palace, I say, "Thanks, Diego. But I'm not coming in."

"What do you mean?"

"There's somewhere else I need to be."

It's five of eight. I have an appointment with Michael Black.

"But your uncle—"

"I know."

"His orders about this were very clear."

"I'll apologize some other time."

And I can feel him staring at me as I walk away.

■ ■ ■

THE SUN NEVER SHINES on the north face of Saint Peter's. On hot days, this is where priests turn up, mosslike, gathering to sneak cigarettes in the long cool shadows. The stone walls are forty feet thick at these corners and rise higher than the cliffs of Dover. Hell itself couldn't warm them.

At this hour, all the other doors are locked. The sampietrini check the basilica at dark, every staircase, every nook. But a sliver of pale light glows beneath this side door. Michael must know a sampietrino who owes him a favor.

I slip inside and drift through the cool air like a grit of sand at the bottom of the sea. Tourists visiting here by day see the marble floor and the sky-high canopy, but this church has more hiding places in between than even most priests know. There are stairways hidden from view, which lead to chapels built into the pillars themselves, where clergy can rehearse and worship away from the eyes of laymen. There are dressing rooms—sacristies—where altar boys help priests vest for Mass. Overhead, tucked behind the stage lights, are the unreachable balconies that even the sampietrini have no way to clean except by dangling from ropes, swinging through the air by the metal hooks screwed into these walls. And connecting everything like arteries is a network of passageways within the walls. Between the inner and outer skin of the basilica are tunnels through which a man can travel around the whole church without ever being seen. For those reasons, no priest ever believes he's alone here. So no priest ever comes here for confidentiality.

Michael knows that. It must be exactly what he's counting on. This is the last place anyone would come looking for two priests meeting in the night.

I emerge from a passage beneath an old pope's tomb onto the main floor of the basilica. All around me is a weightless, twinkling dark. From around a corner comes a sound. A metal click, as of a lock turning.

"Alex?" I hear him say. "Is that you?"

I follow it into the north transept. When Michelangelo designed Saint Peter's, he planned a Greek cross, all four arms the same length. But then a nave was added, making the Greek cross into a Latin one, its long side facing east. Where I now stand is the right crossbeam, the only part of the main floor that is cordoned off to tourists. For most Eastern Catholics, it's an unfamiliar place. Along the walls are the booths where pilgrims come to confess. The confessionals are built like triple coffins, with a priest's stall in the middle and an open compartment on either side. Eastern Catholics, though, confess in the open. Only because of the years I've spent in this basilica do I recognize the sound of the heavy wooden door of a priest's compartment being unlocked.

"Michael," I whisper. "It's me."

The door opens.

For the first time in years, I rest eyes on the living Michael Black.

IT WAS SIXTEEN YEARS ago that he disappeared. Right after the carbon-dating verdict, my father returned to the Turin hotel room they'd been sharing and discovered that Michael was gone. He wasn't on the train back to Rome, or in the office the next Monday. My father tried to track him down, but it wasn't long before Father himself began to disappear into the depression that would become his grave. The search petered out. We never saw Michael again.

Only later did I learn what had happened. On the way out of Turin, an Orthodox reporter had confronted Michael and blamed him for luring a few naïve Orthodox priests into our Catholic humiliation. Michael took away his tape recorder and beat him with it until the reporter ended up in a hospital. Only because the Turin police weren't about to prosecute a Catholic priest for defending their city's relic did he escape punishment. So deals were made, and Michael was sent for treatment. No one could've been naïve enough, in those days, to believe that a few months in a mountain facility would cure him of anything serious. But maybe nobody really believed it was serious. Yet.

He'd always been unruly. His language had been coarse. But Italians understood that he was an American, a cowboy. The real trouble only started after he came back from the mountains. That was when he got picked up by the Secretariat.

There are places in the world where the Church has to fight for its life. Priests are imprisoned. Kidnapped. Even killed on the street. The Secretariat recruits a certain type of priest for those places. The American archbishop who preceded Uncle Lucio in the Governor's Palace was almost as tall as Simon, and twice as burly. On a papal trip to Manila, when a man with a bayonet tried to attack the Holy Father, the American grabbed the attacker and tossed him through the air. Michael was half the size of that archbishop, but in someone's eyes he had those makings.

It was Cardinal Boia who must've seen another kind of potential in Michael. Whenever John Paul proposed a new olive branch to the Orthodox, Boia would send one of his Quasimodos to make sure nothing came of it. A few good slurs, maybe a pushing match or two, and years of diplomatic work could be undermined in hours. Simon blamed Michael for becoming Boia's favorite Quasimodo in Turkey. But I blamed Michael's keepers for recruiting a volatile young priest and convincing him, at his most vulnerable moment, that he'd been right to attack an Orthodox reporter. That he could make a whole career of fighting that way. Priests are institutional men, clay in the hands of the Church. It would've taken a man of unusual strength to shrug off the Secretariat's influence. A man like Simon. And that is hardly the kind of man I see before me.

Michael is shorter than I remember. He breathes loudly, almost panting. A thousand cocktail parties and seven-course dinners have made him fat. He appears uncomfortable, adjusting his sash and making a wordless guttural noise that seems to be a complaint of exertion. He looks rougher than I remember. He hasn't shaved in days. The reason is obvious. It must be hard to work a razor around the divots in his face.

The wounds are still visible. One runs like a seam beneath his left eye. His nose isn't right either; the bridge still bends to one side. He reaches out a hand to offer an American shake instead of an Italian embrace. The first words he says to me, after more than a decade, are, "Damn, Alex. Nobody told me you stayed Eastern. I figured you jumped ship like Simon."

And yet, at the bottom of those words, I hear guilt. His presence under this roof says he's here to repent for what he did to Peter and me.

"Did you meet with Monsignor Mignatto?" I say.

"Lawyers," Michael says with disgust. "Yeah, I did."

"And?"

"He's got me on the stand tomorrow."

Tomorrow. Mignatto wastes no time.

"But I told him," he continues, "I'm not going to lie up there. I don't believe in this garbage. Reuniting Churches. Kowtowing to the beards. And if they ask me, that's what I'm going to say."

"Michael, you told me on the phone that before these people beat you up, they wanted to know about Ugo's research."

He nods.

"What about it?" I say.

He stares at his knuckles. "They thought he discovered something. Something bad for business with the Orthodox. They thought Simon made him hide it. So they wanted to know what it was."

I'm tired of the secrets. "The Fourth Crusade. We stole the Shroud from the Orthodox in 1204."

"No. It wasn't that."

I'm taken aback. "Michael, I'm sure of it."

He's a Roman Catholic. Even after working for years with my father, he may not understand what 1204 means in the East.

But he shakes his head. "It was something Nogara found in the Diatessaron."

"That's impossible. I worked with Ugo for a month on the Diatessaron."

He whistles. "Then you're lucky."

"Lucky?"

"That Cardinal Boia didn't find you before now. You're the one he should've been looking for all along."

Maybe he feels betrayed by Boia. Attacked by his own master. I wonder why it happened.

"Why were you in that airport?" I say. "Were you helping Simon?"

He bristles. "I already told you this."

"Told me what?"

"That I can't talk about what happened."

I throw my head back. I've forgotten. Another oath.

"I told the lawyer, too," he says. "I won't answer questions about that in court."

"Break the oath. Tell the judges the truth."

Suddenly his voice bubbles with anger. "The lawyer and I settled this, and I'm not here to rehash it with you."

"Then why are you here?"

"Because those were my orders."

A chill goes through me. "What are you talking about?"

"Cardinal Boia called me today. He knows I'm in town."

"How is that possible?"

"Your lawyer put my name on some document."

"Did His Eminence threaten you?"

"No. Just gave me a little reminder. And then asked how he could get to *you*."

My pulse is hammering. "What do you mean?"

"He says you shouted at him today. At his windows."

"I was just trying to—"

"Get his attention? Well, it worked."

"What are you telling me?"

"His Eminence wants to meet with you."

I nervously glance around me. "Right now?"

Michael snorts. "Tomorrow morning before the trial reopens. Seven thirty at his apartments."

"Why?"

"I don't know. But for your sake, I hope it goes better than my meeting in the airport."

CHAPTER 31

I STAMMER A FEW more questions, but Michael has no answers. Cardinal Boia's name has a weird effect on him. He begins to fill the silence with praise for his boss. Boia the great man. The defender of tradition. Then his party line: reunion with the Orthodox would weaken our Church, dilute what it means to be Catholic, make the pope nothing more than another one of their patriarchs. Michael's irrationality is returning.

I feel clammy. The chill of the air penetrates under my skin. Finally I say, "I've heard enough, Michael. I'm leaving."

I feel him watching me as I go. If I knew any other way out of this basilica at night, I would take it. As I walk home, I keep one hand on my mobile phone. More than once I think of calling Mignatto. But I know what he would say. Not to listen to Michael. Not to meet with Boia.

I collect Peter from the pharmacists' apartment. He's still wide awake. Rarely have I seen him so eager to leave Brother Samuel.

"What's on your mind?" I ask, slipping the new key into our new lock.

He's almost skipping. "Can we call Mamma?"

"Peter, not tonight."

He frowns. He must think I'm teasing him. After a whole day of separation, I wouldn't really refuse him the one thing he's been hoping for.

"There's something we need to talk about," I say instead.

And then I send him down the hall to wash his face and brush his teeth, telling him to meet me back in his bedroom. He looks anxious. But he obeys.

I open the Bible we keep beside an icon of the Theotokos. She watches serenely as I turn the pages. I wish I could share her calm.

Peter comes back reeking of the ginger-mint toothpaste he loves. He strips down to underwear, then climbs into bed and draws up the sheet to his Adam's apple.

"Peter, I want to talk to you about what's happening with Uncle Simon."

He stares at me. His eyes are suddenly filled with innocence, with the tremulous courage only a child can have, being powerless to stop the things he fears.

"Do you remember Mister Nogara?" I say.

He nods.

"Five days ago, Mister Nogara died."

A wrinkle forms in Peter's forehead. I wait for him to say something.

"Why?" he asks.

Why. The question so distantly beyond my capacity to answer.

"There's no reason to be afraid. You know what happens when we die."

"We go home," he says.

I nod, and it takes a wrenching effort to hide my emotion.

"Now," I say, running a hand through his hair, "you need to know something about his death. We don't understand why it happened. And some people say Simon is to blame. Some people think he hurt Mister Nogara."

Muscle by muscle Peter grows rigid. I can feel him begin to tremble.

"Don't be scared," I repeat. "We know Simon. Right?"

He nods, but the pressure of his body doesn't subside.

"In fact," I say, "do you know where I went today? To a place where people have been coming from all over Italy just to talk about Simon. And do you know what some of them said?"

"What was the place called?" he asks instead.

I hesitate. "It was one of the palaces." I gesture. "Over there."

"Prozio's palace?"

"No, a different one." I persevere. "Bishops and archbishops have been coming there, even cardinals, and do you know what they came to say? That Simon is a very good man. That they know the same thing we do: that he would *never* hurt anyone. Especially not his own friend."

The nodding intensifies, but only because Peter is trying to live up to my expectations. Trying to show he's strong enough to take this awful news. I reach my arms around him and pull him into my chest, showing him he doesn't have to be a grown-up tonight. The relief is so instantaneous, he explodes in tears.

"I know," I say, stroking his hair, feeling his hot tears through my cassock. "I know."

He makes an insensible sound, the cry of a much younger child.

"Oh, my boy," I say, feeling the strange fullness that exists only in these moments of pure dependence. I am his. God made me for this child.

On the nightstand, the Theotokos casts her protective glance over the open Bible. The title above the chapter says: δίκη του Ιησού. *The Trial of Jesus.* Many times we've read it. But when we read it tonight, I hope Peter will start to understand. Tomorrow, I can't know what will happen with Cardinal Boia. I will take a risk that we may both regret. But tonight I can explain to him, in a way he will someday understand, why I have to take that risk.

A Christian life is lived by the example of the disciples. By imitating their virtues, but also by learning from their failures. When the disciples were faced with the arrest and trial of the man they believed in, they abandoned him in fear. They placed their own safety, and the verdict of their priests, above the demands of their consciences.

I believe in my brother as I believe in nothing else on this earth, except for the love of this little boy. And I will never abandon either of them.

So let this be the lesson between us. What I do for Simon, I would do for you. There is one law under God. And it is love.

This is love.

Peter cries, and I hold him. Not until he falls asleep will I let him go.

■ ■ ■

SLEEP WON'T COME FOR me. In the middle of the night I walk out to the living room and sit on the couch. I stare out the window at the moon. I pray.

Before dawn I put the moka pot on the stove. The brothers next door have already showered by quarter to seven, when I ask them to stay with Peter again. On the kitchen table I leave his favorite superhero cup beside the plastic bottle containing the last of our Fanta. Then I write a note, choosing from the words I know he can easily read.

> Peter—
>   *I have gone to help Simon. I will be back as soon as I can. If you need to talk to me, Brother Samuel will let you use his phone. When I get home, you and I will call Mamma. I promise.*
>   *Love,*
>   *Babbo*

I look at those words again—*when I get home*—and they choke me. I'm so glad to be back under this roof. This apartment has been in my family for more than twenty years. It's the only place where I still feel the presence of my parents. And yet I know: Boia could find a way to take it from us. To reassign it to another family. Even Lucio could not stop him. Boia could have the pre-seminary fire me, forcing me out of the Vatican economy. Peter and I would lose our Annona pass, so that we couldn't buy our food tax-free; our gas privileges, so that we would have to pay almost double for fuel in Rome; our parking pass, so that we could no longer afford to have a car at all. John Paul pays a little extra to all his workers with children, and if I were to lose that, too, along with my job, then Peter and I would have nothing. My savings would last us only a few months. What I'm about to do is right. I know that. But I beg God not to let Peter suffer for it.

On my way to the palace, archbishops roll by in chauffeured sedans. Lay workers race past on Vespas. Nuns pedal bicycles. I hurry through the crosswalk on foot, fighting the consciousness of my own smallness. At the first checkpoint the gendarmes sneer when I say, "I have a meeting with Cardinal Boia." But they make the phone call and I'm on the list. Wordlessly they let me by.

My heart thumps as I reach the Secretariat courtyard. I don't know where to go next. Gianni said there was an archway leading to the private courtyard and the elevator. But that archway is sealed with huge doors. I have to backtrack and take the only other elevator I know, down by the Secretariat offices.

The doors open to a different world. These hallways are five hundred years old. They were built to giant scale, two hundred feet long and twenty-five feet high. Their ceilings were painted by Raphael. The priests who march by are Secretariat men, former prefects of their seminary classes, former stars in their home dioceses, men who found the language training at the Academy no harder than the etiquette classes. Even so, many of them won't cut it. The motto here is that a new door opens every time you push another man out a window. I think to myself that Simon never belonged here. He could wipe the floor with these priests. He's already proven he was made for bigger things. And yet they will push him out the window at the first sign of weakness.

I cross into the final wing of the palace. The last checkpoint of Swiss Guards makes its phone call. I'm now a hundred paces from seeing Simon. I keep the thought of him with me at every step. Otherwise the idea of what I'm doing terrifies me.

A priest-secretary greets me at the door. He's thin as a staff, with a cassock so expensive that the fabric shimmers like liquid silk. His hands are clasped in the half-begging, half-praying pose that Secretariat priests use to keep people from embracing them. He gives me a fraction of a bow, then leads me into a library that nothing, not even Lucio's palace, has prepared me for.

On the floor is a red Persian rug the size of a small courtyard. The walls are gold damask. So are the doors, upholstered like jewelry-box tops to make them disappear into the walls when they close. The chairs and footstools and candelabras are gilded. Simon has told me about places in the Secretariat where the tapestries are gifts from Renaissance kings and the gold was brought back by Columbus from America. But the priest-secretary makes no effort to dazzle me with facts. He just leads me to a negotiating table in the middle of the library. He instructs me to wait at my seat, one arm's length away from the chair at the head of the table. And then he leaves.

A moment later, a door on the far side of the room opens. And a great black form enters the room.

CHAPTER 32

WATCHING CARDINAL BOIA approach is like standing in the path
of a steamroller. He fills the doorway, bullies the light out of the room.
"Prepotente," people call him: high-handed, overbearing, bullying. A
man the size of two men, with the ego of three.

I rise from my chair. A cardinal always presents himself to inferiors
for a bow or a kiss of his ring. I don't want to start this conversation
groveling, but it would be worse to ignore protocol.

Yet Boia doesn't bother. He walks straight to the table, lowers a stack
of papers and a tape recorder, and says, "The exhibit begins in twelve
hours. If your brother wants my help, the window is closing."

"Eminence, I won't help you unless I can see him first."

Boia rakes a hand through the air, waving my words away. "My offer is
this. Give me what I want, and I protect your brother from prosecution.
Anything less, and I see to it that he's dismissed from the priesthood."

I don't know what to say. Everyone knows what kind of man Cardinal
Boia is. His cousin was arrested in a tax evasion scheme in Naples. His
brother, a bishop in Sicily, was sentenced to prison for enriching other
relatives with Church property. Cardinal Boia himself throws his weight
behind the pet projects of rich religious groups who thank him with envelopes of cash. He is the face of the old Vatican. For more than a decade
he has flattened every other cardinal who cast an eye toward his job.

He puts aside the tape recorder, as if he's decided not to make a record of what we say here. His fingers begin crawling through the stack of papers. Fat as sausage casings, they lift layer after layer of sheets until he finds what he wants. Finally he slides two folders across the table. The labels say ANDREOU, S. and BLACK, M.

Already I feel myself losing ground. Mignatto has been trying to get his hands on these two personnel files for days.

Then Boia slides a white square of paper between us. A paper sleeve containing a disc. On the front of the disc is written SECURITY CAMERA B-E-9.

I feel his eyes on me as I stare at it. He wants to see the weakness register in my face. This is the key piece of evidence that never surfaced. I'd assumed this footage from Castel Gandolfo was in the hands of Simon's guardian angel.

"These are all copies," he says. "The originals are on their way to the tribunal, to be entered into evidence if I don't get what I want by the end of this meeting."

My traction is fleeting. "I know my brother's here," I say. "I want to see him."

Cardinal Boia growls, "Your brother is *not* here."

In my coolest voice I say, "The Swiss Guards at the checkpoints saw his car drive into this palace. I know he's here."

Boia barks a word. I barely recognize it as a name: Testa. Instantly his priest-secretary appears at the door.

"Father Andreou wants to see his brother," Boia commands.

The monsignor hesitates. "But Eminence . . ."

"Show him. Now."

Testa begins parting the drapes. Sunlight slopes in from the south. The north windows suddenly give way to tiny balconies overlooking the private courtyard below.

"Follow me, Father," he says.

The monsignor leads me into a hallway surrounded by doors, then opens them one by one. Every corridor leads to a new one, branching in a new direction. The floor plan is so disorienting that Simon could be in a room I don't even see.

"Where is he?" I say.

Testa shows me the dining room and kitchen. The chapel and sacristy. Even Testa's own bedroom. He is making a point. Simon isn't here.

I demand to see Cardinal Boia's own bedroom.

"That's out of the question," Testa says.

Yet I feel Boia there, hovering in the doorway again.

"Do what Father Andreou asks," he says.

It's hopeless. Any place they're willing to show me, Simon won't be. "I know he's here," I say. "I talked to the driver who brought him to your private elevator."

Suddenly Boia turns. For the first time, in his eyes, there is a ferocious sharpness. I've made a mistake. I just don't know what it is.

"Come here, Father," he says, stepping onto one of the small balconies overlooking the courtyard. He points and says, "Do you see that?"

On the far side of the courtyard, near the arched entry, is what appears to be a chimney leading from the ground to the roof.

"That," Boia says, "is the elevator shaft. Now follow me."

We circle the halls until we approach the entrance again. "Do you notice anything?" he says, pointing to the inner wall.

There's no door here. No elevator.

Cardinal Boia snorts like a bull. "The elevator goes only one place. So now you know who has your brother."

WHEN HE LEADS ME back to the negotiating table, I hear him order Testa to have the nuns bring us something to drink. Something to eat. I see him put a hand on my chair, not quite pulling it out for me, but making a small gesture of hospitality. I sense a softening in his voice when he tells me I have it all wrong. He knows he doesn't have to bully me anymore. The facts are doing that enough.

"Did you really think he was innocent in all this?" Boia says.

"I *know* he's innocent."

His Eminence smiles thinly. "I didn't mean your brother." He points upward. "I meant *him*."

"Why would the Holy Father put my brother under house arrest?"

"Because he can't risk a scandal with so many important guests in town, and I'm sure he thought your brother would break down and tell him the truth in private."

I shake my head. "The Holy Father must've put Simon under house arrest to keep him away from *you*. From the trial you opened against him."

"If this were a trial *I* had opened," Cardinal Boia says acidly, "you can be sure the witnesses wouldn't be forbidden to testify about Nogara's exhibit. Punishing your brother means much less to me than knowing what Nogara was hiding."

I gape at him. "How do you know witnesses were forbidden to testify about the exhibit?"

He ignores me. "The Holy Father opened the trial because he wants to know if your brother killed Nogara. But he won't let them discuss the exhibit because he doesn't want me to know his plans for tonight. He's been so busy keeping the secret from me that he doesn't realize Nogara was keeping a secret from *him*."

"That's why you invited me here?" I say, repulsed.

His Eminence folds his hands together. "You and your brother have something I want: you know what Nogara found. And in return, I have something *you* want."

I stare at the evidence on the table. So this is how Simon's guardian angel answers prayers.

"Many weeks ago," Cardinal Boia continues, "when I learned what your brother had begun doing with the Orthodox, I asked the Holy Father to summon him back to Rome to answer for it. I thought the problem was solved. But ten days later, I received word that your brother was still making trips, so I had to find a solution myself."

The last sentence emerges in a growl, as if this was when John Paul made it personal. I wonder if Boia's solution is an allusion to the attack on Michael Black.

"Why are you fighting the Holy Father?" I say. "He wants the Orthodox here."

His Eminence lifts a hand over his head and curls a finger toward himself. I don't understand the gesture. Then I see two nuns waiting at the door behind me. Beckoned, they come bearing demitasse cups and a plate of chocolates. When they're gone, Boia throws back the espresso and smudges his mouth with a napkin. Then he pushes his chair back and leans his huge frame into it.

"The idea sounds pretty, you think?" he says, forcing his meaty hands together. "Two Churches, reunited after a thousand years?" He smiles. "But you're the gospel teacher. The one Nogara talked about. You know that isn't what scripture says."

My hands clench into fists under the table. "What scripture says is, *Every kingdom divided against itself will be laid waste, and no house divided against itself will stand.*"

For a second, Cardinal Boia unconsciously bares his teeth. Then he says something I don't expect.

"Tell me something: what does the Beloved Disciple do? In the fourth gospel, what sets him apart?"

I can't imagine what point he thinks he's making. The Beloved Disciple is a mysterious character who appears only in the gospel of John. He is never named except by this title.

Not waiting for me to answer, Boia continues, "When Jesus is arrested and brought before the high priest, the Beloved Disciple goes right in with him, even though Peter doesn't. When Jesus is crucified, the Beloved Disciple is standing at the cross, even though Peter isn't. When Peter rushes to see Christ's empty tomb, the Beloved Disciple runs faster and gets there first. The other gospels never mention this fellow. They say only Peter followed Jesus to the high priest. Only Peter ran to the empty tomb. There was only one true leader of the disciples: Peter. So how can the gospel of John claim to be the testimony of this one man, the Beloved Disciple, when he doesn't even seem to have existed?"

I begin to tell him what he already knows—that the Beloved Disciple is a literary creation, an attempt to justify why John's gospel is so different—but His Eminence cuts me off.

"He's a fiction. He's some other group of Christians trying to say, 'We matter, too. What we say is worth reading. We're just as important as Peter.' But they *weren't* as important as Peter. Our Lord founded the Church on Peter alone. The other gospels are clear about that. Yet these Orthodox patriarchs say the same thing: 'We descend from apostles, too. We're just as important as the pope.' But they aren't. There was only one Peter, and he has only one successor: the pope. No one sits at the table with him. That's what our Lord intended, and I will do everything in my power to keep it that way."

I'm speechless. In all the gospels there is no mention of anything I see around me. No palaces. No cardinals. No Secretariats of State. Boia is the fiction, the power-grabber with no roots in scripture.

"Now," he says, leaning forward again, "your brother needs my help. Tell me what I want and I'll put the original copies of this evidence in your hand." The corner of his upper lip rises. "You can burn them in my fireplace."

He's right. Without this evidence, the tribunal can't convict Simon. But I have nothing to offer him. Only the truth.

When I hesitate, Boia's eyes flash as if I'm about to give him what John Paul has been unable to get out of Simon. And I would, if I knew the answers he wanted.

"Nogara never told me what he discovered," I say. "And I don't think he told my brother either."

Cardinal Boia's eyes narrow.

"In fact," I continue, "as far as I know, the only controversial discovery Ugo ever made was about the Fourth Crusade."

Boia thrusts a finger in the air. "Don't lie to me! *You're* the gospel teacher. *You're* the one who taught Nogara. You know the truth."

I blink at him.

His eyes never leave me as his hand engulfs the tape recorder at his side. His thumb presses a single button, and suddenly I hear an automated voice.

Tuesday, August third. Four seventeen PM.

A pause. Then:

Simon, it's Ugo again. Where the hell are you? Why won't you answer your phone?

His voice is barely recognizable, so full of anger and emotion that it almost quakes.

I won't change the galleries. You and your uncle don't have my permission to alter one iota of the exhibit. The purpose of my work is to present the truth. *Not cater to some political agenda.*

A long silence follows. My hands are already gripping my cassock. This is the same Ugo I remember, fearless in support of the truth, but with a frightening, alien ferocity. His voice is even wilder than I remember it being when we met on the roof of Saint Peter's and he told me he refused to let me work with him anymore. But it's nothing compared to what follows.

When he speaks again, his voice is transformed. The ferocity has vanished. There is almost no trace of life in him at all.

Forget it. It doesn't matter. The real reason for this phone call is to tell you it's over, Simon. 1204 is irrelevant. The exhibit can't go forward. I'm sending you something in the mail that explains what I found. Read it carefully and . . . and call me, Simon. For God's sake. Just call me.

Cardinal Boia stops the recording. I can only stare at him in horror. So this is what the tribunal admitted into evidence yesterday after Corvi confirmed the voice was really Ugo's.

"You had Simon's phone bugged," I say.

I still can't believe what I've heard. Ugo sounded so enraged.

"I was made aware of this voice message promptly enough," Boia says, "that I was able to have your brother's nunciature mail opened and copied before it was delivered to him."

He digs one more sheet from his stack of papers and slides it over to me. My chest tightens.

"Your expression suggests you recognize it," he says.

A photocopy of the letter I found with Simon's day planner. The letter Ugo wrote about their meeting at the Casina.

Cardinal Boia's finger points to a particular line.

I've taken my gospel lessons from Alex very seriously.

This must be how Boia knew who I was.

"The letter is very clear," His Eminence says. "Nogara said he was enclosing a proof. So where is it?"

"I don't know."

"You and your brother are playing games with me. There was nothing in the envelope but this page. I don't know why I bothered to have it resealed."

"I have no idea what Ugo found."

"*Stop lying.*"

I stare blankly at the paper. Slowly it's dawning on me that this letter is not what it seemed.

Boia barks, "Testa!"

The monsignor appears at once.

"Get this man out of here."

"Please," I say. "Don't do this. You're attacking an innocent priest."

But he turns on me and points to the letter in my hand. "I'll find out what Nogara knew. You just ended your brother's future in the priesthood."

CHAPTER 33

THE LETTER. AS soon as I find privacy, I open it again. On the hill overlooking the museums, where the cars and trucks now travel to and from Ugo's exhibit, making their final preparations, I reread it.

3 August 2004

Dear Simon,

Mark 14:44–46	*You've been telling me for several weeks now that*
John 18:4–6	*this meeting wouldn't be postponed—even if*
Matthew 27:32	*you were away on business. Now I realize you were*
John 19:17	*serious. I could tell you I'm ready for it, but I'd be*
Luke 19:35	*lying. For more than a month you've been stealing*
John 12:14–15	*away on these trips—which I know has been hard*
	on you—but you need to understand that I've had
	burdens too. I've been scrambling around to mount
Matthew 26:17	*my exhibit. Changing everything so that you can*
John 19:14	*now pull off this meeting at the Casina will be*
	difficult for me. Yes, I still want to give the keynote.
	But I also feel that doing it compels me to
Mark 15:40–41	*make some grand personal gesture toward the*
	Orthodox. For the past two years I've given

John 19:25–27
my life to this exhibit. *Now you've taken my work and given it a much larger audience—which is wonderful, of course—and yet it gives this keynote a heavy significance. This will be the moment when I officially hand my baby over. The moment when, with a great flourish, I sign my*

Matthew 27:48
life away.

John 19:28–29
So, then, I need to share with you what I've been doing while you were out of town. I hope it agrees with your agenda for the meeting. First, I've taken my gospel lessons from Alex very seriously. I study scripture morning and night. I've also kept up my work with the Diatessaron. These two avenues of investigation, together, have repaid me richly. Brace yourself, because I'm about to use a word that, at this late stage in the process, probably

Mark 15:45–46
horrifies you. I've made a discovery. Yes. What I've found erases everything I thought I knew about the Turin Shroud. It demolishes what we both expected to be the central message of my

John 19:38–40
keynote. It might come as a surprise—or even as a shock—to the guests you're inviting to the

Luke 24:36–40
John 20:19–20
exhibit. For it proves that the Turin Shroud has a dark past. The radiocarbon verdict killed serious scholarship on the Shroud's history before 1300 AD, but now, as that past comes to light, I think a small minority of our audience may find the truth harder to accept than the old idea that the Shroud

Luke 23:46–47
is a fake. Studying the Diatessaron has taught me what a gross misreading we've been guilty of. The same gross misreading, in fact, that reveals the truth about the Shroud.

My discovery is outlined in the proof enclosed here. Please read it carefully, as this is what I'll be telling your friends at the Casina. In the

*meantime, I send my best to Michael, who I know
has become your close follower.*

John 19:34   *In friendship,
Ugo*

This time, reading the text makes me jumpy with anxiety. Something here isn't right. Four days after Ugo wrote this, he sent me a frantic final e-mail. The same day he wrote this, he left Simon an irate voice message. The calm, eager Ugo of this letter is a front. An illusion.

Why send such a message through the mail? Why openly discuss the Orthodox gathering at the Casina? It seems almost intended to draw attention to the meeting. And if Ugo was the one who put this meeting on Cardinal Boia's radar, causing all the last-minute heightening of security and change of venue to Castel Gandolfo, then either he was being careless or he was being spiteful.

Ugo claimed a proof was enclosed here, but Boia said no other page was found in the envelope. *Read it carefully*, Ugo said in his voice message. He repeated those same words in the letter itself. And I have a feeling that if I do, I will somehow find the proof right before my eyes.

I scan the gospel verses in the side column, wondering what I've missed. Ugo and I used this homily paper during his lessons. When two gospels would tell the same story in different ways, Ugo would write down the parallel verses and compare them. It makes me wonder if the body of the letter here is just a sideshow, a distraction. If the progression of the verses is what really matters.

I dig into the column on the left. The first is Mark 14:44–46, which describes how Jesus was arrested before his trial. An armed mob appeared, and Judas identified Jesus to the authorities with the infamous kiss of betrayal. Matthew and Luke agree with Mark's version of events, but Ugo's very next selection is John's version. In it, Judas doesn't kiss anyone. Jesus steps forward on his own, and the mob demands to know who Jesus of Nazareth is. In an eye-opening twist, Jesus' two-word answer—"I AM"—makes the whole mob suddenly fall to the ground.

John is making a theological point: "I AM" is the mystical name of God Himself. In the Old Testament, Moses hears the burning bush command: "Say to the Israelites: 'I AM has sent me to you.'" The point is that Jesus is this same God. But Ugo must be making a point, too: Mark's verse shows that John's verse is theological. It expresses a spiritual truth, but it never really happened.

The next two verses work the same way. Jesus is marched to the site of his crucifixion. But after being scourged and beaten, he's too weak to carry the beam of his own cross. It has to be carried by a passerby named Simon of Cyrene. Luke agrees with Matthew's account, as does Mark, who even names two of Simon's sons to make sure there's no confusion about who he was. But once again Ugo has chosen the companion verse from John, and it's theological. Since Jesus is shouldering the burden for all of us—since he's about to die for the good of all mankind—John has no room for a character who shoulders the burden for Jesus. So Simon of Cyrene vanishes from the text. Instead, John says: "they took Jesus, and he went out, bearing his own cross." Ugo is making the same point as before: John has changed the facts to make a spiritual statement.

As I scan Ugo's column of verses, I notice that this pattern repeats itself again and again. I also notice that many of the verses here are the same ones from Ugo's caduceus drawings. They focus on the two powerful Old Testament symbols—the Good Shepherd and the Lamb of God—that John summons to answer the hardest question in all of Christianity: why did an all-powerful Jesus let us crucify him? These symbols seem to follow Jesus throughout the final days of his life. When Jesus enters Jerusalem, John says, he rides an ass, just like the Good Shepherd of the Old Testament. When Jesus is dying on the cross, John says, he has a sponge of wine raised up to his lips on a stalk of hyssop, a flimsy little plant that could never really have held the weight of a sponge. The other gospels say the sponge was raised on a reed, but John is more interested in symbolism, and hyssop was the plant used to wipe the Passover lamb's blood on the doorposts of the ancient Jews. John even changes the day of Jesus' death so that Jesus, the Lamb of God, is crucified on the same day that the Passover lambs are slaughtered.

This obsession with the Good Shepherd and the Lamb of God is so obvious in Ugo's choices that it must be significant. Yet how these verses can form a proof of any discovery he made, I continue not to see. I feel uncomfortably close, however, to understanding something I couldn't make sense of before.

On the first day of the trial, Ugo's assistant Bachmeier said that Simon had done something odd when he was tasked with overseeing the exhibit: my brother removed one of Ugo's photo enlargements of the Diatessaron. At the time, the accusation seemed absurd. Now I wonder if the gospel verses on that page of the Diatessaron are somehow related to the ones in this letter. If Ugo's proof, whatever it is, depends on seeing *both*.

Time is working against me. The trial has been under way for half an hour. I need to hurry back to the Palace of the Tribunal.

CHAPTER 34

MIGNATTO IS MILLING in the courtyard when I arrive.

"Why are you late?" he demands.

"Why are you out here?"

"We're recessed," he says angrily, "so the judges can consider the new evidence."

Boia.

"The letter," I say.

"And the security video. And the personnel files."

"Monsignor, I need to talk to you."

But at that moment, the gendarmes reopen the doors.

"No, you need to come inside," Mignatto snaps. "We're back in session."

WHEN WE'RE SEATED, THE gendarmes bring in Michael Black. He sits down at the witness table in the center of the room and takes a sip from a glass of water that's already half-drunk. His testimony must've been interrupted by the arrival of the evidence.

I try to whisper to Michael, but Mignatto squeezes my arm. When I steal another look at the photocopy of Ugo's letter, a new thought crosses my mind.

Cardinal Boia compared the Orthodox patriarchs to the Beloved Disciple. The gospel of John was on his mind. I wonder if he was trying to crack Ugo's letter, too.

On the legal pad before me, I write a note—*I need to call my uncle*—and slide it over to Mignatto.

Lucio was with Simon in the museums that day. If Simon took down the photo enlargement, then Lucio must have an idea where he put it.

Mignatto hisses something that sounds like, *It's too late.* I glance around the courtroom, wondering if Lucio might be in attendance, but the only spectator is Archbishop Nowak.

We rise for the entrance of the three judges, then the notary administers the oaths. Michael takes them officiously, as if the rest of us are amateurs and he's the only one here who's been to the Olympics of protocol.

"Please identify yourself to the tribunal," the presiding judge asks.

"Father Michael Black, auditor first class in the Second Section."

The tribunal approaches him deferentially. "Thank you, Father," the presiding judge says, "for agreeing to travel here from Turkey. The tribunal notes your efforts."

Michael nods. On his face is the reserved geniality that Secretariat priests are famous for. Imperturbable. Aristocratic. He makes a surprisingly effective witness.

"Father," the judge says, "did you know the deceased, Doctor Nogara?"

"I did."

"Were you in personal contact with him before he was killed?"

Michael nods. "A couple times Nogara drove ten hours from Edessa to Ankara to see Father Andreou at the nunciature. Both times, Andreou was off on one of his trips, so I made a point of getting to know Nogara myself."

As he says this, Mignatto glances back toward Nowak, waiting to see if he'll object to this mention of Simon's trips. So far, nothing.

"Were Nogara and Father Andreou on good terms?"

Michael makes a sour face. "That's complicated, Monsignor."

"Why?"

"I'll be honest with you. Nogara was a pain in the neck. He clung to Andreou like a tick. My impression is that when Simon saved him from—"

"Father Andreou," the judge says, correcting him.

"When *Father Andreou* saved him from drinking himself to death, Nogara got very dependent on him."

"You seem to have a positive view of Father Andreou."

"I wouldn't say that. I have very mixed views. But he's a special kind of priest. And when people see the things he can do, they put certain expectations on him. Which, unfortunately, he encourages. In my opinion that's a bad recipe."

The judges smell blood. Michael is circling something, putting a good face on a situation he won't quite describe. Mignatto jots a note and submits it to one of the judges, who immediately reads it aloud.

"What were the expectations placed on Father Andreou in this situation?"

Michael turns his head a few degrees before he answers. A sidelong glance at Archbishop Nowak.

"Well," he says, "Father Andreou was working for someone who—"

Nowak lifts a hand in the air. "No," he says.

Michael goes silent.

The judges look chastened. After a moment's silence, one of them says, "Did Doctor Nogara ever say anything to you that would suggest Father Simon Andreou was pressuring him not to discuss a discovery he had made?"

"Yes."

"When?"

"Twice. Including the day before he was killed."

I look at Mignatto. I didn't know Ugo called Michael that day. But Mignatto seems unsurprised. He only stares at one of the judges, who makes intermittent eye contact with him.

"Can you elaborate?" the judge says.

"Not really. Like you said, Nogara thought he had found something important. Father Andreou asked him not to ruffle feathers with it. I asked him what it was all about, but he told me he was waiting to discuss it with Father Andreou."

The judge leans forward. "Do I understand you correctly? On the day before Doctor Nogara was killed, he was waiting to discuss this disagreement with Father Simon Andreou?"

Michael seems impatient. "That's what he told me, anyway."

In the silence that follows, the presiding judge lifts a folder in his hand. I recognize the markings on it. A personnel file from the Secretariat. It must've just come from Cardinal Boia.

"Father Black," the judge says, "could you explain to the tribunal how you received the wounds on your face?"

Michael's lip curls. "No. I can't."

"Why not?"

"Because I took an oath not to talk about it."

Archbishop Nowak seems to be following this intently.

"Can you tell the tribunal *where* it happened?"

"No. I can't."

"An airport, wasn't it?"

"No comment."

"In Bucharest?"

"I said no comment."

The judge removes a photo from the personnel file and lifts it in the air. I recognize it as a copy of the picture I found in Ugo's safe. The same one I now have in my wallet.

"That's you, isn't it, Father Black?"

Michael bristles.

The judge puts it down and raises a second photo, which I've never seen before. It shows the baggage claim where Michael was beaten up.

"What were you doing there?" the judge asks.

For the first time, Mignatto looks concerned. The appearance of the file is a wild card.

"Since you've got all the answers," Michael growls, "why do I need to be here?"

"The investigation report," the judge continues, "says another Secretariat priest was in Bucharest with you. Who was it?"

The muscles of Michael's neck are flexed. His right hand is rubbing the corner of the table. The judge is picking on him. The tribunal is tired of the silences.

The judge says, "You were there with Father Andreou, weren't you?"

"Yeah. That's right. I was."

There's a pulse of silence. Michael has broken his oath. His temper is rising.

"So what was the accused doing in Romania, Father Black?"

Archbishop Nowak raises his hand again and says, "No."

But Michael ignores him. "I'll tell you what he was doing. The same thing *I* was doing. Following orders."

Nowak stands. He ignores Michael and keeps his eyes on the judges when he says, "You may ask about Father Black's injury but not about Father Andreou's trips. Thank you."

"Yes, Your Grace," the lead judge says. Then, as if afraid this will be his last chance to ask it, he poses the question.

"Father Black, who attacked you?"

Michael squirms. The interruption has given him a moment to collect his wits. "No comment," he says.

Wordlessly, the judge lifts a photo from the file. "Taken by a security camera at the airport," he says.

Mignatto and I both crane our necks, trying to see what the photo shows. A black cassock hovers over Michael's body on the floor, staring down at it. The picture is grainy and small. But at the witness table, Michael glances pointedly over at Nowak.

Mignatto's eyes have never left the photo. I hear him murmur, "My God."

"Who is it?" I whisper.

"Tell us what happened, Father Black," the judge says quickly, as if trying to make the most of Nowak's silence.

When I look at the photo again, I still can't make out the face. But in the pit of my stomach, something clenches. The priest standing over Michael's body has the posture of a boxer standing over his opponent.

"Like I told you," Michael says, "he was doing what he was told. And I was doing what I was told."

The dull shock spreads. The breath is heavy in my chest.

The judge lifts the picture of Michael's face again. "You're suggesting someone told the accused to do this?"

"Andreou was sent to meet with the Orthodox patriarch. Cardinal Boia wanted to know where he was going, so I was sent to follow him. Father Simon saw me, and it got physical."

"He almost killed you."

"No. We argued. I'm the one that threw the first punch. He just responded. And he was only there because he was *sent* there."

The presiding judge squints. "Are you defending him?"

Michael smashes a hand on the table. "Like hell! I had to have surgery! They still won't let me come back to work!"

"Then what are you saying?"

"I'm saying that *you*"—he points to all three of them up there, in their silk and ermine cloaks—"don't get it. Everything with you is right or wrong, black or white. But that's not how it is. Down here, you fight for what you believe in. You *fight* for it."

"What on earth are you—"

And this is the moment Michael chooses to turn to me and say, with wild eyes, "Alex, I'm sorry I lied to you about what happened in that airport. But you gotta know something. Simon's wrong about this. He's wrong."

I don't even understand what he means. Everything feels so foggy and faraway. My eyes are fixed on Michael's face. On the wounds that still haven't healed. Simon can't have done that. Can't have.

The judges stop Michael. They tell him his deposition is over. Numbly I stare as he exits the courtroom. Then I hear the presiding judge calling the next witness. The one I fear most.

"Officer, bring in your commander."

A BROODING FIGURE WALKS in, wearing his familiar midnight-blue blazer and patterned charcoal necktie. From a distance his face is all hooked nose and web of wrinkles. But as he approaches, everything converges in his tiny black eyes. Here is the man who sees all, who registers every face that stops to gawk at the pope. Nearly sixty years he has served inside these walls, forty as director of papal security, and on the day John Paul was shot twice and nearly killed in Saint Peter's Square, he hunted down the shooter on foot. Now, taking his oaths, he murmurs the words unintelligibly. And the judges, knowing his reputation, give him this latitude. The Vatican newspaper says he has never granted an interview. Not one, in six decades.

"Commander," says the presiding judge, "would you please identify yourself to the tribunal?"

He studies each monsignor, one by one. Then, in a deep voice, he says, "Eugenio Falcone. Inspector General of Vatican gendarmes."

Without prompting, he reaches into his breast pocket and produces a sheet of paper. His notes.

The sight shakes Mignatto into action. He raises his hand and scribbles something on his pad. I'm just able to read it before he slips it to the judges.

Canon 1566: Witnesses are to give testimony orally and are not to read written materials.

The judges ignore him. The tribunal will listen.

"The deceased," Falcone reads aloud, "was killed by a single gunshot to his right temple from a 6.35-millimeter round discharged at close range. A firearm of this caliber was registered to the deceased, and we have reason to believe it was kept in a gun case in his automobile just prior to the murder."

This statement chokes the judges. But inside it is the missing piece: the object taken from under the driver's seat of Ugo's car was a gun case.

"The window of the deceased's automobile," Falcone continues, "was found to be shattered, and the gun case was no longer present within the automobile. Our conclusion is that the defendant broke into the deceased's car and took his gun in order to commit the murder."

The presiding judge plods into his first line of questioning. "We've heard from a forensic specialist, Doctor Corvi, that you expected to find a particular model of gun. Your prediction was correct?"

Falcone tucks his notes away. The slit of his mouth is thinner than an incision when he says, "We're still searching for the gun case and gun."

"Can you tell us, then, about the medical examiner's finding that no wallet or wristwatch were present on the body of the deceased? Those items were recovered at Castel Gandolfo?"

"No."

"Yet that doesn't lead you to suspect this was a robbery?"

"It leads me to suspect that a robbery was staged."

"Why?"

"The deceased's car was broken into, but the glove box wasn't rifled."

Mignatto dashes out another note and sends it to the youngest judge.

"Eh, Inspector," the judge breaks in, "could you tell us how many days you've been searching for all these items? The gun, the case, the wallet, the watch?"

"Six days."

"And how many of your men have been conducting this search?"

A defensive note enters Falcone's voice. "Twelve per shift. Three shifts per day."

Almost a third of our national police force.

"Have you also had help?"

"From the carabinieri, yes."

The Italian police.

"So where could these items be?"

Falcone glares at the judge. It is said that he can toss a full-grown man off the hem of the pope's cassock like throwing away a tissue. He doesn't answer.

"Right here," the young judge says, "I have the transcript from your police report. One of your agents, Bracco, questioned Father Andreou at Castel Gandolfo. Is that right?"

"Yes."

"How close were the two men standing during the questioning?"

Falcone scowls. He finds the question unintelligible.

"An arm's length from each other?" the judge clarifies. "Across a table?"

"An arm's length."

"So Bracco had a good look at Father Andreou?"

"Yes."

"You told us the killer disposed of the evidence against him. Since an exhaustive search hasn't turned up those items, are you considering the possibility that they were removed from the crime scene?"

"That is our operating theory at this point, yes."

"But how could Father Andreou have removed them with Bracco interviewing him only an arm's length away?"

Falcone's expression sours. He removes a handkerchief from his pocket and scrubs the bottom of his nose. "Andreou would have concealed them."

The judge lifts a photo. "This was taken at Castel Gandolfo by one of your own men, correct?"

"Yes."

"It shows Father Andreou on the night of Doctor Nogara's murder. Do you see what he's wearing?"

"A cassock," Falcone says.

The judge nods. "Commander, are you familiar with what a priest wears under his cassock?"

Falcone clears his throat. "Trousers."

"Correct. That's why cassocks often have no pockets, just slits leading to the pants. Do you know why I mention this?"

Falcone stares grimly ahead. "No."

"At the risk of sounding indecent," the judge says, "it's very uncomfortable to wear pants under a wool cassock in the summer. So some priests simply don't."

The judge raises a second picture, showing Simon squatting near Ugo's body. The bottom hem of his cassock has risen, showing inches of black calf socks underneath. He isn't wearing pants under his cassock.

"Commander," the judge says, "do you see the concern I'm raising?"

I feel a burst of relief. There's no place for him to have hidden anything. When Simon collected his own phone and passport from his greca in the mud, this is why he carried them in his hands all the way home. He had nowhere else to put them.

Falcone continues to stare at the judge. But this time, the judge refuses to bend. The gendarme chief will have to respond.

"The concern is moot," Falcone says finally.

"Why?"

Falcone signals one of the gendarmes at the door, who exits the courtroom and returns with a TV on a cart. "Because," Falcone says, "of what was captured on surveillance."

Mignatto stands. "Objection. The defense hasn't seen this evidence yet. It was submitted only an hour ago."

The presiding judge nods in agreement. "Sustained," he says. "The tribunal will recess for—"

But he freezes midsentence, staring at something behind me.

I turn. In the first row of chairs, Archbishop Nowak has risen to his feet. In his slow, quiet voice he says, "Let this be shown."

"Your Grace," Mignatto says humbly. "Please."

But Nowak says, "It is important. Let this be shown."

The gendarme officer feeds a disc into the machine. For a moment there's no sound in the courtroom except the disc's furious spinning. Then a video begins to play.

It's grainy and soundless. Nothing in the image moves. But I recognize the landscape immediately.

"This was taken," Falcone says, "by the security camera closest to the deceased's car. Less than one hundred feet from where the body of the deceased was found."

In the video, a car flits by on a road. A single tree branch sways rhythmically. Dark clouds scud in the distance. The storm is approaching. I watch with a surge of foreboding.

Suddenly a shape appears on the screen. Falcone presses a button on the remote. The image freezes.

Ugo. He's alive. Walking left to right across the screen, just inside the gate. The sight of him jolts me. He seems so alone.

"Nogara is moving south," Falcone says. "Away from the villa, toward his vehicle." He points to a digital marker in the bottom right of the screen. "Please note."

16:48. Twelve minutes to five o'clock.

I try to orient myself. Ugo is walking away from Simon and the Orthodox. As if planning to leave Castel Gandolfo in his car. This would've been shortly after the last time he and Simon spoke by phone.

Falcone unfreezes the footage. Ugo continues across the screen. If the playback is at real speed, he's walking quickly. Then, at the instant Ugo leaves our field of view, Falcone points to the time again. Still twelve of five.

Now he fast-forwards. Tree branches wave wildly. Drifting leaves race.

"Watch," he says as the footage returns to normal speed.

A new shape enters the frame. Much larger than Nogara. For a moment, in the fading light, it's only a silhouette. But everyone in this room can identify him.

"*Ten* minutes before five o'clock," Falcone says.

Simon is running after Ugo. In mere seconds, he's gone.

Falcone freezes the footage. Mignatto, without even looking at the legal pad, writes a note in giant letters.

TWO MINUTES.

The total time that separates Ugo and Simon in this footage.

Falcone returns to his notes. "The following," he says, "is from our incident report. I quote. Bracco: Father, when you found Doctor Nogara, what condition was he in? Andreou: Not moving. Bracco: Shot? Andreou: Yes. Bracco: Did you see or hear anything before you arrived? Andreou: No. Nothing."

Falcone looks up. He points to the screen. He doesn't say a word.

Simon lied to the police.

———

THE JUDGES PLAY THE footage again. Then a third time. Mignatto insists on it. He wants to hear it with sound. Without fast-forwarding. He wants to see the footage immediately before and immediately after. Maybe he thinks this will dull the judges' shock. Anesthetize them with the repetition. But they see the truth: the defense is groping. Buying time until Mignatto recovers enough to think of something better. As I look at him, I see myself. A flailing man just trying not to drown.

Each loop of the video adds something new. Something worse. Once the sound is turned up, the gunshot becomes audible. Simon undoubtedly heard it. It's all here. Cardinal Boia knew this video was his trump card.

"Monsignors," Mignatto says in a trance, "may we see the film just one more time?"

The presiding judge says, "No. We've seen it enough."

"But Monsignor—"

"No."

To the judges' surprise, Mignatto turns directly to Falcone. In a thin voice he says, "Commander, explain what you think happened after Father Andreou passed by."

The old judge barks, "Monsignor! You will be seated!"

But the lead judge waves his colleague off.

Mignatto continues, "Are you suggesting Father Andreou followed Nogara to his car? Then broke the window to get the gun and kill him?"

Falcone sits impassive. He doesn't answer questions from lawyers.

"Inspector," says the lead judge, "you may respond."

Falcone clears his throat. "Father Andreou knew Nogara owned a weapon. He knew where it was located. It is reasonable to—"

Mignatto cuts in, waving a hand in the air. "No. That's an assumption. You *assume* Father Andreou knew about the weapon. But this is extremely important, Inspector. This man's priesthood is at stake. If Father Andreou didn't know Nogara owned a gun, then he surely couldn't have seen a gun case underneath a car seat. And he wouldn't have broken a window to remove what he didn't know existed. So please be clear. You're making an assumption."

Without the slightest change in tone, Falcone says, "I am not. A Swiss Guard has admitted to providing advice to Nogara about the model of weapon and gun case he should buy. It was Father Andreou who solicited this advice."

I feel bolted to my seat. I know which Swiss Guard Simon would've asked for this advice.

Mignatto fumbles forward. "Nevertheless, the issue—the issue is the sequence of events: you're suggesting that Father Andreou broke the window, then removed the gun, then finally shot Doctor Nogara?"

"Correct."

Mignatto's hand is shaking as he says, "Then, Monsignors, I insist that you play the video again. But this time, instead of watching it, please close your eyes."

THERE IS A SOUND. Late in the footage, I hear a muted noise, different from the deep report of the gunshot. A tinselly pop. I can't tell what it is. It could be the far-off squeal of car brakes on the public road. The rattle of something hitting one of the chain-link border fences. But with my eyes closed, what it most resembles is glass breaking.

Instantly I understand Mignatto's point. If this is the car window being shattered, then the order of sounds is wrong. Gunshot. Then glass breaking.

Mignatto asks Falcone to stop the tape. The silence in the courtroom swells with uncertainty.

The old judge croaks, "What does this mean, Monsignor?"

All eyes are on Mignatto.

"I don't know," he says.

"The sound could be anything," the judge snipes.

"Including," Mignatto says with feeling, "evidence of Father Andreou's innocence."

Falcone grunts dismissively. "The evidence is clear."

Yet he stands corrected.

"No," Archbishop Nowak says softly. "It is not."

Mignatto checks his watch and says, "Monsignors, I request a recess."

"Why?" the presiding judge asks.

"Because it's getting late, and our next witness may be unable to testify since the exhibit begins shortly."

There is a logic here that I don't understand but that the tribunal does. The judges nod their assent.

"Fifteen minutes," their leader says.

Mignatto gets up from the table and begins to walk to the door, but I put a hand on his arm to stop him. "We need to talk," I whisper urgently, "about Ugo's letter."

He is ashen. I can feel his arm shaking.

"No," he says. "Everything else will have to wait."

I FOLLOW HIM INTO the hallway and find Uncle Lucio there. Instead of asking about the proceedings, Lucio begins to guide Mignatto away.

"Uncle," I say, sensing my opportunity, "I need to know what Simon did with the photo enlargement he took down from the exhibit. You were there when he—"

Lucio cuts me off. "I don't know anything about that, Alexander. Now leave us."

He takes Mignatto away toward an empty office. The last thing I hear before they close the door is the monsignor's voice pleading, "Eminence, I've given them something to think about. One more day. Please. You have to reconsider."

I turn and run. I have fifteen minutes. I need to find Leo.

When I get to the barracks and call him down, he emerges from the alleylike courtyard wearing jeans and a T-shirt for his favorite soccer team, Grasshopper Club Zürich. He's holding playing cards.

I try to control myself. To keep my voice low. "Why didn't you tell me Simon came to you about Nogara's gun?"

He throws his hands on his head.

"Tell me everything," I say. "You've got ten minutes."

"Alex, it wasn't me. It was Roger. You know I wouldn't—"

I raise my voice. "Ten minutes! Tell me about the gun."

He rubs at his forearm. "Follow me," he says.

We enter the cool shadows of the courtyard. Sitting around a picnic table are the other men in the card game, some half-dressed in their rainbow uniforms, their multicolored ribbons stripped off like overalls.

To one of them, Leo says, "Roger, a minute."

The man he's speaking to is a giant with a skull like a pipe stem. His huge hands conceal the playing cards entirely.

"Busy," he says.

I step forward. "Roger, I'm Father Andreou."

The man turns. Immediately his cards go facedown on the table. He stands up. Respect for the priesthood is ingrained in these men. "Father," he says, "how can I help you?"

The words are Italian, but the accent is German.

"He needs to see your travel case," Leo says.

Just for a second, the other men at the table glance up.

Roger looks searchingly at Leo, not liking this request.

"Rog, just do it," Leo says.

The behemoth grunts and pulls his straps over his shoulders.

We follow him toward the turret of the Vatican Bank, to a sliver of land the Swiss use as temporary parking on nights when they want to drive into Rome. The car here, a steel-colored Ford Escort designed for a smaller race of men, is Roger's. He kneels down on the cobblestones and reaches into the driver-side foot well. I hear clicking, then a silky zipping noise. Roger rises again to his full height. Without a word, he turns and hands the case to Leo.

It's a black rubber clamshell, rectangular with rounded edges, barely big enough to hold three packs of playing cards side by side. When Leo passes it to me, I'm surprised by its heft. Beneath the layer of rubber is a solid metal frame. Inside is something very dense.

"Simon came to me," Leo begins hesitantly. "He said Nogara had illegally bought a gun in Turkey because he'd been threatened."

"How could you not mention this to me?"

"Hear me out. It was a shotgun. Simon begged me to get it out of his hands, so I told Nogara what he really wanted was a nice subcompact, this peashooter Beretta I knew wouldn't blow his leg off by accident. We got it registered. I swear to you, we took the maximum time with every step, trying to keep it out of his hands as long as possible. Then Simon asked me for a safe way to carry it, a gun case Nogara would have a hard time opening when he was drunk. Those were his words. That's when I handed him over to Roger."

He gives the clamshell back to his partner. "Rog, show him how it works."

"Leo . . ." I say, wondering how he could've sat beside me in the Casa, listening to everything I said about Ugo's death, without mentioning this. How he could've kept this to himself even if Simon told him to keep it quiet.

But his eyes are begging me to wait. Begging me not to ask in front of his fellow soldier.

Grudgingly Roger points to numbered cylinders built into the front of the case. "Combination lock," he says.

Then he turns the clamshell around and points to a reinforced steel tube running along the back. "For the chain," he adds.

"What chain?"

He points down toward the foot well. There, beneath the splitting upholstery of his seat cushion, are the metal sleds that hold the seat to the car frame. Wrapped around them is a sleek black cable thinner than a bicycle chain. It has its own lock, opened by a key.

"The cable ties the case to the seat," Leo says.

Roger demonstrates by chaining it back in place.

"The key removes the chain," Leo says. "But the only way to open the case is with the combination. And if you're not opening it regularly, it's easy to forget the combo. Especially after you've had a few drinks."

I study the dimensions. "You're sure a 6.35-millimeter gun would fit in here?"

Roger snorts.

"Our service piece," Leo says, "is a nine millimeter. Which fits snug in that model. I happen to know it's the same case Simon bought for Nogara."

I lower my voice. "So let's say a stranger didn't have the combination. How could he pry this open?"

Roger smiles. "Try it, Father."

I make a halfhearted attempt to pry it open with my fingers, knowing this is what he wants to see. Then I draw my Casa key from my cassock. I force the edge of the metal fob into the narrow channel between the clamshell's lips. It fits perfectly, but the case doesn't budge. When I press the metal sharply downward, the fob begins to whiten and bend. It would break exactly like the piece I found under Ugo's seat.

"Without the combination," Roger says, "it's impossible."

So this is another oddity about Ugo's death. Ugo was killed by a weapon that—according to the chipped metal on the floor—was never successfully removed from its case.

Leo signals to Roger that his help is no longer needed. The giant locks up his car and lumbers off.

"Listen," Leo whispers, "I'm sorry. I told myself—I was *sure*—it wasn't this gun that killed him. Alex, you've got to understand. That caliber is almost the weakest there is. That's the whole reason I recommended it. And someone would need a crowbar to open Roger's model of gun case without the combo. Nobody could've done that. I still don't believe it."

I recognize his tone of voice. He isn't telling. He's confessing.

"Simon and I were trying to save his life," he says, "by getting him that gun."

I can't stomach this right now. "Did Simon know the combination?" I ask.

"I don't know." He hesitates, then repeats, "Alex, I'm sorry."

But time is running out. The court's recess ends in three minutes.

"You should've told me," I say. "But what happened to Ugo wasn't your fault."

■ ■ ■

I GET BACK TO the courtroom just as the gendarmes begin to close the doors. At the defense table, Mignatto hasn't unpacked his briefcase. There's no legal pad or pen between us. He stares blankly at the photo of John Paul on the wall.

The witness table is empty. The TV cart is gone. Inspector Falcone must be needed elsewhere; security for the exhibit will be tight. When I ask Mignatto if we're finished for the day, he continues peering at John Paul and says, "We'll know soon enough."

The doors open to admit Archbishop Nowak. For a second I wonder if he's our final witness. But instead he takes his usual seat.

I wonder why he's here. Why, with Simon under arrest in John Paul's own apartments, he bothers to come at all, hanging on the words of witnesses who don't know what happened any better than he does. Simon must still be refusing to talk. John Paul could've stopped this trial with a word—could've prevented it from ever beginning—but in two hours the Orthodox will be standing in the museums, waiting to see what Ugo discovered, and the Holy Father needs answers. If that's our timetable, then this final witness is our last chance.

I pull Ugo's letter from my cassock, looking again at the pattern of gospel verses. Trying to imagine what triggered his discovery. Just three weeks earlier, he'd been tracking the Shroud out of Jerusalem in the hands of Doubting Thomas. What could've changed?

But I can't keep my eyes on the page. What troubles me most is the final quarter-hour of Ugo's life. In my bones I know Simon is hiding more than Ugo's discovery. There must be a reason he lied about hearing the gunshot.

The gendarmes open the courtroom door. Mignatto turns to look. His face wears an expression of dull foreboding. His unease makes me turn as well.

The judges have taken their seats. From behind us, I hear one of them say, "The next witness may enter."

The gendarme stands at attention. He calls out, "His Eminence Lucio Cardinal Ciferri."

I watch as my uncle steps into the courtroom.

CHAPTER 35

ALL THREE JUDGES stand in respect. Every gendarme bows. The promoter of justice and the notary rise. Mignatto follows, motioning for me to do the same. Even Archbishop Nowak comes to his feet.

Lucio no longer wears his customary black. He has changed from his priest suit into a simar, the cassock of a cardinal. Like the skullcap on his head, its buttons and trim and sash are scarlet, a color that even bishops and archbishops are forbidden to wear. On top he wears a sweeping scarlet cape reserved for occasions of high formality, and over his heart hangs a baroque pectoral cross. The fourth finger of his right hand glints with the giant golden ring given to cardinals by the pope. This is a clerical show of force. No one here, not even Nowak, can match it.

At the door, a bowing gendarme offers to help Lucio to his table. My uncle refuses. He refuses Archbishop Nowak, too, who offers him the arm that supports the pope. I am awed to see that he glowers at Nowak, evincing a fearsome superiority. Gone is any sign of Lucio's physical weakness. He moves with old-fashioned dignity, erect and chin cocked, with eyes peering downward. It steals my breath because this tall, gaunt specter resembles no one so much as Simon.

Lucio lowers himself into his chair. But everyone else remains standing.

"You may be seated," Lucio says.

The presiding judge says, "Your Eminence, according to the law, your right is to be deposed at a place of your choosing. If you prefer a place other than this aula, tell us your wishes."

My uncle waves his hand. "You may begin," he says.

The judge clears his throat. "You're aware, Eminence, that you may decline our questions? If you fear your testimony might cause harm to you or your family, you have the right to refuse to answer."

"I have no fear," Lucio says.

"Then we ask you to submit to two oaths. One of truthfulness and one of secrecy."

"I will take the first oath," Lucio says. "But not the second."

I glance at Mignatto, wondering what this means. But the monsignor is watching Lucio with dire attention.

"As the law requires, we will hear your testimony anyway," the presiding judge says, sounding concerned. "And since you requested this deposition yourself, Eminence, would you please tell the tribunal the subject you intend to discuss?"

"Am I correct," Lucio asks, "that witnesses have been forbidden to mention my nephew's travels this summer?"

"Correct, Eminence."

"That is the subject I will be discussing."

I'm tense in my seat. The judges glance at each other.

"Eminence . . ." the lead judge says.

"In particular," Lucio says, "I will be discussing how ungrateful my nephew's incarceration seems to me, when he has placed his own career and priesthood in jeopardy, and even refuses to speak in his own defense, all in order to serve the Holy Father, who in return treats him as a criminal."

I'm frozen. Mignatto stares at the table, unable to watch. This is suicide. Lucio came here to wage war on the pope.

In a quiet but firm voice, Nowak says, "Eminence, please reconsider your words."

Lucio responds with a stunning insult: keeping his back turned to Archbishop Nowak, he addresses him.

"You deny it?" he says.

"Eminence," Nowak replies, "we would not be here if your nephew would tell us the truth."

Finally Lucio turns. They sit almost face-to-face, cardinal at the witness table, archbishop in the first seat. In his princely scarlet, sitting at his full height, Lucio leaves no doubt who is the cock and who is the hen.

"You made him a papal emissary," my uncle says. "You consecrated him a bishop in secret. And this is how you allow him to be treated? You abandon him to *this*?"

A knot forms in my throat. A bishop. In secret. My brother: a bishop.

"My nephew, by himself," Lucio continues, "accomplished what your entire Secretariat couldn't. And for that you prosecute him?"

Archbishop Nowak's voice never changes. Never rises in pitch or volume. He has navigated the shoals with every cardinal on earth. His answer is only five words: "Did your nephew kill Nogara?"

"No," Lucio croaks.

"Are you sure?"

My uncle raises a hand in the air and jabs an accusing finger. His voice tightens. Suddenly I understand that everything is not as clear as I imagined.

"If he *did* kill him," Lucio seethes, "it was for *you*."

Behind me, Mignatto makes a sound of disbelief.

Nowak is as calm as a priest hearing confession. "To hide what Nogara discovered?"

Lucio is so gripped with emotion, he can't find the words to answer.

"Please," Nowak says, "tell me about the Shroud."

Lucio shakes his head. "Not until my nephew is free and these charges are dropped."

"Eminence, you know that is impossible. The Holy Father needs to know the truth."

"*The truth?*" Lucio roars, raising his hands. "You swear my drivers to secrecy. You forbid testimony. You let swaths of evidence be suppressed. That is a search for truth?"

Stolidly, Nowak says, "Without these precautions, tonight's exhibit would have been impossible. You know the difficult situation we find ourselves in."

"Because of the Orthodox *you* invited here!"

For the first time, a ripple of anxiety crosses Archbishop Nowak's features. "This is the Holy Father's dying wish. His intentions are the very best."

Lucio lowers his voice almost to a growl. It is a cold, threatening sound I've never heard come out of him before. "If Simon killed that man—*if* he did—then it's because, at every turn, you told him to keep his work secret. You silenced everyone who found out about Nogara's exhibit. And now you act as if you can't see your own reflection in this, when he's accused of doing only what he saw you do, and what you trained him to believe you wanted."

Lucio collects himself. He looks stronger. He will do anything, even destroy his own career, for Simon. Never in my life have I felt so grateful to him.

"Now," Lucio says to Nowak, "I offer you a choice. Free my nephew and dismiss the charges, and I will privately tell you what you want to know. But if you continue to treat him as a criminal, then it will be war between us. The secret you don't want anyone to know, I will put on the front page of every newspaper in Rome. I will stand in front of the Orthodox tonight and tell them everything. I will punish *you* for punishing *him*."

The silence now is unlike any other. No man in this room can remember someone ever speaking this way to a pope or his representative. No man, except me. It is how the Orthodox spoke to John Paul when he visited Greece. The fury that John Paul accepted and shouldered as his own burden. As I wait for Archbishop Nowak to say something, I pray he has the same wisdom as his master.

His Grace stands. His right arm stretches forward, hand hovering in the air. His voice doesn't rise or falter. But in his sad, dark eyes is something new. Something I don't recognize.

"By the authority of the Holy Father," Nowak says, "I end this deposition. I suspend the trial of Father Andreou. And I transfer this matter to the adjudication of the Holy Father."

He bows to the judges on the bench. "The tribunal is thanked for its efforts. This court is now dismissed."

CHAPTER 36

T HE AIR TIGHTENS around me. Every sound in the room is choked
to silence. The judges rise. They mill around, then drift ghostlike out
of the courtroom. The notary stands and then sits again, pecks at his
keyboard, seeming to await further orders. After staring at Mignatto
in disbelief, the promoter of justice packs his briefcase. At last the gendarmes instruct everyone, by order of the Holy Father, to leave.

Mignatto hunches over the defense table, emptied of strength. Only
Lucio sits upright, disregarding everything else—gendarmes, notary,
wreckage of order. He stares at the crucifix over the bench, crosses himself, and murmurs, "Grazie, Dio."

I hear a familiar voice behind me.

"Eminence, your car is waiting."

Don Diego brushes past me.

"Uncle," I say, "what's going to happen to Simon? What's going to
happen at the exhibit?"

But Lucio's focus is elsewhere. When Diego offers to assist him out
of the palace, my uncle redirects him toward Mignatto. "Help the monsignor to our car. Give him anything he needs."

The last thing Mignatto says to Lucio before leaving is, "Eminence,
you have to be prepared. The Holy Father could resume proceedings as
soon as the exhibit is over."

Lucio merely nods. Tomorrow is tomorrow. Today, he is victorious.

"Please, Uncle," I say when Diego and Mignatto are gone. "What's happening?"

He places a hand on my head. The physical weakness is returning. His hand shakes. "We'll know more tonight," he says. "After the exhibit."

He turns and walks away. I begin to ask another question, but he never looks back.

WHEN LUCIO'S SEDAN SLIDES away from the tribunal, I stand outside in the courtyard, trying to orient myself in a world that has changed since I left it. All around me, laymen are walking out of their offices, sent home early to empty the country before Ugo's exhibit. Cars are lined up at the border gates to leave. Black sedans wait near the doors of the Casa. Through the glass hotel doors I see Orthodox priests milling in the lobby. I hear, just faintly, frenzied nuns calling messages in different languages. Orthodox clergy are checking out their valuables from the hotel safe—jeweled crosses and golden rings and diamond-fretted medallions—and I feel like an altar boy watching priests vest in the sacristy, feeling the mystery of the Church gather in the presence of outward signs. My body vibrates with anxious energy. I try to keep myself in this outer world. But inside, everything is raging.

I've always imagined that my father died in agony. When his heart stopped, the pain killed him before the lack of oxygen. He wasn't found in his chair or bed, but on the bedroom floor, having pulled the Greek cross off his own neck. Mona told me I was wrong. She said he suffered, but not the way I thought. Yet I still keep his cross in a box deep in my closet, never to be touched. And to this day, no image frightens me more than of my father on that floor.

The gospel of John says the final words of Jesus on the cross were triumphant: *It is finished.* His mission, completed. But only the theological Jesus could've spoken those words. The earthly Jesus suffered horribly. Mark's description has always shattered me: *Jesus shouted in a loud voice, "Eloi Eloi lama sabachthani?" which is translated, "My God, my God, why have you forsaken me?"* Gospel scholars call this the cry of dereliction. It expresses a suffering so total that God the Son felt abandoned by God the Father. Ugo told me once that crucifixion is like a heart attack prolonged to hours or days. The heart slowly fails. The lungs slowly collapse. The ancient Romans, who set Christians on fire to use them as torches, and carted them into stadiums to watch wild animals devour them, considered crucifixion the worst punishment of all.

These are the two deaths Simon knows best. Our father's and our Lord's. So to say he killed another man is to say he was willing to inflict on another living creature an experience he believed to be the sum of torment. This, from the boy who found his father dead on the bedroom floor. In my heart, I will never believe it.

Yet for a moment at the witness table, Lucio seemed to consider it possible. And even now, thoughts creep into my mind. Ugo seemed so angry in the voice message he left Simon. So hurt. He had probably been drinking shortly before he died, since a man who would take the Diatessaron out of the museum to show it to the Orthodox wasn't acting reasonably. I don't know what really happened in those final minutes, when only God was watching. And though I tell myself there must've been someone else at Castel Gandolfo besides Simon and Ugo—two men were sleeping in that Casa room, and only one man broke into my apartment—the truth is that Lucio's doubt has left a deep impression.

As I walk home, the Belvedere Courtyard is almost empty. No more work trucks, no more commuter cars. Even the jeeps and engines of the fire department are parked in tight formation to leave more room for tonight's visitors. It's coming. Whatever Simon orchestrated for tonight, it's coming.

Peter is so happy to see me. He claps with glee, as if he's waited patiently through this five-act day just to see his favorite actor take the stage. I have more than enough experience in hiding dark feelings from him. I bow as he claps. Brother Samuel looks relieved. Eleven hours with a five-year-old is saintly work for a man his age. He'll have Peter again in an hour, when I leave for the exhibit, but even a saint deserves a break.

"He's been asking all day when you'll be back," Samuel whispers. "He says he gets to see his mother now."

Samuel smiles. But the smile fades when he sees the expression on my face.

"Peter," I say, "please thank Brother Samuel, and let's go home."

Peter pumps his fist in the air. He grins at Samuel, who gives me the most pathetic look, as if to say, *You would really deprive him of this?*

Once we're back inside our apartment, I find myself watching the clock. Without a word, Peter starts tidying his room and putting his toys in piles just so. He lays out his toothbrush and toothpaste. He finds *Pinocchio* and opens it to the last page Mona read. I have to stop this.

"Peter," I say, "come here. I need to tell you something."

He hops into the chair, then hops out of it. He collects the phone from its station on the countertop, then places it on the table in front of him. He sits in his chair and waits.

"We can't call Mamma tonight," I say.

His head stops bobbing.

"When I promised you we could call her, I'd forgotten I needed to be somewhere important tonight."

His eyes grow fat and pearly. Their rims go red. The tears are coming.

"No!" he says.

"I'm sorry."

"You're a liar!"

"I promise, we'll call her tomorrow—"

"No, you promised *tonight*!"

"Tonight is impossible."

He abandons himself to sobs, and now the tears come rushing out.

It will end, though. As every other tantrum has. Inside that five-year-old body is an older soul, accepting of compromise, unsurprised by disappointment.

"We'll find something special for you to do with Brother Samuel instead," I say. "What do you suggest?"

He'll settle for something, I'm sure. Ice cream. A later bedtime. A movie.

Tonight, though, he refuses them all.

"I don't want that! I want Mamma!"

Maybe I've underestimated. Maybe this is not like every other time. I take out my wallet and start to count bills. The next hill over from the Vatican has a park with a video-game arcade, a puppet theater, a carousel. If I don't do something to stop this crying, I know I'll say something I regret. Something about what's really on my mind.

"You can go to the Gianicolo," I say. "Play video games. Ride the merry-go-round."

To show him how serious I am, I pull out the whole stack of bills, reserving only five euros for myself. When I close the wallet, though, something slips out and flutters to the floor.

Peter stares at it. His face changes. His lips curl back.

I look down. It's the picture of Michael with his nose broken and eye blackened. The sight makes Peter start crying all over again. I grit my teeth and push the photo back into my wallet.

"It's okay," I say, pulling him closer to me and staring over his shoulder at my watch. The exhibit begins in forty minutes. "That man," I lie, "just has a bloody nose."

But Peter's body is stiff. It trembles fiercely.

"Babbo," he whispers, crowding himself deeper into my arms. "That's *him*."

"What?"

He digs his face into my shoulder, trying to shield himself completely with my body. In a muffled voice I hear him cry, "That's the man in our apartment."

I FEEL HOT TEARS wetting my cassock. I feel Peter trying to climb into my lap, trying to envelop himself in my robes. But all I can think is: *Michael*.

I have to tell someone. I have to do something.

I stand, but Peter clings to me. He has fistfuls of my cassock. He won't let me put him down.

I reach the phone on the table and call Mignatto, then Lucio. There's no answer.

"Peter, let go. I need to bring you back to Brother Samuel."

He roars hysterically. When I pull him off me, he battles my outstretched arms, lunging at me. His face is sheer panic. I'm abandoning him.

I close my eyes. Calm myself. Kneel.

"Come here," I say.

He runs into my arms with so much force that it almost knocks me over.

"You're safe. Babbo's here. Nothing bad is going to happen."

I stroke his hair. I squeeze him. I let him cry. But it doesn't pass. He's never been so inconsolable. At the tips of my fingers, even as I hold him, I feel the tattoo of my racing pulse. Every passing minute brings the exhibit closer. Michael will be there. I can't stay here. If I don't hurry, I'm going to be late.

I look down at the phone in my hand and can think of only one solution.

MONA ARRIVES TWENTY MINUTES later. Peter is still breathing hard. Only the promise of seeing her has made any change in him.

"Mamma," he squeaks, and goes to her for a hug.

Her first instinct is the right one: to sit down on the floor and let him fold himself into her lap.

"Brother Samuel's going to come over, too," I tell her.

She nods.

"Go to Samuel's if you want, but please don't go anywhere else."

She nods again.

Just seeing him in her arms fills me with guilt. But she doesn't ask why I would leave our crying son behind. She doesn't doubt.

"I don't know when I'll be back," I say.

"Alex," she says softly, "it's okay. Samuel and I are going to take good care of him. Just go."

■ ■ ■

MY HEART THRUMS. TIME is wasting. I'm late.

Gendarmes are posted at the entrance to the Belvedere Courtyard. Over their shoulders I see dozens of black sedans parked inside.

"Which way?" I say.

The gendarmes point north, toward Ugo's old office. "Head that way, Father. You'll see it."

If Michael broke into my apartment, then he didn't fly here for the trial. Everything he said was a lie. He was in Rome all along.

I dial Leo. He doesn't answer. I leave a message warning him to look out for Michael. Finally I see a private entrance unlocked in the museum wall. Inside, printed programs are left curled up on the floor.

He's the one who must've called the apartment, the night before he broke in. Which means he's one of the men who was staying in that room at the Casa.

I pick up one of the programs. In large red letters, a note on the first page says:

WE ASK OUR GUESTS
TO FOLLOW THE GUIDED TOUR OF THE EXHIBIT.

A map shows the route: from here down to the Sistine Chapel, a corridor one quarter of a mile long has been cleared for the exhibit. As I run to catch up, the history of the Shroud flashes by in reverse. 2004: radiocarbon tests refuted. 1983: Italian royal family gives Shroud to John Paul. 1814: Shroud exhibited to celebrate downfall of Napoleon. 1578: Shroud first arrives in Turin. 1355: first known Catholic exhibition of the Holy Shroud. The path runs unstoppably toward the Fourth Crusade. Toward 1204.

That's why Michael sent me to use the pay phone behind the Casa. Because he could watch me from his hotel window.

When I reach the gallery with Constantinople painted on the wall, I stop in surprise. No one's here either. And no part of the exhibit has been removed in the three days since I saw it.

I hesitate, disbelieving. So it's already happened. The Orthodox have learned that we stole the Shroud from them.

There are shoe prints on the marble floor. Body heat still hangs in the air. Then I see them. On the other side of a display case, almost invisible in the darkness, are two Orthodox in black cassocks. They stand in the corner, weeping. Across the glass, one of them meets my stare. His beard is spangled with tears.

But a voice comes from beyond the doorway. A deep, gentle voice, like a father soothing his son. I step forward, recognizing its accent.

Passing between the doors that were kept locked until now, I find myself in a vast, darkened hall. The only thing I see at first are floating heads—disembodied faces peering into the black. Not until my eyes adjust do I make out their cassocks and tuxedo jackets and black gowns. There are hundreds of people here. I start searching for Michael, but it's hard to move through the crowd.

The walls lighten as the corridor continues. Black turns to gray. Gray to white. At the other end, far off, the room seems to glow. Up there, I see paintings on the walls. Down here, though, the walls are almost bare, stenciled with words and mounted with a few old artifacts—coins and bricks—that look like they came from the bottom of a fishing net.

"You now know," Nowak says, standing on a dais at the far end of the hall, "the history of the Holy Shroud. You know that Western crusaders stole it from Constantinople and brought it into the arms of the Catholic Church." His voice goes silent. The crowd is staring. I look up. Archbishop Nowak's eyes are closed, and his fist is in the air. He brings it down, down, down on his chest.

Mea culpa, mea culpa, mea maxima culpa.

My fault, my fault, my most grievous fault.

I move by intuition. The Orthodox are in tight groups, not leaving each other's sides. But the Roman priests, like Michael, are interspersed through the crowd.

"Forgive us, Lord," Nowak says, "for making Your Shroud a symbol of our separation. Forgive us our sins against our brothers."

There's a dead hush. Some old cardinals in the crowd are stony, as if Nowak is going soft, but His Grace forges on.

"Fortunately, Doctor Nogara made a final discovery even more important than anything you have seen so far."

My search for Michael stops. I'm taken by surprise. Archbishop Nowak is about to describe what Ugo found.

"As you will now see," Nowak says, "the Holy Shroud solved our greatest theological crisis in one of the most difficult periods of our shared history. Without it, we could not be standing here tonight, for the Vatican Museums could not exist."

This sounds nothing like what Ugo described in his letter.

"This is the final gallery of the exhibit," Nowak says. "So before we reach the Sistine Chapel, I would like to introduce Doctor Nogara's assistant, Andreas Bachmeier, who will explain Nogara's discovery."

Everyone's attention shifts. As Bachmeier steps up on the dais, I start making my way through the crowd again. Then, just for an instant, I catch sight of something in the crowd. A cassock with a long rip in the back of the collar.

The cassock I cut open at the Casa.

I turn back, but it's gone.

Pushing deeper into the crowd, I try to focus on the faces around me, try not to be distracted by the thought that calls louder and louder for my attention. Bachmeier makes a bow to Archbishop Nowak, then says, "For decades, the world has asked only one question about the Shroud: is it authentic? But Doctor Nogara asked a better question: why did Christ leave it to us? His answer is in this gallery."

All around me, a weird energy is building. Even the Orthodox are looking around, trying to decipher what Bachmeier means. I slip past a herd of them, apologizing in Greek. Then I see it again: the sliver of white in a torn Roman cassock. I move toward it, trying to catch a glimpse of the priest's face.

But he's moving, too. Edging through the crowd. I wait to see where he's going.

"You may wonder," Bachmeier says, "why no art is hung on the walls at the entrance to this gallery. Why there are only words. It's because this is the world into which the Shroud was born." He steps off the dais, pointing to the stenciled quotations. A microphone on his lapel fills the hall with his voice. "The First Commandment of the Mosaic Law says, *I am the Lord your God. You shall have no other gods before me. You shall not make for yourself a graven image, or any likeness of anything that is in heaven above, or that is in the earth beneath, or that is in the water under the earth.* The ancient Jewish people observed this prohibition very seriously. Consider what we're told by their historian Josephus."

Nowak never leaves the platform, but in his deep, rolling voice he intones, "*The Assembly of Jerusalem sent me to destroy the palace of King Herod, because it was decorated with images of animals. But another man arrived there first, and set the palace on fire.*"

As necks crane to see the letters on the wall, the priest in the torn cassock stops. He turns to look at Nowak. From that angle, I can see his face. My whole body stiffens. Michael.

I push forward and reach for his arm, but he's moving away from me. Angling himself toward Archbishop Nowak.

"People ask why the gospels never mention an image on the Shroud," continues Bachmeier. "But imagine how the Jewish community would have responded to the image of a naked, crucified man."

Suddenly Michael steps forward. He makes a move to confront Nowak on the dais, but sheerly by accident another priest walks into his path. Michael sidesteps, and I lunge forward. My fingers reach his sleeve. I grab him.

"This," Bachmeier is saying, "is why the disciples brought the Shroud to Edessa. A pagan city with no prohibition against images. Led by a king who admired Jesus."

Michael spins around. He looks at me, but there's no recognition in his eyes. His pupils are small and tense. His brow is wet with sweat.

"You son of a bitch," I say.

He rips himself away from me and steps up on the platform with Nowak. At first His Grace doesn't register his presence. Bachmeier is saying, "Our early Christian Church, however, was still hostile to images." Archbishop Nowak seamlessly begins to read a quotation. But Michael steps in front of them. I lurch forward to grab hold of him, but he pulls out of my grasp.

At that moment, something swoops before my eyes. A rush of color. Swiss Guards, descending from all corners of the room. Instantly Michael disappears behind a wall of them, engulfed.

There is shock on the faces of the Orthodox in the crowd. I push my way forward. Just for a second, through the thicket of soldiers, I see Michael's white eyes bulging in their sockets, his arms thrashing. He tries to shout, but it's unintelligible. They have clamped something over his mouth. He tries to kick them away, but they're immovable.

A strong hand grips my shoulder and pushes me off. "Back away, Father," a voice says.

But I hold my ground. Michael is roaring, trying to spit out the gag. Two Swiss officers wave for the crowd to part so that he can be hauled away.

"Friends!" Nowak says, lifting his arms in the air. "Please. Forgive this man. He is disturbed."

I start to follow Michael out, but more Swiss arrive, blocking my way.

"I have to talk to him," I say.

They nudge me back.

"Where are you taking him?" I ask.

Then a voice comes from behind me.

"Father."

I turn. Then I take a step back in surprise.

"Your Grace."

The whole crowd is watching us.

Not knowing what else to do, I bow to Archbishop Nowak.

He takes me by the arm and leads me back to the dais.

"My friends," he announces, "many of you know Bishop Andreou. He visited your countries. He was instrumental in what we do tonight. This man is his brother."

He gives them a long look at me. At my beard. My flowing cassock. The point is not subtle. A mixed family, West and East. We can all survive under one roof.

"Thank you, Father Andreou," Nowak says, "for your help a moment ago."

The crowd politely claps. I keep my eyes on the floor. I didn't stop Michael; the Swiss Guards did. This is theater.

When the inspection is over, I begin to step down. But Nowak keeps his hand on me. He won't let me walk away. "Doctor Bachmeier," he says loudly, "please continue."

And when Bachmeier begins speaking again, Archbishop Nowak whispers to me, "Father, your brother would want you to see what comes next."

So I stand beside him, the token Greek Catholic, the antidote to Michael's outburst, as Bachmeier guides the crowd through quotations on the walls. They are the ancient words of Church Fathers, saints, councils of bishops.

God who prohibited the making of graven images would never Himself have made an image.

Images should not be in churches. What is venerated and worshipped should not be painted on the walls.

The names beneath these quotes come straight from the textbooks I teach in pre-seminary. Saint Irenaeus, from the 100s AD. Tertullian and Origen from the 200s. Eusebius, father of Christian historians, from the 300s. Epiphanius, flag-bearer of orthodoxy, from around 400. The audience drifts slowly down the gallery, watching the ancient leaders of our Church breathe fire against images. Watching our religion take a stand against paganism by shunning the paintings and statues that adorn pagan temples of Jupiter and Apollo and Venus.

Only as paganism fades away does the Church's position soften. A pastiche of images on the walls captures it: across the Roman Empire, Christians entering their churches are greeted by paintings and mosaics of Jesus, his miracles, his disciples. There is something miraculous about how quickly it spreads, as if a whole civilization is waking up from a shared dream, a revelation of the divine formula: God is beauty, and beauty moves the soul. The timeless face of Jesus is suddenly everywhere. And yet at this very moment, just as Christian art is blooming, an existential danger rises. When the timeline on the walls reaches the 600s, the white letters become red. They are written in Arabic.

Bachmeier points to the words. "Now we come to the most electrifying event in history since the fall of Rome. Out of Africa marched the unstoppable new religion of Islam. It threatened not only the Holy Land but Christianity's new attitude toward images. Before your eyes are the words of Muhammad as recorded by Imam Muslim. Since I have been asked not to read them aloud in these museums, you may read them for yourselves."

There are murmurs as the crowd takes in the translations.

The most grievously tormented people on the Day of Resurrection will be the painters of pictures.

All painters who make pictures will be in the fire of Hell.

Do not leave an image without obliterating it.

"At the border of Christendom and Islam, Christians came in contact with these ideas," Bachmeier says, beginning to lead the crowd forward again, "and some of our faithful began to absorb them. These Christians slipped into the heresy of believing that art depicting our Lord was evil and must be destroyed. One of these heretics became Christianity's emperor in Constantinople. And in the black year of 726, he launched a campaign we know today as Iconoclasm. A tragedy eclipsing even the Fourth Crusade."

A light clicks on overhead. Letters appear in the darkness, as if written in smoke by the devil. Nowak's voice is pained as he reads them.

"*Churches were scraped down and smeared with ashes because they contained holy images. Wherever there were venerable images of Christ or the Mother of God or the saints, these were consigned to the flames, or were gouged out and smeared over.*"

Bachmeier continues. "The amount of Byzantine art that survived this period is desperately small. The world's greatest collection of Christian art vanished almost entirely. This was a ruthless emperor. He proved to be almost unstoppable."

We come to the end of the hall. Bachmeier points to the final wall, the one separating us from the Sistine Chapel. It is painted an eerie, haunting white. His voice trembles when he says: "*Almost.*"

The wall is so bright I have to look away. That's when I notice that the door leading to the Sistine Chapel is flanked by Swiss Guards.

"One of the most important questions Doctor Nogara posed," Bachmeier says, "was why Jesus left us the Holy Shroud. For seven hundred years, no one knew the answer. But in the midst of Iconoclasm, a Christian monk named John remembered an astonishing fact: in the city of Edessa there existed an image not made by human hands. An image *of* Christ, *by* Christ. It proved that our Lord's new covenant was accompanied by a new art. When God became human, He made *Himself* into an image. By His own incarnation, He shattered the prohibition against art. And as proof of His intentions—like the tablets He gave to Moses—He left behind the Shroud.

"Inspired by John, a small group of old men rose up against the emperor. And together, those men saved Christian history. I present you their words."

Archbishop Nowak's voice is flooded with feeling now. Booming.

"*God-protected emperor, Christ sent His image to King Abgar of Edessa, and even today, many peoples of the East still assemble at this image, in order to pray there. We adjure you, therefore, to turn back to the truth. It would have been better for you to have been a heretic than a destroyer of images.*"

Bachmeier says, "Those words were written by Pope Gregory, Patriarch of the West. But he didn't stand alone. Here are the words of Nicephorus, Patriarch of Constantinople."

"*Why would you punish those who paint Christ's portrait, when Christ Himself left the image of his divine figure on a cloth? It was He who imprinted his own replica, by allowing a cloth to be placed over him.*"

"In Jerusalem," Bachmeier continues, "three more patriarchs sent a letter to the emperor. After that, a full ecumenical council was called. And for the last time in our shared history, the bishops of Christendom spoke in one voice. For all posterity they declared that Christianity is a religion—*the* religion—of art.

"It is therefore my great joy to ask His Grace to open the doors in front of us, and to ask the rest of you to follow him inside. For behind those doors, you will see what our unity, and our Lord's example, made possible."

Even as Bachmeier speaks, Nowak steps forward and makes a signal with his hands. The Swiss Guards at the door part. As if by magic, the Sistine Chapel opens.

A shiver goes through the crowd. Because past this threshold, the Vatican Museums end. The chapel of the pope begins. And on its ceiling is the crowning miracle of art.

As we filter in, however, not a single eye peers upward. My heart pounds. The blood drums in my ears. Because inside this chapel, Michelangelo is not alone. Beside the altar stands a tall golden chair. And in that chair, alone, sits the small, stooped figure of Pope John Paul.

CHAPTER 37

SUDDENLY THERE ARE Swiss Guards swarming around us, finding the Orthodox bishops and leading them to the front. The bishops show no surprise, no confusion, as if they know why they're here.

There's a logjam at the door, a hundred cassocks and tuxedos trying to push forward and see inside, a hundred more stopped dead in the doorway. The guards show the rest of us to red-cushioned chairs on the chapel floor, facing the steps where John Paul sits beside the altar. Already the air feels hot and thin. All around me, cardinals and dignitaries are trying to understand what's happening. Distinguished-looking women fan papers in their laps, craning elegant necks.

In front of us, however, John Paul never moves. I'm startled to see that he looks more decrepit and pained than ever. He wears a permanent frown over the thick mask of his face. Years of illness have transformed his body into something wrenched and misshapen, his torso wide and flat and hunched, the white wings of his simar hanging awkwardly off his shoulders like a tablecloth draped on a stump. He slumps in his specially built chair, the one that his attendants carry everywhere now, designed to prevent him from slipping out of it. A low grinding hum comes from behind the chair. A mechanical motor. All eyes are on the throne, everyone wondering what it will do.

But it's something behind the Holy Father that starts to move: a glass frame, mounted on steel tracks behind the altar. It climbs slowly against the altar wall until it hovers twenty feet over John Paul's head, almost blocking the colossal Christ of Michelangelo's *Last Judgment*.

A gasp comes from the crowd as people see what the frame contains. Catholics in the chapel begin genuflecting, some on their right knees, some on their left, unsure of the protocol for this unprecedented sight. The Orthodox make metanias, Russians and Slavs crossing themselves before bowing, Greeks and Arabs bowing before crossing. But it's the Orthodox bishops who do something all their own. In unison, as if they've been prepared for this moment, they lower themselves to the floor, in full prostration, to venerate God's highest icon.

Never have I felt anything like the hush of this room. The air is so tight that every sound squeezes upward into the outer darkness, like a conclave's smoke. On the wall behind the Shroud, Michelangelo's Jesus lifts his hand in the air, as if commanding time to stop. On the ceiling, electricity gathers in the sliver of nothingness between the outstretched fingers of God and Adam. All of creation, blanketed in the night outside, seems to press its ear against the chapel wall to listen.

I wish desperately that Simon could be here. I wish he could see whatever I'm about to see. Lucio gambled everything on tonight as if it were Simon's only hope. Now it hums all around me: that hope was not misplaced.

A voice speaks up. Archbishop Nowak, standing near the front of the chapel, talking for our poor mute pope.

"Tonight," he says, "we have witnessed the remarkable texts that document the history of the Holy Shroud. And we return, as always, to one text above all. The sacred cloth bears a profound resemblance to the gospel accounts of our Lord's passion and death. The Holy Father has said Christianity must breathe again with two lungs—East and West, Orthodox and Catholic—and here lies Christ before us, wounded by a spear between the ribs. This spear wound was caused by a Roman soldier, as if in anticipation of those Catholic knights who would one day steal this Shroud from Constantinople.

"The Fourth Crusade is a stain on the Christian Church. The Holy Father has apologized for it, and has expressed the everlasting shame of Catholics for our role in it. Yet tonight he has asked me to read aloud to everyone present in this chapel—especially his fellow patriarchs, first among them His All Holiness, Ecumenical Patriarch Bartholomew—a new and special message."

In amazement I stand on my toes and try to see the men he's referring to. The words are almost impossible to believe.

His fellow patriarchs.

First among them His All Holiness.

I knew Simon had invited the Patriarch of Romania here. But far above him in the ancient hierarchy of patriarchs is His All Holiness, the Ecumenical Patriarch of Constantinople, who ranks second only to the pope. This is beyond what I thought even Simon was capable of.

Nowak opens a formidable-looking document. It appears to be sealed in red wax. He reads: "Dear brothers and sisters, as you know, the Holy Shroud has been venerated in Catholic churches for many centuries. Yet until two decades ago, it was owned by the Italian royal family. Only upon the death of the former king, early in my pontificate, was the Holy Shroud bequeathed to the Holy See. I do not mention this to lessen the complicity of the Catholic Church in the sins of 1204. I mention it because of a particular detail in the last testament of King Umberto. That document, rather than bequeathing the Shroud to the archdiocese of Turin or to the Catholic Church, bequeaths it to the person of the Supreme Pontiff. Which is to say, His Royal Highness gave the Holy Shroud to me.

"As pope, I have full, supreme, and universal power over all parts of our Church, so my fellow Catholics may see no need for the distinction I have just made. Yet one of the differences separating us from our treasured Orthodox guests is that the Orthodox Church does not accept the jurisdiction of the pope over his brother-bishops. So I wish to make it clear that, in saying what I am about to say, I am not forcing my will upon other bishops who must obey what I demand.

"Tonight's exhibit has established that the relic known in the West as the Shroud of Turin was in fact stolen by Latin crusaders in 1204. Therefore tonight, in the year of the eight-hundredth anniversary of that trespass, I acknowledge this theft, and hereby restore the Holy Shroud to its rightful caretaker, the Orthodox Church."

There is dead silence in the chapel. Cardinal Boia, in the second row of chairs, shifts in his seat. But it's another cardinal who stands. The eyes of Christendom fall on Cardinal Poletto, Archbishop of Turin.

Soundlessly, Poletto turns toward the Orthodox. He raises his hands in the air. Then he begins to clap.

Everyone stares in disbelief. But I understand what he's doing. I stand and begin clapping, too. I am followed by a Turkish bishop. And finally the dam breaks. Laymen begin clapping. Archbishops. The sound reverberates off the walls. John Paul lifts a trembling hand to cover his ear.

"Please," Nowak says, raising his hands to quiet the crowd. "The Holy Father has asked me to read you one last message."

For once, his voice is heavy with emotion.

"My dear brother patriarchs, please forgive me that I cannot stand to greet you, and that I cannot speak these words in my own voice. As you know, I am approaching the end of my pontificate. The Holy Shroud encourages us to meditate on our mortality, and I am humbled that our Lord has allowed me a pontificate of twenty-six years, when he allowed himself a ministry of only three. Yet Christ's example reminds me how much can be accomplished in a very short time. This is what our predecessors proved by standing together against Iconoclasm. It is what I hope we will do together tonight.

"Since I am no longer able to travel, tonight will be my last visit with you. Therefore it is fitting that I take this opportunity to express the following hope. Never in my twenty-six years have I been permitted to stand together with all of you. And so I ask: will you come forward, in brotherhood, and stand with me?"

Archbishop Nowak stops reading and looks up. Every layman in the chapel bears an expectant look. No one could refuse a pope. No one could refuse *this* pope.

But on the faces of the clergy, I see a different expression. We've spent our lives protecting this man, supporting him as he shouldered the burden of his office. To erase a thousand years of hatred in one gesture is asking too much, even for John Paul. None of us can bear to watch him fail.

And yet, it happens. Not a single patriarch walks up to join him. The only one who even rises to his feet in respect is Bartholomew, His All Holiness.

It strikes John Paul like a blow. When he sees they aren't moving, his one good hand clamps down on his chair. His body hunches forward as if it might fall. From nowhere, two helpers materialize at his sides. They place hands on him and whisper in his ear, trying to finesse him back into the chair, but John Paul pushes them off. They look to Archbishop Nowak for support, but he sends them away.

Now it's just the two of them up there, Nowak and John Paul. They trade looks, debating something invisible, speaking the language of forty years spent together. Maybe Nowak is begging him to save face, but if that's it, then John Paul ignores him. He begins pushing himself out of the chair again, trying vainly to get up. So, like a good son, Archbishop Nowak helps him.

More than a year has passed since John Paul took a step under his own power. People say he can't even stand. Yet he stares down the assembled patriarchs of the Orthodox Church across a marble staircase, as if he will climb down these steps if he has to.

All at once, I understand what he's doing. What problem he's trying to solve. In ancient times there was only one man allowed to sit in a gold chair, and that was the emperor. No matter how many reasons the Orthodox have for not joining him on that platform, the most obvious is that no Orthodox will honor a pope on a throne. Not even if that throne is a gilded wheelchair.

With his good arm, John Paul grabs Nowak's cassock and pulls on it for balance. He flexes every muscle that still answers to his mind. And though they are one hundred and fifty years old together, these two men somehow bring each other safely down the stairs to the chair of the Ecumenical Patriarch.

Bartholomew is visibly worried. He steps forward to keep John Paul steady. But John Paul is already bending his knees and folding his legs under himself. With Archbishop Nowak's help, he lowers himself into a painful kneel.

His All Holiness reaches over and grabs John Paul's hands, trying to keep him up. "Please, Holy Father," I hear him say in a surprised voice. "No." But John Paul clasps the patriarch's right hand, bows his head, and lowers his lips to kiss it.

That is when it happens.

To Bartholomew's left are the other patriarchs of the ancient tetrarchy: Ignatius of Antioch, Theodore of Alexandria, Irenaios of Jerusalem. All are white-bearded and black-robed. All have hard, unflinching faces, like saints in holy icons. But they're also younger than John Paul. And when they see him stooping at their feet, the oldest patriarch from the most honored See, they don't know what to do.

On Bartholomew's left, across the aisle, are the patriarchs of the younger Orthodox capitals: Maxim of Bulgaria, Ilia of Georgia, Pavle of Serbia. Alexy of Moscow has sent his second-in-command. But on his far side, at the very end of the row, is the man who will change everything. Patriarch Teoctist of Romania.

He is almost ninety years old. Five years older than John Paul. Not long ago he became the first Orthodox patriarch in a millennium to invite a pope to visit his country, an offer John Paul gladly accepted. Now Teoctist is prepared to make an even bigger gesture.

The ancient patriarch pushes himself up from his chair on two shaking legs. Then he stands beside John Paul.

John Paul's eyes follow him. When Teoctist reaches out a hand to help the Holy Father, the mask of John Paul's face crumbles. His eyes fill with tears.

Now the true whitebeards come: Maxim and Pavle, old as the dust. They rise from their seats as if something is at stake here, something beyond protocol and history. The Christian principle of love. Respect for the See of Saint Peter. They, too, stand. Between them sits Ilia of Georgia, barely more than seventy years old, a mere schoolboy. To honor his elders, he stands up as well.

Now it's all momentum. One by one, to Bartholomew's left, the other patriarchs rise. The crowd in the chapel roars. Each time a new bishop comes to his feet, the ocean of black thunders its approval.

Silently Nowak inches back. He makes himself almost invisible, disappearing by half steps, acknowledging that the men at the front of this chapel belong to a world that the rest of us—even Archbishop Nowak—do not inhabit. They are the giants we pray to meet in heaven. I pull the cross out of my collar and squeeze it, wanting to send up this moment to my parents in heaven. To send out this moment to Simon in his cell.

The patriarchs huddle and bow their heads together. And in the whole thousand-year history of our divided religion, there is no precedent for what happens next.

A voice rises from their midst. I can't tell whose it is. But the voice begins a chant. Not in Italian, or in Latin, but in Greek. One by one, the other patriarchs join it. In unison, they deliver the profession of faith made official seventeen centuries ago, at the very first council of all Christian bishops.

Πιστεύομεν εἰς ἕνα Θεόν, Πατέρα, Παντοκράτορα, ποιητὴν οὐρανοῦ καὶ γῆς, ὁρατῶν τε πάντων καὶ ἀοράτων . . .

We believe in one God, the Father Almighty, Maker of heaven and earth, and of all things visible and invisible . . .

I shiver. It is happening. Before my eyes, in my own lifetime, it is happening. And my brother isn't here to see it.

But someone else is: one of the Swiss Guards has left his post at the door to find me in the crowd. Leo doesn't say a word, but he puts a hand on my arm. He knows what this moment means to me.

When the profession of faith ends, an unsteady hush follows. The crowd is waiting, wondering what will happen next. In the huddle of patriarchs there are searching looks. Even these ancient men—nearly old enough, together, to reach back to the Fourth Crusade—don't know the answer. But they're wordlessly negotiating something. Not what they will do next, but who will do it. Which leader will speak for them all.

There's no question who it should be. The Orthodox know it, too. Saint Peter was the leader of the apostles, so the highest honor must go to Peter's successor. The pope. They are waiting for John Paul to speak.

But John Paul didn't bring these men here to trump them. Instead he turns to the Ecumenical Patriarch and whispers in his ear.

The patriarch's pale eyes flash. He smiles. Turning back to John Paul, he whispers his agreement. Then, to everyone in the chapel, the patriarch says, "In honor of this moment, let us pray in silence."

No sooner has he spoken the words than I feel Leo's hand on my arm again. This time it's more insistent. He's been biding his time to tell me something. I quickly follow him to the exit.

"We have Father Black in custody," Leo says. "He says he needs to talk to you."

■ ■ ■

EVEN AS I FOLLOW him, I'm in a dream. I feel myself moving, but my heart remains back there in the chapel. One thousand years: we are coming together again after one thousand years. Tonight, in heaven, there is a ticker-tape parade. Old popes lift their hands in blessing. Saints smile. Angels beat their wings. From now on, when people talk about the chapel that Michelangelo painted, they will remember John Paul in it, and the place where he rebuilt our Church.

Even if Mignatto's right—even if Simon's trial isn't over yet—tonight my brother had a hand in history.

MICHAEL IS UNDER LOCKDOWN in the barracks.

"Why does he want to talk to me?" I ask.

"He says it's about Simon." Leo puts out a hand in warning. "But Alex, there's something not right about that man. We brought him in earlier this week for starting a fight over a parking ticket. Be careful."

A parking ticket. Probably the same one I found at the Casa alongside the books stolen from my apartment.

Leo leads me down a dank hallway. Toward the end, we stop. "Do you want me in there?" he asks.

I tell him I need to do this alone.

He unlocks the door, then pushes it slightly open.

The cell is the size of a closet. Michael sits on a bare mattress. I keep my distance.

"So," he says, without looking up. "Are congratulations in order?"

I say nothing.

"This is wrong for our Church," he continues. "You'll see. Reunion is a mistake."

"Did you kill him, Michael?"

He snorts.

I want to grab him by the cassock and shake him. Simon was right about him all along.

"Who were you sharing that room at the Casa with?" I say.

He ignores me. "You know, Nogara told me you abandoned him, the same way Simon did. You brothers are exactly the same. Agenda as long as my arm, and no loyalty to anyone but each other."

I turn and start to leave.

"You two wouldn't answer his phone calls," Michael says quickly, "so he settled for me. *That's* who I shared the room with."

The bottle of Grappa Julia in the trash can. The calls to my apartment from a Casa phone number. The person who slept on the floor of Michael's room that night was Ugo.

He pulls a cigarette from a pack, then realizes he has no lighter. He tears it in half and hurls it across the room. "Damn it!"

A cold sensation crawls up my spine. So Michael had no partner in this. He did everything alone.

"Why did you break into my apartment?" I say.

"You know why."

"But Simon was at Castel Gandolfo. You must've seen him there."

"I sure as hell did not."

Suddenly, though, it clicks. It seems so clear. Why Simon has refused to say a word about what happened. Why Michael came looking for Simon as soon as he got back from Castel Gandolfo.

I say, "My brother saw *you* there, didn't he?"

Michael pinches the bridge of his nose. "I wasn't at Castel Gandolfo."

"You were inside Ugo's car. Trying to get his gun."

"I don't know what you're talking about."

"I found a sliver of your hotel key in his car. It broke off when you tried to open his gun case."

"It must've been Nogara's. I wasn't even there."

"You came to our apartment because you realized he saw you."

He leaps up and shouts, "Whatever he said to you, he lied!" He digs his fists into his temples. I step back.

Immediately Leo enters the holding cell. Michael backs away and turns to stand in the corner, facing the wall. He runs his hands through his hair again and again.

"You let Ugo stay in your room," I say, "so you could follow him to Castel Gandolfo."

Michael says nothing.

"What did you think you were going to do?" I say.

He turns and shouts, "You think I planned to *kill* him? Go to hell, Alex!"

Leo steps toward him, but I motion him back.

"Why is Simon protecting you?" I say. "Because it was an accident?"

Michael's face is the color of liver. He grabs the metal frame of the bed and grips it. He turns to Leo and chokes out, "I didn't kill anyone. His *brother* killed Nogara. I wasn't even there."

"We're done," Leo says, opening the door.

But Michael lifts a hand in the air. "Please. Give me one more minute with him. Alone."

Leo shakes his head. But I ask him to wait outside.

Michael stays in his corner. He presses his back against the wall. His eyes look around the room, one place at a time, as he tries to collect himself. This was the best man my father could find for an assistant. It must've been obvious, to anyone who wasn't a child, how troubled he was. How desperate my father must've been if this was the best he could do. Maybe Simon was old enough to see those things. But I was still a boy.

"You know what they're saying I'll be charged with?" he says in a voice that rattles with emotion.

"What are you talking about?"

"For what happened tonight. They say I'll be charged with an attack on the Holy Father." His eyes are swimming. His voice tries to sound angry but can't disguise that he's frightened. "You know what I could get for a charge like that?"

I do. Here, at last, is justice. The punishment for attacking a pope is automatic excommunication and possible dismissal from the priesthood.

"I was fair to Simon in my testimony," he says. "All I'm asking is for your uncle to put in a good word for me."

He says it so earnestly that I wonder what he can possibly be thinking, except that he can no longer count on Cardinal Boia for help.

"Explain something to me," I say.

He nods, mistaking this for an opening. A negotiation.

"How did you open Ugo's gun case? Did he tell you the combination?"

Michael emits a thin, nervous laugh. "That lunatic was so paranoid he had three bolts on his apartment door. You think he told me a combination?"

My God. He did all of it. Everything. When Peter and I went to Ugo's apartment, we found broken glass on the floor. Michael couldn't pick the locks on the door, so he climbed in through the window.

"Leo," I say, knocking at the door, "we're done here. I'm coming out."

Michael stares at me uncomprehendingly. "So you'll help me?"

They were right, sixteen years ago, when they sent him to that treatment facility in the mountains. They knew the sort of help he really needed.

Leo opens the door and waits for me to exit.

"Pray, Michael," I say. "Ask for forgiveness. Then you need to confess."

CHAPTER 38

I HAVE TO FIND Lucio and Mignatto. We can end Simon's trial tonight.

On my way home, the streets of the Vatican village are quiet. News of the exhibit hasn't leaked yet. Or maybe these good Roman Catholics, discovering that they've given away the Shroud, are waiting to see what tomorrow holds.

When I get back, I hear Mona's and Peter's laughter coming from behind Brother Samuel's door. I leave them be. When I let myself into the apartment, everything's black. Neither Mignatto nor Lucio answers when I call. Even Diego isn't picking up at the palace.

I sit at the kitchen table and wait. I unfasten my outer cassock. I breathe. When I close my eyes, even for an instant, the darkness fills with thoughts of Ugo. Memories of him. Gratitude for what he made possible tonight. Tomorrow, millions of people who never knew him will hear that the architect of John Paul's exhibit was killed in the act of bringing a pope's dream to fruition. And they will think of him as a martyr. A hero. He never wanted anything to do with a reunion of the Churches. But if he'd been there tonight, maybe he would've understood.

I peel off my sweaty inner cassock. A tiny hope begins to take root in me. I try to ignore it, but the longer the phone stays quiet, the bigger it grows. Maybe Simon is free. Now that the exhibit has accomplished its purpose, maybe Lucio and Mignatto have gone to bring him home.

I shoo the idea away, busying myself around the apartment. But

Mona has done the dishes, and Peter's room is already clean. So I take a quick shower to scrub off the residue of my meeting with Michael. Then, just as I've changed back into clothes, I hear a knock at the door. I hurry to let Peter and Mona in.

Standing at my threshold, instead, is a man with silver hair. A layman in black suit and tie. He's not one of my neighbors. I've never seen him before. But he looks at me as if my face is familiar.

"May I help you?" I say.

"Father Andreou?"

A tiny flame of panic flickers at the bottom of my throat.

"Alexandros Andreou?" he repeats.

Alexandros. The name on my official documents. There's something in his hand. An envelope.

"Yes, that's me. Please tell me what's going on."

He hands me the envelope. It's engraved with the words PREFECTURE OF THE PONTIFICAL HOUSEHOLD. Above the words is John Paul's coat of arms. This man is a cursore, one of the pope's private messengers.

"What's this?" I murmur.

But the cursore only says, "A car will be waiting outside your building thirty minutes before your audience." He offers a slight bow. "Good night, Father."

Then he turns around and slips away.

I tear open the envelope. The card inside says:

YOU ARE SUMMONED TO THE PRIVATE APARTMENTS OF HIS HOLINESS
TO BE DEPOSED AT TEN O'CLOCK.

My heart pounds. I don't understand. As Simon's procurator, I can't be a witness in his trial.

But the rule book has changed. The pope is above the law.

Numbly I go to my closet. I look for my best clean cassock. For my iron. But in the hallway, I stop. Out the window of Peter's bedroom I can see the palace. Cardinal Boia's windows are dark. All along the top floor, though, the lights are on.

The thought of those apartments gives me a slippery feeling at the bottom of my stomach. I'll have to prepare everything I'll say. If Michael hasn't confessed by morning, then I'll need Mignatto's help.

I'm pulling out the ironing board when I hear a key turn in the lock. Peter's voice rises as the door opens.

"And usually, in the jungle?, they have poison that could kill you, but it's only poison because they eat bugs that have poison, so in the zoo, they don't eat the bugs?, so they're not super poisonous. Or at all."

I take a deep breath and step out of the closet. My foot lands on something sharp, and I stifle a curse. It makes Mona notice me as I enter the hall. She smiles.

"Tree frogs," she explains.

Then she notices the look on my face.

"Babbo!" Peter cries, racing toward me.

I step forward and quickly lift him onto my shoulder so he can't see the uncertainty in my eyes. I hand Mona the card from the cursore.

She whispers, "Is this a good thing?"

"I don't know."

Peter is ecstatic. The story of his adventures since I left comes out in a river of unintelligible sentences. I hold him in my arms and want to tell him that the man who broke into this apartment will never come back. Our home is truly ours again. But a few hours with his mother have already washed all the darkness from his life.

"Thank you," I say to her.

Yet she's already walking away.

"You're leaving?" I ask.

She continues into the kitchen and finds the first-aid kit in the cabinet. "Your foot's bleeding," she says.

Peter looks down and points to a trail of red dots.

"Mona," I say as she returns, "would you stay a little longer? I need to meet with someone to prepare my testimony."

"What did you step on?" she says, kneeling to pull something out of my heel. She drops it into my hand. It looks like a red pebble.

I wait for her to answer.

"I'll stay however long you need," she says without looking me in the eye.

She starts to bandage my foot, but I reach down and do it myself. She takes back her hands and doesn't follow me when I walk to the sink.

The red washes off the pebble. It's a piece of glass.

Mona is behind me. In a quiet voice, so that Peter can't eavesdrop, she says, "You've done a wonderful job with him. He's so thoughtful. So curious about everything. Being with him makes me wish . . ."

I stare at the glass.

"Makes me wish," she continues, "I hadn't missed so much of his life. I can't tell you how much I regret that."

I step back. I look at the spots of blood leading back to the bedroom. I feel the first prick of fear.

"I know I don't have a right to ask this," she says, "but I would love to see him more often."

My legs carry me down the hallway. Mona's voice trails off. The spots lead to my closet.

A sensation wraps around me like a tentacle. I kneel and search the carpet.

"What's wrong?" Mona says behind me.

There's nothing else here. Not another crumb. But in the corner of the closet, I find a twinkling of glass dust. Something was hidden behind the ironing board.

"Mona," I call back, "I need you to take Peter back to Brother Samuel's."

She doesn't ask why. Hearing my tone, she just tells Peter to get his pajamas.

It could be glass from Ugo's apartment. From the broken window Peter found.

But old panes of glass don't break into pebbles like this. This is modern glass. Tempered glass. The kind used in car windows.

I wait until I hear the door close behind them. Then I take everything out of the closet. Every pair of shoes, every cassock, every shoebox on the top shelf. Nothing.

When I empty the laundry bag, I find a mildewed towel that must be Simon's, from the shower he took when he came home from Castel Gandolfo. But his cassock from that night is missing.

I run through everything I can remember. After Simon showered, he limped in here to dress with his muddy cassock in his hand. But I never saw him put it in the laundry bag. We left and spent the night with Leo and Sofia in the barracks. We didn't come back until the morning.

But Simon did.

That night, he said he couldn't sleep. He came back here and started cleaning up.

Please, Lord. Let this not be true.

I check the trash cans. They're all empty. In the small plastic can in the bathroom, though, stuck to the bottom, is the same dusting of glass.

My body is leaden. I look around the bathroom. This was the first place Simon had a chance to be alone. He came in here to shower and came out in nothing but a towel.

There aren't many hiding places. A drawer beneath the sink. The toilet tank. The vent grate. All are empty.

But I'm looking in the wrong places. A man of Simon's size wouldn't look down. He would look up.

Standing on the countertop, I prod the ceiling tiles up, one by one. Each rises with the same resistance.

And then, one doesn't.

I lift it. I reach into the darkness.

My hands shake as I pull out the cassock and lay it on the floor. Simon's very best robe. The one Lucio bought for his Academy graduation. The knees are muddy. There's no glass to be seen.

My body is rigid as I reach down and turn out the French cuffs. The inside of the right cuff is powdered with glass dust.

I close my eyes. Simon is standing in the rain beside Ugo's car. He unfolds the French cuff. Pads his knuckles with the rich, thick fabric. Knows, like any boxer, to protect his hand. It takes him just one blow to shatter the glass.

My lungs take long, shuddering breaths. I stare at the ceiling. I know something else is up there, but I don't want to touch it.

A single coil dangles down from the opening where the ceiling tile was. A loop of black wire.

When the judge asked Falcone how the murder weapon disappeared right under his nose, Falcone had no answer. Because no gendarme would dare to look under a priest's cassock.

I thought the bruise around Simon's thigh was from wearing a cilice. I realize now my brother tied the gun case around his thigh.

I slump down the wall. Taking the phone from my pocket, I dial Leo. He answers almost immediately.

"You told me," I mumble, "you arrested Michael earlier this week. A fight over a parking ticket."

"That's right."

"Tell me what happened."

"I don't know. That's just what Colonel Huber told me."

I wasn't even there, Michael insisted.

"I need you to find out," I say.

He shuffles papers and returns to the phone. "It says Black got into a fight with two officers because we booted his car. Not sure why we did it, but the report says he got violent about it."

I can guess why. To keep him from leaving the Vatican. To keep him away from the Orthodox meeting at Castel Gandolfo.

"Saturday afternoon?" I say.

"How did you know?"

Saturday is the day Ugo was killed.

"After you arrested him, what time was he released?"

"Just after six, it says here."

By then, Ugo was dead. I was on my way to Castel Gandolfo. And the only thing on Michael's mind was to get even with Simon.

That's why he came to our apartment.

■ ■ ■

I REACH BACK INTO the ceiling. My hand follows the black chain to its source in the darkness. At the end I feel the rubberized surface of the gun case. I can't bear to look at it. But its weight tells me the gun is still inside.

You can't have done this. There's nothing more evil in the world.

I sit on the floor with my head pressed against my knees. My body tightens until my hands are white on my cassock, balled in fists. The knuckles dig into my cheeks.

Ugo was a good man. An innocent man. You can't have killed a lamb.

I push back against the racking shudder in my chest. My teeth are clenched so hard that my eye sockets hurt when the tears come out.

I try to pray. But the prayer slips away like smoke, dissipating into nothingness. When I stare down the hallway, I see the coffee table where Ugo and I reviewed his gospel work. In my ears is the sound of his voice on the telephone, calling me at all hours with questions. The traces of him press in around me—the letter in my cassock; the work diary I took from his apartment; the stacks of homily paper in my bedroom, black with verses he wrote and crossed out and insisted I correct—as if the hours and days of life contained in them have condensed into something heavy and accusing. I lift myself into the bathroom doorway. It's the only thing I can think to do. The only place on earth I feel I can go for help.

Standing on the countertop, I reopen the ceiling and put the cassock and gun case back. I clean the glass dust off the floor. Then I head for the door.

CHAPTER 39

Don diego answers the door to Lucio's apartment. He explains that Lucio's gone. Meeting with Mignatto. I push inside and tell him I'll wait.

The waiting, though, is endless. Diego watches me pace the apartments. Finally he says, "Your uncle told me what happened at the trial today. Is that why you're here?"

I hold myself together. But I can't even look at him.

Diego inspects his hands. Quietly he says, "Come with me."

He leads me out of Lucio's office and into a room I have almost no memory of. My uncle's bedroom.

"Maybe it's best," he says, "if you wait for His Eminence in here."

He closes the door after himself. And it takes me a moment to understand what I'm looking at.

The hospital bed is angled up, surrounded by medical devices and trays of pills. There are three large vases of flowers and a standing wardrobe. And otherwise, in this sprawling bedroom nearly as big as my apartment, there is not a single other thing except what hangs on the walls. Mementos cover every inch of space like icons on the wall of a Greek church. I see a photo of Lucio at his consecration. A newspaper article about a piano concert he gave as a young man. But every other framed object is of *us*.

My mother when she was young. My parents at their wedding. I cover my mouth, seeing two entire rows of Peter. Beside them are corresponding pictures of me: at baptism; on my name day; being held in my mother's arms. My ordination. Winning my seminary prize for gospel studies. We are half of my uncle's waking world. We, who never seemed to mean anything to him.

The other half is Simon. Two entire walls, floor to ceiling, filled with pictures. A toddler walking through the Vatican gardens, holding Lucio's hand. Riding a tricycle in Lucio's dining room. A baby in his proud uncle's arms. In that picture is something I've never seen before: my uncle truly smiling. Then comes every stage of Simon's priesthood. Academy milestones. Nunciature posts. And, finally, an empty frame containing nothing but a silk skullcap. It is amaranth red. The color of a bishop.

My eyes return to the hospital bed. To the platters of plastic vials and the breathing apparatus. Only when I hear the door open behind me do I turn.

Lucio hobbles in on his cane. He bears no resemblance to the cardinal who tried to save Simon's life from the witness table. He struggles to make it to his bed. Yet he waves Diego away and stops when he's beside me.

"Uncle," I murmur, "I found his cassock in my apartment. I found the gun case."

His eyes fall. They seem so tired.

"You knew?" I say.

He doesn't answer.

"For how long?" I ask.

"Two days."

"He told you? Even though he didn't tell me?"

And yet, seeing everything on these walls, I begin to understand why he might.

Lucio removes his pectoral cross and places it in a small jewelry box by the bed. "Alexander," he says, "you know better than to think that. Your brother never confides in me. His only family is you."

He moves the four-legged cane so that he can reach a tube of ointment in a drawer. Each hand struggles to rub the medicine into the withered joints of the other.

"Then how did you know?" I say.

"Would you mind opening that for me?" he says, gesturing at the wardrobe.

It's filled with old cassocks and the smell of mothballs.

"See it there?" he says.

"Which one?"

Then I realize he isn't talking about the cassocks. He's talking about what's behind them.

Propped against the back wall of the wardrobe is a giant photographic enlargement of a page from the Diatessaron. The one Simon took down from Ugo's exhibit.

"When I was in seminary," Lucio says in a scratchy voice, "I was a gospel man, like you."

I spread the hangers apart. My arms reach inside and edge the photo out. I feel rigid.

"I don't know what he did with the Diatessaron," Lucio says. "I could've sold many tickets to an exhibit about that manuscript. But once it disappeared, my fears were confirmed."

The page is nearly as tall as I am. I prop it against the wall, against the pictures of my own childhood. And almost instantly, I feel as if a glass has shattered inside my heart. Because seeing the ghost of the ancient stains that our restorers removed, I understand.

I scrabble in my pockets for the letter Ugo mailed to Simon.

"If you're looking for a Bible," Lucio says, "I have one here." He reaches under his pillow and produces it. "Ignore my notations. I'm sure you'll see it before I did."

But all I feel is a lancing pain in my chest. "A pen," I whisper. "Give me a pen."

He hands me one from the nightstand.

I kneel and unfold the letter across his cold marble floor. Then I do exactly what the Alogi did almost two thousand years ago. In his letter, wherever I see verses from John, I cross out the text.

3 August 2004

Dear Simon,

Mark 14:44–46	*You've been telling me for several weeks now that*
~~John 18:4–6~~	~~*this meeting wouldn't be postponed—even if*~~
Matthew 27:32	*you were away on business. Now I realize you were*

~~John 19:17~~	~~serious. I could tell you I'm ready for it, but I'd be~~
Luke 19:35	lying. For more than a month you've been stealing
~~John 12:14–15~~	~~away on these trips—which I know has been hard~~
	~~on you—but you need to understand that I've had~~
	~~burdens too. I've been scrambling around to mount~~
Matthew 26:17	my exhibit. Changing everything so that you can
~~John 19:14~~	~~now pull off this meeting at the Casina will be~~
	~~difficult for me. Yes, I still want to give the keynote.~~
	~~But I also feel that doing it compels me to~~
Mark 15:40–41	make some grand personal gesture toward the
	Orthodox. For the past two years I've given
	my life to this exhibit. Now you've taken my
~~John 19:25–27~~	~~work and given it a much larger audience—which~~
	~~is wonderful, of course—and yet it gives this~~
	~~keynote a heavy significance. This will be the~~
	~~moment when I officially hand my baby over. The~~
	~~moment when, with a great flourish, I sign my~~
Matthew 27:48	life away.

	So, then, I need to share with you what I've
	been doing while you were out of town. I hope it
~~John 19:28–29~~	~~agrees with your agenda for the meeting. First, I've~~
	~~taken my gospel lessons from Alex very seriously. I~~
	~~study scripture morning and night. I've also kept up~~
	~~my work with the Diatessaron. These two avenues~~
	~~of investigation, together, have repaid me richly.~~
	~~Brace yourself, because I'm about to use a word~~
	~~that, at this late stage in the process, probably~~
Mark 15:45–46	horrifies you. I've made a <u>discovery</u>. Yes. What
	I've found erases everything I thought I knew
	about the Turin Shroud. It demolishes what we
	both expected to be the central message of my
~~John 19:38–40~~	~~keynote. It might come as a surprise—or even~~
	~~as a shock—to the guests you're inviting to the~~
Luke 24:36–40	exhibit. For it proves that the Turin Shroud
~~John 20:19–20~~	~~has a dark past. The radiocarbon verdict killed~~
	~~serious scholarship on the Shroud's history before~~

1300 AD, but now, as that past comes to light, I
think a small minority of our audience may find the
truth harder to accept than the old idea that the Shroud

Luke 23:46–47   *is a fake. Studying the Diatessaron has taught me what*
a gross misreading we've been guilty of. The same
gross misreading, in fact, that reveals the truth about
the Shroud.

My discovery is outlined in the proof
enclosed here. Please read it carefully, as this is
what I'll be telling your friends at the Casina. In the
meantime, I send my best to Michael, who I know
has become your close follower.

John 19:34   *In friendship,*
Ugo

I hear my voice shaking when I utter those two words.

"A fake?"

Lucio doesn't answer.

But I realize, as I stare at the lines of Greek on the photographic enlargement, that I don't need him to. My heart has gone cold. My body feels brittle. *This* is what Ugo meant. *This* is what he found.

The page of the Diatessaron before me combines the testimony of all four gospels about the end of Jesus' life. About his final moments on the cross. But not his burial. Not the Shroud. Not yet. Ugo spent weeks studying every detail of the burial accounts, only to make his discovery where he didn't expect it.

The damning fact isn't what the gospels say about the cloth. It's what the gospels say about the *wounds* on the cloth.

■ ■ ■

THERE ARE NINE LINES of text on this Diatessaron page that stand out. The reason they stand out is that our conservators removed the blot of censorship left by the Alogi but couldn't get it all. A hint of the ancient stain remains, making these nine lines darker than the ones around them. Thus any passerby can tell they must've come from the only gospel the Alogi objected to: John. And this simple observation is what will doom the Shroud.

The seven lines include John 19:34, the last verse Ugo quoted in his letter. The significance of John 19:34 is hard to see straight-on. But it's much easier to see when approached from the very spot where Ugo was the last time we worked together: the story of Doubting Thomas.

Doubting Thomas is John's creation. No other gospel claims Thomas needed to see and touch Christ's wounds. But there's an oddity about the Thomas story that Ugo had noticed in our final meeting: namely, a very similar story is told by Luke. According to Luke's version, Christ appeared to the frightened disciples after the Resurrection, and in order to prove that He was a resurrected man rather than a terrifying ghost, He showed them His wounds. Ugo realized that a comparison between Luke's story and John's story would reveal the details that John had changed. And the most visible difference was that John had focused the story on Thomas—so that was where Ugo, in turn, focused. Later, though, he must've noticed the much smaller, and yet far more destructive, difference: that the wounds mentioned in Luke are not the same as the wounds mentioned in John.

In Luke's story, Christ shows the disciples His hands and feet. His wounds from the crucifixion. But John adds something more. Something new. He says Thomas put his finger in a lance wound in Christ's side.

Where did the lance wound come from? No other gospel mentions it. Only John himself does—earlier in his own narrative, at a crucial symbolic moment: the moment where the Good Shepherd and the Lamb of God are finally fused together. These are the very verses shown on this Diatessaron enlargement, John 19:32–37:

So the soldiers came and broke the legs of the men crucified with Jesus. But when they came to Jesus and saw that he was already dead, they did not break his legs, but one soldier thrust a lance into his side, and immediately blood and water flowed out. An eyewitness has testified, and his testimony is true; he knows that he is speaking the truth so that you also may believe. For this happened so that the scripture passage might be fulfilled: "Not a bone of it will be broken." And again another passage says: "They will look upon him whom they have pierced."

No other gospel says that either of these two incidents ever happened. So where did John get this?

Not a bone of it will be broken: this is what the Old Testament says about the Passover lamb.

They will look upon him whom they have pierced: this is what the Old Testament says about the Good Shepherd.

John's theology has reached its summit. At the moment of Jesus' death, Shepherd and Lamb converge. The two snakes of Ugo's caduceus meet. The gospel stops dead in its tracks to point out that these are symbols, that they come from the Old Testament. John is saying, emphatically, *This is why Jesus died. Like the shepherd, he laid down his life for his flock. Like the lamb, he saved us with his blood.* John even says these events came straight from the testimony of the Beloved Disciple. In other words, they express a symbolic truth that is essential to understanding Jesus Christ. On earth, however, in history, *they didn't really happen.*

Of all the wounds on the Turin Shroud, the bloodiest is the spear wound in Jesus' side. Yet the earthly Jesus was never pierced in his side. This wound is no more historical than the armed mob that Jesus magically knocked off its feet by saying, "I AM." No more historical than the sponge raised on the limp stalk of hyssop. They all belong together, to the same family of symbols, because the writer of John made all these changes for the same reason: to make his point about the Shepherd and the Lamb.

Which means that the forger of the Shroud—whoever he may have been, whenever he may have worked—made the same mistake as the author of the Diatessaron. By merging the testimony of all four gospels together, he erased the difference between theology and history. He created a terrible, heartbreaking mishmash. Putting the spear wound on the burial cloth is no different from putting a crook in Jesus' hand because he was the Good Shepherd or a coat of wool on his shoulders because he was the Lamb of God. When the Beloved Disciple says his testimony is "true," he means it in the same way John does when he calls Jesus "the true light," or when Jesus himself says—only in the gospel of John—"I am the True Vine" and "I am the true bread." To be literal about these symbols is to miss their beauty and importance. The genius of John's gospel is that it refuses to be bound by an earthly straitjacket. John's spear wound gestures at the truth that lies beyond mere facts. The Shroud, then, does the same. It is a powerful symbol—but it has never been a relic.

I've spent my life combing these verses for meaning. Yet when Ugo came to me, wanting to show me what he'd found, I closed my eyes. And Simon did infinitely worse. So this is why my friend died. Because I taught him how to read the gospels. And because he had the bravery to speak out about what they revealed.

CHAPTER 40

I WANT TO FALL to my knees. I have never been so blindsided by my own failure. The anguish is a cord wrapped around my chest, tightening, tightening. My body is unsteady. But my eyes are fixed on the Greek letters of the Diatessaron photograph. They accuse me of having been a hypocrite. A fool. I ask my own students to read carefully, to search for complexity and meaning in the evidence God puts before us, and here I have known my own gospels as dimly as I knew Ugo, who suffered with a secret that would have tortured and haunted any believer in the Shroud but that must have been unspeakable hell to him, salting the whole earth of his life, laying waste to him before he ever arrived at Castel Gandolfo. And Simon, who knew how he suffered, seems to have chosen to end his life with even more suffering. If that's true, then it makes my own brother, whose heart I thought I understood as well as I understand my own, as much a stranger to me as the man on the Shroud.

The words slip out into the stillness of Lucio's bedroom.

"What do we do, Uncle? They want me to testify tomorrow."

He lifts himself off the bed and hoists himself up on his cane. He doesn't put a hand on me. But he comes and stands by my side, unmoving, as if to remind me I'm not alone.

"Do you still have his cassock?" he says.

"Yes."

"And the gun case?"

I nod.

He lets go of the cane. For a moment he stands on his own legs. Peering at the verses of the gospels, he frowns the same way he does when reading the newspaper for its obituaries. These old friends. These memories of happier times.

"If you bring those items here," he says, "I can arrange to have the garbage trucks come at dawn."

"He killed Ugo! How can you not care?"

"He took a fish to feed a multitude. You think he should sacrifice his entire future for that?"

I jab my finger at the photo of the Diatessaron page. "He killed Ugo to hide what we were giving the Orthodox!"

Lucio cocks his head and says nothing.

"Does the Holy Father know?" I ask.

"Of course not."

"Does Archbishop Nowak?"

"No."

The air is still. Nothing moves except a red dot on one of the medical machines, racing forward, forward.

"Did your mother ever tell you," he says finally, "that your great-grand uncle led the voting after the eighth ballot in the conclave of 1922? He almost became pope." Lucio smiles foggily into the air. "And that man was nothing compared to Simon."

"Don't, Uncle."

"He could wear the white someday."

"Not anymore."

Lucio raises an eyebrow, as if I'm missing the point.

"I don't see that you have a choice," he says.

I stare at him. Maybe he's right. He has put words to this powerless feeling. Nothing remains but different ways to reconcile ourselves to what must come next.

"We'll give them what they want," Lucio says. He points to the Diatessaron page. "We'll explain that they made a terrible mistake by giving the Shroud to the Orthodox. And when they ask us to keep quiet, we'll agree. As long as Simon isn't punished."

I shake my head.

"Alexander, even without the cassock and gun case, they have enough evidence to convict him. There's no alternative."

"He *killed* for this. Ugo *died* for this. Simon would rather be convicted than let a reunion with the Orthodox fail."

Lucio sniffs. "It would be naïve to assume the Holy Father will tell the Orthodox just because we tell him. The Orthodox don't even read the Bible the same way we do. To them, it's all factual."

I glare at him. "The Shroud is a fake! He's not going to give them a fake."

Lucio pats me on the back. "Bring me the cassock and the gun case. I'll take care of everything."

I stare over his shoulder at one of the photos on the wall. Simon, at about Peter's age. He is sitting in our father's lap, looking up at him. In his eyes is a perfect admiration. Beside them is our mother, who peers into the camera and smiles. There is something indefinable in her eyes, mischief and wisdom and peace, as if she knows something no one else does. Her hands are covering the slightest bump in her belly.

"No," I say. "I can't do that. I'll find another way."

"There *is* no other way."

But already, as I look at that photo, my heart begins to break. Because I know, better than I have ever known anything, that he's wrong.

OUTSIDE, THE MOON IS full. The air is soft with powdery light. I walk as far as the garden by Sister Helena's priory before I stop and loop my fingers through the metal fence to hold myself up. I close my eyes and breathe. My chest begins to heave.

I love him. I will always love him. He never planned to do this. He came to Castel Gandolfo without a weapon. He could've run away from what he'd done, but instead he called the police. And while he waited for them to arrive, he took off his raincoat and knelt beside his friend to spread it over him.

A wind rushes through the garden, bending the stalks away from me. The plants pull at the soil as if to run from their own roots.

I imagine the size of Simon's hand. The size of the gun in it. Leo called it a peashooter. The smallest, least powerful weapon he could find. One giant finger looped against that trigger must've left no room to move. All it took was a tiny nudge.

I would do anything to believe it was an accident. Except that there is no accidental way the gun could've been in Simon's hand.

I sit down. My fingers claw at the hot soil. He could've confessed. They would've asked him why he did it, and that's when he could've kept silent to protect the Shroud. Instead, he let the silence protect himself, too. That choice, even more than what he did to Ugo, makes him a stranger to me.

I was fourteen years old when he told me he didn't want to be a Greek Catholic anymore. He sat me down and explained that on Sundays he would still walk me to our church, and come back afterward to pick me up, but from now on he would be going to Mass, not Divine Liturgy. I never understood why he wanted to leave. We both loved our Greek church. To see our father appear from behind the wall of icons, glittering in golden robes, fresh from the altar, where no laymen were allowed, had been one of our few opportunities to believe he was an important man. But that day, I told Simon I would leave our Greek church, too, because no matter where we went on Sundays, I wanted us to go together.

He refused. He forced me to stay. He made sure that I was tonsured as an altar server in the Greek church. He made sure the priests there continued my Greek lessons. From that day on, whenever he asked me about the girls I was interested in, the first ones he mentioned were always the daughters of families from my Greek congregation.

He shouldn't have been able to become a Roman Catholic. Canon law says the rite of the father is the rite of his sons. But Simon asked Lucio for help. And my uncle, who never wanted anything more in the world than a nephew to continue our family line, finally realized what Simon could be. That was the moment he began to steal my brother away from me, to set him on the road where even I knew he belonged.

So every Sunday morning, I polished the shoes while Simon ironed the clothes. We shaved together in the mirror. And then he walked me to my church and put me in the arms of my parish. And left me behind.

He has been preparing me, all my life, for this moment. And all my life I have been resisting it. He became a Roman Catholic because his work with me was finally done. It must've almost killed him to be a father to his little brother. He knew he was made to outgrow our village, our home, our father's small shoes. But he stayed with me as long as he could. As Lucio said, there was really no choice. In a Christian life, maybe there never is. Simon buried himself in order to raise me. The imprint of that decision is the watermark on every other feat he's ever performed. That willingness to surrender everything. To sacrifice all. Future; priesthood; even the life of a friend.

If you love something, die for it. That's the message of the gospels. *Whoever loses his life for my sake,* Jesus said, *will save it.* I hate my brother for what he did. I hate him more for what I have to do tomorrow. But as I think about the account we're about to settle, I also feel relieved. It is finished. The odyssey of being his brother. The fear of the destination. The unpaid debt. The wondering what we were made for. Tomorrow, it is finished.

This is what we were made for.

I COUNT THE STEPS. I touch the new lock on the old door. I watch the new key as it turns. When I step inside, Mona and Peter look up with the same expression. As if I've come home too soon. As if I've woken them from a wonderful dream. Peter slowly crawls out of her lap to welcome me. The sight of him makes me want to hide my face and cry.

"Peter," I manage to say, "it's bedtime. Please go brush and wash."

He looks at me and doesn't argue. I've never worked harder to hide my feelings from him. Yet he senses them. His heart tunes automatically to the same frequency of sadness.

"Go," I repeat.

I follow him and numbly watch him run the water. The cake of soap slips out of his hands, so I put it between his palms and hold his hands between mine as we lather.

"Babbo, why are you so sad?" he whispers.

From behind me, Mona says softly, "I don't think he wants to talk about that right now, Peter."

But in the same mirror where Simon and I used to shave together, he watches me. Those blue eyes. My brother's eyes. My mother's eyes. In the photos on Lucio's wall, even my uncle used to have those eyes.

"Get in your pajamas," I say.

For a moment, as he changes clothes, he is almost naked in front of us. And the mother who has never seen him in underwear glances away. Around his thighs, briefly visible when he contorts himself to pull on his pants, are faint rings where the leg holes of his underwear fit snugly. I think of Simon's bruise.

He rushes into bed and turns to me. "Is Simon okay?" he says.

But I tell him we aren't going to bed. "Follow me."

When we get to the door of the apartment, he says, "Where are we going?"

I motion for Mona to come, too. Then I lead them up the stairs to the roof.

It is like standing on the deck of a ship at night. The ocean below us twinkles. Wash on a clothesline billows like signal flags. Across the channel is John Paul's palace. Beneath us, like fishing boats, are the buildings of our village. Supermarket and post office. Autopark and museums. Rising above them all, white as baptism, is Saint Peter's.

Holding my son in my arms, I step almost to the edge of the roof, so that he can see everything. Then I say, "Peter, what's your happiest memory here?"

He smiles and looks over at Mona. "Seeing Mamma," he says.

She touches his cheek and whispers, "Alex, why are you doing this?"

"Peter, open your eyes as big as they'll go," I say, "and look at everything. Then squeeze your eyes closed tight, and make a postcard in your mind."

"Why?"

I kneel so that we're at the same level. "I want you to remember everything you see tonight."

And I think: *Because we may not see it very much anymore. Because this isn't one of those times when we say see you later. This is a time when we say good-bye.*

With a quaver in his voice he says, "What's wrong, Babbo?"

"No matter what happens," I whisper, "we'll always have each other, you and I. Always."

Into this child's life God has put only one example of love that never fails. I am it. From the bottom of my heart I mean those words. *No matter what happens.*

"Are we going to live at Mamma's house?" he asks.

My throat closes. "Sweetheart, no."

I feel broken. I lift him in my arms and squeeze almost as hard as I can.

"Then why are we here?"

There is no answer he can understand. So I lift him in the air and point to all our favorite places. I remind him of the things we've done here, the adventures we've had. The way we used to sit in the shade of the trees below us, throwing pieces of old bread to the birds, watching people drop letters into the big yellow box at the post office and imagining the countries they were destined for. The night we climbed to the top of Saint Peter's to watch the fireworks for John Paul's silver jubilee, and we saw John Paul sitting in his own window, watching them, too. The winter morning we came out of the Annona, the village supermarket, and our plastic bag broke and the eggs cracked all over the street and Peter started to cry until—a miracle—for the only time in his life, it started to snow. Remember, Peter, that magical feeling. How, in an instant, every particle of sadness can be swept away by the smallest gift of God's love. He watches us. Cares for us. Never, ever abandons us.

God bless Mona, she comes to my rescue. When I am empty and exhausted, when Peter wants to hear more stories but my memories are growing darker and darker, she begins to tell him about when we were young. About what I was like as a boy.

"Mamma," he asks, "did Babbo used to be good at soccer?"

Mona smiles. "Oh, *very* good."

"Even as good as Simon?"

The muscles under her eyes tighten. "Peter, in every way, he was better."

I carry my son back downstairs. He frowns when he sees the apartment again. He tucks himself in bed, then gets up. He closes the closet and checks that it's really shut. We pray. Mona holds his hand, and somehow that's enough. I turn out the light and see fingernails of moonlight reflecting in the wet of his eyes.

"I love you," I say.

"I love you, too."

And for a second, my heart feels full again. Wherever this child is beside me, that's where I will call home.

MONA FOLLOWS ME BACK to the kitchen. She runs a hand through her hair. She stands and takes down one of the cups from the cabinet, filling it with water from the tap. All this time, she doesn't speak.

Finally, she puts her cup down and sits beside me, wresting my hands from an open Bible that happens to be there. An open Bible she has been reading to our son.

"Alex, what are you about to do?"

"I can't talk about it."

"It's not your job to save Simon. Do you understand that?"

"Please," I say. "Don't."

She nudges the Bible back at me. "Look in there, and tell me something. Who saves Jesus?"

I stare at her, wondering what she can possibly mean.

"Show me," she says, "the page where he wins his trial."

"You know he doesn't w . . ."

My words trail off. But she waits. She says nothing. She wants to hear me speak those words.

"Jesus," I say, "doesn't win his trial."

Her voice is quieter now. "Then show me where everything ends happily ever after because his brother comes to save him."

"So I should abandon him? Just run away?"

Her expression is crimped. She hears the accusation. Her eyes slip.

"No matter what you do," she says, "nobody's ever been able to control Simon. Nobody's ever been able to change his mind. If he wants to lose this trial—"

I rise from my chair. "We're not having this conversation."

But for the first time since her return, she won't bow and scrape. "There is only one life in your hands, Alex. And it's his." She points toward the bedroom. "But you've filled his head with stories about two people he never sees. You've let him believe that the two most important people in his life are never around. Even though the most important person in his life is *always* around."

"Mona," I say, "I have a chance to give Simon his life back. I owe him that."

Her lip curls. "You don't."

But she doesn't understand. "No matter what happens to me," I say, "I'll still have Peter. If he loses his priesthood, he'll have nothing."

She's about to say something awful, but I won't give her the chance.

"When I'm done tomorrow," I tell her, "there are going to be consequences. One of them may be that Peter and I can't stay here anymore."

She starts to ask why, but I push on.

"Before anything like that happens, it's important to me that I be honest with you. Ever since you left, there's nothing I've wanted more than to get our family back together."

She's already shaking her head, trying to rewind the tape, trying to make this stop.

"I used to dream about the three of us," I say, "living in this apartment. I wanted that more than I've ever wanted anything in my life."

Suddenly she begins to cry. I have to look away.

"But when you came back," I say, "everything had changed. It's nothing you did wrong. You did everything right. I love you. I always will. But everything else has changed."

She is staring up at the ceiling, trying to dry her eyes. "You don't owe me an explanation. You don't owe me *anything*." Her eyes come down, settling on mine. "But I'm begging you. Put yourself and Peter first. Just once. Forget about Simon. You've worked so hard to give Peter a good, happy life here. Whatever you're about to do, remember that this place is his whole world."

I love her for these words. For this fierce defense of her husband and son. But I can't take much more of it. I need to finish this.

"Mona, I don't know where Peter and I will live if we have to move. All I know is, we would be somewhere outside the walls." I hesitate. "And if you wanted, you could join us."

She stares at me in silence.

"I'm not asking what your plans are," I say. "But I realized, tonight, what mine are. I want my family together."

She reaches over and folds her arms around me. She begins to sob, digging her fingers into my skin.

"Don't answer me," I say. "Not tonight. Wait until you're sure."

She tightens her grip. I close my eyes and hold her.

It's done.

I have loved this life. In the future, whatever it may hold, I will stare up at the walls of this country and thank God for the years He gave me inside them. As a child, I watched the sun rise over Rome. As a man, I will watch it set over Saint Peter's.

CHAPTER 41

For an hour she watches me pace the living room, knowing what I'm rehearsing in my thoughts. Finally she says, "Alex, you need to sleep." And before I can refuse, she takes me by the hand and leads me toward the bedroom. She waits for me to follow her inside. Then she locks the door after us.

It has been almost five years since I slept with my wife. The old mattress sighs at the return of her long-forgotten weight. She doesn't undress. She just removes her shoes and makes me lie down beside her. She turns out the lights. And when they're off, I feel her fingers running gently through my hair. I feel her breath on the back of my neck. But her hand never strays. Her mouth never comes any closer.

All night, my dreams are violent. Twice I rise in the dark to pray. Mona sleeps so lightly that she gets up to join me. Then, in the darkest hours, I'm swallowed by a loneliness that makes me desperate to wake her. To tell her what I'm about to do. When I think of what Simon has done to keep this secret, though, I turn over and say nothing. I twist in the sheets, and when I hear her asking if I'm all right, I pretend that I'm asleep.

Before dawn I slip out of bed and begin to prepare. I lock myself in the bathroom and stand on the countertop. I wrap Simon's cassock in a towel, then put it in a garbage bag. I put the gun case in a small plastic bag from the grocery store. When I return to the kitchen, I place the small bag beside me on the table.

Then I work over my story, pouring cup after cup from the moka pot, paging through the Bible on the table to be sure I remember the verses well enough to leave no opportunity for anyone to second-guess me. I force myself to think back to the night Ugo died, searching for details I might've forgotten. It doesn't need to be perfect. It just needs to be convincing.

Mona appears a half hour later. Soundlessly she inspects my inner and outer cassocks, my best pair of shoes. On the kitchen table she lays out my keys and the summons from the cursore. She doesn't ask about the small plastic bag. She must see that it contains something hard and dark, wrapped in a length of cable, but she never says a word. Every time she glances at her watch, I check my own.

Peter is sleeping when I kiss him on the forehead. I sit on the edge of his mattress and stare across the room at the empty bed where Simon used to sleep long ago. Beside that bed I used to pray with my brother. Across the space between these mattresses we used to whisper in the dark. Before the memories can undo me, I leave the room.

By half past eight I'm outside, the small bag hidden under my cassock, the garbage bag left in a dumpster across the border in Rome. There's enough time for me to walk a final lap around my country. Instead I leave the gates and walk into Saint Peter's Square to mill with the early crowds and feel the kiss of spray from the fountains. I watch the Jewish peddlers set up carts and the sampietrini set out chairs for an outdoor event that must be coming later in the afternoon. Mainly, though, I watch the laypeople. The pilgrims and tourists. I want to experience this place as they do.

The sedan arrives promptly at nine thirty, driven by the papal butler, Angelo Gugel. Signor Gugel lives in our building. One of his three daughters used to babysit Simon and me when our mother was still alive. But there are no affectionate greetings, just a polite "Good morning, Father." Then he drives me by the Sistine Chapel to the palace road. As we slip through, the Swiss Guards salute. When we reach the Secretariat, a folding wooden gate opens, revealing an archway. Beyond is terra incognita. John Paul's private wing of the palace.

The courtyard is small. The walls seem immensely high, giving me the sensation of standing at the bottom of a pit. The earth is crossed with shadows. On the opposite side, two guards sit in a glass-paneled kiosk, watching us. But Gugel drives in a circle and returns to the archway, stopping so that my door is opposite an entrance in the wall. When he lets me out, he says, "Father, this way."

The private elevator.

He inserts a key and operates it himself. When the car stops, Signor Gugel pushes aside the metal grate and opens a door. The flesh of my neck tingles.

We have arrived. I am standing inside the Holy Father's apartments. In front of me is a sitting room furnished with odd pieces of furniture and a few potted plants. No Swiss Guards anywhere. Leo says they aren't allowed inside here. Gugel leads me on.

We enter a library with walls of gold damask. Beneath a towering painting of Jesus there stands a single desk. On the desk is nothing but a gold clock and a white telephone.

Gugel points to a long table in the center of the room and says, "Please wait here."

Then, to my surprise, he leaves.

I look all around me, tense with feelings. Every night of my childhood I stared at the windows of this top floor, wondering what these rooms contained. What it was like for a poor soldier's son from Poland, who grew up in a small room on the rented floor of another family's house, to live in the penthouse of the world's most famous palace. John Paul haunted so many of my thoughts in those days. Gave me strength against so many fears. He, too, had his parents die when he was young. He, too, once felt like an outsider in this city. For what I'm about to do, I am a traitor to my own guardian angel.

More men are ushered into the library. First comes Falcone, the gendarme chief. Then the promoter of justice. Lucio arrives with Mignatto in his wake.

Then, from a different door, Simon.

All the rest of us stare. Lucio's arms reach outward. He shuffles forward and raises his hands to Simon's cheeks.

But Simon's eyes are locked on mine.

I can't move. He seems cadaverous. His eyes are sunken. His ropy arms could encircle his torso twice. I feel the gun case pressed against my ribs. Simon motions for me to come closer, but I steel myself and don't respond. I've prepared myself for this moment. It's important now for us to keep our distance.

A moment later, Archbishop Nowak appears at the door. "Father Alexandros Andreou," he says. "His Holiness will see you now."

I FOLLOW HIM INTO a smaller, more secluded room. I recognize it as the private study where John Paul makes his appearances to the crowds in Saint Peter's Square. Bulletproof glass fills the enormous window, but behind the window is a modest desk littered with folders and papers to sign, the dossiers that arrive unstoppably from the Secretariat. They have so outpaced the pope's ability to return them that they now choke the room, standing in stacks around the desk. The mounds are so large that at first I don't see who sits behind them.

I freeze. He is only an arm's length away. But he looks nothing like the man I saw in the Sistine Chapel, who found the strength to kneel at patriarchs' feet. This man is frail and sunken, with small, narrow eyes that barely conceal his pain. He doesn't move except to breathe. He looks at me, but there's no moment between us. No connection, no greeting. Humans are thrown in front of him as fast as they can appear and disappear. He might as well be staring at a mannequin.

Nowak says, "Please be seated, Father." He gestures to a chair opposite the desk, then sits beside John Paul, serving in a capacity I don't understand.

"His Holiness," he continues, "has studied the evidence that the tribunal gathered. He wishes to ask you a small number of questions."

The Holy Father doesn't budge in his chair. I wonder if he will speak at all.

"Yes, Your Grace."

"Very well. Please begin by explaining how you knew Doctor Nogara."

"Your Grace, I met him—"

But Archbishop Nowak makes a polite gesture of correction.

I force myself to meet John Paul's unwavering stare. "Your Holiness, I met Doctor Nogara through my brother. Doctor Nogara found a missing manuscript in the library, and I helped him read it."

This registers as just another fact. Nowak doesn't pursue it. Instead he asks, "How would you characterize your brother's working relationship with Nogara?"

"They were good friends. My brother saved his life."

"Yet I have heard the voice message from Doctor Nogara. It indicates they were not on friendly terms."

I choose my words carefully.

"When my brother began to travel on his missions to the Orthodox, he couldn't spend as much time tending to Nogara. It upset them both."

I watch Nowak's expression. I need to make sure he remembers the demands on Simon's time. The source of Simon's obligations. Just a few feet from here is the private chapel where the Holy Father would've performed the rite of consecration to make Simon a bishop.

"But the voice message suggests," Archbishop Nowak says, "that Nogara made a discovery which complicated their working relationship. Were you aware of this?"

I brace myself. "Yes. I was."

"What was the discovery?"

"He found a manuscript of an ancient gospel called the Diatessaron."

Nowak nods. "The one that is now missing."

"I helped him to read the Diatessaron," I continue. "Until that time, Doctor Nogara hadn't realized that the gospels have different testimony about the Holy Shroud. This was the origin of his problem."

"Go on."

Now I begin my own job of weaving verses. I must do it perfectly.

"The most detailed description of Jesus' burial," I say, "is in the gospel of John. The other gospels say Jesus was buried in a σινδόνι, 'shroud,' but John says όθονίοις, 'cloths.' John also gives us the most specific description of the empty tomb, and it corroborates his first one: the disciples didn't just find the όθονίοις, 'burial cloths'; they also found the σουδάριον, the kerchief or napkin, that had been wrapped around Jesus' head. This would obviously be problematic for any image on the Shroud."

Archbishop Nowak frowns. He seems about to ask another question, but I push forward, heaping up evidence, burying him in Greek. At all cost, I must keep him away from the lance wound. I must keep him looking in the other direction, at all the minor details where John's discrepancies don't match the Shroud, because Nowak will know Ugo should've brushed them aside, since no one turns to John for hard facts.

"These problems are deepened by John's testimony about the ἀρωμάτων, 'burial spices.' The other gospels suggest Jesus *wasn't* buried with spices, since the Jewish Sabbath had come and the burial took place in a hurry. But John says a huge weight of spices—μίγμα σμύρνης καί ἀλόης ὡς λίτρας ἑκατόν, 'a mixture of myrrh and aloes about a hundred pounds' weight'—was used. And this is a problem, because the scientific tests on the Shroud haven't found any trace of burial spices. Without belaboring the point, Your Holiness, Nogara felt that our most detailed testimony about Jesus' burial was John's, and that John's account did not support the existence of the Shroud. Nogara went to Castel Gandolfo to say as much to the Orthodox."

Archbishop Nowak's soft features sag with concern. His brow is heavy. His hand is folded pensively over his jowls. "But Father, did you not explain to him about the gospel of John?"

"I did. I explained to him that it's the most theological. The least historical. That it was written decades after the others. But he knew the Orthodox would be less likely to apply a scientific reading to the gospel. He knew the Orthodox were more likely to feel that John needed to be taken at face value."

Nowak rubs his temples. He seems pained. "That is what Nogara discovered? A misunderstanding?"

I nod.

He grimaces. When he begins to speak again, I detect a change in his voice. The question at the tip of his tongue is no longer legal, no longer scriptural. It is deeper than that: it is human. The worst, I hope, is over.

"Then why," he says, "was Doctor Nogara killed?"

Now is the time to scratch at the old scabs. They bleed so readily. "My father spent thirty years here trying to reunite our Church with Orthodoxy." I bow toward John Paul. "Holy Father, I know it's impossible to remember every priest who works inside these walls, but my father gave his life to a reunion. You invited him to these apartments once, before the carbon-dating was announced, and he was so honored. He was devastated when he heard the radiocarbon results."

For the first time, there is a twinge in John Paul's mouth. It deepens his frown.

"My brother and I," I continue, "were raised to believe in that work. It was upsetting to think that the Orthodox, on their historic visit here, would be hearing something disturbing. My brother tried explaining that to Doctor Nogara. But it didn't work."

Archbishop Nowak's brow casts shadows over his eyes. "Then I would like to understand the events of that night. You arrived around six thirty, after Nogara was already dead. Is that correct?"

Now the difficult part begins. "Not exactly, Your Grace."

He shuffles papers on the desk, trying to sift facts from pages of testimony. "That isn't when Signor Canali opened the garden gate for you?"

I am tense in my chair.

"It is when he opened the gate," I say. "But that's not when I arrived."

He looks up darkly. "Please explain."

My heart is with Simon. It has always been with Simon.

"Your Grace, I called Guido Canali in order to create the appearance that I had arrived at Castel Gandolfo later than I actually did."

John Paul tries to turn his head to glance at Nowak but can't. His hand stays clamped on the arm of the chair. Only his eyes peer across at his old priest-secretary.

"What are you saying?" the archbishop asks.

"I was there before five o'clock," I say.

The time shown on the surveillance video.

Nowak waits.

"I found Doctor Nogara at his car," I say. "We got into an argument."

Here is the darkness I've spent my priesthood trying to stamp out of myself. The emotions no good man should even feign. But my performance doesn't need to be perfect. Nowak knows these feelings even less well than I do.

He raises a hand to interrupt. "Wait, Father. We need someone else here."

My breathing is shallow. My lungs feel tight. With a notary, it will become official.

Archbishop Nowak lifts the phone and says something in Polish to someone on the other end. A moment later, the second secretary, Monsignor Mietek, opens the door. But the man he ushers inside is the last person I want to see.

"Inspector Falcone," says Nowak, "the Holy Father would like you to hear the testimony that is being given. It seems Father Andreou is about to confess to the murder of Doctor Nogara."

CHAPTER 42

Nowak offers the gendarme chief a chair and explains what I've said. Then he instructs me to proceed.

I don't know where to begin again. With Falcone here, I have to keep meticulous track of every detail.

"My brother," I say, "must've come out of the villa looking for Nogara and me. He saw us standing by Nogara's car."

4:50 on the surveillance video. Simon passes by.

"Where was the car parked?" Falcone asks.

He's testing me.

"In the small parking lot south of the villa," I say, "just inside the gate."

"But *why*?" Archbishop Nowak says, impatient at the interruption.

The lies come more and more easily. "All I could think of was my father," I say. "He never recovered from his humiliation in front of the Orthodox. I couldn't let that happen to Simon."

Falcone interrupts again. "How did you know about the presence of the gun?"

I had hoped to rush through this part of the story. Even now, I can't square this circle. Simon must've had keys to the chain of the gun case. Yet he didn't have the keys to the car. He must've known the combination but had to break the window with his fist. There's something here that, even now, I don't understand.

"Nogara came back to his car," I say, "to get his lecture notes. While he was pulling them out of his glove compartment, I saw the gun case under his seat. It didn't look like it was closed all the way. I don't know why I did it. The sight of that case just changed something in me."

John Paul's lips are parted. He breathes through his mouth. I am disgusted with myself.

But Falcone is relentless. "So you took the gun out of the open car?"

"No. Ugo closed the door and walked away. We were arguing with each other. He didn't care what would happen when the Orthodox found out. He thought the exhibit was destroyed. I . . . I told him I wasn't going to let him do it. I threatened him. That's when I went back to his car for the gun."

Archbishop Nowak nods. He must see it on one of the pages in front of him: my hair found in the foot well of Ugo's car.

But nothing distracts Falcone. The human conflict is irrelevant. All that matters to him is the gun. "You knew the combination to the case?"

"No. As I told you, it wasn't completely shut."

"Then how did you remove the chain?"

"I didn't. Not until I needed to hide it later. Then I used Nogara's keys."

Falcone scowls. "From his dead body?"

I can't hold his stare. I simply nod.

"Go on," Nowak says.

"I caught up to Ugo when he was walking back into the gardens. I only meant to scare him. But he wouldn't turn around to look at me, so I had to come right up to him. He saw the gun. He put up one of his hands to protect himself. When his hand hit the gun, the gun went off."

I watch Falcone, certain he will remember that the autopsy found gunshot residue on one of Ugo's hands. A single bullet wound at close range.

"Where was your brother as this happened?" he says.

"When Simon heard the gunshot, he came running. He got down on his knees and tried to revive Doctor Nogara, but it was too late."

I haven't invented this last detail. I believe it's the explanation for the mud on Simon's cassock.

"I didn't know what to do," I continue. "I begged him to help me."

Archbishop Nowak glances up from the pages in front of him.

"Your Grace," I say, "my brother would do anything for me."

John Paul suddenly lurches to one side, wincing, as if these final words have dealt him a blow. Nowak rises to help him.

But Falcone never takes his eyes off me. In his low, almost inaudible voice, he asks, "What exactly did your brother do for you?"

He doesn't realize that my story, from this point forward, is almost watertight.

"He got rid of the wallet and watch," I say, "while I got rid of the gun."

"Whose idea was it to create the impression of a robbery?"

"Mine. I only found out later what my brother's idea was."

Falcone is waiting to pounce. Waiting, but failing to see an opportunity.

"The last thing he told me," I say, "was to get my car. Drive down the mountain and wait until everyone from the meeting had left. Then call my friend Guido and tell him I'd just arrived from Rome. Simon said he needed to go back to the meeting, but then he would meet me again in the gardens."

"There is no evidence to suggest," Falcone says, "that your brother returned to the meeting."

He doesn't see that this is the crux of my story.

"He lied to me," I say. "He never intended to go back."

Falcone looks bemused.

But Archbishop Nowak seems to understand. He thinks like a priest. He must see that there's finally a reason at hand for my brother's silence. Me.

His sad Slavic eyes study me, neither disgusted nor compassionate. They convey only that Middle European familiarity with tragedy. His hands organize the papers on his master's desk.

Falcone, though, isn't satisfied. "What did you do with the gun?" he demands.

I am, like the serpent, victorious. Reaching inside my cassock, I remove the plastic bag containing the gun case. The proof that silences all doubt.

As Falcone stares at it, I see a slow transformation in his eyes. The pieces are finally arranging themselves. The only fact he cares about is finally in evidence.

"Your brother," he says, without any hint of feeling, "has been protecting you?"

But before I can answer, Falcone's head suddenly turns. He's on alert, as if he's seen something out of the corner of his eye.

Then I see it, too.

The Holy Father is moving. His right hand—his good one—is bobbing in the air, signaling to Archbishop Nowak.

His Grace lowers himself beside John Paul's ear. Then a voice comes out of the ancient body. A husky, faint voice too hoarse for me to hear.

Nowak glances at me. There's a change in his face. Something tumbles through his eyes. He whispers something back to John Paul, but I can't understand their Polish. Finally the pope's head nods. I'm frozen in my seat.

Falcone watches warily as Nowak takes the handles of the wheelchair. The chair rolls forward. Around the desk it comes. Past Falcone. Toward me.

The eyes are fixed on mine. A hypnotic Mediterranean color, a pelagic blue. They swim with life. He has missed nothing.

My body tightens. My backbone curves. He sees through me. I'm a faceless priest to him, one of tens of thousands, but he can recognize a lie as surely as he can sense the change of weather in his bones. The pain in his face tells me that he *feels* it.

When he's inches away, he signals for Archbishop Nowak to stop.

I don't know what else to do. I crawl out of my chair and lower myself. It's customary to kiss the pope's ring or bend down to kiss his shoe, to make a gesture of abasement, and I would make myself invisible if I could, to hide myself from him. Nothing is beneath me.

Nowak reaches down and touches me on the ribs. "His Holiness wishes to speak to you."

John Paul's arm moves. For an instant the white sleeve brushes electrically against the bare flesh of my hand. Then he reaches out and puts his heavy palm down on my cheek. Over my beard.

I feel him shaking. Rhythmically, incessantly. The cadence of his disease. Under the tremulous hand he transmits a pure, sweating heat. With this one gesture, he tells me he has seen enough. He is about to speak his mind. He opens his mouth and croaks something.

I can't make out the words. I glance at Archbishop Nowak.

But John Paul strains and raises his voice.

"Ioannis," he says, pressing his hand deeper into my beard.

I stare up at him, frozen. Wondering if I heard right. But Nowak warns me not to say a word. The Holy Father is not to be interrupted.

"Ioannis Andreou," John Paul says.

He is confused. In the darkness of his mind, he looks at me and sees the man he remembers from more than fifteen years ago.

Then he finds the strength to finish.

"Was your father."

The breath catches in my lungs. I dig my fingers into my palms, trying not to show any emotion.

"You," he says in an almost inarticulate voice, "are the priest with the son."

He fixes on me with the oceans of those eyes, and suddenly I am reduced to my barest atom.

"Yes," I say, fighting the tightness in my throat.

John Paul glances at Archbishop Nowak, asking him to finish the thought. The exertion is becoming too much.

"His Holiness sometimes sees you with your pupils," Nowak says, "when he's driven through the gardens."

I ache. My shame guts me.

John Paul bobs his hand in the air, gesturing toward himself. "I," he says. Then he jabs his hand in the air, gesturing at Nowak. "And he."

Nowak translates, "His Holiness was a seminary teacher, too. He was my moral theology professor."

It is wrenching to keep his stare, to avoid looking away. John Paul plunges his hand one more time toward his chest. "And," he says in a rattling whisper, "I had a brother."

I finally have to close my eyes. I know about this brother. Edmund. Older by fourteen years. A young doctor in Poland. He died of a fever from a hospital patient.

The Holy Father's voice surges with feeling. "We would do anything. For each other."

There are only two reasons he would say this to me. One is that he believes my testimony. The other is that he knows why I'm lying. When I open my eyes, I will know the answer. So, for an instant, I can't bear to.

Then the silence unnerves me. I look.

The wheelchair is moving away. Archbishop Nowak is pushing it out the door, toward the library. His Grace turns to motion for me to come after him. The last thing I see, before following him out, is the look on Falcone's face. I can't read it. The old policeman doesn't say a word. But he's fingering the gun case and dialing a number on his phone.

■ ■ ■

"THE CHARGE IS DISMISSED," Archbishop Nowak says to the assembled group in the library. "We have heard a confession."

All around there are looks of shock. I watch the incredulity spread. But Simon rises.

Every eye turns to look. He is a Mosaic presence, ten ells tall. His black shape pulls electricity from the air like a lightning rod. Nowak pauses, taken aback by his forcefulness. And in that pause, my brother says: "He lies."

Mignatto and Lucio turn against him, objecting. The promoter of justice watches in disbelief.

"He *lies*," Simon repeats. "And I can prove it. Ask him what he did with the gun."

"He has produced the gun case," Archbishop Nowak explains.

Simon blinks. He cannot imagine the lies I've woven.

But he has one last hope. Turning to me, he says, "Then open it for them."

Nowak looks as if he's about to cut Simon off. But John Paul rakes his hand through the air, allowing it.

Everyone in the room stares, waiting.

"I don't know the combination," I repeat to Nowak. "Ugo never shared it."

Simon peers down at me. And there is such heart-splitting love in that look. Such astonishment. As if I should have known it was impossible for me to succeed at this, but he is amazed, shattered, that I would have tried anyway.

His voice is slow and broken. "Holy Father, you won't find the gun inside that case. I buried it in one of the flower beds in the gardens, where I buried Ugo's wallet, watch, and hotel key. I can show the gendarmes the spot."

I'm frozen. Before I can say anything, Falcone enters the room. He is carrying the case. And the clamshell is open.

"Your Holiness," he murmurs in a concerned tone.

When he shows John Paul the contents, I feel Mignatto's eyes on me. Yet I can't take my own eyes off the case.

Simon is right. Where the weapon should be, there is only that cursed, rotted thing. Deathless. Invincible. Its gnarled leather umbilical cord no longer binds the manuscript tight. The stitches that attach the cover flaps together, making the Diatessaron almost waterproof, are open. Had it fallen into a puddle of rainwater that night at Castel Gandolfo, the way it once fell into the Nile, it might've been soaked through. But the gun case has served impeccably. Tucked inside it like a bookmark is a white sheet of paper on which I can see Ugo's handwriting. The notes for his presentation to the Orthodox.

Archbishop Nowak carefully lifts out the manuscript. But it is John Paul who raises his good hand and motions toward the notes. Nowak hands them to him. And for a moment the room is silent as he reads.

Piece by piece, the mask of his face crumbles. He is in anguish. Nowak slowly pries the sheet away. But instead of reading it, he turns to me and says, "What is the meaning of this?"

Simon intervenes. "My brother didn't know the book was in there. His confession was a lie."

Falcone reaches into his back pocket for his handkerchief. He spreads it over his palm and gently lifts the gun case from the Holy Father's hands.

I scramble for words, trying to cobble together anything that would change this. That would mitigate Simon's guilt. But my brother's expression as he stares at the gun case is so horrified that my thoughts go to pieces. He shrinks from the cold appraisal in Falcone's eyes. He can't even look at me.

The police chief shuts the clamshell. But he does not move it from Simon's eyes. The sight is agony for Simon, and Falcone knows it.

"Take it, Father," he says.

Simon recoils.

There is no trace of humanity in the gendarme chief's eyes. "*Take it*," he repeats.

"No."

"Open it."

"I won't touch that thing again."

"Then give me its combination."

Numbly Simon says, "One, sixteen, eighteen."

The same combination as the vault in Ugo's apartment. The verse from Matthew that establishes the papacy.

Falcone dials in the digits. Before pulling the clasp, he glances back at Simon. There's something between them that I don't understand.

"Your brother took you by surprise, didn't he?" Falcone says.

Simon's face is blank. "You don't know what you're talking about."

Falcone's fingers pull. The lock does not open.

Simon is paralyzed. He glances at me as if Falcone and I are in collusion.

The old police chief turns the case and considers it from all angles. Then, for the first time, he turns away from Simon. He addresses John Paul.

"Holiness, one of the reasons the Swiss Guards recommended this gun case is that its combination is set by the manufacturer. It cannot be changed." He lifts a scrap of paper in his hand. "I have just called the factory. And 'one, sixteen, eighteen' is not the combination."

Consulting the scrap, he turns the dials one at a time. The lock clicks open. I feel the breath slip out of me.

"Father," Falcone says to Simon, "I saw it in your eyes."

Archbishop Nowak murmurs, "Saw what, Inspector? What does this mean?"

Falcone stares at the gun case as if it has beguiled him. Darkly he says, "There was gunshot residue on Doctor Nogara's right hand." He extends an index finger down the edge of the clamshell, making the shape of a pistol. "His shooting hand."

The tone of his voice says everything.

The expression on Simon's face tells me it's true.

CHAPTER 43

"SIMON . . ." I SAY.

He doesn't answer. He looks dimly at the gun case.

Archbishop Nowak squints at me, trying to square my confession with Falcone's demonstration.

But I know. At last, I understand. The relief is so intense that I don't feel, at first, the crushing sadness of how Ugo really died.

"The only person who knew the combination," Falcone says, "was Nogara. He was the one who opened it."

Simon says nothing. He will maintain his silence to the last.

"But he wouldn't have had to break the window to enter his own car," Falcone says. "So what happened, Father?"

It's Mignatto who says, almost in a whisper, "The surveillance video."

The two minutes between Ugo's arrival and Simon's. It was almost the first thing Simon said to me when I got to Castel Gandolfo.

He called me. I knew he was in trouble. I came as soon as I could.

"But why," Falcone repeats, "did you break the window of his car?"

This explains the sequence of sounds Mignatto heard in the footage. Gunshot. *Then* glass breaking.

Simon still doesn't speak. But he doesn't need to.

"Because," I say, "the gun case was inside the car."

"But Nogara had already opened the case," the promoter of justice protests. "It was empty."

But it wasn't empty. Simon wouldn't have locked a case he couldn't reopen. The case must've been locked before he ever got to it.

"*Ugo* put the manuscript in there," I say.

It was pouring that night. He was protecting the Diatessaron.

In a hushed voice I say to my brother, "How did you know?"

Simon wouldn't have saved the gun case unless he'd known what was in it. And he couldn't have known what was in it unless Ugo told him.

My brother still doesn't speak. But I think again of those two minutes separating him from Ugo.

"Did you catch up to him," I say, "before he died?"

Simon raises a hand to silence me. Then the thumb and forefinger of his hand come together until they almost meet. Almost. And he stares at me, bottomlessly, through that tiny gap.

I'm mute. If only those giant strides had been a fraction longer. A fraction faster. I can see Simon now, in my mind's eye, just fifteen years old, standing on the narrow balcony of Saint Peter's, reaching out his hands to prevent that stranger from jumping. I wonder how close he came this time. What final words passed between him and the friend whose life he thought he had already saved.

But not even the beginning of an explanation comes from my brother's mouth. The room is silent. At last Archbishop Nowak speaks in a faint voice. In his hands are Ugo's lecture notes.

"Why would you hide this from us?" he asks. "Both of you?"

I look to Simon. He doesn't want to look at Nowak, but he won't disrespect him by continuing to look away. The muscles of his neck tighten. His nostrils flare.

"Why," the archbishop repeats, "would you hide it?"

Even now, Simon still doesn't utter a sound. But a weaker voice speaks up. It chokes out a question, and the room goes perfectly still.

"Why did this—" John Paul says, "—poor man—take his own life?"

The greatest crime of Judas was suicide. It was not long ago that suicides were refused Church funerals. Denied cemetery plots. Shame, though, isn't why Simon hid the truth.

John Paul thumps his hand down. He moans, "Answer me!"

At last Simon weakens. The cloak of silence drops.

"Holiness," he says, "Ugo never knew how much the exhibit meant to you until he saw the patriarchs at Castel Gandolfo."

John Paul frowns.

Archbishop Nowak says, "You didn't tell him he would be addressing the Orthodox?"

Simon says nothing. He refuses to blame anyone else.

But John Paul croaks, "You did as I asked."

My brother won't trace any of this back to the Holy Father. Instead he says, "I begged him not to tell anyone what he'd discovered about the Shroud. I pleaded with him. But Ugo insisted on telling the truth. He came to Castel Gandolfo to tell the Orthodox what he'd found. But then he saw who was in the audience. He never knew, until that moment, what his exhibit was going to make possible. He couldn't live with himself if he lied to you about the Shroud, but he couldn't forgive himself if he destroyed your dream with the Orthodox." My brother's face is agony. He lowers himself to his knees. "Holy Father, I am so sorry. Please forgive me."

I think of Ugo, alone, arriving at Castel Gandolfo with his notes and his manuscript, prepared for the bravest act of his life. To disown the Shroud he had considered as precious as a child. To sacrifice it in the name of truth. My brave friend. Fearless to the end. Even in that awful, terrifying final act.

John Paul murmurs to Simon, "Why would you not tell me this?"

My brother struggles to compose himself. Finally he says, "Because if you knew, then you would never have offered the Shroud to the Orthodox. And if we had nothing to offer them, then we had no hope of a reunion. Ugo was willing to die for this secret. His choice was my choice, too."

I have seen thousands of pictures of John Paul. He is one of the most photographed men in history. But never have I seen him like this. The lines of his face converge in pain. His eyes squeeze shut. His head lolls back, tensing the muscles in his great thick neck. Archbishop Nowak lowers himself and whispers concerned words in Polish.

There are trails of reflected light down Simon's cheeks. Not a hair of him moves.

Quickly Nowak announces, "We will recess until the Holy Father wishes to reconvene." Then he wheels John Paul into the adjoining study and closes the door.

A moment later, a different door opens. Monsignor Mietek, the second secretary, abruptly enters. Looking pale, he says, "I will see you all down on the service elevator now."

We're led away in a herd. As we wait in the hallway, Mietek keeps a finger on the elevator call button. When the car comes, he shepherds us inside and touches the button. Only at the last instant does he place a hand on Simon's forearm and say, "Not you, Excellency. You are to remain."

It happens so quickly that I barely see Simon as the doors close between us. He's staring back at me. Not at anyone or anything else. But behind him, in the distance, a door has opened. Archbishop Nowak stands in it, looking at my brother, who sees nothing but me.

CHAPTER 44

I WAIT FOR HIM the rest of the morning. Then into the afternoon. I watch from my apartment windows as the treetops begin to sway. As litter in the cobblestone fairways begins to shift and scatter in the rising wind. Rain is close at hand. Just past five, there's a rapid knock at the door. I rush to answer it.

Brother Samuel. His face is pinched. His voice is agitated when he says, "Quick, Father Alex. You have to go downstairs."

I race down. But what I find, instead of Simon, is a small procession. Leaving the door of Health Services are two deacons carrying candles, led by a cross-bearer. Then comes a priest chanting quietly, followed by Ugo's coffin.

In the lot outside, no hearse is waiting. Instead, the procession walks down the village streets, into the spitting rain, and turns left just before the border gate, entering the Vatican parish church.

A metal bier is waiting in the empty nave. The coffin is lifted onto it, Ugo's feet facing the altar. Every motion is gentle and thoughtful and silent. I feel short of breath. I step outside and phone Simon again. Still no answer.

Just inside the door, the priest places a funeral notice on a board. CALLED TO ETERNAL LIFE. UGOLINO LUCA NOGARA. The vigil will be tonight. Mass in the morning. Graveside ceremony to follow.

As I watch him spell the words, I feel the rain at my back, splashing off the steps, spattering my cassock. When he's gone, I lift the board and place it outside, in the open air, where passersby will see it. But there's no one on the streets. Thunder rolls in the distance.

From the door of the church I look across the road at the papal palace, waiting for Simon to appear in the archway. This brief vigil will be the only time for eulogies. Once the funeral Mass starts, none will be allowed. But there's not a living thing in sight.

Finally I go to the coffin and pray. The closed casket feels like an accusation. Surely the morticians could've covered up Ugo's wounds, but there's a message here, in the hasty way Ugo was brought to this church, in the way his announcement was buried on this overlooked board, in the way no villager is coming down after seeing a coffin travel through these streets. They will say it was raining. They will say they didn't know Ugo. They will say anything except that it was a suicide.

I sit in the first pew and offer my prayers. Then, to fill the silence, I talk to him. I tell him about his exhibit. I tell him what a success it was. I look at the coffin when I speak, but in my mind I am talking to the still-living Ugo, in whatever place he now finds himself.

Just before dark I hear someone enter the church. I turn and see Ugo's assistant, Bachmeier. He takes a middle pew and prays for almost a quarter hour. When he's done, he comes forward and puts a hand on my shoulder, taking me for the bereaved. Ugo thought this man never cared for him. Before Bachmeier goes, I thank him.

When he's gone, the parish priest comes up to me. "Father," he says, "you know you're welcome to stay as long as you want. But if you're waiting out the storm, I'm happy to lend you my umbrella."

I explain that I won't be leaving. That my brother will be here soon. The priest keeps me company a moment, asking how I knew Ugo, admitting that he didn't know Ugo well himself. A funeral silence is so different from the silence of a baptism or wedding, so unlike the hush that builds with hope and expectation. To fill it, the pastor asks about my Greek rite, about the ring on my right hand. And though I don't want to talk about it, we are all ambassadors for our churches and traditions. Married six years, I tell him. Eighth-generation Vatican priest, and my son's only dream in the world is to be a professional footballer. He smiles. "Your cassock's still wet," he says. "May I dry it for you?"

I decline and let him drift away.

Midnight comes. The candles around the coffin burn their brightest. Suddenly the air behind me changes. The noise of the rain is dampened. Something large is blocking the sound. I recognize the way it makes the air part; I recognize the long strides of the quiet footfalls as they approach.

He kneels beside me. His silhouette is gold in the candlelight. My fingers grip the coffin rails. With one stabbing breath, he reaches his hands across the casket, as if to hold Ugo in his arms. Then he lowers his head against the wood and moans.

I watch his hand reach into his collar. His fingers remove the chain from around his neck. On the end of it, beside the Latin cross, is a ring. A bishop's ring. He closes his palm around it and puts it on the casket. Then he turns and puts his hands on my shoulders. We clasp each other.

I whisper, "What did they do to you?"

He doesn't hear me. His only answer is, "I'm so sorry."

"Did they dismiss you?"

From the priesthood. From the only life we have ever known.

He answers, "Who gave Ugo's eulogies?"

"No one. Nobody even knows he's here."

He clamps his fists together and presses them against his jaw. He rises and peers at the wood of the coffin. His gaze seems to stare down through it.

"Ugo," he murmurs.

His voice is thin, the volume of a prayer, not a eulogy. I step back, giving him space. But the silence is so pure that I can hear even his shallow breaths, even the dry rasp before his words.

"You were wrong," he says. "God didn't abandon you. God didn't let you fail."

He bends over, almost stooping, the way I imagine he did long ago, finding our father on the floor after his heart attack. Wanting to cradle, to give comfort even in death. His words are stern but his hands reach out into the darkness tentatively, tenderly, seeming to find this wooden box so unyielding and cruel. Mighty the boundary that even these mighty hands can't shatter. And I think, as I watch his great form lower itself to the edge of the coffin to whisper to his friend: how I love my brother. How impossible it will be to think of him as anything other than a priest.

"Ugo," he says, so severely that I know his teeth are clenched, his emotion barely willed back, "God put *me* there to help you. *I* am the one who failed you."

"No," I say. "Simon, that isn't true."

"Forgive me," he whispers. "O God, forgive me."

Unsteadily, he makes the sign of the cross. Then he hides his face in his hands.

I put my arm around him. I pull him against me, holding him there. His massive body shudders. The flames of the candles bow low and rise again. I look down at those giant hands now balled up in fists, digging into his thighs, and silently I join in his prayer. I beg forgiveness for us all.

■ ■ ■

WE WAIT TWO DAYS for punishment to be handed down. Then four days. A week passes. No phone call. No letter in the mail. I become unable to get Peter out the door for school on time. I burn dinner. My distraction is becoming total. Each new day of waiting changes the scale of waiting yet to be done. It may be weeks. By October, I realize it may be months.

I visit Ugo's cemetery plot often, keeping out of sight of the mourners at other headstones, not wanting to scandalize villagers with the sight of Simon or me by Ugo's grave, not knowing what they might have heard. After so many days of praying from afar, the distance begins to feel symbolic. When Ugo abandoned me, I kept him at arm's length. I never let him reenter my life. And though this is a small sin in the world of laymen, it is a significant one for a priest. The Church is eternal, proof against all setbacks, so whatever may happen to the Turin Shroud, I know in my heart that Catholics and Orthodox will someday reunite. But the life of a single man is precious and brief. Guido Canali told me once about an old man at Castel Gandolfo who has no other job but to collect eggs from the henhouses without breaking them. *A job*, Guido said, *you might figure anyone could do, except it takes special hands.* I often think of those words as I stand in the graveyard. They seem equally true for priests.

During breaks in my workday I visit the exhibit. It satisfies an appetite that gradually comes to feel like an addiction, the need to see people interacting with Ugo. He remains here, some part of him intact. These galleries are a reliquary, holding the best of a good man. And yet it causes a churning uneasiness in me to see these thousands of innocent people staring at the walls, reading the placards and stenciled letters, following Ugo's timeline of Christian art. The relic they've come for isn't the memory of a dead friend but the cloth of Christ, still mounted in the Sistine Chapel, so in their eyes this exhibit is a reliquary of a different sort. A vessel so ornate and impressive—paintings so grand, manuscripts so old, a confession so frank that we stole the Shroud from the Orthodox—that it convinces them the relic is authentic. Droves of them react the same way, with nods of understanding and agreement, then gradually with tongues clicking and even hands clasped over hearts as if to say, *I knew it*. The exhibit has given the world permission to believe again. So has the news that the Holy Father is returning the Shroud to the Orthodox, which most of Rome seems to have absorbed not as a milestone in Church relations, but as proof that Ugo's exhibit is the gospel truth about the Shroud. If only John Paul could see the people in these galleries, he would know what I know. I will miss having Ugo so close by. But this show can't go on.

On October the twelfth, I am called into the office of the preseminary rector, Father Vitari, for the only unscheduled meeting I have ever had with my boss. Vitari is a good man. He rarely complains that I have to bring my son to work sometimes or ask for days off when Peter's sick. Even so, there's something oddly hospitable about the way he sits me down and asks, right off, if he can get me anything to drink. I notice that my personnel file is on the desk. Sadness settles over me. The small but insistent fears that have hovered around me like flies, the uncertainties about the future, now go quiet with expectation. So this is how it will happen. Mignatto said the verdict would come in the form of a court document, but I see now that it would be easier to sweep the problem away quietly. It couldn't be difficult, in a country of priests, to find a replacement gospel teacher.

Yet Vitari lifts the file in his hand and asks if I realize I've been working at the pre-seminary for five years. "Five years," he repeats, and then smiles. "That means you're due for a raise." I leave with a handshake and an appreciation card signed by all my boys. I leave, also, trembling and almost sick. That night, the dreams begin. I'm a boy again, watching the crate of blood oranges fall on Guido at the train station. Watching the jumper in Saint Peter's fall through the air to the floor. I feel a pinch in my chest, as if a finger is nocking an arrow on my heartstrings. Before long, even in daylight, it comes to seem as if something is rattling inside me, a bass note of anxiety like the far-off vibration of an approaching train. I'm afraid. Whatever's coming, I fear it.

ONE MORNING, THE DIRECTOR of the museums announces that the exhibit will end ahead of schedule. Someone, possibly Lucio, slips word to the press that Church politics are to blame. A journalist at *l'Espresso* develops this into an article saying John Paul pulled the plug because he feared the Orthodox would take umbrage. After all, we can't continue to make money off the relic we promised them. So on the show's final day, I return to say good-bye. The crowds are astonishing. The exhibit will set records beyond even what its creator could've imagined. I can barely see the walls through the oceans of people. Ugo is fading away.

That night, the Shroud leaves the Sistine Chapel. John Paul's spokesman announces that for reasons of security the cloth's location can no longer be disclosed. This seems to mean we're preparing to send it east. But when I ask Leo if the Swiss Guards have seen a major shipment leaving any of the gates, they haven't. I repeat my question every day until he's just as puzzled as I am that the answer never changes. After a while, a reporter at a press conference asks for an update and the papal spokesman explains that the logistics are complicated and the negotiations private. In other words, don't expect news about the Shroud or the Orthodox for a while.

Soon the other priests at my Greek church in town begin to ask me if the rumors are true. If John Paul's health has become an obstacle. If he's dying too quickly to navigate the next steps with the Orthodox. I tell them I wouldn't know. But I do know. The rumors are true in a way my friends can't understand: this has surely become, for John Paul as it once was for Ugo, a matter of conscience. He would sooner die than base a reunion on a lie. And so, with time as his ally, that is exactly what he plans to do.

There's a parable in the gospel of Matthew about an enemy who comes in the night and sows weeds in a man's field of good wheat. The man's servants ask if they should pull up the weeds, but their master says to wait, or else the good may be lost with the bad. Let everything grow until the day of harvest, he says; then the wheat will be reaped and the weeds will be burned.

I didn't mean to sow those weeds. Not in Ugo's life, not in John Paul's. But in the silence that surrounds the Shroud now, I hear the master telling his servants to wait. Not to reap yet. And I wait for the day of harvest.

MONA SURPRISES ME BY asking to join Peter and me again at a Greek liturgy. Then, two days later, she suggests we go back for another. The third time, she finds a way to ask when I last confessed. She thinks it will do me good.

My wife doesn't understand: I've tried. Yet never in my life have I felt more immune to the power of forgiveness. A nurse always believes in a cure, but unlike Mona's patients at the hospital, I have brought this on myself, and there is no medicine.

Slowly, though, I find that the woman coming to my aid is no longer the woman I married. Rather, she is the wife and mother who left behind husband and son, who lived for years in tortured solitude, and who stands before me now as a virtuoso of the self-recrimination I'm only beginning to learn. She is helping me because she loves me, because she knows this darkness and has its map. There is indeed no medicine. But there is a journey I no longer have to make alone.

In mid-November, the sampietrini begin raising scaffolding in the middle of Saint Peter's Square. Each year they build a nativity scene bigger than the last, veiled with fifteen-foot curtains until a revealing on Christmas Eve. Peter walks the perimeter like a detective, inspecting debris, eavesdropping on workmen, searching for holes in the tarp he can peek through. When the Greek forty-day fast before Christmas begins, Roman Catholics have already filled the markets with holiday sweets, cheeses, and cured meats, none of which an Eastern Catholic can eat. This year it comes as a relief to me. While Mona and Peter go shopping in Piazza Navona, I continue on alone to visit Simon.

He is staying in a small church just outside Rome. The pastor has taken him in like a stray cat. The Secretariat has placed Simon on temporary leave, and guilt has driven him out of the Vatican walls, so he serves food at a community kitchen in the evenings and helps at a Catholic shelter most nights. I assist him sometimes, and in the small hours that follow, when the bars have closed and Rome almost sleeps, we return to his little church and sit side by side on a pew.

At first we keep ourselves to the familiar topics. But one night at a time, the tap opens wider. He seems to be undergoing a second priestly formation here, stripping off the coats of Secretariat varnish and sanding down the grain of our father's old ambitions to see what remains. I listen, mainly. I sense he's bracing me to hear some conclusion he's come to about his life. On this spot, long ago, Saint Peter was fleeing the persecution of Emperor Nero when he had a vision of Jesus. "Domine," Peter asked, "quo vadis?" *Lord, where are you going?* And the vision replied, "Romam vado iterum crucifigi." *I go to Rome, to be crucified again.* At that moment, Peter understood God's plan for him. He accepted martyrdom, letting Emperor Nero crucify him on Vatican Hill. There is a church in Rome for every station of a man's life, and this one is the church of turning points. Some night soon, I keep telling myself, I will share news of my own with my brother.

It's four miles from Simon's church back to the Vatican gates. Four miles is a long way to walk, but a pilgrimage should not be driven. The walk home takes me by the Pantheon, the Trevi Fountain, the Spanish Steps, all in the dead hours of dark. There are still a few tourists and young couples in the piazzas, but they're as invisible to me as the pigeons and night traffic. What I see is the Academy where Simon once studied, the square where Mona and I met on our first date, the hospital in the distance where Peter was born. At each milepost, I make a small prayer. In each neighborhood along the way, my eyes linger over the clotheslines strung over the narrow streets, the soccer balls left on doorsteps, the holiday lights in the shape of La Befana or Babbo Natale and his reindeer.

Four miles on a December night cuts like a river between penance and prayer, and when I reach home, my own feelings of foreboding are more muted. I check the answering machine in case there is word of a verdict. But the verdict is always the same: Peter is asleep and barely moves when I kiss him on the forehead, and when I crawl into bed, Mona whispers, *You're freezing, don't touch me with those feet.* She smiles and slides over, nestling against my chest, and fits herself into the emptiness that only she can fill. For a second, on those nights, I am tense with amazement all over again. I reach out to hold her. *Is he doing better?* she murmurs. Because she has found a new place in her heart for the brother-in-law who used to fill her with misgivings. Then I kiss the back of her neck and I lie to her. I say that Simon seems better every time I visit him. *He needs to know he's forgiven*, she says. And she's right. But to make him believe those words takes a higher power than mine.

The last thing Mona always says, before falling asleep, is, *Did you tell Simon the news?* I touch her bare back. The soft unguarded slope of her shoulder. For years I have lived with one foot in yesterday. Now I can barely sleep for thought of tomorrow. Did I tell him the news? No, I did not. Because I believe I will have more time.

Not yet, I tell her. *But soon.*

ON THE TWENTIETH OF December, just before dawn, I get a text on my phone. Leo.

Baby boy born at 4:17 AM. Healthy, 7 pounds 3 ounces. Alessandro Matteo Keller. With thankful hearts we praise God.

I stare at the screen in the dark. Alessandro. They've named him after me.

A second message appears.

We want you to be godfather. Come visit. We're downstairs.

Downstairs. Sofia delivered at Health Services. They have a Vatican baby.

When Peter and Mona and I arrive, Simon is already there. He is holding the newborn, enveloping it in his immense hands the same way he used to do with Peter. In his eyes is the fragile vigilance I remember so well, the protectiveness snowed over with awe. He looks like the big brother who once raised me, the boy disguised in a man's body. When Mona comes up to run a tender finger across the blue cap on the little child's head, I am suddenly choked by the sight of them both. I watch as Simon gently lowers Alessandro to let her hold him. But first she reaches out her hand and puts her palm on Simon's chest, in the space over his heart where a bishop's pectoral cross should be. He stares down at it, and his eyes are big and searching. I hear her whisper, *Whatever you did, Ugo forgives you.*

The words crush him. As soon as she takes the baby from him, Simon murmurs his congratulations to Leo and Sofia, then finds his way to the door.

I find him upstairs, in the hallway outside our apartment, sitting numbly among the packing boxes. I should have told him. I should have, but I knew he wasn't ready.

Simon stands. He says, *They can't do this to you.* He says, *They can't make you move out.*

I explain. No one is making us. We want to be a family again. There are just too many ghosts in this place.

He stares at the door to the apartment, the door to which his key no longer works, and he listens as I describe the new place we've found. On the way back from visiting him at Domine Quo Vadis, I tell him, I fell in love with one of the neighborhoods. Two of Peter's school friends live in the same building. It's Church-owned, which means rent control. And with two incomes now, Mona and I can afford it.

Simon blinks. He says something convoluted about a savings account he opened for Peter. It's not much, he says, but Mona and I are welcome to use it for our deposit.

I have to turn away. He looks harrowed. I begin to say I'm sorry, I meant to tell him, but he interrupts and tells me: "Alex, I asked for a new posting."

Our eyes search each other. We seem so far away.

A new posting: back into Secretariat service. *Domine, quo vadis?* To Rome, to be crucified again.

When I ask him where he requested to be sent, he tells me it's nowhere specific. Anywhere far from the Orthodox world. With sudden passion he says there are Christians being killed in the Middle East, Catholics being persecuted in China. There is always a cause, and the cause is still all. I look at the open box beside him, on which Peter has tried to write the word *kitchen*. Our own little china, swaddled in butcher paper. I offer him a hand up. I ask him to join us for Christmas dinner.

THE CURTAIN FALLS ON Christmas Eve. The nativity scene in Saint Peter's Square is grander than ever, a stable as big as an inn. Peter is delighted by the life-size ox and sheep that surround the manger. Mona and I take him ice-skating at Castel Sant'Angelo. We return only for Holy Supper.

According to Eastern tradition, the youngest child keeps lookout for the first star in the sky on Christmas Eve. So Peter keeps watch at his bedroom window while I scatter straw on our table and Mona lays the white tablecloth, symbols of the manger in which the baby Jesus was placed. Simon places a lit candle in the loaf of bread in the center of the table, symbol of Christ, the light of the world. As we sit down to eat, we leave the door cracked and an unoccupied chair at the table, recalling that Jesus' parents were travelers in this season, dependent on the hospitality of others. In past years, this was a melancholy moment, peering across at empty chair and unclosed door. An occasion for brooding on Mona. Tonight, my heart brims. If only Simon could experience the same peace.

Just as we're about to eat, a sound interrupts us. A knock. Followed by a creaking of the door.

I look up. My hand drops its piece of bread. Monsignor Mignatto is standing in the doorway.

I stumble to my feet. "Please," I say, "come in."

Mignatto looks nervous. "Buon Natale," he says. "My apologies for intruding."

Without seeming to realize it, Simon whispers, "Not this. Not tonight."

The monsignor's face is lifeless. He glances around the room, seeming to notice the absence of furniture except this table and these chairs. The walls are a quilt of ghostly patterns where picture frames have been removed and packed up.

"This is our last dinner here," I say under my breath.

"Yes," he says, "your uncle told me."

His trepidation is so heavy. I look for some sign of why he's here, but I see no briefcase, no court documents.

Mignatto clears his throat. "The Holy Father's decision will be issued tonight."

Simon stares at him.

"I've been asked to confirm," Mignatto says, pressing on, "where the news should be sent."

"Right here," I say.

Mignatto adds, "I would like to be present when it comes."

I start to agree, but he continues, "However, I was instructed otherwise. So whatever the news may be, I hope you'll call me, Father Andreou."

Faintly, my brother says, "Thank you, Monsignor. But there's no need. I know there's no appeal."

Mignatto's eyes fall. He says, "Even so, I may be able to offer perspective. Or comfort."

Simon nods, but in a way that says there will be no phone call. We will not see the monsignor again.

For a moment, the silence is perforated only by the muted caroling of our neighbors, by the sound of children shouting excitedly in the stairwell. There is joy tonight, elsewhere.

"Monsignor," Simon says, "I'm grateful for everything you did for me."

Mignatto gently bows his head. He steps forward and gives Simon a handshake. He repeats, "Buon Natale. All of you."

LICK BY LICK, THE candles on the table hollow themselves out. Mona and I read Peter the gospel stories of Jesus' birth—Luke's story of the manger, Matthew's story of the three wise men—but Simon merely stares. His eyes are empty. The light in them is dying. It is just past eleven when Peter falls asleep. We place him on a sheet on the floor. The bed frames and mattresses are already in the moving truck.

Mona turns on the television for the broadcast from Saint Peter's Square. Midnight Mass used to be our tradition with Simon until having a newborn made it impossible. People are queued in the piazza, thousands of them, black silhouettes dwarfed by the century-old Alpine fir that has been mounted in the square as John Paul's Christmas tree. Mona's fingers slip between mine and squeeze my hand. I kiss her on the forehead. Her eyes never leave the screen; she hangs on every word of the broadcast. But I go to the kitchen and pour drinks. Simon, who has delivered toasts for cardinals and ambassadors, raises his glass but can think of nothing to say. I lower myself beside him.

"Whatever happens," I say, tapping his glass.

He nods. He smiles.

"We'll get through it," I say.

He drapes a hand across my shoulders. Out the window, in the darkness high over John Paul's palace, there is a star in the east. His stare is locked on it. I close my eyes. Somehow, this is the moment I know. My brother is gone. His body is beside me, but the rest has slipped away. He is here only for our sake, to let us believe we've kept him afloat.

"We love you," I say.

His eyes seem blank. He says, "Thank you for always making me feel like part of your family."

When he finishes his drink, he stands to wash out the glass. I think to myself: *eleven years.* That is how long the priesthood has been his family. Since his first year of seminary. One-third of his life. Which means tonight he may experience what no man ever should: to become an orphan for the second time. He reaches for his pack of cigarettes, but he's interrupted by a knock at the door.

The sound makes Peter wake up.

I look at Simon. The glaze in his stare is gone.

I step forward.

"Fathers Andreou?" says the man at the door.

A layman in a black suit. I recognize him. John Paul's private messenger. The cursore.

He holds out two envelopes. One is engraved with my name. The other with Simon's.

I hand Simon's to him, and he closes his eyes. Mona stands and walks over to us.

I have dreamt of this, and lived in dread of it, but at this moment my fears are silent. I am filled with an unfamiliar stillness.

Trust in the Lord with all your heart. In all your ways submit to Him. He will make your paths straight.

My brother, though, has never looked so frightened. Mona reaches out an arm and says, "Simon . . ."

Peter stares at the messenger. Then he rises, walks toward Simon, and places his head on his uncle's hip, wrapping his arms around his uncle's waist. With the might of Samson, he squeezes.

I open my envelope first. The words inside are not what I imagined. I turn back to the cursore.

He waits.

"Simon," Mona whispers, "open it."

My brother's hand is unsteady as he unseals the envelope. I watch him scan the lines. Looking up at the cursore he says, in a thin voice, "Right now?"

The cursore nods. "Yes, Fathers. Follow me. The car is waiting."

Simon shakes his head. He backs away.

Mona glances over Simon's shoulder at the paper in his hand. Something flickers in her eyes. She says, "Simon, go."

I stare at her.

"Trust me," she whispers. Her expression is electric. "Go."

IT IS THE SAME black sedan as before. Signor Gugel opens the rear door with the same impersonal expression. The cursore sits in the front passenger seat. I can hear Simon breathing beside me.

Gugel and the messenger don't speak. High above us, in the windows of the top floor of the Belvedere Palace, Peter is staring down. I watch him until the window disappears from sight.

The streets are empty. The offices dark. Earlier tonight, when Mona and Peter and I walked home from ice-skating, huge flocks of starlings threw themselves across the sky like a net being cast over Rome. Cast, and drawn back, and cast again. But now there are only the stars. Simon's fingers touch his throat, plucking at the band of his Roman collar.

The car reaches the palace entrance. Then continues past it.

"Where are we going?" Simon says.

Silently we sweep across the road that cuts behind the basilica. The Palace of the Tribunal comes into view. It, too, disappears into the dark.

The courtyard of wet cobblestones looks like black glass, like the Tiber on a choppy night. Simon is leaning forward, placing his hands on the front seats. My phone buzzes. A text from Mona.

Are you at SP?

I type: *Almost. Why?*

The car slows. Gugel cuts the engine and steps out, opening an umbrella. "Fathers," the cursore says, "follow me."

To the south is the gate separating us from Saint Peter's Square. Out in the rain are the hundreds of faithful who would stand here on Christmas Eve even if the sky were falling, the world ending.

The cursore leads us through the side entrance. In the sacristy, a few old priests are vesting frantically. My own pre-seminary boys are here, dressed in red cassocks and white surplices, helping the old-timers into their robes. Two of them come rushing toward us, pushing a clothes rack on wheels. "For you," one of them says to Simon.

It's a choir cassock, the kind worn by a priest attending another priest's Mass.

Simon stares at it. "No," he says.

My heart is thudding. The robe is purple. The choir cassock of a bishop.

My phone buzzes. Mona's answer.

Special homily tonight.

I signal to my boys not to listen to Simon. To do their jobs. They can vest a priest faster than any altar boys on earth. And though Simon begins to protest, he must sense what's about to happen. If he stays in his black cassock, then he is about to be mistaken for a bishop in mourning. And on this day, the day of our Lord's birth, there can be no mourning.

Simon lowers his head. He takes a deep breath. Then he extends his arms. The boys strip off his black cassock and slip on the purple one, the white rochet, and the capelike purple mozzetta. On top goes a pectoral cross.

"This way," the cursore says, moving faster now.

The passage looks like the marble doorway to a sepulcher. I glance over my shoulder. One of my boys lifts a hand in the air as if bidding us good-bye.

In the passageway, the air is changing. Growing warmer. Vibrating with noise. My skin tingles. We travel through another doorway—and suddenly we've arrived.

The ceiling vanishes. The walls rise infinitely to the basilica roof. The vibration has become a deep, cosmic murmur.

"This way," the cursore says.

The sight stops me short. All my life I have attended a Greek church that can hold two hundred people. Tonight, from the high altar over the bones of Saint Peter to the stone disc near the entrance where Charlemagne was once crowned, this basilica holds ten thousand Christian souls. The nave is so full that laymen have given up searching for seats and have begun crowding the side aisles. The congregation bristles and pulses, spilling to the edges of sight and beyond.

The cursore leads us forward. The altar is surrounded by ring after ring of the faithful, rising in dignity as they approach. First the laymen, then the nuns and seminarians. We reach the monks and priests, and I stop, knowing my place. I see other Eastern Catholic priests here, and some of them, recognizing me, make room.

But Simon won't leave my side. The cursore gestures for him to continue, yet my brother stops as well. "Alex," he whispers, "I can't."

"It's not your choice anymore," I say, forcing him forward.

The cursore leads him through rows of ambassadors and royalty, chests glittering with medals. They reach the priests of the Secretariat, and I watch Simon hesitate before stepping in. But the cursore touches him gently on the back. Not here. Continue walking.

They come to the rows of the bishops. Men far older than Simon, some twice his age. The cursore stands back, as if this is as far as his kind may come, but Simon only stands and stares like an altar boy. The bishops, seeing one of their own, begin to part. Two of them reach out, clapping hands on Simon's back. My brother takes a step forward. Beyond them, in the innermost circle, a cardinal in white and gold—the colors of tonight, of hope and exultation—turns to watch. I can see the emotion in Uncle Lucio's eyes.

The cantor starts to sing. The Mass has begun. Simon's head is bent down, not looking at John Paul. He seems to be sunk in some private battle. His body shudders. I see him cover his face in his hands. Then a sound rises. Voices. The Sistine Chapel Choir.

Lord Jesus Christ, only Son of the Father, Lord God, Lamb of God, you take away the sin of the world: have mercy on us.

A procession of children brings flowers to a statue of the baby Jesus. They smile and giggle. The sound lifts Simon's head. As the homily draws nearer, I pray that Mona was right.

The book of gospels is brought to John Paul, and he kisses it, making the sign of the cross. Ten thousand people go utterly silent. The clicking of cameras stops. There is not even a cough. Here is the only pope many of us have ever known. We all surely know, in our bones, that this will be the last time we see our Papa at this high altar. Through this man, God has made miracles. I pray He will do it one more time.

John Paul's voice is low and slurred.

"Tonight, a child is born to us. The Christ child, who offers us a new beginning."

I watch Simon. His eyes are fixed on the Holy Father.

"The evangelist John writes that 'to those who did accept the Lord, he gave power to become children of God.' But what does this mean? How are *we* to become children, like the Christ child, we who are heavy with sin?"

Simon flinches. His shoulders sag again, and he leans forward as if to grip the rail in front of him.

"It is possible only because the child who comes in darkness brings a message of hope: no matter how we have sinned, our Redeemer comes to bear those sins. He comes to *forgive us*."

For a moment, my gaze is drawn upward to the pier where the basilica's relics are kept. I think of the Shroud. I wonder if it is hidden in the reliquary between those walls of stone. If, for now, Ugo was right. Saint Peter's is the Shroud's new home.

"We cannot serve the Lord without first welcoming His forgiveness. Tonight, the Christ child offers us all a new beginning. Let us take it."

The microphone is moved away from John Paul's mouth. The same perfect silence falls. Something has changed in Simon's posture. His head isn't hanging on his neck. The Creed comes, then the prayers of the faithful. When the Holy Father raises the host for consecration, a bell tolls and ten thousand voices sing, *Lamb of God, you take away the sins of the world. Have mercy on us.*

On all sides, priests begin to offer communion. Seats empty, forming lines to receive it. *Adeste fideles*, sings the Sistine Chapel Choir. *O come, all ye faithful.* Simon watches the other bishops around him. Yet as their ranks thin, he can't seem to pry his hands from the rail. Can't take a step forward. An archbishop in front of him turns and shakes his head, as if to say Simon mustn't receive communion here.

Nowak.

His Grace takes Simon by the hand and leads him away. They weave through the other bishops, toward the aisle that leads back to me. But instead of turning in my direction, Nowak brings Simon toward the high altar.

My brother shakes his head. They stop. For a moment, at the foot of the stairs that lead down toward the bones of Saint Peter, or up toward Pope John Paul, they are motionless. Nowak says something to my brother. I will never know what it is. I will always prefer to keep this moment a mystery.

When the words are spoken, His Grace puts both hands on Simon's shoulders, and my brother stands at his full height. He looks up the stairs. In the Holy Father's hand is the host. Far above us all, in the windows of the dome, is the veil of heaven, torn by the stars. Simon makes a small prayer, crosses himself, then takes the first step.

I watch my brother rise.

ACKNOWLEDGMENTS

THIS BOOK TOOK ten years to write. The following people helped me finish it—and helped prevent it from finishing me.

No one understands Father Alex and his world better than my long-suffering literary agent, Jennifer Joel of ICM, who not only read but marked up four thousand draft pages of *The Fifth Gospel* over the course of a decade, including almost a dozen passes over this final version of the novel. Midstream in that process, catastrophe struck and my initial book contract was scrapped, so Jenn waded into the worst publishing climate in recent memory with nothing but my half-finished manuscript and a determination to fight for my survival. She postponed business trips and canceled family vacations. She traveled hundreds of miles to visit me at my home because she refused to give up on this novel and its maddeningly slow author. I defy anyone to find a literary agent who has given more to a book, ever.

Jofie Ferrari-Adler at Simon & Schuster took me on when I was heartbroken and cynical, eight years into a novel that still wasn't done. He put on no airs and gave me just what I needed: the freedom to do the things I do best, the wisdom to fix the things I don't, and no runaround in between. His infectious love of this business even convinced me, all over again, that the world of books is a joyful place to call home.

Many priests, canonists, and professors made crucial contributions. Surely no institution on earth has better reason to doubt the motives of novelists than the Catholic Church, but to my surprise I received generous help at every turn: seminary instructors, Church lawyers, and prominent Catholic scholars not only answered my questions in detail but sometimes spoke openly about their experiences at the Vatican. Special thanks go to Father John Custer for many hours of generous assistance helping me understand Eastern Catholicism and the life of an Eastern Catholic priest in Rome; to Margaret Chalmers and Father Jon Chalmers for their guidance on penal cases under canon law, a subject that has not received full justice in these pages but that would have been utterly bungled without their unstinting help; and to John Byron Kuhner, who had already studied with the papal Latinist by the time we were reading Augustine and Ignatius as undergraduates together, and who made short work of correcting my Greek and Latin.

Many newfangled technologies prevented a years-long research process from becoming a decades-long one. Google in particular deserves recognition for the wealth of tools it has placed at the hands of researchers. With a working knowledge of only English and French, I resorted to scanning my own books in other languages and reading them via Google Translate. I made almost daily use of Google Books, mining its stockpiles of scholarship on ancient Christianity, its old Baedeker guides of Italy and the Papal States, and its hard-to-find texts on clerical clothing. Google Maps helped me diagram the layout of the Vatican village in more detail than any of the various books I own on the subject, while letting me keep tabs on the progress of the city-state's endless construction projects. More recently, Google Street View has made it possible to take high-resolution tours around the perimeters of both the Vatican and Castel Gandolfo. Also deserving of great thanks are the many newspapers—above all *The New York Times*—that during the past ten years bravely digitized their archives. I discovered wonderful and sometimes astonishing things about the Vatican in those old pages.

Jonathan Tze, who seventeen years ago helped hatch the idea behind *The Rule of Four*, became one of the first victims of this novel's endless birth pangs. After long months of helping to research a different storyline, he watched the material lead me in another direction. Years later, though, he generously reprised his inspirational role by helping me imagine *The Fifth Gospel*'s final scenes. There are few better things to a writer than creative companionship, but one of them is constant friendship.

Dusty Thomason is this book's godfather. Even before the publication of *The Rule of Four*, he and I spent a week together in Greece researching a follow-up novel we intended to write together, which neither of us envisioned being set at the Vatican. Then life intervened, and we found ourselves working on different projects on different coasts. Still, Dusty helped shepherd me through endless drafts of this manuscript—and through the *selva oscura* they led to. Most importantly, in the eighth year of this process, when the book seemed on the brink of failure and my family was on the verge of a darkness I still cannot contemplate, Dusty refused to let us suffer. He rescued the people I love, simply out of love for me. Not even a thirty-year friendship brimming with acts of inexplicable kindness prepared me to receive a gift like that. No thanks will ever suffice. Just writing these words brings me almost to tears.

The last of these acknowledgments is the hardest. The world is full of writers who believe they are making important sacrifices for their art. But a husband and father who volunteers his family to share in those sacrifices is either heartless or a fool. Beginning in 2006, and continuing in an almost yearly cycle, I believed I was close to finishing this book. Whatever the problem was—the bottomless research, the interweaving of the threads of the plot, the work of getting Alex's voice just right—the solution was always just around the corner. For nine years this is what I put my family through. My wife wouldn't steal from me the optimism I was surviving on, but she knew the truth. And when the worst finally came, and it knocked me on my back, she was the one who lifted me up and carried me to the finish line. Never have I met anyone who cares less about material things or the prospect of losing them. Never have I met anyone who shows by daily proofs that love, truly, is all. I gave this novel everything I had. But she gave it even more. This book begins and ends with Meredith.